NIGHTSHADE

by

Shea Godfrey

NIGHTSHADE

ISBN 10: 1-60282-151-8
ISBN 13: 978-1-60282-151-4

This Trade Paperback Original Is Published By
Bold Strokes Books, Inc.
P.O. Box 249
Valley Falls, NY 12185

First Edition: May 2010

Credits
Editors: Cindy Cresap and Shelley Thrasher
Production Design: Stacia Seaman
Cover Design By Sheri (graphicartist2020@hotmail.com)

Acknowledgments

Thank you to my family and friends for your patience and support. Thank you for letting me be creative in whatever way I have needed to be. Your generosity in accepting me as I am and encouraging me to be an artist in a society that no longer promotes individuality or celebrates creativity has always been a part of my every day. I am grateful for you and I appreciate you. Thank you.

Dedication

A change came o'er the spirit of my dream.

—Lord Byron

To Lyoness
The Killy Mountains
The SiegeWood
Gillencoe
Cooley's Blue Drink
The Far Outpost
The Taurus Mountains
To Greymear & Senegal
Cullidan's Gap
Sha-Karam
The Plains of Ishlere
The Lanark River
Sheildag
White Horn Keep
Brayburn
Bailentrae
Marban
The Wick Willow Islands
~ARRAVAN~
Dynn's Town
The Towerwood Tangle
Dunbarle
Emmerin Gap
West Sligo
~The Lowlands~
Raven's Run River
Kastamon City
Lake Aurora
The Gonnard Forest
The Green Hills
AvLyn Keep
Lokey
Kenton
The Menath
The Kult River
Armasha River
The Black-wood Forest
The Dark Ridge Mountains
The Taljah River
Topms Town
The Bay of Alirra
Murphy's Landing
Eleven Blue Waters
Hockley
Antioch City
South Antioch
The Sandista Valley
Yellow Rock Ridge
The Sellen Sea
Hollow Sun
Kura
To Wei-Jinn & Artanis

CHAPTER ONE

Winter 1032
The Year of Attia's Spear
The Jade Palace, the city of Karballa, Lyoness

The dogs attacked when they caught the scent of Princess Jessa-Sirrah's flesh, brought up short by their leads after a violent rush. The chains scraped against the marble floor and dragged along the smooth stone as the dogs retreated, the iron links that had cut into their flesh easing when they did so. The broad, muscular animals were bred for killing, the black hair on their backs bristling and their claws left long for the hunt. When their barking rose, it echoed against the domed ceiling high above.

Jessa walked straight among them, a dark green sari wrapped about her lower body in turns of silk and draped forward over her left shoulder with a long-sleeved golden choli blouse beneath it. She wore a burka that covered her head and face, though it was not quite long enough to hide the ends of her hair.

The men lounged upon the dais. The raised platform curved about the head of the vast oval room like a horseshoe and closed in on the wide aisle that led to the throne at its deepest point, the Jade Throne, which was the seat of all power within the land of Lyoness. The massive chair was made of purest gold, its surface littered with polished hunks of jade, some as broad as a man's hand. Its back rose nearly six feet with a wide cushion of rare Damascus silk upon its seat.

Seven chairs lined each side of the curved platform, smaller by far than the throne but no less gaudy, each made of gold and decorated in some way, though not with jade. Jade was the province of the throne and these were the chairs for the sons of King Abdul-Majid de Bharjah of

Lyoness. Only twelve of the seats were occupied, one upon each end of the broken circle left empty for the two sons that had not lived.

Jessa was the only daughter of King Bharjah, and her brothers watched with interest as she strode to the foot of the throne. Several smiled at her with lazy contempt. Some were amused. She tried to walk with strength and grace. Though the dogs frightened her, she could keep her shoulders back and hold to the center of the aisle. One of her brothers threw his goblet of wine at the nearest animal and the dog spun about, his jaws snapping loudly. During the laughter a second goblet was tossed, another dog hit upon the back of the head and goaded into rage.

Jessa stopped before the foot of the Jade Throne and bowed her head amidst the commotion. She closed her eyes and tried very hard to steady her heart.

"Enough," King Bharjah said quietly. "Serabee."

The man who stood behind the throne, the Lord Serabee El-Khan, stepped forward and spoke. Tall and thin, he wore only black and had two swords fastened to his belt, one low on each hip. Throwing daggers were also attached to the wide leather, and he rested his hands on them in an easy manner. He was pale and his head was shaved clean, his facial features long and harsh.

The dogs heard the softly spoken words, as did Jessa, his spell weaving its way into the very air of the room. The animals slinked away as Serabee's majik touched them.

King Bharjah smiled as his sons let their laughter fade and the dogs became submissive. Once powerfully built, in recent years he had lost his imposing physique. He reclined upon his throne in silk and sandals, a light blue robe about his shoulders, his long braids of dyed hair falling onto his chest. Bharjah displayed no gray hair despite his advanced age, and those who dyed it dark black had no tongues with which to speak of such vain inclinations. His beard and mustache, long enough to curl, featured several tiny braids that dangled from the tip of his chin and were adorned with small pieces of jade. "Remove the headdress, Jessa-Sirrah," he ordered.

As Jessa pulled at her burka, her hands trembled. She bent her head and removed the heavy silk.

"Pretty cunta," her brother Malik-Assad taunted, and the others laughed as a sharp whistle cut through their amusement. The dogs responded and dragged their chains in search of attention.

Bharjah lifted a lazy hand and the laughter died away.

Jessa stood before her father with her face lowered, her attention on the rise of the dais as she counted the turns of jade within the stone.

"Look at me."

Jessa obeyed. She studied his face, careful to avoid his eyes. One could become trapped within them, for their darkness was not of color but of spirit, and their dominance and violent sway could devastate. To keep her wits about her and her fear at bay she had to avoid his gaze. She noted that his complexion was ashen and his skin shadowed beneath his lids and puffy about his cheeks. A thin sheen of sweat on his face suggested discomfort, for the air was still cool.

"You shall be the last piece of jade within my tower," he said.

Jessa did her best to ignore the hooded tone.

"What have you to say to that?"

"Whatever is your wish, my Lord King."

Bharjah chuckled and looked to his right, observing his eldest sons. "You should take note, you rabble." He laughed louder. "Respect!"

Sylban-Tenna, Bharjah's firstborn, was seated at Bharjah's right hand. He stared at Jessa's body, something shadowed flaring within his expression. "She's a good little rabbit," he said.

"Up!" King Bharjah snapped, and the power of his eyes instantly caught Jessa. "I have a use for you." Her brothers sat straighter in their seats. "You will travel with Trey-Jak Joaquin and the Lord Serabee El-Khan into the heart of Arravan. You will marry their firstborn."

After a heavy silence, the shouts rang out, more than one prince pushing to his feet in shock and rage. The dogs began to bark and the noise level escalated, flooding the pillared throne room.

"Enough!" Bharjah shouted.

The silence was instant.

"If you do not like it, then you are free to…" His expression was almost playful. "Then you are free to complain to Serabee. And your brother Joaquin, of course." He smiled and sought out Joaquin, who was but a few years older than Jessa. He was seated on the left side of the platform near the end and had not shouted or moved, nor shown any discontent at the announcement.

"Joaquin?" Sylban-Tenna's dangerous tone moved in the distance between him and his younger brother like a dagger, though Joaquin merely smiled.

"Yes," Bharjah said with apparent satisfaction. "On your toes, Sylban."

The shouting began again and Jessa stood in the center of the storm. One of the dogs, set loose from its chain, rushed across the aisle and was met instantly by two others.

"You may leave," Bharjah said above the din, never once distracted from Jessa.

She stood extremely still, mindful that if she moved, the dogs would react. At least one of them was now free from its restraints.

Bharjah lifted a hand and Serabee walked down the right side of the dais in answer. The uproar abruptly halted as he moved, the still-chained dogs pulling back as he passed.

He reached into the fight without pause. The largest dog yelped in pain as Serabee tore it from the conflict by the neck and flung it from the dais, where it landed in the aisle with a snapping of bones and a heavy thud. The other dogs scattered and Serabee turned, focusing a subtle challenge on Jessa.

"Leave it," Bharjah ordered. "Find your ugly witch woman, Jessa-Sirrah, and prepare for your journey. You will depart at the first turn of the spring moon."

"As you command, my Lord King." Jessa bowed her head then turned away. During the long walk back down the aisle she could feel the weight of the moment. When she approached the wounded animal she hesitated and a strange rush of understanding engulfed her as he tried to crawl. Crawl to where, Jessa had no idea, but she recognized the instinct. She stepped around his hind legs and kept moving as the animal whimpered.

Yes, child, keep going. You cannot help.

The unexpected words slipped like smoke through Jessa's thoughts and she breathed in relief as she searched for the source of the warning. She quickened her pace as a new majik moved within the air and was certain Serabee would sense its presence as well. As she left the carpeted aisle for polished marble she saw only shadows, the sun's rays through the enormous terrace doors bright and sharp as they slashed across the chamber.

Jessa waited on the wide veranda beyond her rooms, the cushioned bench she occupied one of her favorite places as she viewed the landscape beyond the palace grounds. In a seldom-used wing of the palace she had made her home, and she had more freedom than perhaps her father had intended when, years ago, he had ordered that she be kept out of his way.

It was still chilly, the winter season reluctant to relinquish its power to the softer winds and warm rains of the spring. The sky was deep blue, streaked with gold that layered into rich pink as the sun slid beneath the horizon. The stars were born within the sky like flints struck upon the weight of its impending darkness, the constellations slow to form.

"You did well."

Jessa looked to the voice. "Radha."

Lady Radha was small and thin, her white hair short and tossed by the breeze, the fine curls blown about her wrinkled face. Her tanned skin blended with her black skirt and dark tunic, and several fringed shawls were draped about her shoulders. Her eyes, the palest of blue, ruled her weathered face with a glorious sort of power. She had been Jessa's guardian and companion since the moment of Jessa's birth, and she attended to the duties of her position with total love and a cunning sense of responsibility.

"I did nothing but bow my head," Jessa said. "I didn't know you were there."

Radha considered Jessa's words and assessed her mood, even as she measured their place in a broader tapestry.

The presence of a royal daughter had always been a curiosity and a nuisance, and the fact that Radha had kept Jessa but a ghost amid the palace life was deemed a worthy service. Jessa was there only when summoned, which had always fascinated and pleased Bharjah. Only Radha occasionally tempted him with Jessa's presence, allowing Bharjah to take credit for her loveliness or her skills, and thus earning her some status.

Jessa was the one thing of beauty that Bharjah had ever produced, and Radha's skill in handling him had secured Jessa at least some measure of protection from his many sons.

Radha laughed as she walked across the terrace stones and stopped beside the bench before she sat next to her charge with a flutter of shawls and fringe. "That was the point of my spell," she said, certain that though she had been watched closely for decades and always bowed to Serabee's apparent dominance, never once had anyone discovered the truth of her abilities. Once nursemaid and now servant to the Princess Jessa-Sirrah, Radha was a high priestess and shaman in the service of the nomadic Vhaelin Gods.

"You will leave this place at last." Radha studied the beauty of Jessa's face and saw how troubled she was. "Arravan is said to be a most attractive land, green and ripe with plants and flowers. Blooming things that a woman of Lyoness might only dream of."

"Yes. And so I shall go from being Bharjah's chattel to being the slave of a stranger, meant to serve him in his bed and keep my eyes down still. I know very well what traveling to Arravan means for me, Radha. Do not try to dress this up as some sort of grand adventure so I might sleep tonight. I am being sold."

Radha squeezed her hand. "I wasn't. I was just happy that we shall see some green things."

Jessa let out a breath of laughter. "And what else are you happy about?"

"The Vhaelin speak favorably upon this, child. I have seen it within the Waters of Truth. Strong portents," Radha replied, recognizing Jessa's doubt. "Do you think you know what the heart of an Arravan king might hold?"

Jessa pushed back the hair that had blown across her face. "I know exactly what the heart of a king may hold, Radha. The land he rules is but a formality." A touch of temper flared within her expression and Radha smiled at the sight of it. "Must you always bait me? Have you nothing better to do, old woman?"

Radha laughed happily. "Not a thing."

They glared at one another, neither backing down. Radha smiled and Jessa scowled back at her.

"Would you like me to find out about him? About his family?" Radha asked. "Perhaps you might sew him a pretty shirt while we wait for spring to arrive."

Jessa yanked her hand free and rose from the bench, then strode to the terrace railing. "And perhaps I should have you beaten for your insolence," she said, though Radha knew that she would never order a stranger beaten, much less her.

"I shall find out what we need to know, you needn't fear. And perhaps you might consider the reasons why you're being sent as a possible bride for the son of your father's greatest enemy, yes? It is a good question."

Jessa turned about and then rested against the wrought iron. "*Possible*?"

"Bharjah knows little about Arravan etiquette, I think. It is the woman who must agree to the contract and no one else, and before the witnesses of her choosing. Use your mind, girl. It's that nuisance that has been hiding beneath all of your curls and rotting with disuse since the weather changed," Radha said. "I've taught you better than to sulk and bow your head when you might look about you instead."

"Yes, Radha, thank you for reminding me that I've been found lacking."

Radha laughed.

"Joaquin has been busy, I am thinking," Jessa mused.

"How so?"

"For Serabee to be given over to his authority? There is a deeper play and Bharjah is at the heart of it, whether Joaquin knows it or not."

"And?"

"And what?" Jessa said. "What does it matter?"

"Perhaps what you will find within Arravan will not be what you expect."

"And perhaps a year from now I will be ripe with child and mocked by an entirely different country. A unique sort of distinction, to be an amusement to half the known world. I'm not sure that many women may claim such a pleasure."

"You are the Nightshade Lark and the Woman within the Shadows, Jessa," Radha said with strength. "You are a mystery to Lyoness but you are here, make no mistake. No one laughs at you. You are the only child of the Blood that people do not fear or hate, and you are a great source of curiosity. You are the wish they do not know enough to make, for what need do a conquered people have for dreams that don't come true? But you are on the edge of everything and they know it. The people do not speak of you within the same breath as the others. You are spoken of with clean air."

Jessa ignored the words as she considered her future. "An heir of Bharjah's blood upon the throne of Arravan."

"Perhaps." Radha could feel the challenge within the silence she was met with. "Do you think that is the deeper play, then? It is about as deep as the bowl I soak my feet in."

Jessa laughed. "Yes, I'm sorry. It was a poor effort."

"The world is wide, my child," Radha said softly. "You have clawed at the door since you could reach it, searching for your chance. When the spring moon rises and we leave upon the road east, it shall be a road that you know nothing of and the world shall open to you. You will leave the Jade Palace behind. You shall move beyond the specter of your brothers and the stench of Bharjah's presence."

Jessa studied her hands for a moment and then turned about, gazing once again upon an unknown distance. "Yes, I shall trade one cage for another and have Joaquin stepping on my shadow as always."

"Perhaps."

"Yes, and if not that, then what?" Jessa said. "Whether I am a possible bride or one that has already been bartered and paid for, Bharjah's wishes were quite clear and my choice must be yes. I'm not sure where that leaves my *chance*."

"You do not know everything," Radha said. "We shall consult the Waters."

"No. I have no wish to see what they hold."

"Why not?"

"Because I am tired of my gods taunting me!" Jessa answered with unexpected anger. "I show them respect and I practice their arts, yet they give me *nothing*. Your spell is not what you think, old woman. It never has been."

"My spell is fine. It is *you* that cannot hold what they show within your head," Radha said. "Or perhaps your heart."

"My head is quite capable, thank you," Jessa replied. "And my heart has nothing to do with it."

"What is it you have seen that you're so afraid of?" Radha asked, not for the first time.

For years Jessa had been plagued by what the spell had shown her, sulking within her visions and her temper flaring easily at any mention of them. She held them tightly to her heart, claiming that she could not remember or that they were smoke within her thoughts. Whether or not Jessa was being honest Radha had no idea, but it was a mystery she had tried to solve for many years. She suspected that Jessa lied, though for what reason she could not decipher. Jessa did not seek the Waters as she once did.

Jessa searched the stars of the warrior Attia's spear and did not answer for Radha to hear, though she heard Jessa's whisper on the rising breeze. "And my heart…my heart is very tired and of no use to anyone."

CHAPTER TWO

Spring 1032
The Lowlands of Arravan

Jessa stood in the long grass and stared down into the green lands of Arravan. Their caravan had traveled for nearly three weeks and had reached the well-guarded border at the Emmerin Gap, passing from Lyoness beneath the curious eyes of several thousand soldiers. First the Eastern Forces of her father bowed to their knees as they passed, and then the Western Army of Arravan gathered at the strongholds of the Gap, showing their might as they stood tall. Within the same week they had crossed the Taljah River and entered the Lowlands, traveling deeper into the country that might well become her home.

The land had changed in subtle ways as they had moved east from Karballa, but once they had crossed the Taljah, Jessa's knowledge of the world had swung like a pendulum from what was familiar to what was extraordinary and uncommon. The world had come alive. The weather was warm and the rains more frequent, the earth transforming into an exotic landscape of growth and vitality.

Radha was right, I've never seen such color, Jessa thought as the breeze washed over her. The sun was setting as the sky grew dark, thin clouds drifting high up and pushed to the north by the wind.

Their party consisted of one hundred of her father's soldiers that answered to her brother Joaquin. The men rode sleek, beautiful horses. The steeds of Lyoness were famed throughout the world, the envy of all who saw them. Within the camp the broad canvas tents had been set quickly and the red flags of Lyoness had been raised, almost as if warning any who saw them. Jessa could smell the cooking fires and the meat roasting above the flames, though it did little to stir her appetite.

Arravan soldiers had met them at the border between the stone citadels of the Gap, more than double their own number and led by the First Councilor to the King of Arravan, a man called Armistad Greyson. He was older, most likely in his fiftieth year or more, his hair streaked with gray. His crisp black uniform bore the insignia of the Kingsmen, the elite guard of Arravan that protected the High King himself.

Lord Greyson had insisted Jessa leave her wagon and remove her headdress, so that he might look upon her face. Joaquin had agreed to his wishes and Jessa had obeyed, meeting the stranger's eyes for but an instant before she bowed her head.

He had been a kind man and thanked her in a quiet voice, then begged her forgiveness that such a formality was necessary.

She had not expected to be treated with respect. The man had ignored Joaquin and spoken directly to her. She was uncertain of the reason for the ritual, though. She had never met a man of Arravan and so how should he recognize her? They might have sent a girl from the streets. When she had suggested this to Radha, she had laughed and kissed her cheek.

In the growing darkness she could see the many campfires of the Arravan soldiers farther along the road and amongst the trees that were blooming to the south. And behind us as well, I should imagine, she mused, though no fires signaled their presence. Jessa knew they were allowed very little liberty, and once through the Gap their numbers had become insignificant. These were the Lowlands, and they were a most holy place to both countries. Arravan would protect them at all costs.

It was said in Lyoness that the world had birthed the First Man within the soil of the Lowlands and that the god named Hamranesh did not like the damp and cold, and so walked west until he found the comforting heat of the desert. There he called forth his wives and servants from the fires of the sand, and thus gave blood to Lyoness. The land he was born of, however, was still sacred beyond all other places.

The Lowlands were said to have also been the birthplace of the gods of Arravan. Firstborn and most powerful, the god Gamar was said to have roamed these hills and considered the servants he might create and what gifts to bestow upon them. While deep in this contemplation he failed to notice the subtle birth of his cunning sister Jezara or the screams of the earth when his dark brother Amar was born after her.

That indifference had led to the rivalry between them all, and though Jezara and Amar would bow to Gamar if forced to, both of them were their own entities and decidedly powerful. Or so it was told and Jessa did not dispute the claim. Though Hamranesh was the main deity worshipped within Lyoness, Jessa followed the ways of the Vhaelin and her gods taught respect for all faiths. The Vhaelin were champions of free will; to them nothing was more sacred than to be allowed the devotions of your choice.

Jessa knelt and set her hand upon the damp earth, closing her eyes. She could feel the pulse and the life, and something deeper as well. Perhaps the blood of their southern gods, coursing through the rivers far beneath the earth. Perhaps the shudder that the land gave when the sun creased the world at the end of the day. Perhaps merely her own pulse. She would have to wait and see.

It was a holy place, though, and she understood that now, standing upon its soil. The place was rich with life and it was said that those who tilled and worked the soil within the Lowlands tilled the flesh of gods. It was so in Arravan and it was the same in Lyoness.

The Lowlands were the greatest source of dispute between their two lands, and Jessa realized it was here that the war would be waged for her hand. Arravan had seized the Lowlands several generations past, and in that victory over Lyoness they had endangered what her family held most precious: the assertion that the blood of the Bharjah line hailed directly from the veins of Hamranesh.

Jessa knew it was a lie, but the claim was a potent one and had been made since the first of her blood had seized power.

What is the truth of this place? Or did you give birth to all gods, even my own?

The Vhaelin walked the Ibarris Plains, but where they had come from was a long-standing mystery. In the city of Karballa their followers were scattered and few, but Jessa had learned at Radha's knee and had known from the start that the Vhaelin were hers to keep and pay homage to, no matter where she made her home. Perhaps it was here, in this most holy of places, that all gods were born and sent out into the world.

She could not deny her excitement. She could not deny her joy at being freed from her prison of the Jade Palace. That she was quiet in this happiness and careful of her emotions seemed only prudent to her. Despite the fresh air she encountered each morning, air that held the remnants of a thousand dreams of freedom, she knew that they were a lovely illusion.

Joaquin still dogged her steps, as did Lord Serabee El-Khan. And whether this would change if a son of Arravan wanted her for his bride, she had no idea. She was Joaquin's advantage over his rivals and she could do nothing about it. She did not doubt he had played a significant role in brokering the contract for her hand. Now he would be closer on her heels than ever before. *But what shall it gain you, my brother, if Arravan's son finds me lacking? Or more to the point, what will that mean for me?*

If she returned in disgrace to the Jade Throne, Bharjah's plans, whatever they might be, would be dashed to nothing because she was not beautiful enough. *Or not enticing enough for a son of the Blood to get his sons upon. Not sweet enough, perhaps, in my temptations. How awful I shall feel, you old butcher, to disappoint you.*

She had no clue how to seduce a man. And she had no such desire. She still believed the words she had spoken to Radha, that she would be exchanging one cage for another. *Though perhaps the cages of Arravan are prettier, and I might gain some small amount of liberty if I am the mother of his sons.*

Her annoyance was sudden and fierce. She was joining a game already in play, and she would be forced to move the pieces on the board with great care if she were to win some measure of contentment. Her only remaining task was to decide whom she would rather be a pawn to.

She did not like the complete uncertainty of her position. She had never possessed even the smallest degree of power and had always been but a step away from someone's blade. And now she was being sold, her body offered up as the vessel for a stranger's seed. She felt ill and her head throbbed, but this was perhaps the only currency available to her, to open her legs to him and offer her spirit. With years of practice behind her, she changed the direction of her thoughts, her heart hardening to stone as she searched the far horizon.

She needed more information about what to expect and more confidence in order to meet it with grace and dignity. Radha had unearthed some small scraps of information about the family that would greet her, and some of their history as well, though not as much as they liked. Lyoness was unkind to the legacies of any but those of Bharjah's blood. Radha had promised more and Jessa hoped that she could deliver on that pledge.

Jessa knew she was to visit a small family and that the High King, Owen Durand, had taken but one bride in his lifetime, to whom he was married still. This woman, Cecelia Lewellyn, had borne him five children, three sons and two daughters. Radha assured her that their knowledge would increase as they traveled farther into Arravan, but for now, Jessa understood only that the Durand reputation was far different from that of her own blood.

She took a deep breath and cast a final glance across the landscape, with its richness and utter beauty. She rose and returned to camp, lifting her skirt above her boots when the grass grew tall and smiling at the novelty of such a simple thing. If she were to finally receive a clear answer from the Vhaelin as to her fate, it would be in a place such as this, upon sacred and holy ground.

"*Vhaelin essa ahbwalla*," she whispered in blessing as she walked.

Beneath the first full moon of spring, Jessa would seek the Waters of Truth.

❖

Radha spoke the words that would bring the truth. The changes that took place in Jessa's face caused her to proceed with caution. The abundance of power Jessa possessed was vast but well-hidden, rushing blindly through Jessa's soul and, for now, unattainable. It had been that way since Radha first held her. The mark of the Vhaelin surged so fiercely in Jessa's tiny body that when she had cried, Radha caught her breath. Jessa's mother had felt the power also, laughing that first time and weeping in her happiness at the singing of her gods.

When Radha called upon the Waters of Truth she could sense Jessa's buried potential struggle to free itself, even as she had in that first breath. Its staggering promise made the stars hang like ripe fruit, ready to tumble from the sky if Jessa could only seize her strength and call them down.

Radha lifted her hands to the brass bowl that sat between them, the ancient metal vibrating against her skin. Jessa's eyes were closed as she sat cross-legged before the low table, her hands within her lap.

"Look, Jessa," Radha said, "and see what the Vhaelin would show you."

Jessa took a deep breath and let it out slowly, opening her eyes.

Jessa's eyes were unfocused and blind in the majik, soaking up the light in a shocking fashion. No one Radha had ever known understood the power of the trance as Jessa did. *You give yourself so completely, my love, that you lose your control.* "Jessa, pull back."

Not responding to Radha's order, Jessa became trapped in the waters of the bowl, the dark liquid swirling slowly toward the center in smooth ripples as the scent of sage and obee root wafted around them.

She saw nothing but the words, the letters and runes floating before her and slipping into order as if written in blood in the air. She saw Radha as but a shadow, a figure of smoke beyond her comprehension. Their tent had receded into darkness, though she could still sense the things within: the pillows of her bed and the trunks for travel, the lamps that hissed and filled her head like the buzzing of summer bees.

The water was the purest of light and her eyes reacted to it with pain. She grabbed the edge of the table even as her mind let go, her consciousness pulled within the shallow depths of the bowl as if they had no end. The breath that she took felt as if it might be her last.

Jessa saw the midday sun high above the hard-packed earth of a courtyard and watched as her boots touched the steps of her carriage and carried her to the ground. A light dust rose from the contact and scattered as she felt someone firmly grip her hand. The touch was like the bitter cava root, for it lingered and tainted the things that followed it. It was Joaquin.

The stones of the structure rose before her, black rock set within dark mortar, its massive presence oddly soft and warm as the sun spilled against its surface.

"What do you see?" Radha whispered. It was unwise to interrupt a vision or to prompt the seeker, but if Jessa were telling the truth about the loss of her visions, there would be questions.

"Blackstone Keep," Jessa said.

Jessa saw him instantly within the greeting courtyard, dressed in some form of state regalia, his lips curling up under a dark beard and mustache that covered the skin about his mouth. He was handsome, his eyes blue and deep as they caught the sun beneath a shock of black hair. But the sun is at your back, Jessa thought, and was uncertain where or when she thought it. His expression was one of surprise and delight as he spoke to her. The gold medallion about his neck flared boldly against his white tunic and she reacted, wincing in pain.

Jessa was trapped by the movement of water against the side of the bowl, caught within a rush of vertigo as a ribbon of brilliant blue pulled at her senses and coaxed her into the recesses of a much darker pool.

She heard the sound of her own laughter and the tone was strange to her ears. This was not as she was used to laughing, hidden and covert so as to not draw attention to herself. This laughter was open and full, so full, in fact, that she could feel the joy in her chest as if she would drown if it were not released.

Jessa's face felt flushed. She blinked in surprise, the touch of something soft and familiar gliding against her skin and teasing her lips. It was hair, and she ran her fingers through it, laughing once more as she took the curls in her grasp. A hand wrapped about her wrist, then skated down the inner surface of her arm, the caress sending a shiver along Jessa's spine.

She felt the press of a body on top of her and her blood surged at the heat and the softness of the flesh, at the weight and the scent of it, at the intimate connection of her body against another. She lifted her legs with slow enjoyment, wrapping them in a possessive manner around slim hips. She smiled at the lips against her throat. They were full and moist in their warmth as they pulled at her skin, and the tongue was sweet as it tasted of her flesh, teeth nipping gently.

Jessa's shoulders trembled and her head dropped back. "I smell…I smell the ocean," she whispered, and heard a tender voice beside her ear but failed to understand what was said.

"What do you see?" Radha asked again.

Laughter rose within Jessa's throat once more and she set it free. She lifted her left hand and it trembled, the bangles she wore on her wrist clinking in a soft rain of sound.

"And musk," Jessa said, surprised.

"But what—"

Jessa's head tipped forward with a jerk and she plunged her right hand into the bowl. The water splashed and Radha grabbed the small table to keep it from overturning. The waters were not to be disturbed, and Radha hissed in warning as a cloud of steam mushroomed from the confines of the bowl.

"A child," Jessa spoke in a strained voice. "A child of the Durand line."

"Do you bear him a son?" Radha was shocked. *But that cannot be! That is not what the Vhaelin promised.*

Jessa opened her eyes, her pupils expanding completely until nothing but black was left. She was blind to all but the truth.

Radha jerked her hand away, startled as a thick finger of water curled from the bowl and snaked about Jessa's arm, winding its way upward.

Jessa felt the kiss upon her lips but it was too quick. The flavor on her tongue was the most delicious taste she had ever encountered and she wanted more, she was certain of it. Her lips were sweetly bruised and full with kisses. *I know this taste. Vhaelin essa, I know this.*

Jessa saw a face and her entire body filled with heat. The eyes before her were utterly beautiful. "Is what you see different than what I see?"

Radha could smell the pungent burning of the bowl as the brass began to warp. The container was slowly being drained as the water continued its climb and soaked the silk about Jessa's right shoulder. It spread like blood across the garment as she seized the spell completely. "No, Jessa!"

Torchlight filled the tent as the flap was thrown open and the wind blew in. Radha turned with a shout of warning.

Joaquin rushed forward, his vicious boot sending the table across the tent. The bowl spun away as Serabee stepped close behind him, his pale expression savage at the sight of the ancient brass.

Jessa felt the spell break like a fist against her chest. She gasped and reeled away from the light with a cry of agony. The world around her coalesced into a cruel focus as she saw her brother's hand. Pain washed through her nose and right cheekbone at the vicious blow.

He straddled Jessa's body on his knees, and his right hand closed hard around her throat. Jessa clawed at his thick wrist with both hands and kicked in panic.

"Stupid cunta." He shook her and Jessa's head snapped back. "You would work majik with the Kingsmen but half a league away?"

She struggled to breathe, her bracelets jangling with a harsh music.

"Careful, my Prince!" Radha said. "You would offer damaged goods in this affair?"

Jessa could see the thrill in his expression at her helplessness, and it was not an unfamiliar moment. He cupped her breast with his left hand, squeezing with violence. "Little rabbit," he said in a mocking tone.

Radha spoke yet again. "Careful, my Prince."

"What have I told you, dear sister," Joaquin said, "about consorting with this witch?"

"My Lord?"

Joaquin turned at Serabee's voice, the low timbre of the words seeming to cut through his enjoyment. Jessa fell away as he shoved her and then stood up. "Will you see to this witch once and for all? Or must I do everything myself, now that we've left the curried favors and hand-kissing of my father's presence?"

"I will do what I can, my Prince."

Joaquin considered Serabee for a heartbeat, then smoothed his tunic. For an instant, in the midst of her own confusion, Jessa could see that he was still adjusting to the idea that a man of Serabee's considerable power was his to command. "See that you do."

Joaquin left the tent as Serabee looked at Radha with a knowing expression. "Be careful, Lady Radha." He smiled. "There are no hidden passageways here for you to hide within or to use in making good your escape."

Radha returned his smile. "Lord Serabee El-Khan, I thank you for the warning and advise you of the same, in the coming months."

Jessa glanced at them as she tried to order her thoughts. She saw only the shadows of ancient enemies, however, a Lord of the Fakir and a High Priestess of the Vhaelin. Gods that had been mortal foes since the birth of the sun itself, their history awash in murder and honorable combat, the blood spilt upon both sides stretching back through the ages. Their combined energy dragged at her senses, Serabee's quiet laughter cutting at the base of her skull like a dull blade.

Serabee bowed his head and then spun about, tossing the canvas behind him as he took his leave into the night. Radha fell to her knees and grasped Jessa by the shoulders with gentle hands.

Jessa lifted her face and searched the shadows that swam above her bed. The darkness divided and a form shifted within the gloom, fighting to free itself. She reached out as her emotions swarmed up and broke through the walls she had built. She tried to recapture the heart of her vision and her eyes burned with sudden tears.

Don't leave me, Jessa, please.

Jessa sobbed at her name spoken so, for it was said with such sweet desperation.

She collapsed against Radha and began to cry. Radha glanced beyond her toward the far corner of the tent. "Hush…" Radha brought her face close. "Hush now, child."

The nausea swelled up in Jessa and she pushed free with weak hands. Her entire body ached, pinpricks of pain that moved within her blood like thorns. Vertigo pulled hard in the pit of her stomach and a cold sweat raced across her skin, her breath becoming short and strained. Her body jerked as her stomach pushed into her throat and she shoved it back down, trying to assert her will.

Radha came close once more and took hold of Jessa's waist, catching her when her arms gave out.

"Forgive me," Jessa whispered.

"It's all right, child."

Jessa felt confused as her eyes began to focus again.

"Who do you look for?" Radha whispered.

"Radha?"

"Yes, child, all is well."

Jessa fixed her gaze within the darkness near the ceiling of their tent, and for a time she searched with as much purpose as her strength could summon.

"Do you remember, child?"

"What happened to the bowl?"

"You have destroyed it. I should have known better, child. It is this place. The land beneath us is a stronger bowl."

"'Tis a holy place."

"Yes, there is too much power here. It is too easy to lose control."

"Your spell is not what you think it is, old woman," Jessa said softly.

"My spell is fine."

"What did I say?"

Radha hesitated. "You said nothing."

You lie, my Radha.

"What do you remember?"

"I remember nothing." Jessa gave as she was given, for she remembered the scent of the sea and lips upon her throat, soft and filled with warmth.

"Not a face?"

"No," she answered, and this time she told the truth. Joaquin had destroyed her trance too soon. She wiped at her nose and the back of her hand came away touched with blood. "Only smoke."

"I will fix the bowl," Radha said.

"I don't *wish* for you to fix it."

"Then what do you wish for?"

"To look up one day and understand. I wish to say, *Vhaelin essa yellam nee-ellow*." She pushed onto her right hip and tumbled over into a pile of pillows. "And thus praise my gods for smiling upon me."

Radha seemed to ponder her statement. "Perhaps you should meditate."

Jessa turned her face to a pillow, forcing her emotions down. This was the moment she always feared, this overwhelming sense of failure and betrayal. The knowledge that she was too weak and thus had abandoned the shade of her lover to the endless darkness of the spirit world. That her gods would give her but a taste of what was sweetest, then steal it away with such heartless indifference. That they could be so cruel when she had done nothing but serve them. "Be silent, old woman," she said. "Just… just for once, please."

Radha held her tongue, respectful as she turned away.

CHAPTER THREE

Late spring 1032
The city of Lokey, Arravan

The dice rolled across the boards, everyone in the main parlor of Madam Salina's House of Courtesans waiting with anticipation. The bones hit the surface of the overturned table and leapt back, tipping and then falling still.

Some three dozen spectators reacted, the parlor erupting with cheers as the Princess Darrius Lauranna Durand stood back and laughed, throwing her arms up in victory as the crowd swamped her.

Lord Bentley Greeves, jostled as the crowd surged around him in celebration, watched his friend with a broad smile. He knew what was said about the Princess. She was backwards in a world where such a passion was not fully accepted, especially for one of her station. She refused to deny that she reserved her love and desires for women and not men.

And at the moment, Darrius was as beautiful up close as she was from afar, and appeared to be just as wild as the rumors claimed she was. She was tall and her body was lean and powerful beneath her black uniform and white tunic, her shoulders, so he'd heard it said, were the sort that a woman could hold on to when in need of some leverage. And her hips, her hips were slim and her trousers hinted at a behind that was firm and delicious. Her thighs? He'd heard women give delicate moans at the sight of those strong legs.

And the hair. It was all heavy golden curls that were thick and natural and sinfully lush. It had been tied behind her neck when they arrived, but now it was not so and she was all the more beautiful as it spilled down her back to just between her shoulder blades. Her face was pleasing in the extreme, noble lines and chiseled cheekbones, a nose that was true above full lips, her skin soft-looking with just a hint of a tan. But it was her mouth that he caught people dreaming over, men and women alike.

The Golden Panther, he thought, the nickname given to Darrius when she was but a child, and from her sleek looks and the rich color of her hair, it was no surprise that it had stuck.

When Darrius had openly declared herself to be backwards, announcing to the world that she desired the company of women over that of men, she had created a long-lasting scandal. Conversation and debates had abounded, and more than a few factions within the Court of King Owen Durand had complained, some even speaking out against his youngest daughter and demanding that she conform to the dictates of her station.

She had refused, and her father had not forced the issue. It had all been petty politics, though, and so for those not immediately involved in such concerns only one thing mattered. The residents of Lokey loved Arravan's youngest child well, and whether she enjoyed the touch of a man or a woman made little difference.

The backwards women of the city desired her, though Bentley knew that Darrius honestly had no idea, no matter how many times he brought up the subject. And though her reputation was wild, not one courtesan could lay an honest claim to having shared her spirit with Darry. Not all courtesans would entertain those of the same sex, but very few would have turned down a client of royal blood, be they male or female. And even if a courtesan were undecided, one look into those unique eyes would most likely tip the scales in favor of a tryst, for her right eye was a rich emerald in color and her left a deep sky blue.

Darrius scooped up her gold and eyed her large opponent. "Well played, Sir Littleton," she said. "Just not your night."

Arton Littleton was no gentleman and he knew it. He was also extremely drunk. He stepped his three-hundred-stone, six-foot-six-inch frame into the circle of spectators and looked down his nose at her. "Do you mock me?"

"Darry, be nice now," Bentley said from the edge of the crowd.

Darry began to pocket her coins, smiling. "Yes, I am mocking you, Sir Littleton, but only a bit."

His nostrils flared wide.

"You've lost all night and still you bet more than your share," she said, her eyes never leaving his. "You should've known better, my large friend."

"If you weren't who you are…" He took another step.

"And who might that be?" Darry gave her heavy pockets a shake. "The woman who just took all of your coin, that's all. If you feel I've cheated you in some way, then take the first swing and with my blessing."

Bentley cringed. "Bloody hell."

Darry laughed. "Bentley don't be such a—"

Arton Littleton's right fist took Darry in the side of the head and sent her sprawling into the crowd. The big man laughed as several people tumbled to the floor beneath her. He spun about and held his arms high as a nervous cheer rippled through the crowd.

"You want my hammer in your ear as well?" Arton asked, shaking his fist.

Bentley blinked at him. "You've just hit the High King's daughter in the head."

"She said I could."

Bentley considered that. "Yes, but she's drunk."

"So am I."

"I am as well, actually, but this is all beside the point."

Arton frowned in confusion. "You want the hammer?"

"No, now see, this is what gets you into trouble, Arton," Bentley replied simply, tapping his fingers against the massive knuckles. "Someone tells you to bet all of your money and so you do. Someone tells you to hit a pretty woman in the head and so you do. It's a terrible pattern I see forming, and I think it might be the root of a more serious problem."

"What in the seven hells are you talking about?"

"I'm not sure. I was just waiting for Darry to get back up."

Arton spun about more quickly than Bentley would have thought for a big man in such a drunken state, but Darry was ready for him. Her right boot landed between his legs in a well-placed shot, and a collective groan moved through the crowd as Arton grabbed his crotch, falling forward onto his knees with a boom. Darry swung the empty pewter pitcher and it clanged against the side of his head.

Arton Littleton tipped to the right like a felled tree and slammed into the floor.

Bentley smiled. "Were you taking a walk?"

"I was trying to remember who I was," Darry said.

"And you are?"

"I haven't a bloody clue." She laughed and turned with a start.

Someone's shoulder hit her in the ribs and she let out a grunt as the body attached to it knocked her into several chairs and a table that skidded and tipped over beneath their combined weight. Bentley was caught up as the crowd surged, taking a fist on his left shoulder and shoved into the fight with a grin.

❖

Bentley sat on the cushioned bench behind the round table and stared at the parlor. Darry lounged against his body doing the same. Less than a dozen patrons were left and the mess had been cleaned up quickly, the damaged furniture dispatched for firewood. A fire blazed in the hearth and a lute was playing. The entire room was completely altered from its chaos of several hours earlier.

The windows behind them were closed to the night, though the louvered shutters allowed the ocean breeze to enter. The scent of the sea cut through the pipe smoke and ale, as well as the heady perfume that seemed to occupy every corner. A bar ran along the southern wall, fronting the kitchens and the corridor that led to the private baths.

Of the establishment's three stories, the upper two were reserved for the courtesans and their patrons. It was a place less rich and opulent than some, but its reputation was of the highest order. Madam Salina's did not cater to the Bloods of Arravan society, but offered pleasure and respite to its backbone and callused hands.

"How much gold do we have left?" Bentley asked.

"What we won or what we came in with?"

"Either."

"I'm not sure."

"Do we have enough to pay for this delicious Ravonese gold?" He took up his goblet from beside the empty wine bottle.

"I thought you already paid."

"You have all the coin."

"Oh, right," she said. "I didn't order it, Bent."

"Neither did I. I shall be scrubbing plates, I know it," he mumbled. "We win the biggest roll of the bones all night and it pays for furniture."

"And a bodhran."

"A bodhran?"

"Yes. Someone's head went through the drum."

"And here you thought your music lessons would never be of use."

"It was him or me."

"One would think that a princess would have better manners."

"And four bottles of Kenton Rose."

"My favorite vintage."

Several minutes of companionable silence passed and then, "Do you think it's safe to go home yet?" she asked.

Bentley noted the touch of melancholy. "We can stay as long as you like. We can even get a room, if you want."

Darry took a long breath and let it out slowly. "I drank too much."

"Are you drunk?" he asked. Darry made a good show of drinking and her reputation was such that everyone assumed she favored the grape, but he knew that she was rarely if ever drunk. She was too careful for that despite that she liked her fun.

She had fallen last in line of the royal children, and though that fact should have given her more leeway as the babe of the family, her life had been far from carefree. The eldest, Malcolm, was heir to the throne and a decided presence in Darry's life. It was no secret that he disapproved of her. As a consequence, Darry had been forced to step carefully, forever glancing over her shoulder for the blow of his condemnation.

The beautiful, red-haired Emmalyn was next behind Malcolm, and her generosity and graceful spirit made her much beloved. Bentley knew that Darry worshipped her sister and loved her terribly, but what she did not appreciate, perhaps, was that the feeling was mutual. Emmalyn was much like their mother, strong and filled with a presence that drew others to her side with little effort. She was also a touch like Darry, though her wild streak was somewhat reserved and showed itself more in her sharp tongue than her behavior.

Jacob was the middle child and a scholar of considerable renown. He was a man of quick wit and deep thinking, a diplomat and a member of the King's Council, his thirst for knowledge and clever mind having made him a confidant to both his father and Malcolm. He was betrothed to the Lady Alisha Pfinster, and their wedding was set for Solstice Eve but some three months away.

Wyatt was two years older than Darry and her beloved. He was dark-haired and quiet, and he let his sword do the talking. A warrior of uncommon strength and cunning, he had quickly risen in the ranks of their father's command. When Darry had taken to the sword as a girl, Wyatt had defended and watched over her, and they were thick in their blood and their love. That Wyatt now commanded the Arravan forces along the Greymear border to the east surprised no one.

And then there was Darrius herself, last in line.

Bentley observed her with a tilt of his head, his heart full at the sight of her. She was bolder than he ever dared and more generous and loving than anyone he had ever known. When they had met at the age of eight, it had taken but a minute to know that he loved her. *And not as many think.* He had been under serious attack from four of his eight brothers, and Darry had waded in and started swinging as their mothers had stood on the wide southern terrace of the royal retreat at Lake Aurora. Darry had announced unabashedly that he was not to be harmed. Their mothers laughed as she took his hand and they walked free from the mob, relatively unscathed and heads held high.

They had sat by the lake for hours and built a fortress of sticks and mud, and Darry had let him decide everything, asking what he thought and if he felt they should have a moat. No one had ever asked what he thought, and when they shook hands at the completion of their magnificent structure, he knew that he would always love her. It was the most wonderful summer of his life.

He had known that she was backwards before she did, perhaps, and had waited patiently for her to sort through her feelings as they had both tried to understand them. And he had never once wished her to be other than she was, for to him, she was his match in life, not love. "Are you drunk?" he asked again.

"A little, I think," she said. "But not much. I feel rather good, actually, aside from the dent in my head…and the teeth marks in my finger."

Bentley chuckled. "Much more entertaining than a formal dinner of tight collars to welcome your brother's Lyonese treasure."

That Malcolm had agreed to meet with the only daughter of King Bharjah of Lyoness to explore a proposal of marriage still stunned Darry. Arranged marriages had fallen out of favor over two hundred years ago, when her own ancestor had taken the daughter of a sea captain for his bride and made her a queen. Marriages of convenience and unions for political and social gain still existed but were no longer preferred.

Lyoness. The flames in the hearth across the parlor held Darry's attention. *What do you want with Bharjah's daughter, Malcolm?*

Early that morning Darry had stood in one of the far guard towers and watched the Lyonese caravan arrive, careful not to be seen as the covered coaches rolled into the courtyard. She had seen the Arravan flags raised and the banners had caught in the sun, blue and black and silver. Her family had stood in wait, dressed in their finest to greet Bharjah's children and their small entourage.

Armistad had first introduced the Prince Trey-Jak Joaquin and a tall man dressed in black that Darry assumed was his councilor. She had heard Jacob comment that he was a Lord of the Fakir and he looked the part, pale and lean and cold, even from a distance. The Fakir were extinct in Arravan, but the cult members had never been known for their warmth no matter where they hailed from.

The Princess Jessa-Sirrah had stepped from her coach with the help of her brother's hand and Darry had leaned close against the stones of the window ledge, trying to see her properly. All that Darry could determine, though, was that her hair was black and lustrous and the sari she wore was a blood crimson that caught fire in the sun upon her shapely figure. She had been followed by a servant, a small woman dressed in blacks and fringe, holding the silk drape that trailed behind her mistress.

The Princess Jessa-Sirrah had been introduced then, bowing low in proper etiquette and only touching hands with the women. Darry's mother and her sister Emmalyn broke from the greeting line to flank her, taking possession of her almost at once, and Prince Joaquin looked somewhat startled as she was led away from his authority.

Darry had not stayed to watch the men in the courtyard. Instead she drifted down the shadowed stairs, then moved through several back corridors and a secret tunnel that led to the eastern arch. She and Bentley were supposed to be in the city of Kenton, having claimed an assignment to avoid the formal greeting and the fanfare of the welcoming banquet that would begin when the sun set. She would catch all seven hells for her absence, but she preferred that to being trapped beneath the insufferable weight of courtly etiquette.

She and Bentley had finished their duty quickly and returned at once, determined to hide in Lokey until the furor died down at the arrival of the royal guests from Lyoness. It was a good trick and they knew it well, stealing their liberty from under the nose of their Commander, Grissom Longshanks, one of the most hardened veterans the Kingsmen had ever known.

"Do you think he'll marry her?" Bentley asked.

"Arravan and Lyoness have been enemies for almost three hundred years," Darry said, thinking aloud. "When we last went to war over the Lowlands, King Bharjah himself killed my uncle, or so it's said. He killed the future King of Arravan. Thousands of men died and nothing was gained, and the throne went to my father.

"A skirmish here and there, a minor advance to test the strength of our defenses at the Gap, but nothing to indicate more. So why the overture toward Malcolm when Bharjah knows that my father will make any final decision? He extended the proposal to Malcolm for a reason. To put the idea out there and let Mal stew upon the repercussions, to let him wonder and spin his own webs. I have no doubt that Mal has known of this for half a year or more."

"Without telling your father?"

"To have direct contact with Bharjah or his envoy without my father's interference? Malcolm would be drooling at the prospect. Though my father knew nothing about it until after Mal sent his response. He pissed on his boots with that, but Mal's always had a good aim, yes?"

"Because your father would've knocked him in the head otherwise."

Darry smiled. "Maybe. Yet the past month has been spent preparing for their arrival. A few council meetings after the fact and my father gives his consent to the visit?" She still did not understand. "He might've ordered the Western Army to turn them back. What harm would that have done? My father hates Bharjah and Bharjah hates him. If that gave insult what would it matter? Would Bharjah ride to war for that?"

"Would he?"

"No," Darry said. "No doubt he was shocked in the first place that his offer was even considered, much less accepted."

"And they were not turned back."

"Precisely. There's something much deeper going on here. Jacob and my father have been behind closed doors for hours."

Bentley knew that Jacob was considered an expert on Lyoness, and it was rumored that he controlled a network of spies it had taken him years to install across the unfriendly border to the west, the information they supplied second to none.

"Jacob knows something, and that knowledge somehow intrigues my father. It's all I can think of that would make him willing to even consider this entire thing. And whatever Jacob knows you can be sure that Malcolm knows it as well, and perhaps even before Jacob did. It's what spurred him into accepting Bharjah's proposal.

"Obviously Malcolm thinks this gamble with Bharjah's daughter is a good one. She'll stay here for weeks before they're allowed to be alone together, and months before the word *marriage* is officially spoken. He's buying time."

"Buying time for what?" Bentley asked. "As soon as he took Bharjah's offer it was certain your parents would be involved. What time does that purchase when your father will lead the negotiations?"

"None that I can see at this point. But it was Mal's opening move, setting the board to his advantage."

"Does he seek the throne before it's his?"

"Why would he?" Darry asked. "The throne is his birthright and he has spent his whole life preparing to claim it. But if he could bring about peace with Lyoness and secure the Lowlands once and for all? It would grease his path to the throne with scented oils and petals of roses. He sees some great victory in this scheme that will do just that."

"And so what information do they have?"

Darry laughed. "As if I would know? I'm the backwards indiscretion, remember? My father would no more share such knowledge with me than he would dance with me on Solstice Eve."

Bentley heard the taint of unhappiness once again and knew that she had drunk more wine than usual. She would never have made such a comment so casually were she not a tad in her cups, not even to him.

"Bharjah offered up his daughter like a prized piece of meat and Malcolm snapped at her like a hungry dog. My father has agreed to let them come and to see how this all plays out. That's all I know for certain and, to be honest, all I care to know. If thirty years from now Arravan has a king of Lyonese blood, this will be the best gamble that Bharjah ever made. No doubt I shall be long dead by then. Killed in a bar fight most likely."

Bentley's heart stuttered. "No doubt," he whispered. "Shall we have a big funeral?"

Darry smiled at the assumption they would go together. "I've just bought a bodhran, so perhaps we might have music as well."

"You should've broken a fiddle then."

"I hear that she's very beautiful," Darry said after a time, remembering her brief glimpse of the princess and how her sari had caught the sun.

"The Nightshade Lark?"

"Named so for her dark hair and famous voice," Darry said, wondering what Bharjah's daughter would be like. There was little mystery about her many brothers. They were said to be as their father—hard, cruel men. Of the Princess Jessa-Sirrah, however, very little was known.

"Perhaps she looks like her father."

"Don't jest, Bentley. She's being offered up like a sacrifice. She deserves our respect and best manners."

Bentley smiled.

After a while the barkeep approached, setting another bottle of Ravonese gold on their table, then taking up the empty one.

"We did not order such," Bentley said. "And though it's a rather delicious, fruity vintage, I think you have most of our coin already."

"Compliments of the Lady Marin Corvinus," the man said, and walked away.

"Corvinus. I believe I might know that one," Bentley said.

"Someone likes you, my pretty."

Bentley searched the room until his eyes fell upon the courtesan. Dressed in lace stockings and an ivory-colored corset with ties of green ribbons, she lounged in a cushioned chair as if it were a throne. Her face was beautiful, heart-shaped and delicate, and she eyed them with a secretive smile.

"Sweet Gamar's mustache. Sit up, Darry." Bentley filled his goblet again and stared across the room, searching for an invitation from the courtesan as he took a slow drink.

Darry's arms were on the table and her left hand played at the cuff of her right sleeve. "Is she pretty?"

"Decidedly so."

"I've a few golds in my pockets yet," she said as he refilled her cup.

The courtesan's head tipped back slightly and her lips parted as Darry took a drink, her gaze filled with more heat than the fire that blazed within the hearth. "Sweet Jezara," Bentley said. "Best save that gold for yourself."

Darry's brow came down in confusion.

Bentley laughed at her frown and reclined against the bench. "The wine was not for me. Look for yourself, by the hearth."

Darry set her wine down and let her eyes wander, taking in the woman's lovely curls, the red within the buoyant strands flaring in the firelight. She followed them down along the smooth neck and then farther still, admiring her gorgeous curves and the cut of the corset. Her legs were long and smooth, and Darry's blood heated in a wicked manner. She swallowed and turned away, warmth of desire starting at the base of her spine and spreading outward as she stared into her goblet.

"So what will you do, my kitten?" Bentley asked.

"She looks like—"

"She wants to kiss you?"

"Yes."

"Like she wants you beneath her on the cool sheets of her bed?"

Darry closed her eyes, only to have her mind latch hold of Bentley's suggestion. She could almost feel the woman moving beneath her, their skin slick as they thrust together on tangled sheets.

"She's very beautiful, Darry."

"I can see that," Darry answered in a tight voice.

The music in the parlor changed to a ballad plucked on the strings of the lute and meant for lovers. Darry let out a slow breath at the change in tempo. She could feel the woman's mouth on her, relinquishing herself to the absolute heat of it, the Lady Marin's tongue taking control and those hands on her breasts, lips clinging and pulling upon her flesh until…

And what would be the price, she wondered, for a moment's worth of pleasure? To risk her hard-won freedom for an indiscretion that Malcolm could very possibly use against her, despite the joy she might feel at the coupling. It was too easy and Darry knew it, acknowledging where she was and that the whole room would watch. She had not recognized any patron as one of Malcolm's men, but they did not have to be paid for at the moment, to be given his coin in the end. *Don't be a bloody fool, Darry. You're being careless.*

She had been in love once, and though she had proceeded with caution and as much discretion as she had been capable of, she had pursued her love with all of the wonder and enthusiasm that youth and a sense of invincibility might lend. But she had learned there were no guarantees, not even in love. *Or perhaps especially in love.*

Bentley could see the battle taking place within Darry. Her situation was complicated and he knew that better than anyone. That she deprived herself the comfort of a lover was no secret. She respected her family's position and the problems her heart might pose. Her sense of honor was deeper than any he had yet encountered, and she always kept in mind that a casual dalliance on her part might become a weapon to be used against the crown. She had to consider Prince Malcolm as well, and the fact that he waited for her to stumble, eager to assert his control in some way. What Malcolm would do when Darry decided to free her heart and declare her full independence at last, neither of them knew, but Bentley understood that she would never do it lightly and without great deliberation. And she would do it for nothing less than love.

He regretted having teased her, even in such a small way. "Let us go, my friend, yes?"

"Yes." Darry pushed her wine away with a careful hand. "Yes… before I forget what I'm fighting for."

CHAPTER FOUR

"You look fine." Bentley pulled at Darry's sleeve, keeping her from fussing with her collar. "If you don't stop, I'll have to piss."

"I thought I was the nervous one."

"You are, but you know I can't manage when you fidget about." His hands wiggled in front of his face as they walked along the balustrade. "If *you* can't handle it how am I supposed to?"

"Poor baby."

Darry saw her sister, Emmalyn, and then she saw the woman who stepped onto the wide terrace from one of the guest chambers.

"Sweet Jezara, is that her?" Bentley asked.

The woman wore a sari, as was the fashion in Lyoness, its silk draped about her curvaceous figure in a manner that was more suggestive than the dresses of Arravan. Her hair was a lovely spill of black curls that fell down her back. A veil clipped within the strands covered her face beneath the eyes.

Darry's heart skipped as she surveyed the woman's body and followed her movements, noting the bangles and bracelets on her wrists and the way her hands moved with grace as she closed the door.

Bentley straightened his own collar. "If she looks like her father, I shall spread my legs for him and bat my eyes."

Darry laughed.

Jessa took a jagged breath at the laughter and stepped back, a sudden fist closing within her chest as she turned. Her shawl slipped from her arm, and Jessa stared as it pooled on the stones at her feet. *Stop being so jumpy, you fool.*

Darry hurried her step as the princess knelt to retrieve the garment. She slid to a knee as she took up the silk with careful hands. "It appears I wasn't quick enough," she said with a smile.

Jessa met her eyes, her gaze moving from one eye to the other and taking in the shocking difference in color. The woman before her possessed a green eye on the right and a deep blue on the left, her expression filled with warmth. Her strong face was framed by wide golden curls that were stark against her black uniform, the high collar of the tunic rising along her neck.

So you must be the warrior, the backwards daughter they call the panther. Vhaelin essa, but you're lovely. A stutter of fear moved within her chest and she considered its weight, still caught beneath the woman's eyes.

"'Tis a lovely shawl, Princess," she said.

Not fear. It did nothing to push Jessa away but drew her forward instead.

"This is my sister, Princess Jessa," Emmalyn said, stepping up. "Captain Darrius Lauranna Durand. Her duties occupied her elsewhere upon the eve of your welcoming banquet."

"I'm sorry." The Princess Darrius's hand was still extended. "I didn't mean to startle you."

Jessa placed her hand within the Princess's. The feel of the strong hand about her own caused a pleasant flutter within Jessa's chest and she smiled beneath her veil. "*Tu an rayza masha-anna*," she breathed, tightening her grip as she rose and stepped close.

Darrius took a small step backward as etiquette demanded, releasing Jessa's hand and holding forth the shawl. "I'm afraid you must translate, my Lady."

Jessa found her tongue at last. "Thank you," she said, taking back the shawl. "You're most kind, Princess."

"And you're most welcome," Princess Darrius said. She glanced at her sister and lifted her elbow out. "Might we escort you to dinner?"

Emmalyn slipped her right hand in the crook of Darrius's arm. "By all means. Lady Jessa, this is Lieutenant Bentley Greeves."

Bentley stepped forward and lowered his head in deference. "Princess, I am most honored to make your acquaintance," he said formally. "If you would allow me the privilege of being your escort, I would be most pleased."

Jessa bowed her head in return. "I must enter the great hall with my brother, Lieutenant Greeves, but until then I will most humbly accept your arm."

"Off we go." Emmalyn turned to Darry and set them in motion. "Malcolm has promised a feast of delights. It wouldn't do for us to be late."

"Yes," Darry said, "that would be a sin."

Emmalyn cast her a sideways glance. "You're looking rather splendid in your dress blacks," she said.

The uniform had been specially tailored to fit, the jacket flaring at the waist and falling just past Darry's slim hips over a starched white tunic, her black trousers hugging her strong legs and tucked neatly into calf-high black boots polished to a brilliant shine. On the left breast was the embroidered emblem of her command, a golden mountain panther stitched with an expert hand. On the right were the insignia that announced her rank and several service medals as well, denoting that she had served along the borders of Lyoness and Greymear. She had also sailed for a year with the royal navy, patrolling the Sellen Sea aboard the Queen's own clipper, the *White Zephyr*.

Not even their brother Wyatt had managed to accomplish that. Their father had frowned upon such a duty as too dangerous. Darry, however, had gone when her opportunity to do so had arisen. The fact that their father had said naught against Darry for it and had refused to send for the ship's return still troubled Emmalyn. She was unsure why he had argued for Wyatt's safety and not Darry's.

Darry had been just seventeen, and it had been a very long year for those left behind. A year in which their mother had barely spoken to their father, her anger and worry so thick that from solstice to solstice the royal family had been at war within itself.

That war had ended only when Darry walked through the palace gates in her bare feet and worn, weathered uniform. She was as dark as an island native and grinning wildly. Wyatt had been so jealous that Emmalyn had thought he would burst, but he had worn it well and still swelled with pride when the *Zephyr* was mentioned, trumpeting their sister's service as if she had conquered the world.

"Darry?"

"Hmm?"

"Nothing." Emmalyn tightened her hold upon Darry's arm as they stepped from the stairs into the grand foyer. "Just wondering where you were."

They neared the doors of the great hall and Darry straightened her shoulders at the sight of their brother Malcolm and the Prince Trey-Jak Joaquin. "Just wishing I was a farmer's daughter, Em, and you?"

"Bloody well glad you're not."

Darry smiled in full, drawing Joaquin's gaze. She met his hazel eyes and nodded in deference, to which he bowed, as was custom. His brightly colored tunic and waistcoat were a startling shade of green beneath his tan jacket, the embroidery on the lapel and the piping along the jacket cuffs a matching green. His head was shaved extremely close, but he had a long braid hooked forward over his right shoulder. "The Princess Darrius, yes?"

"Prince Joaquin," Darry said. "A pleasure to meet at last."

"I'm glad you could join us this evening. I was greatly disappointed that you could not be present at the welcoming banquet."

His accent was thick and clipped, giving the Arravan words a harsh sound that Darry had not noticed with the Princess Jessa. "Alas, but duty called. A soldier goes where they're told. Is this not true in Lyoness?"

His smile was instant. "It is true for those not of the Blood, yes."

Darry ignored the taunt. "But I am just a captain, good Prince, not a commander such as yourself or my brothers."

"Well, you have limitations," Joaquin said. "A woman cannot expect to be of the same standing as a true soldier."

Darry tried very hard not to respond.

Malcolm stepped forward, his blue eyes severe. He wore his own uniform but a vest of silver closed about his white tunic, the decorative buttons onyx and flaring within the light. The jacket sported silver frogging that matched the piping along his trousers. His dark goatee and mustache were trimmed neatly, his thick black hair combed back from his face. "Emmalyn, allow me to escort you?"

"I believe your sister wishes to say something first," Prince Joaquin said quietly, his attention fierce upon Darry. "Princess?"

Darry smiled at last, taking Emmalyn's hand and guiding her to Malcolm. "Only that you should enjoy your meal, good Prince, for I hear it will be an absolute feast of delights."

As Malcolm took Emmalyn's arm, Darry refused to meet his glance. She never took her eyes from Joaquin.

After a span of time that infringed upon proper etiquette, Joaquin looked past her. "Jessa, *hootun ahshee*."

Darry stepped aside as Jessa let go of Bentley's arm and started forward. Darry smiled and then she winked. Jessa appeared surprised, then lowered her eyes as she stepped past her, her brother taking hold of her elbow.

Bentley stepped close, allowing Darry to lean against him in her leisure. They watched as Prince Joaquin escorted Jessa into the hall. Jessa's face was lowered and her steps matched those of her taller brother. She had surrendered to his authority in all things, even his gait. "Isn't he just as sweet as a peach," Bentley said with a lisp of mocking. "Such a clever boy."

"I'm thinking he doesn't like me."

"Liking has nothing to do with what he thinks of you, or what he might enjoy doing about it." Bentley chuckled. "Your beauty would appear to cast a wide and salacious net, my inferior female friend."

Darry returned her attention to the great hall, sighing as Joaquin held out Jessa's chair and took her hand. The Princess sat with grace, never lifting her eyes. "What a truly unpleasant thought. I'd rather have him drag me behind his horse." Bentley offered her his elbow and she took it. "Darling, always the gentleman," she purred, blinking her lashes.

"Let us do our duty and drink your brother's best spring wine," he said, "before you goad our foreign dandy into dragging you off by the hair and I'm forced to defend your rather dubious honor."

"By doing what? Confusing him with your wit until he decides which fist to beat you with?"

Bentley's step faltered as he sucked down his laughter. Darry merely kept walking, eyes straight ahead as they crossed the room. When they neared the table Bentley pulled out the chair to the right of Jessa's and Darry flipped her short coattail back and sat as Bentley claimed the seat beside her.

Jessa turned her head slightly as Darrius took up her goblet. She noted the small scars that adorned Darrius's skin and her fingernails that were trimmed close and neat. It was the hand of a soldier, the strength evident and revealing that her rank was far from ornamental.

At the head of the long table and seated to his father's right, Malcolm stood, drawing everyone's attention as he lifted his goblet. "Again, I welcome our guests from the western lands. Tonight, in honor of their stay, we have prepared a meal of Ibarris venison from the land of the Green Hills. I bid you enjoy."

Goblets were raised and Joaquin nodded at the honor.

The servers entered from the kitchens carrying trays laden with food: leeks and peppers in a thick wine sauce, freshly baked breads, and steaming platters of rare venison and spiced potatoes. The hall filled with the smells as plates were set before the guests accompanied by pitchers of spring wine and chilled water, as well as a sweet juice made from unfermented grapes.

Jessa closed her eyes at her plate. The sight of the venison sent a swell of nausea through her and a rush of heat within her chest. While considered a luxury to most, venison was forbidden to the followers of the Vhaelin. The stag was a sacred animal and the messenger of her gods. Jessa was trapped. If she didn't eat the delicacy provided by Prince

Malcolm she would insult him and her brother would make her pay for the slight.

Jessa felt something brush against her right arm and she opened her eyes.

Princess Darrius lifted Jessa's plate smoothly and replaced it quickly with her own. Jessa stared at the plate of fresh fruit and a thick fillet of smoked fish decorated with spicy red peppers. Startled, she looked at the Princess, who picked up her knife and fork, surveying her new dinner.

"He doesn't know, Princess," she said, stabbing the steak of venison. She placed it on top of Bentley's, who lifted his cutlery out of the way as she did so. Darrius set her fork down and reached for a pear from the bowl in front of her. "I do not care to eat venison on principle. The animal is much too beautiful to end up on my plate merely because someone was good with a bow. I don't approve of such an unfair fight," she said. "The cooks know this."

Jessa watched as Darrius cut her honeyed pear in half and then returned to the inviting food before her. She lifted her own fork and tried to find her tongue in response to the unexpected kindness. "Thank you."

"You're welcome. *Vhaelin essa ahbwalla*."

"*Ahbwalla essa*," Jessa automatically responded, startled yet again as the words of the Vhaelin blessing passed her lips. She looked once more at Darrius, who was studying the edge of her knife. "You worship the Vhaelin, Princess?"

"No, I do not. But you do, yes?"

"I do."

They stared at one another for the span of several heartbeats and Darry flashed a grin, the dimple pressing into her left cheek. "You shall have to explain to me, then, how I might avoid their Blood Fires."

Jessa looked at her, confused.

"I said I do not worship them, not that I didn't believe," Darrius said. "My mother tells me frequently that I shall wind up somewhere unholy for being such a terrible cad. I'm merely trying to avoid the more unsavory destinations."

Jessa laughed. That was the last response she had expected to hear. "If you're destined for the Blood Fires of the Vhaelin, Princess, I'm afraid there's naught you may do about it."

"Then I shall have to enjoy myself more while I am able. It shall take some effort, I think," Darrius said, then chuckled. "Eat your dinner, my Lady."

Jessa returned to her plate, delighted if not somewhat confused.

She rarely felt at ease with anyone, much less a stranger, but "at ease" described her condition exactly. And wonderfully off balance as well. The feeling was not at all unpleasant.

Darry cast her gaze down the table, running straight into the stern appraisal of Prince Trey-Jak Joaquin. She returned his stare and then smiled without guile, giving a small wave with her knife still in hand.

Emmalyn watched her. "Darrius."

Darry contrived an expression that embodied innocence as honeyed-pear juice coated her lips. "What?"

Emmalyn looked as if she could hardly keep herself from laughing. She often said that though Darry walked a fine line, she did so with such enjoyment and unrepentant daring that it was extremely difficult not to share in her humor. "I swear to Gamar, if Mother doesn't skin you alive I shall do it for her."

Darry swallowed awkwardly as Bentley laughed at the reprimand. "What've you done now?"

"Nothing," Darry said, reaching for her wine.

Bentley made a face and returned to his venison, carving a sizeable piece. "You don't actually need to *tease* him," he said so only Darry could hear. "He'll still want to fuck you."

Darry sputtered into her wine, closing her eyes to avoid the back spray as Bentley smiled in satisfaction.

She swallowed and cursed, setting the goblet down and reaching out. Jessa's fingers brushed hers as she placed a napkin in her palm. Darry wiped carefully at her mouth and left eye, praying silently that her mother's attention was occupied elsewhere. She cast a furtive glance to her left but Jessa appeared to be enjoying her meal with a hint of a smile.

❖

Jessa moved unseen within the shadows of the night, the spell she had cast familiar to her lips. Her cloak was pulled close about her body and its hood was wide and dark, enclosing her face. She had removed her bangles and veil, and her slippers were as silent as dust upon the stones. The spell did not make her invisible, but it allowed her to blend within the shadows and even the light, if need be, disguising her form as just another turn of darkness within the night.

Blackstone Keep was a magnificent structure, and even though the towers of the Jade Palace pierced the sky, she was discovering that it could not compare to the royal seat of Arravan. The outer curtain encompassed almost three times the space, and the stones of its walls were a mixture of granite and black rock, the combination not only beautiful but nearly impenetrable, their color having given the palace its name. The outer walls stood nearly thirty feet high and eight feet thick, and she gauged it to be two leagues or more upon each side.

The inner curtain stood taller yet, the towers and ramparts allowing for an easy defense in support of the outer ward and beyond. Though it was clearly designed for defense, the architect had also kept beauty in mind. The inner ward was wonderfully open, every measure of space planned to perfection with living quarters on all sides of the residence, with spiraling staircases and sweeping rises. Arches of cut marble and carved blackwood prevailed, with massive doors of teak that swung on pins of steel, making their massive weight irrelevant. And windows were everywhere, stained glass and open casements that required only the shutters be closed against the elements. Unexpected skylights opened high within the ceilings, protected by thick panes of glass that allowed a surprising amount of sunlight to fall within the building. Even the moonlight passed through them, illuminating the corridors with its pale glow.

Carpets and heavy tapestries adorned the walls, brilliant scenes of Arravan's history on display. And within the inner bailey were the gardens and the keep with its great hall, the foyer, and a solar. The Queen's Library and the lesser halls for minor functions surrounded these, with the kitchens at the heart of it all. The throne room was there as well, connected to the council chamber and the great hall, though Jessa had yet to see the throne of Arravan itself.

Many of the rooms and private chambers within the residence had two entrances, one that led into the closed interior and one to the outer balustrade. Slanted roofs offered protection from the rain and elements, yet provided the feel of a walk outside, despite the fact that the stones beneath were high above the ground. Some of the chambers, such as her own, were built within odd spaces that allowed for both entrances as well as a balcony, the stone jutting out upon smooth corners and curved towers.

As Jessa moved along just such a terrace walk, keeping close to the inner wall, she realized that she had never been in a more welcoming place. She had yet to know the people, though her opinions were forming quickly, but the palace itself had been constructed with obvious love and care. She was certain hidden corridors and pathways known only to a few existed, for such was the nature of a palace. It was clean and open, and much too inviting not to acutely appreciate it.

As she neared one of the open staircases that would take her down to the main level, she stopped beside the stone rail and tried to gauge the size of the barracks and the stables, the latter bordered by fertile green paddocks and straight planked fences. She took in the bulk of the massive armory and the wide practice yards beyond the barracks with its watch bell tower. She could see torches within the towers of the outer wall and light from the guard posts near the main gate.

She could smell the sea and lifted her face toward the Bay of Alirra, seeing the lights of Lokey spread beneath the palace and spill in twisting streets toward the harbor. Several ships were anchored there, waiting through the night tides upon their moorings and the massive piers. She wondered how the palace might appear from below to one of those ships sailing into Arravan's largest port.

When a distinctive voice intruded upon her explorations, Jessa stepped back from the rail and drifted through the shadows along the wall, waiting, then catching a second voice. Common sense told her to avoid them, but her curiosity took hold and she searched them out instead, silent as she descended the stairs. As she neared the bottom the voices began to take shape. Jessa spied the deepest shadows and slipped within their protection.

"Do you think I didn't see you?"

"I didn't think of you at all, actually."

Prince Malcolm faced Darrius as she sat on the rail. Darrius had removed her jacket, which lay neatly beside her. "This was a formal function, Darrius, not a *tavern* for you and your friend Greeves to make a mockery of."

Jessa found the darkness beneath the staircase and drifted into the thickest part of its gloom, standing as still as the stones behind her.

"We did no such thing and you know it," Darry answered in a tired voice. "I'm sorry if you thought so. That wasn't my intention."

"You engaged the Princess in conversation? As if she were just another guest at my table?"

Darrius's eyes were sharp. "It is our father's table, Malcolm, not yours. And I treated her as I would a friend. For the love of Gamar, you had her seated half a world away from the people she knows. Did you not consider she might be nervous?"

"She knows her place," Malcolm snapped. "As you never have."

"And what place is that?" Darrius asked.

"Must I renew my objections and tell you yet again the shame your behavior and you cause me?"

Darrius laughed. "Not what my place is, you bloody fool, *hers*."

Malcolm took another step, and from Darrius's perch on the rail they were nearly of the same height. "Take care how you speak to me, Darrius."

"Or what?" she asked, reclining casually. "When you're the lord of all the world you may banish me to whatever dark hole you see fit. But until that time, never forget that I carry the same blood as you, and it comes with certain rights and privileges. Calling you a fool is perfectly within those rights, I assure you."

Jessa smiled in surprise.

Malcolm's response was slow to form, his hands clasped behind his back. "Then what did you mean?"

"Malcolm," Darrius's tone softened, "you're bartering for the hand of another human being. This isn't a horse that you bid for or land you must trade for. She's a *woman*, Mal, a beautiful and striking human being. You sent for her and Bharjah wrapped her in bright colors and obeyed, though we both know for reasons of his own. If you truly wish to court her then *win* her, Mal, seduce her until she says yes out of want, no matter the question you would pose. Not because her father or her pig of a preening brother tells her to. Don't presume to just *take* her. She's not yours for the taking. She belongs to no one but herself."

Jessa felt a stirring in her chest at the heartfelt words. To be defended by anyone was not something she had ever come to count on. Only Radha had stood by her. But for a stranger to stand up and voice compassionate words in her defense was something she had never envisioned happening.

Malcolm's smile was cold. "Is that what you would do then?"

"Yes," Darrius replied. "That's exactly what I would do."

"You really have no clue as to what needs to be done or how things work, do you?"

"I know what's important."

"And what might that be? Playing at being a man?"

Darrius gave a breath of laughter. "Yes, Malcolm, that's exactly what I mean."

"Is there not a tavern you must be at, Darrius? Someplace suitable to your backwards behavior? Should you not be drunk?" His tone was callous. "Should you not be begging to kiss the sweat from between a barmaid's thighs by now? You may leave the important things to those of us with the intelligence and authority to handle them properly."

Jessa was startled at the sexual reference and considered his words as she watched Darrius for a response. She understood that Darrius was backwards. Radha had made good on her pledge for more information. She had not, however, truly considered the heart of the matter until that very moment. *I do not think she would have to beg, you fikloche. Bloody well* look *at her. They must stand wanting beyond her door.*

Darrius was very still and Jessa felt the sudden tension, an air of danger about Darrius as if any reaction were possible. She saw that even Malcolm felt it, for he took a silent step back, creating some distance between them as his hands fell open to his sides. Jessa understood the reason beneath his words at once. She was familiar with the tactic. As any one of her brothers had done a thousand times, Malcolm sought to provoke Darrius into a retaliation he might take advantage of.

"Do you remember that summer at Lake Aurora, Mal?" Darrius met his eyes. Her expression held nothing but a sincere smile. "When we would race every morning from the southern terrace to the waters, and Wyatt and Jacob would always win? And I would be so angry that I couldn't keep up?

"And you decided that racing in teams would be more fair, so you chose me?" Darrius's laughter was filled with warmth. "And then we raced, and you pushed Jacob into the lairien bushes and tackled poor Wyatt into the dirt, yelling for me to run. 'Run,' you yelled, and you were laughing so hard and I was running for all I was worth, running so hard that I thought my legs would fly off."

Malcolm's eyes narrowed, his left cheek twitching slightly.

"I remember that," Darrius said softly. "And how you spun me around and we fell into the water, laughing until we nearly drowned, and Emmalyn crowned us with laurel wreaths. And we paraded about until Mother made us stop, even though she was laughing too. Do you remember that?"

"No," Malcolm answered simply. "I remember my sister very well, though, before she became ill. Before she became whatever it is that you are now. Stick to your taverns and the bastard sons that are your friends, Darrius. Stay out of the affairs that are taking place here. If you don't, you may find that dark hole sooner than you would like."

Darrius laughed and sat up straight. "Whatever you say, sweet brother," she said. "Is there any tavern in particular that you would like me to seek out? The Blue Porpoise perhaps? I hear they have an ale that will get you drunk within a single tankard. A boastful promise if ever I heard one."

Malcolm turned away. "That will do nicely, thank you."

Jessa's eyes never left Darrius's face, even as Malcolm passed close and disappeared beyond the angle of the stairs above her.

"Sweet dreams, my Prince!" Darrius called, setting her hands on the wide rail and bumping her boot heels against the posts. After a time she looked down.

Jessa stood very still, her chest tight as she held to her cloak. She could hear a lark somewhere, the night bird she was named for in her native land singing out within the darkness. The urge to step from the shadows rose up within her like an unexpected tide, surprising in its need as she struggled against it, against the overwhelming impulse to walk into the open, if only to stand beside Darrius while she thought whatever she might be pondering.

Jessa took a silent step forward, and then another.

"Darry?"

Jessa retreated awkwardly at the voice, recognizing Lieutenant Greeves as he moved from the shadows farther down the walkway.

Darry spied him within the moonlight. "Bentley." Her voice was rough and she cleared her throat. "I have orders from our Prince."

"Yes? And what are they?"

"We are to get drunk with all good speed."

Bentley spread his arms and bent back at the waist. "At last." He sighed dramatically. "An order I can follow in all good conscience!"

Darrius laughed as he approached, giving her his back. "Ah, my mount." She pushed from the rail and wrapped her arms about his neck. He grabbed hold of her legs as they hugged his waist from behind, and they laughed as he stumbled. "My jacket, if you please, good steed."

He let out a grunt and moved sideways as Darrius snagged her coat. "Have you been eating pastries again?" he said, taking hold behind her knees.

"Only the ones with butter and cream frosting."

"Well, stop it."

"Yes, my friend." She kissed his neck as they moved along the walkway.

"I mean it, Darry."

"*Fine*." She sighed. "You're a weak little thing, Bent. Buck up, will you?"

"Yes, dear. Shall we round up the troops?"

"By all means! Let us see if Darry's Boys can reduce the city of Lokey into some rather pretty rubble, shall we?"

"Indeed," he said, turning his head as they passed by the alcove beneath the stairs.

Jessa almost gasped aloud as he met her gaze, her heart seizing at his hard look of recognition, his expression filled with warning. And then they were past her, Jessa retreating until she bumped into the wall behind her, Darrius's infectious laughter floating in their wake.

❖

Radha stood at the balcony arch in the curve of the north wall and watched Jessa sit in the moonlight. Jessa's eyes were closed and her face was raised to the light. How much Jessa resembled her mother, the beautiful lines of her face and the elegant curve of her neck. Even her body was reminiscent of her, voluptuous and graceful in its form yet never too obvious in any feature.

"What troubles you, child?"

"If the Veil of Shadows is cast properly, is it still possible to be seen?"

Radha narrowed her eyes. "Were you seen?"

Jessa did not answer.

"At times." Radha moved back into their spacious chambers. "If the desire to be seen is strong enough, the charm may transform. This happens only when you're careless."

"I wasn't careless."

"If you were seen then you were careless."

Jessa searched the night sky, gauging the direction of the constellations and finding the stars of the warrior Attia. The Princess Darrius was not what she had expected, not in any way.

She thought of Darrius sitting alone on the railing of the walkway, her hair catching the moonlight. Her expression had been so sad in that brief instant before she lowered her face, left in the wake of her brother's attack. Jessa also remembered the words Darrius used to challenge him. She had met his malice with a memory that sounded so lovely Jessa had felt a fierce stirring of envy.

Jessa smiled, remembering the laughter into the wine at the banquet and the grin that Darrius had tried to stop as she wiped her face. Laughter stirred within Jessa once again, only this time she released it. *And what do those eyes look like, I wonder, when your full humor is upon you? Such colors filled with laughter and not sadness, I would very much like to see that. Before you're cast into the Blood Fires of the Vhaelin for being a cad.* She smiled more freely and the heat of a blush rose along her neck.

CHAPTER FIVE

Darry ran, her bare feet sure within the thick grass despite the morning dew. She rushed through the hedgerows of the gardens at a rapid pace. The air burning her lungs felt good. Darry tasted the sharpness of the hedges with each breath. Their scent filled the back of her head and flooded her with the flavor of new things.

She bolted down a separate path near the heart of the main gardens, never stopping, pushing herself faster. She laughed, breathless as she ducked her head and broke through the corner of a hedge in a sharp turn, leaves flying in her wake. She could smell the water.

Jessa walked along the edge of the clearing in the early morning sun. She trailed her hand through the ivy and verdant leaves of the hedge. The small white flowers of hamesroot were in full bloom and tangled within the branches, teasing her fingers and stirring her sense of touch.

The bluish-green water of a pond was set within the small glade, the land it occupied low within the center of a natural depression and fed by a spring near the eastern edge.

It was a place of serenity and undeniable beauty, the colors rich and fulfilling, and as Jessa moved along the southern hedges, she wondered how deep the water might be at the center. When summer was high in Lyoness and the heat at times unbearable in its arid oppression, the mosaic tiles on the bottom of the reflecting pool in the western courtyard of the Jade Palace showed, bereft of water. The comparison appalled her.

The Princess Darrius burst into the clearing in a rage of movement and Jessa stumbled into the solid presence of the hedge. She spoke the runes of her spell upon sheer instinct, the Veil of Shadows rising like a surge of heat erupting from the earth.

Darrius tossed her tunic into the air behind her and slowed her pace only long enough to awkwardly discard her trousers, hopping as she lifted one leg and then the other. She was left only with short breeches that clung to her strong thighs and backside and a sleeveless homespun that reached her belly. Darrius sprinted into the shallows of the pond, sliced into the water with a flat dive, and disappeared beneath the surface.

Jessa knelt beside the hedge and waited, her heart pounding as she spied the discarded clothes. Darrius came up for air in a splashing of water.

She swam for a time, exploring the confines of the pool and laughing with simple pleasure. The sound caught against the water with a subtle echo. When she ducked beneath the surface once more Jessa stood up slowly, not wanting to lose sight of her.

Darrius's feet speared into the air and her legs wavered. Jessa smiled as Darrius walked on her hands beneath the water and tried to keep her balance. She tumbled over eventually and disappeared with a splash before surging to the surface and pushing smoothly toward the shore upon the southern edge.

Jessa caught her breath as Darrius pushed her curls back and they slapped against her shoulders. Her clothes clung to her form, her breasts high beneath the homespun and firm in their shape, her nipples raised. Jessa's chest filled with heat as she took in the rigid muscles of Darrius's stomach and the clinging breeches, her tight backside utterly on display as she turned and pulled at the material.

Stepping from the pond, Darrius grabbed her hair and wrung out the water with certain hands. Her breeches slipped low on her slim hips but she let them be, taking a few more steps and glancing about.

Jessa held her breath as Darrius stood very still and stared across the distance between them. Radha's words about being careless swept through Jessa's thoughts and she put more strength into the spell, feeling it pull at her blood as if it were an insistent hand on her arm.

Darrius turned again and sat on the grass, then lay down with her hands behind her head as her legs stretched out, her feet but inches from the water. The sky was becoming light as the sun rose higher.

Jessa took one careful step and then another, watching Darrius's prone form and seeing no reaction. She moved then, making for the nearest opening in the hedge and trying not to rush her escape. She was wary, though the Veil of Shadows would mask her movements. Perhaps she would be a breeze in the leaves of the hedge, or a ripple on the water, though either way she would not be the intruder that she actually was.

"I can hear you."

Jessa stood absolutely still, closing her eyes as she let out a slow breath.

"Are you planning to scold me for not being proper?" There was amusement in Darrius's voice. "No one likes a nag, you know."

Jessa turned smoothly and let the Veil of Shadows slip away. Darrius had not moved from where she lay, her thoughts still within the sky. If Jessa walked away after being acknowledged she might give insult, and yet if she approached it would...*it would what? She's the one who's running about half naked and jumping into ponds as if she were something wild and...something wild and beautiful.*

Jessa squared her shoulders and walked into the clearing, trying to decide how the rules of etiquette applied to the situation.

"I don't know why you didn't come in." Darrius sighed. "The water's nice and cool."

Jessa stopped at Darrius's discarded tunic and considered the ease of the words and her familiar tone. She picked up the shirt, giving it a shake. *And who do you think I might be, that your current state of undress is of no concern?*

"You used to come in."

Jessa picked up the trousers as well, still approaching. Her heart was pounding but she felt the innocent misunderstanding with a touch of enjoyment.

"I remember when you'd throw off everything," Darrius said, grinning as she closed her eyes to the brightening morning. "And in you went like a bloody fish."

Jessa stopped near the top of Darrius's head. She held the high ground in more ways than one. "I don't recall that."

Darrius jolted at the unexpected voice.

Jessa stepped back as Darrius was on her feet in a heartbeat, spinning about. And then her bare feet slipped on the wet grass.

"No!" Jessa lunged as Darrius's legs kicked out and she fell back, but Darrius hit the water with a splash and met the bottom. She slid in the silt and then scrambled to stand. Jessa eased closer in concern, forgetting that she had yet to fasten her veil. Darrius pulled at her breeches, which were slipping from her hips, splashing to the side until her feet found solid ground.

They stared at one another. Jessa's vantage point had changed now and her confidence seeped away.

Darry studied Jessa's face, seeing for the first time her full beauty. Her cheekbones and chin were sculpted in fine lines and her lips were ample and wide, though the darkness of her eyes stood out above everything. The black curls and braids of her hair fell against her tanned complexion, which was a warm shade of light caramel that made Darry feel like sighing. Jessa's eyes seemed lit from within. Her nose completed the picture in a perfect manner, a tiny bump upon the bridge just enough to add a touch of delicious character.

Jessa smiled and met Darry's silent appraisal.

"Look at you," Darry said with a grin. "You're beautiful." Then Darry realized what she had said and let out a nervous laugh. "I mean… well, that's what I meant, actually, yes," she said, and felt a blush invade her face. "But I thought…" Darry looked down at herself, pulling at her breeches. "I thought you were my sister."

Jessa followed Darry's movements and blushed also. "I am not."

"Yes, I see that now, thank you."

Jessa held out her hand again. "Come out of there."

"Why don't you come in?"

"I beg your pardon?"

Darry considered Jessa's startled tone and frowned as she tried to remember the rules of etiquette. She was not speaking to just a beautiful woman but to a daughter of royal blood. "Did I just insult you?"

"Was it proper for you to ask me that?"

"Was it?"

"No."

"And I'm standing in my breeches."

Jessa tried very hard not to look down again, for Darrius's body was extremely pleasing, all sleek muscles and smooth skin. "Yes," she replied quietly. *Don't look down, don't do it*. But Darrius's breasts were clinging to her tight shirt just beyond the edge of her focus, the dark nipples on display. *Don't, Jessa.* "Give me your hand, please," Jessa said, her blood hot within her veins.

Darrius obeyed and Jessa pulled her from the water. She let go of Darrius's hand and waited, confident that Darrius would say something. But Darrius merely pulled at her shirt again, looking somewhat perplexed by the stubborn material.

"Put this on, my Lady." Jessa offered the tunic. She would not have thought anything would make Darrius shy.

Darrius took it in silence and shrugged into the sleeves, flipping her hair to the side then flinging it back. Jessa closed her eyes at the water that dusted her face and the silk of her blue sari.

"Bloody hell."

Jessa laughed. "You're right, it's cold."

"I'm sorry, Lady Jessa, truly. I didn't mean to do that."

Jessa was still smiling as she held out the trousers with one hand and wiped at a cheek with the other. "It's only water, Princess."

Darrius took her pants back. "I didn't just ruin that, did I?"

"I think," Jessa spoke kindly, surveying her sari as she quickly brushed it with her hands, "that it would not be the first lady's dress you've ruined." And then she realized how her words must sound. "I mean, you don't seem well suited to women's fashions, Princess…I mean, what you wear…"

"Not what a lady usually wears."

Jessa stepped back, trying to compose herself. She wanted to be understood. "I like what you wear very much," she said. She had never met a woman who dressed as a man, but considering what she had seen thus far, Darrius's unique fashion was highly appealing and more than agreeable to her personality. "You are…they, I mean, they suit you most wonderfully."

"When I'm actually wearing them."

"Well, you look, I mean you look very fine…" Jessa's tongue stumbled into her private thoughts quite against her will. "You're just, you're quite lovely without them, too." Mortified, she wanted to sink in the ground and disappear.

Darrius smiled at the words. "I tried this fashion, actually, but my mother didn't approve."

"And why not?"

"It doesn't go with my boots."

Jessa laughed. "You're quite mad, I think."

"Maybe a little," Darrius said.

Jessa tried to settle her scattered thoughts and the first one to take root was that her veil was not yet fastened. She quickly took possession of the silk.

Darrius took a quick step and reached out with a gentle hand, guiding Jessa's hand away from the veil. "I'm standing here half naked, my Lady," she said with a slow smile. "If you raise your veil you would leave me all alone. Please don't."

Jessa felt the fingers about her hand tighten for a heartbeat then release her before she could return the pressure. The lost opportunity slightly dismayed her.

"Seems only fair, yes?"

"Yes."

"And I have another idea." Darrius spoke as if in secret. "If you will allow me? Why don't we stop being so nervous and just be friends? I could use a friend. What do you say?"

"You have many friends already, I think," Jessa replied with quiet certainty.

"But none of them are you." Darrius gave a brilliant smile. She held her hand out and then brought it back with a quick frown, wiping it on her damp tunic before she presented it again. "What do you say, Princess, shall we shake hands on it?"

Jessa considered the strong hand before her.

"It's what friends do in Lyoness as well, yes? They make a bargain and shake hands?"

"Yes." Jessa slipped her hand into Darrius's, finding the touch against her own impossibly warm and inviting. She had never been offered such a thing before. "I would like that very much, thank you."

Darry shook her hand with gentle enthusiasm and Jessa laughed. "And so now is it proper if I ask?"

"Ask what?"

"If you'd like to go swimming."

"No."

"No, it's not proper, or no, you don't want to?"

Jessa laughed again. "No, it's not proper."

Darrius slowly let go of Jessa's hand. "I'm not very good at this."

"At what?"

"At being proper, I suppose. I try, but things come out wrong."

"You're doing fine, not to worry, my Lady."

"Call me Darrius, or Darry, if you prefer," she said. "Friends have no need of titles, Jessa. Even etiquette allows for that."

Friends. Jessa found herself smiling yet again. "So I will see you at dinner then…Darry?" Darry had been absent from each function since the night of her argument with Prince Malcolm, and Jessa suspected his words were the cause. *As was I, yes? His cruelty resulted from your kindness toward me.* "It's been two nights since you saved me with smoked fish and peppers, and I've seen you nowhere. Your duties will allow you to attend?"

"For certain. I'll request my commander to relieve me of night duty."

"Honestly?"

"You asked me, Jessa, and so I shall come. As I said, we're friends now. You shall have a hard time getting rid of me."

"Then I will look for you." *I asked and so you shall come. It cannot be so simple as that, can it?*

"Off you go then," Darry said. She looked at her bare feet. "I have to find my boots."

"I'll save you a seat. Next to mine."

"And I'll be wearing clothes. With any luck you'll be able to recognize me."

Jessa laughed as she turned, and Darry watched the curls and braids of hair against the drape of her blue sari and the sway of her hips as Jessa hurried from the clearing toward the path that would lead her to the keep. The sound of her bangles and bracelets was like birdsong in the air, and Darry could hear them long after Jessa had moved through the hedges.

She frowned as an ache moved along her spine, though whether it was from her wet clothes or the beauty that had unexpectedly graced her morning she had no idea. She tossed her trousers over her shoulder and traced her own path back through the gardens. "Bentley was right." She walked awkwardly for several steps as she tried to adjust her breeches. *If she looks like her father…bloody hell, but she's altogether fine.* "And I'm frolicking about in my breeches," she mumbled, then laughed at herself, a genuine rush of excitement rising at the prospect of getting to know such an appealing woman. *Mal can rot for all I care.*

She ran then, making her way back along the path at a furious pace. She knew the twists and turns like the palm of her hand, and when she reached the small circular clearing where she had left her boots and socks, she looked up at the marble fountain sitting in its center.

From the heart of the sloping marble bowl, the carved granite of a scantily clad woman rose, her right arm outstretched. The water flowed in a smooth stream from the tips of her fingers. She bore round hips, and the robe that looped about her round hips in a low-slung manner ascended her body and covered a single breast, the other left exposed and decidedly on display.

"My first sweetheart," Darry said, and seized a boot, grinning at the truth. She was halfway into her right boot then yanked it off, grabbing at her trousers instead as she thought of Jessa's braids.

"Darrius!"

Darry let out a grunt of surprise at the all-too-familiar voice. Her left foot caught in her trousers as she turned on a heel and lost her balance, then hit the ground with a solid thud. "Seven *hells.*" She huffed and rolled onto her back, her arms flopping out as she blinked into the sky.

"Darrius Lauranna, what are you doing?" her mother said with a laugh. "By the gods, have you lost your mind?"

"It's been a splendid morning thus far, yes," Darry said.

The High Queen of Arravan stood tall in a pale blue skirt and simple white tunic, her fading red hair pinned behind her neck. Her face was quite beautiful, laugh lines showing at her deep green eyes and her fifty-four years exposed only slightly within her graying hair and smooth complexion. "Should I even ask what you're doing without your pants on?"

"You're free to ask, of course. But I don't really know if you want the truth." Darry sighed as the watch bell within the main bailey sounded. "Perfect."

"You're late." Her mother's hands landed on her hips. "You'll be mucking the stables."

Darry rolled over and found her feet, then yanked up her trousers and tied the drawstring as quickly as possible.

"And no more night duty," her mother said as Darry slid on the grass and retrieved her boots and socks. "I've spoken to Longshanks about his ill-conceived duty schedule, and though he didn't appreciate my tone, at least he understood my annoyance. He was most happy to put you… what?"

"I'll be digging postholes for a bloody *month*."

"What've you done now?"

Darry moved forward in a rush and her mother accepted her kiss of greeting with a pleased smile. And then Darry was running and sliding around the fountain, then making for the bailey up the quickest path.

"Dress blacks, sweet Cat!" her mother called.

Darry sprinted along the path until it curved into the smooth stones leading to the solar and the minor halls of the keep, turning to the left beneath the portico and heading for the barracks and stables. The hard-packed earth of the bailey came up fast, and as she turned with the lane she tried to stop her momentum.

Darry felt her father's hands tighten on her arms and push her away gently. His salt-and-pepper hair still showed traces of black, brushed back from his clean-shaven face. He was tall and still strongly built and wore his age well, though he was a tad heavier about the waist than when in his prime. "You're a bit *wet*, Darrius," he said, surveying her clothes and then his hands.

"Yes, sir."

"A nice long run?"

"Not really, sir."

"Swimming?"

"Sort of, sir."

"Sort of swimming?"

"Yes, sir. I, ah, fell in the pond."

His brow went up in question as the bells of the tower sounded for a second time. "You're late, Captain."

"Yes, sir. May I go, sir?"

"On your way then."

"Thank you, sir," Darry said, and bolted.

Owen Durand watched her run, noting the speed and the strength with which she moved. Her comrades yelled upon seeing her and he heard laughter as Jemin McNeely, who was quite possibly the largest man Owen had ever seen, jogged forward. Darry called out as Jemin bent at the waist and lifted her up, catching her at the knees as she tumbled down his back with laughter. Bentley smiled and yanked her boots away, then held them up as if they were trophies as Jemin carried her toward the barracks, their friends spilling out of the way at his booming voice.

Owen continued along the path, smiling contentedly.

CHAPTER SIX

The summer deepened slowly, and life within Blackstone Keep had settled into its new routine. Owen and his sons engaged in daily council meetings, intent upon treating with the Lyonese delegation.

The ladies of the palace had a different agenda, and Cecelia negotiated her own sort of council. Their days contained activities that were no longer commonplace but had a subtle air of importance. Things had been even more hectic within the past week for they were planning the official ball that would introduce Prince Joaquin and Princess Jessa-Sirrah to the Blooded society of Arravan.

Darry had always made it a habit to disappear rather smoothly at this point in the season, leaving the details to others, saying she had to train for the Solstice Tournament. And while she did in fact train with relish and dedication, this season she had been strangely underfoot.

She sat cross-legged in her chair, her hair tumbling forward as she held her embroidery. Darry had always been good with the needle but she hated it immensely. It was too small and she moved too quickly, the patterns for lace and other disciplines requiring a patience she rarely had. That she sat thus, in her chair between Emmalyn and Jessa with her boots on the floor and her legs so, was a horrible breach of etiquette, but Cecelia had not the heart to correct her. Darry was making a true effort.

Jessa watched Darry as well, and though Cecelia could not hear what was said, the ghost of Darry's voice floated across the sunlit study. Jessa's shoulders shook, her eyes on her lace as she laughed.

Darry was an object of extreme interest to Jessa, and Cecelia had yet to decide why. It might have been Darry's manner, for she could not hide her boldness for long. Jessa had most likely not encountered such a woman before. Lyoness was not a land that allowed a woman her independence, and Darry tended to kiss her freedom with relish upon the throat until liberty spilled her rewards with a sigh.

It might have been that she was a soldier and dressed as a man, though her womanly virtues were unmistakable no matter the clothes she wore.

And it might have been that she was backwards.

In Lyoness the openly backwards were put to death, and though it had not been discussed, Cecelia knew that Owen had to take Darry into consideration as he negotiated with Prince Joaquin. Darry, especially since she was highborn, blatantly displayed the differences in their cultures. If and when might it become an issue? Cecelia had not missed how Joaquin stared at Darry with annoyed interest. But Jessa, she noticed, appeared fascinated.

A few hours here and there, such as now and during meals, at some point each day Darry found her way onto the chair beside Jessa, and Jessa welcomed Darry's sudden presence with sincere enjoyment. Their conversation seemed to consist of simple things as far as Cecelia knew, but they appeared exceedingly at ease with one another, and Darry was very attentive when Jessa was near.

And if they were not beside one another, they sought each other out, Jessa showing a true intensity of purpose when Darry was across the room from her instead of by her side. Darry had helped Jessa adjust to her new surroundings with respect and humor, and Cecelia was grateful in more ways than one.

They have become friends. The bell tower rang, interrupting Cecelia's musings.

Darry gave a winning smile. "Ah, well." She stretched out her legs and dropped her feet to the floor. "It appears that I must leave you for more important things, such as staring into the sun and standing for hours in one place."

"Give me that." Emmalyn held out her hand out for the delicate handkerchief that Darry had been sewing.

"So you may claim it as your own?" Darry said. "My Lady Jessa, if you would keep this for me, please. My sister is most cunning and will steal my hard work."

"Yes, of course, Lady Darrius," Jessa said quietly, taking the offering.

"Darry, apologize to your sister," Cecelia said in mock reprimand. "Your sewing is not as good as hers. What use has she for your threads?"

Darry picked up her boots as Emmalyn laughed at her expense. "Fine. I take time from my busy schedule—"

"Mucking stalls," Emmalyn mumbled beneath her breath.

"To spend *time* with you, and I become the object of ridicule."

Jessa lowered the handkerchief to her lap, holding tight to her laughter.

"I would like to see you shovel shit as well as I can, Emmalyn."

"Darry!" Cecelia laughed.

"I'm quite good with a shovel," Darry said with pride, making for the door.

Jessa stared at the embroidery. She looked up quickly and Darry caught her eyes as she walked backward beneath the arch. Her smile was true as she disappeared into the corridor, her dimple pressing sweetly in her cheek.

"I will expect you at dinner, Cat!" Cecelia called.

"Let me see, Jessa?" Emmalyn asked. "She's been hiding that piece for a week."

Jessa studied the thread that moved in delicate chain links about the outer edges of the handkerchief. A rose flowered upward into a near-perfect rendering of a nightshade in full bloom. A flush of heat spread along the back of Jessa's neck.

It had been meant for her. Darry had spent her time thinking of her with every thread and careful stitch. *Oh, Darry, it's lovely. It's so...it's simply lovely.*

"Jessa?"

"So you might steal it?"

Emmalyn laughed as Jessa placed Darry's gift beneath her length of unfinished lace. "She has corrupted you. We should've seen it coming."

Jessa smiled, trying to hide the tremble of her hands as she picked up her needles.

"Does she still tend to miss stitches?" Cecelia asked.

Jessa could detect the small mistakes that Darry had made as the sable thread had flowed into the green, and the tiny gaps near the base of the petals. "No," she answered quietly. "It's perfect."

Prince Joaquin took up his goblet at the dinner table, finding what he sought farther down the table. Serabee had informed him that Darrius had spent the afternoon sewing with the other women of the keep before attending to her duties, and he had yet to get over his amusement. Her bold manner and offensive dress, her blatant lie of wearing a sword was all absurd, and her engagement of the womanly arts was a challenge he could not pass up. It was time he stirred the pot somewhat to see what poured out.

That Malcolm was complacent in their negotiations and unwilling to broach several key subjects in the presence of his father had not escaped Joaquin's notice. He was being treated as a pawn and he did not like it. He was an equal player in the game with more at stake than anyone, and though Malcolm acknowledged that fact when they spoke in private, he did not treat him with the proper respect in council. Arravan's arrogant son needed to learn there would be a price for that.

Malcolm wanted a piece of Lyoness, and he was willing to do just about anything to win it, including marrying Jessa-Sirrah. Joaquin wanted the Jade Throne and all that came with it. He wanted Sylban-Tenna destroyed and the others of his father's line either dead or in chains, preferably the latter so he might enjoy the sight. His dream was simple, if only he could hit upon the right plan before the others did. *Now* was his moment, but his play would depend upon Malcolm's, and Malcolm was acting his part like a nervous girl who hid her secrets and played the trembling submissive to her father's authority.

It was time to shake loose their caution and step boldly, whether Malcolm was prepared or not. Joaquin had always known that blood would be shed in the end. *Though on this night, it shall merely be his pride.*

"Will Captain Darrius be joining us on our hunt?"

Malcolm lifted his eyes from his plate. "No, she will not."

Owen eased back in his chair at the head of the table, his goblet in hand as he studied Joaquin. He had been expecting some sort of challenge for several days. Malcolm had been on the receiving end of several short-tempered comments as of late. Their negotiations were slow, but forming a lasting treaty with Lyoness had never been attempted. They had much to consider, and beyond that, the timetable had been set by Bharjah's offer of his daughter's hand in marriage. The protocol involved in such a venture was complicated at best, and the one thing they had now was time. And if Jacob's spies were right, a little more time was all they might need.

If Owen could believe the missives sent back across the Lyonese border, Bharjah was swiftly dying and all would change in a heartbeat if one bright morning the Butcher of the Plains did not awake with the sun. Perhaps Joaquin knew this, perhaps not, but the young man certainly had *some*thing planned for his part in the negotiations; it was written within his every expression. That he and Malcolm had become thick was no secret either, and though Malcolm loved his games, too much was at stake right now for Malcolm to overstep his bounds.

"Seems a shame," Joaquin said. "If she is allowed to pursue manly virtues, then she should be permitted the hunt."

"She'll not be joining us, Joaquin," Malcolm repeated.

"But surely her beauty, despite her dress, would allow us a bit of entertainment while away from the feminine comforts," Joaquin said, pleased by Malcolm's reaction. *You are weaker than I thought, Malcolm. You'd not last a week within the shadow of the Jade Throne, nor even a day beneath my father's wrath.*

"Entertainment how?" Owen asked.

Joaquin turned to his right, straight into the unwavering gaze of the High King of Arravan, and a tremor of apprehension rippled through his stomach at the steady question within Owen's eyes. "I am curious as to her skills, that is all."

"You wish to mock her?"

Joaquin sat back slowly. He had meant to spar with Malcolm, for Joaquin had discovered almost at once that Darrius was Malcolm's bane. If Joaquin was to put him in his place, she was the key. Owen, on the other hand, was a unique opponent. "Not at all, my Lord. But in my land a woman knows her place and is kept within it. Your daughter is somewhat of an oddity."

"But you're no longer in Lyoness, are you, Joaquin?"

"Perhaps if she could demonstrate her *skills*, I would not find her so impolite. As to her manly dress and behavior only, I assure you, my Lord." Joaquin knew the comment encompassed more than enough to insult. "If she truly has value as a soldier in your command that is a different matter. But I find that fact hard to believe so I wonder, why is she allowed to play at this game? Does it merely amuse you to let her do so?"

Silence suddenly encompassed them, the other conversations at the table having tapered off. The Queen sat unmoving, her eyes upon her husband as a fire of slow temper rose within her expression.

"Perhaps this is a conversation better suited for after dinner, Prince Joaquin," Jacob said. "I waited some time for my dinner and I would like to enjoy it."

"Yes, but you see my dilemma, Prince Jacob?" Joaquin said. "I am to deal in treaty with your father's throne and have yet to determine the seriousness or the tone of these negotiations. We have spoken in council for many days as to the state of affairs between our two lands and the history of war between us. These are serious matters, yes?"

"Of course. But they are matters unrelated to my dinner."

Joaquin ignored Owen's quiet laughter. "So how might I treat with a throne that allows a daughter of the Blood to expose herself in such a manner? It's hard to know if this is a frivolous pursuit allowed out of indulgence or a serious threat that speaks to the minds of your people. Am

I to sanction a union between Malcolm and my innocent sister, who has never been exposed to such widely accepted immorality, shall we say?"

"Perhaps we might see if the weather will affect your ruminations as well." Jacob's tone had turned somewhat cold. "We're expecting a blow from the south, I believe, that might upset your thoughts on any number of things."

"If her value as a woman is so slight that her skills as a warrior are a better asset to the Arravan throne, I might accept her uniqueness," Joaquin said. He was surprised that the weakling Jacob had come to her defense. He was always quiet in council and seemed to have very little standing for a man of the Blood. "I understand your need for an ample supply of warriors, even if you must employ your women to find them."

"*Enough*." Cecelia pushed her chair back and rose to her feet, looking down at Joaquin.

"Perhaps a walk in the gardens, Cecelia," Owen said, interrupting her before she could say what was obviously on her mind. "For the ladies at the table, so we might finish this conversation without insult to anyone."

"I mean insult to no one." Joaquin met Owen's heavy gaze. "I merely wish to know if all your officers are of the same amusing caliber. And if they sport the same inclinations as your daughter. It is a reasonable question."

"You seek to provo—"

"Why don't you ask her," Owen said. "Ask her," Owen repeated, "if the men in my command are of the same caliber as she."

Joaquin reacted swiftly. "Lady Darrius?"

Darrius stared at the table. "Yes, my Lord?"

"Are the officers within your father's command of the same caliber with a sword as you?"

"No," Darry answered. "They have cocks and I do not."

Joaquin was uncharacteristically silent, clearly undone.

"Or were you talking about the *other* sword?"

Owen let out a bark of laughter.

"Yes, actually, I was." Joaquin's tone was snappish.

"Because if you were talking about the male anatomy, I consider them to be at a disadvantage. But since you were not, you have my apologies."

"A disadvantage?"

"Yes, well, your cock does not allow you the time or the inclination, does it?"

Joaquin frowned. Jacob was grinning as he cut into his fish.

"The time or the inclination for what?" Joaquin demanded.

"To discover what truly pleases a woman."

"*Darry*." Cecelia smiled and ducked her head.

"Though you can piss standing up," Darry said, "which is an advantage, I'll give you that. But back to the proper sword, yes?"

That Joaquin was insulted showed clearly in his demeanor, and though it was obvious that he wished to respond, nothing came out when he opened his mouth.

"But I see that perhaps I've maligned your prowess as a lover. This was unintended, my Prince. I'm sure that your lovers, and they are legion I have no doubt, I'm certain that you have satisfied them all. Their screams were from pleasure, no doubt." Darry chuckled, dangerously close to mocking. "And their sobbing was that their prayers had been answered. I was speaking of lesser men, I assure you, who do not handle their swords with care."

Owen watched as Darry took up her goblet. *By the Gods, woman, but you have your mother's wicked tongue.*

"But I shall never know if that's actually true, for you see, I do not fancy having your cock between my legs. I shall just have to take it on faith."

Malcolm sat back in his chair with a beseeching expression. Owen ignored him, though, caught by the clever spin of words as he considered Darry with thoughtful pride.

"And I believe," Darry continued with a smile, "that unless you wish to challenge me to a duel right here and now, before dessert—which I hear is a lovely pie of spiced peaches with a dark sugar crust—that you must show the same faith in *my* skills and assume that I have earned my rank at least in some measure, based on the same exacting standards that others must meet."

They stared at one another, neither looking away as the silence grew thick.

"Some of life's mysteries, my good Prince, are meant to be savored," Darry added quietly. "Let us not ruin them, and before dessert? It really is in bad form."

Joaquin held her eyes for a few seconds more, then glanced away, lifting his goblet. "Then let us drink to those mysteries, Princess. Until one or the other, or both, may be solved."

Owen's jaw twitched. *Don't make me spill your blood, boy, for I'll do so without a thought if you would be so careless. Arravan's panther shall not have the* chance *to gut you, before you've met her father's sword.*

Darry lifted her wine in return. "There shall be only one question answered between us, Joaquin, and you must trust that I shall be the one who decides which mystery it will solve."

They both drank, Darry the first to set her chalice down before returning to her plate. "Shall we find a deck of cards after our pie, Emma? We've not had a game of Suns for some time."

Cecelia turned to Owen. "I shall see to the kitchen, Owen, with your leave?"

"Of course. My compliments to the cooks."

"I would like a match very much, Darry," Emmalyn said.

"Excellent."

"So what is the best game at this lodge of yours, Malcolm?" Joaquin looked down the table, then returned to violently slicing his meat, his knife blade scraping against his plate.

Jessa listened as several conversations sprang up, everyone eager to wipe away any remaining effects of the awkward confrontation. She had never witnessed such open mockery of a man, and a son of Bharjah at that. Her heart was pounding as a heady rush of victory settled in her chest, smothering her embarrassment that Joaquin had thrown such innuendo at a woman of royal blood. Spoken in front of Darry's parents, it was a terrible breach on many levels, despite the overtly sexual tone of Darry's challenge.

She studied Darry and noted that though she moved the food about her plate she made no real effort to eat it. Darry set her fork down and reached for her goblet. A bloodstain darkened the white tablecloth beneath where Darry held her knife. She was gripping the edge of the blade where it met the handle, her knuckles white with the force.

Jessa reached for the pear that sat beyond Darry's plate. "Let go, Darry."

The colors of Darry's eyes were tainted with emotions she had not anticipated, and as Jessa sat back she was ashamed of her joy at Joaquin's defeat. *I didn't think of that, Darry, forgive me. Vhaelin essa, but I didn't... you're not alone, Darry, I promise.*

CHAPTER SEVEN

"You're as restless as a bloody cat," Radha growled in her scrape of a voice. "Sit down!"

Jessa moved from where she paced before the hearth and flopped onto the divan across from Radha's heavily stuffed chair. "I will be expected to sing."

"Perhaps not." Radha's needle moved with precision within the silk of Jessa's dress.

"It is a formal ball, Radha. There will be musicians and players, most likely."

"Yes. And is that why you've been stalking about for the past two days?"

Jessa tipped onto her back and stared at the ceiling. She pulled at her robe, shifting with annoyance and then settling with a sigh. "Leave me be, old woman."

Radha studied Jessa for a time before returning to the dress. "She has been making herself scarce, child, that's all." She laughed, the sound like pebbles caught underfoot. "They have cocks and I do not." She laughed harder. "I would've given a piece of my soul to have heard that."

"It was not as pleasant as you might think," Jessa said, "to see that *fikloche* get his own handed back."

Radha's laughter faded and she started on the seam once again.

"She was all alone," Jessa spoke almost to herself. "And I just sat there."

"And what would you have done?"

Jessa had no answer. Radha moved along the seam and then knotted the stitch and brought the dress to her mouth where she bit cleanly through the thread. She searched the basket on the table beside her for the spool of blue.

"She is a backwards woman." Radha threaded her needle. "In such a life she must defend herself. No one else will do it."

"I could've tried to be brave."

"At what price?"

"What does it matter the *price*?" Jessa pushed to her feet and walked back to the hearth. "I have always been trapped, Radha, and so it is no matter what I do or feel. But to see her so, it wasn't right."

"You know little enough about her to be making such a statement."

"I know enough."

"And what is it that you know?"

"That she's kind and good. And that she has courage. I can talk to her and she speaks to me as if I were someone other than Bharjah's daughter, as if I was just *me* and that is enough for her." She smiled. "And she makes me laugh."

Jessa considered her stay at Blackstone Keep since she and Darry had shaken hands at the pond and made their pact to be friends. She thought of their time each day, always in the midst of others, yet even so she realized how dull and heavy things seemed without her presence. *I am missing you, Darry.*

She was surprised how much she had come to rely on Darry being here and how she waited with anticipation each day for that hitch within her heart that warmed her blood so wonderfully when she first saw Darry. And it did not stop there. For a minute or for an hour, it made little difference. *She makes me feel as if I belong somewhere.*

"And she's very beautiful," Jessa whispered, as thoughts of the pond turned to the memory of Darry's wet clothes clinging so suggestively to her body. *And when she smiles at me my stomach does wonderful things.*

"What was that?"

"Nothing," Jessa answered. She closed her eyes. "They will want me to sing." She turned abruptly. "I would look into the Waters of Truth, Radha."

"You cannot. The water is very different here and I've not yet found the proper herbs. I still discover the city, and the things I need are not offered in the open markets."

"Yes, and while you prowl about the castle at night and move through the city by day, I am stuck having tea and waiting to be sold off for the highest bid! Are you not *done* with that yet?"

Radha laughed, ignoring her. "What need have you for the Waters, child? Had your *fikloche* not interrupted us on the road, do you think you might have seen what you are needing now?"

"I am needing nothing."

"Your vision lies within you, you know that," Radha said, concentrating on the tight stitch. "If you would but meditate, most likely you would remember better."

"I'm sick of meditating. Either the Vhaelin will show me or they will not. My sitting about in a stupor waiting for my gods to give me a sign is becoming a waste of my time." She turned on Radha. "I said nothing to you? I must have said something."

"Not that I can remember." Radha did not look up. "What will you do when your vision comes at last, Jessa? Will you accept what it shows you, no matter what it is? Perhaps your sons will be of the Blood, perhaps not. A vision granted is but one path."

"But I remember feeling…I felt so—"

"You felt what?"

"*Alive*!" Jessa said. "Damn you, Radha, I *know* you're lying."

"Then you should meditate. I cannot do everything for you."

"I do not *want* to meditate," Jessa said between clenched teeth.

"Then what would you rather be doing?"

"I would rather be *living*," she said. "I shall be in the bath, not that you care, you heartless wretch."

Radha grinned.

"I will have to sing, mark my words."

Emmalyn handed the bulky packages delivered from the tailor into Darry's arms, noting the dusty uniform and the sword at Darry's side. "I almost opened them," she said, eyeing for the hundredth time the soft parchment wrappings that were tied with string. "Tell me you don't have a dress in there." Darry was utterly stunning in a dress, but they had not suited her temperament or her wild spirit since she was a girl. If she wore one now it would bring the court to its knees with shock and rumors. *Malcolm would keel over.*

"I don't have a dress in there."

"Where have you been? Mother and I went looking for you, and Longshanks told her that he sent you on an errand, then received a tongue-lashing like I haven't heard in years."

"I had to do a bit of riding, yes." Darry smiled. "I have a present for you."

"What?"

"I said that I have a present for you."

"What is it?"

"A Solstice gift, of sorts."

"What is it?" Emmalyn asked again.

"You're very pushy."

"Darry."

"Do you always lie about in the middle of the day in your dressing robe?" Darry asked, surveying her up and down. Her hair had been done for the ball, piled in flaming red curls atop her head and spilling onto her shoulders. She had yet to put on her dress and so stood in bare feet and a simple gray robe. "And though you look ravishing just as you are, I'm fairly unimpressed with the duties of the eldest daughter if this is how you're allowed to spend your days."

"You would do well to get ready yourself," Emmalyn said. "Your hair will take hours to dry."

"My hair is fine."

Emmalyn was less than convinced. "Mother will flay you alive."

"It won't be the first time," Darry said with a grin. "My skin grows back."

"Where's my present?"

"Close your eyes."

Emmalyn lowered her brow in annoyance.

"Do you want it or not?"

"We're not to exchange gifts until the Solstice, Darry."

"This isn't your Solstice gift. I said it was a *sort* of Solstice gift."

"Just give it to me."

"Then close your eyes."

Emmalyn growled and closed her eyes, though but a moment later she heard the hinges of the door and looked. "Where are you going?"

Darry turned on her. "You're bloody well impossible, Em. I left it in the hall, is that all right with you? Close your eyes!"

"Is it very big then?" she asked, smiling.

Darry stared at her.

Emmalyn closed her eyes. "Is it big?"

"Not too big," Darry answered. "But the box is very pretty. If you look before I say you can I'll take it back, I swear to Gamar."

"*Fine*," Emmalyn said. "I promise."

Darry proceeded into the hallway and pulled the door closed.

Lord Royce Greyson stepped away from the wall, a smile spreading like sunlight across his handsome face. He was six feet tall and his shoulders were strong beneath his dusty black jacket and tunic, his unshaven face dark with stubble. Royce straightened his jacket and sword.

Darry liked the way his clothes fit his well-built frame. They were a bit dusty from their ride on the furious road south, but he was a handsome sight nonetheless. *And I'm not in love with you, my friend.*

Darry chuckled at his boyish smile. "I don't suppose you brought her anything, did you?"

Royce frowned.

Darry took his hand and pressed a small brightly wrapped box into his palm. "*Men*," she said. "Put it in your pocket," she ordered, and he did so. "And people wonder why I seek my pleasures elsewhere."

Royce's eyes lit up and he planted a kiss on her cheek. "I shall pay you back."

"Darry?" Emmalyn called. "What in the seven hells are you doing?"

"Keep your eyes closed, woman!" Darry yelled over her shoulder. She unbent his collar, patting some of the dust away, then licked her thumb and smoothed down the twist of curling hair above his left ear. "I'm fixing the paper!" she called. Darry met his gaze. "They are combs for her hair, in case you're wondering. And you're damn right you'll pay me back. They're from Master Fina's."

"You'll make me a fine sister, Darrius. Like the one I always dreamt of but never had. Thank you."

Darry flushed at the words and took him by the shoulder. "Wyatt has some rather smashing clothes that will fit you for the fête. I've set them on his bed. And please, Royce, remember that though you're betrothed, if our mother finds you in her daughter's rooms in the middle of the day, you shall be running for the Green Hills with the entire guard intent upon your ass."

"*Darry*?" Emmalyn called.

"Are they closed?" Darry asked as she pushed the door inward, Royce crowding her from behind. She elbowed him in the stomach and he retreated.

"They're bloody well *sewn* shut."

Darry opened the door completely and pulled at Royce's jacket, sending him forward. The expression on his face when he saw Emmalyn made Darry's heart skip, not only in happiness but with envy. He stood very still as he took in the sight of the woman he loved, and after a few seconds Darry shoved him again.

Emmalyn's head tipped to the side. "Is that you?"

"All right, Em," Darry said. "You may open them."

Emmalyn obeyed instantly, her gaze catching on Darry for but an instant before her shoulders jerked at another person standing so close.

Royce touched her face as their eyes met. "Look at your hair," he whispered. "You're so beautiful, Emma."

Emmalyn shook her head in shock, then threw her arms about his neck. "Royce!" Her hands slid through his hair as his lips lowered onto hers.

Darry smiled in satisfaction as he pulled Emmalyn close. She turned away and picked up her packages.

Emmalyn's hands moved down his chest as they kissed. She slipped them about his waist and then his hips. "Wait, *Emma*," he mumbled against her mouth. His hands went to her face and he kissed her again, ignoring his own plea.

Emmalyn pulled back. "Not the hair, love."

"All right," he whispered as his hands dropped to her shoulders. "Darry said," he tried to speak and then kissed her again. "Your…mother would…"

Emmalyn gave a start. "*Darry*," she said. *I said it was a sort of Solstice gift*. Darry was gone and the chamber door closed tight against any intrusions. "Darry," she said again.

"You can't keep touching me there," Royce said quietly, "and expect me not to mess up your hair."

Emmalyn laughed. With slow and deliberate purpose she drew her right hand around, stopping at his belt buckle, then inched lower to touch him elsewhere. A lovely tremble tripped along her spine when his body reacted. His fingers caressed her mouth as his eyes darkened with want.

"May I touch your hair now?"

The need within his voice made her knees weak. "Yes," she answered, moaning as his lips covered hers once more.

❖

Darry stood upon the balustrade and considered Jessa's door.

She had been gone only a short time, yet she had waited for this moment since her first night on the road. Sitting beside her small fire and enjoying the night air, she had looked back to the south and wondered what Jessa's day had been like. She had wondered what color her sari had been and if her hair had held more braids or less. Their number seemed to change each day and counting them had become a lovely pastime that Darry indulged in as often as possible. She had missed making Jessa laugh, or at least trying to. Jessa's delicate humor made her feel special, somehow, that such a beautiful woman had been charmed by her, if only a little.

She had realized as well that she liked very much how quiet Jessa was. Life was never quiet for Darry, and she had not known how much she would enjoy such a thing.

Of her many thoughts while she was away, those of Jessa had been uppermost. It pleasantly surprised her how much she now welcomed Jessa's presence in her daily life.

Just to be next to her made Darry happy, and Jessa's scent of jasmine haunted her in a pleasing manner throughout her days. She was not immune to Jessa's beauty either, but she supposed that could not be helped. The way her sari curved to her breasts and draped about her hips enthralled Darry. *I'm only human…and I've done nothing untoward. Anyone with a bloody heart that beats would notice how sweet her body is.*

She kicked the dust from her boots, feeling trapped as she tried to put her attraction aside. *I've not forgotten why she's here or who she is. But we can be friends, just as we pledged. There's no harm in that, even though I find her…* Darry let out a long breath. *Find her what?*

"Bloody well fucking lovely," she whispered. *But just friends.* Somewhere deep in her heart she knew it was true, despite her thinking of Jessa in ways that she should not. They were friends, and it had been some time since she made a new friend. Remembering that innocent pledge once again, she stepped forward.

Radha opened the door to her knock.

"Lady Radha." Darry gave a slight bow of her head. "You're looking well on this fine day."

"And you are looking road-worn, Princess."

Darry chuckled. "Yes, but that's because I wore out the road."

Radha laughed.

"I was wondering…" Darry faltered. She shifted the packages in her arms. "I mean, would it be all right if I spoke with your Lady for a few moments? I know she must be busy preparing for the fête, but I would just like to pay my respects. If that's all right?"

"Would you stand in wait?"

"Of course," Darry answered with a grin. "I would wait forever if needs be."

Radha studied her closely and Darry stared back, wondering suddenly if she had said something wrong. The old woman moved and Darry let out a nervous breath as she disappeared into the chamber.

Radha pushed open the door to the expansive privy. Jessa stood with a towel about her legs as she dried her body from the bath. "You have a visitor."

"Unless it is the Queen, Radha, I don't want to see anyone before I have to. Please send them away."

"As you wish," Radha answered.

Darry pushed the packages more tightly beneath her left arm. *Maybe she won't want to see me. Maybe you should've just*—she straightened as Radha approached. "She will see me?"

"No. She's very nervous about this evening."

"Why? Did someone say…" Darry realized her tone was too forceful and she stepped back. "My pardons, Lady, I didn't mean to…" She let out a breath of frustration. "I mean, has someone made her feel, did my brother—"

"She is afraid they will make her sing."

Darry considered Radha's answer, imagining herself standing in the Jade Palace and singing before its entire court of strangers, of being judged so openly and made to perform for the pleasure of others. And though Jessa was known as the Nightshade Lark for the beauty of her voice, no doubt it was not as pleasant as some might think to be on display in such a manner. Standing before the future King of Arravan, caught beneath his appraising eyes as the whole world watched, could be demeaning.

"She'll not have to sing, my Lady," Darry said with confidence. "You have my word."

"And how will you stop such a thing if the court desires it?"

"I shall think of something."

"No doubt," Radha said. "Off you go then, child, to wash the road from you, I should think. Before your mother sees you thus."

Darry bowed her head and stepped back. "Lady Radha."

Jessa walked from the privy, tying her robe as Radha closed the door. "Who was at the door?"

"It was not the Queen, so what care do you have?"

"One day you shall be dying and ask for help in one of your riddles, and no one shall lift a finger to save you for want of knowing what you really need," she said sarcastically.

Radha laughed, picking up the dress. "She was not a queen, it is settled."

"Yes, thank you old woman, for telling me what I've…" She raised her eyes slowly. "For telling me—*Shivahsa*!" Jessa cursed, rushing to the balustrade door and throwing it open. The door crashed against the chair beside it as Jessa stepped over the threshold.

Darry turned at the disturbance and smiled as Jessa slid in a rush onto the terrace in her bare feet and robe.

"Jessa," Darry said as her eyes followed the fall of dark hair to where Jessa's robe fell open between her breasts. The garment was tied loosely about her waist. Darry raised her eyes quickly at the stirring within her, her attention caught yet again by the silken fall of Jessa's hair. *At least a dozen—*

"Where have you been?" Jessa's hands played with the tie of her robe. "Are you all right?" She took hold of Darry's right hand and caressed the fading cut on her palm, the slight wound but a pink line of irritation.

"All is well," Darry said, suddenly very content as Jessa's touch warmed her blood. "I wanted to see you."

"Yes." Jessa smiled as Darry's fingers curled about her own. "Yes, you as well."

"I know you're getting ready, but I'll—"

"Where have you *been*?"

"I rode north to bring a friend home for the fête tonight, and for the Solstice celebrations to come."

"A friend?" Jessa asked. "An escort?"

"No," Darry answered, curious as to the spark within Jessa's eyes. "Emmalyn's betrothed, Royce Greyson. He was stationed in Marban. His family holds lands along the Lanark River and he was detained by orders from the Commander there to make maps, but our Longshanks is of a higher rank."

"I hadn't known Emmalyn was to be married."

"They wait to make the announcement until after Jacob and Alisha's ceremony. Emmalyn has no wish to steal from Alisha's joy. You will keep their secret?"

"Of course," Jessa said.

"She doesn't want the fanfare again either, I suppose."

"Again?"

"Again?" Darry asked, smiling.

Jessa laughed softly. "You said 'again.'"

"Ah, yes." Darry tried to keep her mind from drifting. Jessa had fewer braids than she had first thought, and she paused to collect her words. "Emmalyn is a widow." She stepped closer, smelling the scent of jasmine and finding it most pleasant and yet more subtle than she remembered. "Her first husband was killed when he fell from a horse. It was a terrible accident that took him soon after they were wed. They were married during the summer festivities, like the ones that fast approach. It can be a sad time for her."

"So you sent for him."

Darry shifted her parcels, looking sheepish. "Well, sort of. It's not really my place, but I had something that Longshanks wanted badly enough in exchange for his help in bringing Royce home. A horse named Dragon."

Jessa stared at her for several heartbeats, then laughed with pleasure. "You traded your horse so your sister could be with her beloved?"

Darry looked at the stones between them, enjoying the sight of Jessa's toes. She shrugged. "He is named so for a reason. He's a most ornery animal and his breath is very hot before he tries to bite you."

"A good bargain then," Jessa said softly, liking the way Darry looked when she was uncertain. Her brow would come down and a shyness would steal into her posture, so much strength and force of will made almost quiet.

"Yes." Darry shifted her packages once again and stepped back. "Your hair is so very beautiful, Jessa." Then she murmured, "Bloody hell," as if her words had leapt forth before she could think better of it.

Jessa lifted her hand to her braids, thanking the gods for them since Darry admired them. "Thank you."

"I should let you finish getting ready."

"Yes, I suppose…and you as well? Your hair?"

"Bentley shall have to help me with it."

"Lord *Greeves*?"

"For certain. He likes to, actually, though don't tell him I told you. He wouldn't speak to me again, I think, should that secret get out."

Jessa tried not to laugh. "I will say nothing."

Darry backed up another step. "I thought of you while I was away… and I missed seeing your face. It is nice to have a new friend."

"Yes," Jessa said. *I missed your face as well, Darry. I missed…I missed so many things about you.*

"Do not be nervous tonight, with so many people. It's only a party, yes?"

"I know. I shall try not to be. I will look for you."

"Then I shall look forward to being seen," Darry said. "Princess," she bid, and bowed her head.

Darry turned and walked away. Jessa gazed across her strong shoulders and down the center of Darry's back, then drifted lower still. A hard wave of pleasure turned within her stomach and bled downward, lighting within her thighs. She swallowed awkwardly and let out a rough breath. *The way you walk, Princess. Like the panther you are named for.*

"Will you stand for all the world to see?" Radha said from the door as Jessa jumped in surprise. "Without your veil? In your robe and naked toes?"

Jessa laughed, hurrying back into the room and hugging her. Radha slapped at her arms and Jessa kissed her cheek. "Finish my dress!" she said, though she had no anger in her voice.

Radha pushed from the embrace with a flutter of shawls and black fabric. "Next time ask who it might be that is knocking at your door."

Jessa shut the door and flopped onto her back. *You make me feel so alive, Darry.* She smiled slowly, feeling the heat on her cheeks. She tipped her face away from the room, not trusting her feelings to Radha. *I am awake now.*

Her blood moved with excitement and her thoughts raced, tumbling this way and that. Her skin tingled with expectation, her hands still wanting to touch Darry just a little, just a bit. When she did so, Jessa could feel Darry's strength, could feel it invade her own body and her flesh react, becoming stronger in return, becoming more of what it should be.

She felt like a woman in Darry's presence. *A woman. Not a piece of chattel to be wagered like coins on a table.* She felt her body like never before, and each movement she made had a purpose somehow, as if she were meeting a need she had never known was there.

She had no idea what Darry would say next, none at all. And she would respond without her normal care, which was wonderful. It was so astonishing to speak her mind without censure or caution. Anything she said would be acceptable, somehow. No matter what passed her lips, Darry could be trusted with it.

And the way your eyes fill with warmth. You always look so pleased by what you find, even though it's only me. And I like it when your tongue is nervous for want of the right word, Darry. I like it so very much.

CHAPTER EIGHT

Cecilia surveyed the great hall of Blackstone Keep and considered the evening to come with a strict eye for details.

The hall was filled to capacity. The entire Court of Arravan had turned out for the formal fête to welcome the Lyonese Prince and the woman who might marry the heir to Arravan's throne. The doors to the two minor halls that bordered the vast chamber had been thrown open to allow for their numbers, and the white stone solar as well. The gardens beyond were lit with hanging lamps to ward off the darkness.

The dais at the north end of the room was occupied by a troupe of Greymear musicians, lute players and more than one bodhran, the largest of the skin drums standing as tall as the man who wielded the batons. Arravan flutes and fiddles of varying sizes were evident, and a hurdy-gurdy as well, the instrument known mostly within the walled city of Sha-Kiram on display and ready to produce its unique sound.

Along the north and east walls, long tables stood end to end, their surfaces covered with platters and bowls of food, everything from spiced meat delicacies to colorful displays of sliced fruits and sweet breads.

The massive tapestries that hung upon the walls had been cleaned and brushed, depicting everything from the Durand family tree to the battle of the Ishlere Plains. Ornate poles extended from the balcony, the platform bracing the chamber upon its southern end. Flags hung down and swayed gently, the Lewellyn crest of Cecelia's family and the Durand shield bold and colorful as they flanked the silver, black, and blue banner of Arravan.

The guests had been arriving by coach for nearly an hour, passing through the main gates in a steady stream. The guard set upon the main gate was Longshanks's own staff, their dress blacks offset by swords and baldrics.

Within the palace the Blooded society of Arravan was fast turning out. Lords in their finest clothing or the uniforms of their chosen service. Swords were worn and daggers as well, many ornate and purely for show, though all of them were the thin rapiers of gentlemen.

The women held to the arms of their escorts and traveled about the room with a purpose, clearly leading their men in a dance of casual mingling. Their dresses were of the finest materials, many of the skirts wide and sweeping, some bearing short trains of lace that fluttered above the polished floor. Every neck was adorned in some way, either by jewels so precious they had been passed down for generations or by subtle tokens purchased for the occasion. Hair was curled and held with pins or delicate ribbons, or straight and falling in lustrous waves, some ladies revealing their locks in their full length, more than one head of hair cascading well below the waist.

Serving men circulated about the room offering pewter chalices of wine—a delicate spring red that was light in its flavor—and narrow tankards of ale both light and dark. As the night reached the appointed hour the musicians began to play, a simple composition that introduced each instrument's song into the air fast becoming crowded with conversation and perfume.

Cecelia moved along the wall behind the dais, her hair pinned loosely behind her neck and falling between her shoulders, her dress of ivory and blue whisking about her legs. She spied Margery Tuanna, the Queen's lady, and lifted her chin with a smile.

"Have you seen Darry?"

"No, my Lady," Margery said. "I'm told she rode in earlier today, though, looking as if she were wearing the road from here to the Green Hills. And she did not come alone. She brought Lord Greyson home, my Lady."

Cecelia laughed. "Damn her to all seven hells, why didn't I think of that? I shall have to apologize to Grissom Longshanks now, I should think. He must have had a hand in that one, for all he sat there and didn't say a word while I carved him a new ear."

"There's Emmalyn now," Margery said as the music gained in volume. Emmalyn entered on the arm of Lord Royce Greyson. "I must see to the kitchens, mum."

"Thank you, Margery," Cecelia said, her heart giving a delicate tug at the joy on Emmalyn's face as she held to Royce's arm.

Emmalyn's dress was dyed the deepest emerald and all the more beautiful for its simple lines. Her hair was piled atop her head and spilled in curls down her neck in flames of rich color. Royce stood beside her as if he were the happiest man in Arravan. His black trousers and suit of silk were offset by his simple white tunic and the silver-studded belt and scabbard that held his sword. Cecelia recognized the outfit as belonging to her son, and he wore it almost as well as Wyatt did.

"Wyatt," she whispered. She would speak to Owen about bringing him home. He was scheduled to arrive for Jacob and Alisha's wedding, but a week or two early seemed like a splendid idea.

Amongst a cluster of men near the throne room upon the opposite side of the dais, Owen and Armistad Greyson greeted Emmalyn and Royce. Cecelia found Malcolm near the main arch, his First Councilor Marteen Salish by his side. They were both in their dress uniforms of black, though Malcolm's vest was a deep blue silk. He stood among his peers and their ladies, Marteen's sister Melora and her husband among them. Lord Boris Greeves was there with his wife Serina, yet another of the infamous Greeves men making an appearance. Cecelia knew that if she were to look about she would find nearly every child of Lord Silas Greeves present.

The Lord Serabee El-Khan stood off to the side in his black clothes, his shaved head shining in the lamplight and his dark eyes prowling about the room.

Prince Trey-Jak Joaquin stood within Malcolm's close-knit crowd as if he were an intimate confidant. The Princess Jessa-Sirrah stood beside her brother and Cecelia let out a breath of admiration at her beauty.

Jessa's dress was a unique mixture of both Lyonese and Arravan fashions. Cecelia was impressed at the beauty of it and wondered if Jessa had made it herself, for it was a style she had never seen. A rich, cream-colored silk, dyed in its fabric was an ocean of glorious blues that spilled down her shoulders and poured over the bodice. From the top of the neckline it was very much in the style of the saris she was wont to wear, but as it moved down her body it changed in an understated manner into a fuller skirt of Arravan's latest fashion.

Cecelia noticed then the way Jessa kept her eyes to the floor, only raising them when she was spoken to. Lord El-Khan stood very close to her at all times, his eyes falling occasionally to her hair and the tanned skin of her neck, a curious look passing over his face when he did so. Everything about his close attention bordered on offensive, yet he never crossed that line. It seemingly made Jessa uncomfortable, though she accepted his presence with the same quiet grace she displayed in everything.

Always so tentative, Princess. Cecelia tried not to stare. *And you do not look very happy to be here, a lamb among jackals, trapped in a conversation that interests you not a whit, no doubt. And within arm's length of the man who will be King of Arravan and perhaps your husband, at that.*

Cecelia crossed the floor before the dais and moved through the spill of music. As she neared the opposite side of the floor, Emmalyn fell in step beside her.

"You look bloody smashing, Mother," Emmalyn said. "Shall we rescue our stunning guest?"

Cecelia took her arm. "Royce looks rather happy to be here."

"I believe he is, yes."

"I shall take care of the Prince if you would but spirit her away," Cecelia said. "Where is Alisha?"

"Here, my Lady." Cecelia looked to her left as Alisha stepped close. "I shall take care of Melora, for no doubt she'll curry favor and follow poor Jessa about the room."

"Sweet Alisha," Cecelia said, "you're smarter than my son, which makes me somewhat nervous about the grandchildren you shall give me."

Alisha laughed. "You're not the only one nervous on that account, my Lady. No doubt I shall be over my head from the start."

"Into the breach, girls."

Jessa straightened as Cecelia drew near, noticing her determined smile even as Joaquin tightened his arm upon her hand. The guests around her parted to allow Cecelia entrance into their clique, and Malcolm's talk of hunting the Green Hills faded as he greeted his mother with genuine affection.

Joaquin pulled his arm away and stepped back, giving a bow.

Jessa felt the heated presence of Serabee and a spear of nervousness pierced her stomach. The Queen was speaking of the musicians and asking if Joaquin would perhaps dance a Lyonese galliard, when a hand slipped into her own.

Jessa found Emmalyn's eyes and they were filled with warmth, so Jessa pulled smoothly to the side in a deft maneuver that avoided both her brother and Serabee, affording her an almost casual exit from those of Malcolm's circle.

"I never leave a friend behind," Emmalyn said as she guided them back across the room, breaking into the open near the dance floor. "Don't look back."

"Thank you, Princess."

"Emmalyn, remember?"

"Yes, I'm sorry, Princess," Jessa replied, trying to find her balance after being freed from both her brother and Serabee. "No…I mean I'm sorry, Emmalyn."

"No apologies. Try again."

"Bless you to all the gods you love, Emmalyn," Jessa replied with absolute sincerity, glad for her veil beneath so much attention. "*Vhaelin essa ahbwalla*."

"And now for some wine while we wait for Mother and Alisha to return from the war."

They loitered near the doors to the solar and Emmalyn took hold of two goblets from one of the servers, handing one to Jessa as they searched back through the hall. Boris Greeves laughed with Cecelia, and Alisha nodded as Melora gestured to the musicians.

"How did you find our Melora?" Emmalyn asked as the woman in question smoothed at her burgundy skirt. The auburn-haired Melora was beautiful as always, but it was a clever beauty without warmth.

"I was wishing that she had not been found."

"Your sentiments are not unique, you must trust me."

"Your court is extremely large," Jessa said. The difference between Bharjah's court and Arravan's staggered her. "I hadn't thought there would be so many people…even though I expected there would be."

"Not to worry, Jessa. We shan't let them run you to ground."

"Thank you."

"Here come our comrades." Emmalyn smiled as her mother and Jacob's future wife moved across the dance floor. "No doubt your brother and mine will be talking blood sport more openly now."

"Wine, quick now," Alisha said as she approached, Jessa lifting her untouched drink and offering the chalice. "Thank you."

Cecelia called out as she neared and a tray of wine was brought immediately. Cecelia took up two goblets and handed one to Jessa. "All better, my girl?"

"Yes, thank you, my Lady."

"Where is Darry?" Alisha asked.

A murmur of voices rose as if in answer and rolled through the hall, starting in the crowded foyer and spreading inward. Someone gave a shout and the mass of people about the entrance began to part.

The Princess Darrius Lauranna moved beneath the arch as the throng gave way, Lord Bentley Greeves on her right a single step behind and Lieutenant Arkady Winnows at her left as the three moved in unison.

"Blessed Gamar!" Cecelia exclaimed.

"Holy seven hells." Emmalyn smiled. "Not a bloody dress, Darry."

Jessa's breath caught within her throat, her heart pounding in a sudden rush. Darry's hair fell in shining golden curls onto her shoulders, completely free of ties or combs. Her black jacket was of the deepest silk Jessa had ever seen, the material so dark and shimmering that it made Darry's movements seem all the more sleek. Her white silk tunic was open at her neck and plunged down her chest until it disappeared beneath a golden vest of gypsy silk. The unique fabric was washed through with tendrils of black, a lovely smoke of darkness captured in the opulent gold material. If not for the close-fitting vest her tunic would have breached every rule of etiquette. The cut of the garment was so blatantly sensual that new rules would no doubt be discussed in the weeks to come.

At her neck she wore the gold medallion of her family on a thick linked chain that flamed as she moved. On the left arm of the jacket, stitched by the finest of hands, a golden mountain panther seemed to climb from the flared cuff at her wrist up the entire length of the sleeve, its image filled with detail and melting colors the likes of which Jessa had never seen until this instant. At Darry's waist was a belt studded with gold. Darry's left hand rested on the hilt of a fine-blade rapier with a golden hand guard, the elegant metal twisted in a thin, ornate design. Her trousers were of the same material as her jacket, and as the long coattails fell to the backs of her knees her boots rose in their high polish, the toe caps made of gold and soaking up the light.

On each side of Darry, Bentley Greeves and Arkady Winnows were dressed in the same stunning uniforms, though the panthers that adorned their jackets covered the left shoulder and climbed down onto the chest, the animal caught in attack above their hearts. Bentley's blond locks and neatly trimmed mustache were a match to Arkady's flaxen hair, which was combed short and neat about his clean-shaven face.

"That's Damascus silk," Cecelia whispered. "She'll have emptied the bloody treasury."

Bentley seized two goblets of wine from a tray as they moved to an empty space at the end of the dance floor, staking a cavalier claim. Darry accepted her drink with a smile, the gesture open in its affection for him. She took a drink and turned to Arkady, handing him her chalice, which he drank from.

"Oh, well, that was entirely too bold." Alisha chuckled in a wicked manner. "Is she allowed to do that?"

"No," Emmalyn said, trying not to laugh and failing miserably.

Owen observed his daughter and held his back a tad straighter, his shoulders stretching his black dress uniform.

Bentley spoke in Darry's ear, causing her to flash a rebellious grin. The three of them were beyond appealing, and though the cut of Darry's tunic caused Owen a surge of discomfort, he could not deny that the three of them were altogether exquisite.

"Let us watch our Lyonese Prince," Armistad Greyson said.

"Malcolm ignores her," Owen replied as Malcolm looked anywhere but at his sister. *Or at least you try, my boy. If you'd but learn to respect her, you might have an easier time of it.*

"Aye, but Joaquin doesn't."

Owen let out a huff of amusement. "Look at him bristle." He glanced back at his daughter and her escorts. "Good Gamar, the sun has shone only for them."

"Aye, my Lord, they are a sight. I forget sometimes how beautiful Darry is."

"Yes," Owen said. "She has the look of my mother, with her hair like that."

"The hair. Queen Marget's hair, you're right."

"I do believe that my daughter is taking up a piece in the game. Though it's different from Mal's, or what mine must be."

"And what piece will it be?"

"She's taken up the gauntlet." Owen laughed softly. "She means to wield the blade before our enemies. Look to our young guest."

Joaquin's hand had fallen to his sword, his ringed fingers gripping the hilt as his body tensed. He clearly recognized the challenge of another warrior's presence and his stance had changed accordingly. His shoulders stiffened and his legs were braced as if he would draw his sword at the slightest provocation.

Darry stood flanked by her escort, smiling in such an open and sensual manner that Owen felt surprise at first. He raised a brow as Arkady Winnows leaned much too close, whispering into her hair as she stared across the room toward the arch. It was an intimate move and not Darry's way with her men. There was true love between them, impressive and unto death, but that was not the power she now wielded. This power spoke of all manner of things at her disposal: the power of death that a warrior has, and the power of life that a lover might hold.

Owen realized that Darry still suspected Joaquin of using the latter without thought or care as to the lover, and he did not disagree with her assessment. The man had a sense of malice about him, and though it was slight, it was always present. This was but a continuation of their clash at the dinner table, and Darry was clearly winning.

"They begin to flock," Armistad said.

The attention Darry commanded was undeniable, and her challenge was open to the Lyonese Prince and anyone else who cared to see it.

The music from the dais stopped and the players readied for the first official tune, drawing everyone's attention. The floor cleared in response and the singer stepped forward as the strings began to rise around her. The bodhran sounded, its beat rolling softly at first and then laying claim to the center as the sticks beat and the pipes deep and rich pulsed within its beat. A single fiddle cried out its challenge.

"The Mohn-Drom!" someone called, and scattered applause moved about the room along with the sound of voices rising in surprise and excitement.

Armistad laughed. "An impossible dance to begin with!"

"Darry," Owen said as the singer gave a slight nod. He turned just in time to see Darry smile in answer as Arkady Winnows took her hand and led her forth, their entourage parting and shouting the challenge.

The Mohn-Drom was the most suggestive and sensual of all the courtly dances, and rarely was it played at such a function. It was also the most difficult and intricate dance that Arravan had ever produced, and only the most natural and talented of dancers could complete its turns and complex footwork. It was a dance meant for lovers, and its many clinches and patterns were meant to imply and mimic the most heated of moments between them.

Someone called out to Darry and she laughed, unhooking the sword from her belt. She tossed the weapon and its sheath to Bentley, who reached out in an absent manner and caught it, after which he took a drink of his wine. A cheer went up and laughter moved through the crowd as Darry sent him a scathing look.

Cecelia turned to Emmalyn but found her eyes captured by Jessa instead, and her comment died upon her lips.

Jessa stood as straight and still as if she were made of stone, though the veil that hid her face moved as she breathed, short and quick. She stared at the dance floor with a startling intensity, though the veil still hid the deeper truth of Jessa's expression. Cecelia stepped closer in concern and followed her gaze as the singer's voice pierced the air and the bodhran beat low with its bass sound. The strings flared hard within the call of the pipes as the Mohn-Drom began.

Darry swirled gracefully onto the center of the floor with Arkady close upon her hip, her arms above her head and then behind his neck as he stepped close and dipped her backward. Darry's hair caught the light and flamed with a life of its own.

They moved, executing the complex steps of the Mohn-Drom with grace and confidence. Their bodies touched in a bold manner. Arkady's hands were lower than Blooded custom would dictate on Darry's hips as their legs intertwined and they circled tightly about the center of the floor. The music swelled and flowed over them, allowing them entrance into the realm that only music can create.

They twirled, Darry ducking beneath his arms and spinning, then she was pulled close and Arkady's lips brushed her neck. He caught her hand and spun back into her arms, normally a move played by the woman, but his elegance was undeniable as he relinquished control of the dance and Darry changed her steps with flair. The mandolins and the lute increased their melody as the singer sang notes but no words, the pace increasing. And then Arkady was in control once more, leading them in an intricate pattern as they spun as one, and the crowd sent up a cheer.

Cecelia had never seen her daughter so exposed before, so openly on display at such an official function. Some in the crowd seemed offended by her deliberate audacity, but most appeared in some measure captivated. Darry was desire personified as Arkady chased her with determination though she would not give in. They were both caught up in the Mohn-Drom. Darry's body was sybaritic as she moved, almost too much for propriety. She pulled back before she gave affront, though, and it was as if an enticing dream had come and gone.

Darry stepped and spun away from Arkady as he reached out. His hand swept her hair aside and caught the collar of her jacket at the exact moment the music crashed and stilled. Darry stood like a statue, looking over her left shoulder. Then the music burst forth and Arkady pulled the jacket, releasing Darry from its silken confines. Arkady chased her, tossing the garment that Bentley caught on his arm as if he had been expecting it. Arkady detained her from behind and slid his right hand across her stomach as his lips found her neck, while his left hand brushed low upon her breast. Darry reached back and slid her hand up his firm backside, pulling him even closer.

"Seven hells, Mother," Emmalyn breathed. "Where did she learn to dance the Mohn-Drom like that?"

Arkady's fingers opened, seeming confident as he teased Darry's breast. Darry's flesh rose beneath the pressure of the caress and her breast eased toward the edge of her tunic.

"That cannot be taught."

They both turned. Jessa's quiet words were filled with heat.

"Probably not." Emmalyn's attention returned to the dance floor. A hiccup of sound passed her lips. "Bloody hell, how does she do that with her *back*?"

Cecelia looked at Jessa, her curiosity rising slowly at the paling of Jessa's dark complexion. Jessa's shoulders trembled slightly, as if a coiled energy trapped within suddenly begged for release. It seemed to spark and move down her arms; her hair shifted about her shoulders though the breeze from the courtyard had stilled.

A wild cheer went up and Cecelia reacted. Arkady and Darry spun in a wide circle, tattooing the floor with their steps.

Darry was flush against his body, her right hand held out high in his left as their legs moved so close and swift that it was hard to separate them. Darry's face turned to the side as Arkady pressed his lips to her temple. As they spun, Darry was elsewhere, caught within the music completely as they twirled through the difficult movements.

The strings were on fire and the giant bodhran was booming its beat, and then Arkady let her go. His boots slid gracefully along the polished floor as he let his momentum carry him. Darry spun beside him, keeping pace in a dizzying display of balance as they cut onto the center of the floor, where Arkady pulled her into his arms as the final notes burst with an explosion of sound.

In the sudden silence that shook the room Arkady held Darry's left thigh tight against his hip as she arched back from him, and he placed a rather insolent kiss on the soft skin between her breasts.

The hall erupted.

Darry laughed and slid her hands through Arkady's hair as they straightened, then she stepped close and spoke to him as he laughed as well. People crowded onto the floor and they were swamped, unable to escape the adulation.

Jessa watched Darry's partner lean close and kiss her. Darry moved and time slowed for Jessa. Darry smiled and lowered her face as if she had suddenly become aware of what they had done. Arkady seemed startled and stepped back as though he had just realized he had kissed a Blooded woman at court.

Darry's gaze shifted, cutting across the room through the crowd.

Jessa caught her breath and returned the stare, her blood scorching her veins with a pain so sweet and unknown that her thoughts failed completely. It was only then, when her mind was clear of everything, save for those eyes, that her vision blossomed within her thoughts as clear and heated as the moment she had first seen it.

Eyes were lifted and Jessa caressed the face so close to her own, caught beneath their spell. Lips met in a slow, open kiss and Jessa shuddered with both desire and contentment. The eyes that held her spellbound...

The eyes before her were both green and blue.

The skin was soft and filled with heat against the palm of her hand, life and blood and promise alive beneath her touch...

It was Darry's cheek that she touched.

Darry's face was before her, so near, so beautiful as her taste lingered like fire on Jessa's lips and filled her tongue. "Is what you see different from what I see?"

Arkady bent close once again, and he spoke only to Darry, stealing her eyes away. Jessa tightened her hand around her chalice in a violent surge of irritation. The goblet was unable to withstand the strength of the Vhaelin that moved within her blood and the pewter bent oddly beneath the grip and spilled wine on her hand.

Jessa blinked and stepped back in a daze. "*Belowsha*!" She pulled her skirt out of the way and a dizziness followed heavy behind the curse. Jessa felt the supple kiss upon her lips once more. Her senses spun and she blinked, looking up as her head tightened with a rush of blood.

"I have it," Emmalyn said quickly, taking the chalice from Jessa's hand.

Heat flooded Jessa's cheeks and she tipped to the right. Cecelia stepped up fast with a hand on Jessa's back. The hall seemed to recede within her sight and a fog of darkness swarmed about the edges of her vision.

"It's too close in here," Cecelia said. "Jessa?"

Jessa caught her breath as Darry took the offered kiss without hesitation, her lips parting as Darry's tongue moved within her mouth, teasing against her own.

"Jessa." Cecelia's tone was rigid with worry as Jessa tipped closer.

"*Vhaelin essa yellam nee-ellow*," Jessa answered roughly.

Emmalyn took the cloth napkin that Alisha held out and wiped Jessa's hand. "I don't..." Emmalyn said nervously. "I don't understand."

"Let's get some air," Cecelia said as Jessa closed her eyes.

Darry's lips were tender beneath her ear. Jessa laughed as Darry's hair trailed in curls across her face. A rise of pleasure trembled in her stomach and then between her legs, pulsing in reaction to the attention.

"Jessa?"

Darry moved between her thighs and Jessa cried out with pleasure, her legs possessive as they wrapped about slim hips and her hands grasped with want and urging. Her body thrust in perfect rhythm with the strong flesh against her own.

Jessa set her hand in an iron grip around Cecelia's arm and straightened. "*Vhaelin essa...*" Her voice broke and she swallowed harshly. "*...yellam nee-ellow*."

"I'll get some water," Alisha said.

"*Essa ahbwalla*!" she exclaimed in a breath. A violent tremor shook her. "*Shivahsa*."

"Jessa, answer me," Cecelia said.

"Yes, my Lady," Jessa said, trying to compose herself. "Yes, I'm sorry." She looked to Emmalyn for help, trying to steady her voice. "I felt...I felt a bit dizzy, that's all. It's very hot in here, yes?"

"Yes." Emmalyn took hold of Jessa's arm, grasping it firmly. "Yes, you're right."

Jessa laughed again. "Yes, yes it is."

"Too many people?"

Jessa nodded, pushing down her emotions. "Yes."

"Off to the patio then for some fresh air," Cecelia said with quiet authority.

"Some air might be nice," Jessa said, wanting to laugh again.

"Then a turn about the gardens," Cecelia added.

"My pardons, Majesty," Joaquin said as he invaded their small circle. "But my sister will sing now."

Jessa's stomach gave a violent lurch at his words.

"Nonsense," a strong voice declared in open defiance. Darry smiled at Jessa. "Emmalyn and I have promised to show the Princess the inner gardens, for there are orchids that bloom only in the moonlight."

"Orchids?" Joaquin said.

Darry had donned her jacket and sword and seemed unconcerned as she faced Joaquin, her left hand resting casually on the hilt of her weapon. "Surely after the Mohn-Drom, a Lyonese ballad might stall the festivities, despite the beauty of the voice that sings it." Darry turned to the dais as a swift galliard began to play and the floor filled with dancers.

"Perhaps another night, my Lord?" Emmalyn said. Joaquin put his back to the dancers as the music quickened. "Perhaps a gathering less crowded and hot, yes? I'm shocked that Malcolm would even suggest such a thing. It's bad form, actually. Tonight is only for your introduction, do you see?"

Joaquin considered her words. He found Emmalyn to be proper and beautiful in all that she did, and a woman who seemed to know her rank, unlike her sister. Malcolm had praised her earlier in the evening as well for her insightful knowledge of both etiquette and those at court. "Yes," he said, taking advantage of Malcolm's name. "Yes, he used poor judgment perhaps."

He was not beyond taking advice, and in a situation such as this, mired beneath the annoying protocol of a strange court, he decided it might be best to respect her instincts. The Mohn-Drom had indeed set a blistering pace, and though he hated to admit it, the backwards bitch was right. Jessa's voice was not the proper weapon at the moment to establish a Lyonese presence before the Bloods of Arravan. *A smaller gathering, where I might see everyone's reaction...without the yellow hair's presence to steal my play.*

"Perhaps we might dance later?" Darry said, turning his attention.

"I would like that."

"But not the Mohn-Drom."

"A galliard perhaps?" he said.

"Perhaps."

Joaquin bowed his head and stepped back. "As you wish, Princess." He nodded to the others. "Enjoy your walk." He made his way back along the dance floor, the pace of the music picking up with a fierce swell.

"What did I miss?" Alisha asked as she entered their circle, holding out a goblet of chilled water.

"My life being saved," Jessa whispered as she accepted the chalice. She unclipped her veil and drank deeply.

Alisha smiled at Darry. "I see you still have your clothes on."

"And they're very lovely clothes, Darry," Emmalyn added.

"Do you think so?" Darry grinned, brushing at her vest. "They aren't too showy?"

"No, Darry, they're not."

"They're beautiful," Jessa said, *as are you, Darry.* She wanted to laugh again, seeing Darry's sultry beauty. *Darry, what have I done? What have...ahbwalla, but you...bloody hell, Darry.*

"Well, then," Darry replied. "I consider my gold well spent if you find them pleasing, my Lady."

Jessa smiled at the playful tone. "You dance with great skill, as does your partner."

"Thank you, Jessa. Arkady has a fine step and clever hands, but I didn't..." Her grin brought forth her dimple. "I didn't mean to cause such a spectacle."

"A spectacle indeed." Cecelia straightened Darry's collar with a gentle hand. "You do look extremely dashing, Cat. Though I would've preferred a less suggestive dance. And we shall talk about that tunic on the morrow."

"Mother," Darry laughed, "don't scold me when I'm having such fun. You know how I hate parties."

"Yes, your wallflower behavior is notorious."

"I take after my mother."

Emmalyn slipped her hand within Jessa's. "Malcolm is near the dais. Off we go before the hounds return in force. Alisha?"

"I must find Jacob."

"Does the Royal Tart care to join us?" Emmalyn asked Darry.

Darry laughed as they walked away. "*Tart*?"

Jessa searched over her shoulder and her dark eyes punched the breath from Darry's lungs, sending her stomach over in a pleasing flip of response. *Sweet Jezara, but you shouldn't be looking at someone so without a bit of warning, Jessa.* The voices of the crowd and the volume of the music brought her back to the room with a vengeance. *Bloody hell and mangy hounds, I danced the Mohn-Drom before the entire rotting court of Arravan.* She turned with a wry smile and offered her arm to her mother. "Will you join us, my Queen?"

"I suggest that you leave me before I make you change that shirt. And well played, Cat."

"What've I done now?"

"What *have*n't you done today?" her mother asked. "You'll make my heart give out, I've always said it."

"You also said I would grow horns if I didn't wear a dress to my tenth birthing-day celebration," Darry said as she turned to walk away.

Cecelia laughed. "Yes, and if you hadn't thought that would be a splendid idea," she said, "it might've worked."

CHAPTER NINE

Darry stood beneath the bossa tree, its branches ripe with thick green leaves and seasoned red berries that hung low and shielded her within the shadows.

Jessa sat on one of the stone benches scattered throughout the gardens, bathed in the blue light from one of the colored lamps as Emmalyn knelt before her. "Are you truly all right?" Emmalyn asked, touching Jessa's hands.

"Yes, Emmalyn, thank you. I was just…it was very close, as your mother said."

"You do not have to sing if you don't want," Emmalyn said. "Not ever, Jessa, if it's not your wish."

"It's not so simple as that."

"I know. But you need only tell someone—myself or Alisha, or my mother. Or Darry, of course," Emmalyn added. *Did you dance the Mohn-Drom to save our lovely guest, my sister? It was a clever gamble if you did, and I shall keep you in pastries for a year.* "We will try to help you."

Jessa nodded. "You should find your friend…Royce?"

Emmalyn smiled instantly. "How do you know of Royce?"

"I know only that you love him. It was plain to see and I heard his name spoken."

"He's been gone for many weeks."

"He'll want to dance with you."

"Yes. He can wait, though."

Jessa shook her head. "Please go to him, Emmalyn. It would make me happy. And I would enjoy a moment to myself."

"Are you sure?"

"For certain. Go and dance with your beloved."

Emmalyn nodded and stood. "I'll come find you."

"All right."

Emmalyn kissed Jessa's cheek, a gesture that obviously startled Jessa. Emmalyn smiled, pulling lightly at a braid.

Jessa smoothed at her skirt and closed her eyes, then pressed the back of her hand to her forehead. She saw within her mind's eye as Darry walked beneath the arch and her heart beat fast at the image. She reached for the single bracelet cuff that Radha had allowed her to wear, searching beneath the silk of her left sleeve to find its carved metal glyphs. "*Patroona tu an eesha*," she whispered.

Radha's words echoed in her head. *And what will you do when your vision comes at last, Jessa? Will you accept what it shows you, no matter what it is?*

I should've known it anyway, for no one has ever struck my blood so deeply before.

Am I backwards then? Darry is backwards. Her love is for women. She wants the touch of a woman, and...she wants. What do you want, Darry?

Jessa closed her eyes tightly to bar the image of the man's hands on Darry's body and the way he had fondled her breast with a lustful touch. And he had kissed her. "*Fikloche piton*," Jessa said under her breath, her anger flashing.

She shook her head in surprise.

And what am I to do about it anyway? I am here for Malcolm to judge and that is my path. And though the Vhaelin preach free will in all things, I've known little enough of such matters. What would a woman such as Darry find within the likes of Bharjah's chattel? I'm not much of a prize for one so bold, be they man or woman.

Bloody hell, but she's lovely. You're so beautiful, Darry.

Are these the thoughts of a backwards woman? Wanting to touch her, her skin, wondering what her kiss would... A surge of pleasure blossomed in her chest and spread in a wondrous manner. She felt Darry's weight between her thighs once more and caught her breath, a heavy pulse of desire aching sweetly between her legs. *Essa ahbwalla...* She pressed her hands to her thighs and pushed...*that's rather lovely, yes.*

A breeze lifted and Jessa turned her face, taking a slow, sweet breath. It swept her hair away from her face like a gentle touch, and the scent of lilacs filled her head.

Darry had stepped deeper into the shadows as her sister passed, uncertain of why she hid but following her instincts as always. She waited until Emmalyn was beyond the curve in the hedgerow before turning back and finding Jessa.

Darry's heartbeat quickened as Jessa savored the breeze, a warm flood of appreciation filling her chest. She took a deep breath and expelled it slowly. *Such an amazing woman, yet you may never have her as you wish to.*

Darry looked to the ground at her feet and thought of that long-ago night when she had seen Aidan for the last time and how everything had ached so with want that her hands had shaken as never before. Aidan was the only lover she had ever truly known, and her memories could not help but emerge as her emotions stirred at Jessa's beauty.

What she felt now was different. It was more, and it was terribly fierce, even in its innocence. But Aidan was all she had to compare it to, so her thoughts tumbled backward in time. Their last tryst, it had been almost a week since they had met alone and she had been set upon seeing Aidan no matter the cost. She had known something was wrong, had felt it in her bones.

And it was a lie. She *was a lie. Well, no...that's not true. She was real enough, as was everything we shared, the pleasure and the words we spoke. And though we were young, I can't believe that what we whispered was all a dream. Though I remember well the cold words you spoke that night, Aidan, instead of finding laughter and the taste of your kiss.*

Your cruelty was most certainly not a dream.

Darry's mouth had a bitter taste as she recalled her first lover. Her only lover, as far as the word mattered, for though she had known other women, she had not been in love since. *It never occurred to me, Aidan, that I would not be enough. That the love I gave would mean so much less than others might offer. Not sweet enough. Not smart enough to know what you needed. It hadn't occurred to me that my love wasn't strong enough to be what a woman needs.*

She made out the shadowed hilt of her sword and twisted her left hand upon the pommel. She had, as of yet, been unable to answer many questions where her heart was concerned. What would her family do if she were to love in the open, with no regard for the consequences? Would a royal daughter with a backwards bent be accepted? Or would she be disowned, as no doubt Malcolm would campaign for. She and Aidan had hidden themselves from both of their families, and seeing now how it had all turned out, it had been the best for all concerned.

"*Hesha anna, shaloona tu mahdree*?"

Darry looked up at the soft voice, not so much startled but confused as to how someone could be standing so close without her knowledge.

Jessa saw the sadness in Darry's eyes and wanted to smooth her hand along Darry's cheek. Would that soothe the almost-animal ferocity that played just beneath? The question surprised her so deeply she was unable to move. *What am I to do now? Do I ignore this? Can I even do that?*

"I don't understand," Darry whispered.

"Why do you look so sad?"

And then it was gone, the honesty and raw emotion of what Jessa had seen. It was replaced by a clear expression, one that was just as true but held nothing of the answer to her question.

"I was thinking of someone who's no longer here," Darry said. "A friend. From a very long time ago."

Jessa reached out tentatively and grasped Darry's hand. "I'm sorry."

Darry studied their hands and gently squeezed Jessa's fingers before letting go. "Just a stray thought. I'm sorry to have upset you."

"You did not upset me, my Lady, but I—"

"Darrius," Darry interrupted. "Or Darry, remember? Please call me either. I'm not much of a lady."

"You did not upset me, Darry."

"You are well, though?"

"Yes," Jessa answered, suddenly nervous, although it was a strange sort of wonderful that made her so. This was the first time since their encounter at the garden pond that they had been alone. *With nothing and no one to steal you away. Was it you, Darry? Was it you the wind caught and stole from me like smoke?*

"I hope," Darry replied. "I hope I didn't offend you when I suggested you shouldn't sing. I would like to hear you sing very much, but there were so many people."

"I did not want to sing, Darry, not at all. And I was looking for you and couldn't find you. Until you arrived, that is."

Darry grinned. "I thought with the crowd I would let you know where I was."

"Yes. *Everyone* knew where you were, didn't they."

"Perhaps." The humor was thick within Darry's voice as she glanced into the leaves above. "I think Bentley enjoyed it all very much, at least. He's very bold."

And you are not?

"I didn't mean to take you from your rest. If you'd like to be alone."

Jessa could see Darry's hesitation and wondered if she was nervous as well, though she thought not. A wave of warmth blossomed deep within her chest. *I saw you beneath the bossa and I wanted...I wanted.* "You promised me flowers, Darry. Orchids that bloom in the moonlight."

"Orchids," Darry said happily. "I promised, yes."

"You did."

"But not within these gardens." Darry leaned forward as if she shared a secret. "They grow within a very different garden."

"There are *more*?" Within Lyoness, one garden was a paradise unrivaled. More than one was unheard of.

"For certain. Will you come with me?"

Jessa nodded and Darry stepped to the side, lifting the low-hanging branches back as Jessa moved through the opening.

"There is a story behind these orchids." Darry gestured to the path that wove from the clearing and to their left.

"Then you must tell it to me."

"May I tell you first how very beautiful you look?" Darry asked. "I've never seen such a dress before, interweaving Lyonese and Arravan styles. You wear it extremely well. No other woman here looks quite so lovely."

Jessa blushed as the compliment cut deep. "Thank you."

"I think that the dressmakers of Lokey will be even busier now, before the Solstice festivities."

Jessa frowned as they walked, not understanding.

"You will have created something of a stir," Darry said. "The women of court will want to partake in such a new fashion."

Jessa laughed. "I shall tell Radha then. She'll be most amused."

"Lady Radha?"

"Radha made my dress."

"Truly?"

"Yes."

"She doesn't seem, well, she seems more the type for herbs and healing soups for when your stomach aches. And for scolding you when you've not taken a bath as you should, no matter that you are a woman full grown."

Jessa laughed in earnest. "For certain."

"To the right, Jessa," Darry said as another path opened before them. "And did she knock you on the back of the head when you disobeyed?"

"No," Jessa answered, amused.

"My mother used to." Darry's hand rubbed there. "She has a cracking good swing, and she wears a ring that if it catches you just right? It can cause a strange echo to rattle in your skull."

Jessa laughed yet again.

"Sort of like a coin within an empty bucket."

"Are you saying that your head is empty?"

"I have been accused of that, yes."

"I don't believe it," Jessa said.

"It's true." Darry spied the path before them. "It's just here."

Jessa felt Darry's touch at her elbow and she faced the hedgerow on their right. "This is a garden?"

"Look closer."

Jessa studied the riot of vegetation and saw within the plants an irregular shape to their growth and a channel of deeper shadows that lifted from the ground. "There's a door!"

Darry nodded and reached to her vest. "It is my mother's garden," she said, looking troubled as she pulled at one of the black buttons. She tried carefully to detach the chain that was looped around it. "Fancy clothes with their bloody buttons can be a good-for-nothing nuisance."

Before she could stop herself Jessa covered Darry's hands with her own. "What are you doing?"

"Key. This is the Queen's Garden. It requires a key."

Jessa pushed Darry's hands aside and untangled the chain from the beautiful button. Her heart was racing and she wondered what she was doing, though it felt so right to be doing it, to be standing so close. "You'll pull it loose," she said in quiet reprimand. "And you should try the laces of a Lyonese corset if you wish to experience a nuisance."

Jessa let the delicate gold chain slide through her fingers. She pulled the catch free and smoothed at the vest once more. As she realized what she was doing, she stilled her hands, the heat from Darry's body searing her skin.

Their hands met as Darry took the chain, a crooked stone key hanging in the air between them. "Do you wish to open it?" she said with a grin. "It is the only key other than my mother's."

"How…" Jessa cleared her throat lightly, finding it too hard to breathe standing so close. "Did she give it to you?"

"When I was a girl," Darry said. "I was…struggling with some things, and she said that we might share it. It made me feel special, that we had a place just for us."

Jessa raised her hand and Darry laid the key in her palm. *Still warm from your body*. She closed her eyes as the stone seemed to vibrate against her skin. "Is it all right that I go in?"

"Yes," Darry said, "I want more than anything to share such a place with you."

"You do?"

"I can think of no one better. Open the door, Jessa. Let me show you the Moonblood orchids."

Jessa stepped to the ivy-covered door, spying the keyhole as she pushed a cluster of leaves away from the handle. The key slid within the opening and she turned it. The door popped open in answer.

Darry took Jessa's hand and led her beneath the gate, careful of Jessa's dress before she retrieved the key and pushed the door shut. "I give you the Queen's Garden."

Jessa tightened her grip around Darry's arm and her senses filled at the presence of a thousand flowers. The plants still held some of their colors. The lamps from the palace were many and filled the night with a golden glow.

Tall stalks of sunflowers shot up from within batches of foxglove and hyacinths, and tulips and drooping bluebells were so heavy that they were falling over. Flowering ivy exploded up a trellis made of weathered wood, and periwinkle sprawled everywhere, wild and chaotic as it lay scattered among the rest.

"You have chicory!" Jessa exclaimed, and Darry let go of her hand as Jessa moved deeper in the garden, cupping the delicate blue buds that would open only in the morning light. Jessa laughed with joy. "It is my Radha's favorite. She likes it in her karrem." She turned to the blue flag, closing her eyes as she pressed her nose to the silken petals. "And lupine," she said in a whisper. "Lupine dies so quickly in the clay of Amendeese Province. It's good for healing salves if cured properly."

Darry moved into the clearing near the center of the enclosed garden, then walked beyond.

"Nightshade…" Jessa said, admiring the black and violet petals she was partly named for. It produced a potion that if boiled down would make men see things that were not there, and it was said that it could drive them mad unto death.

Jessa turned to ask if there were oxeye daisies, but the words caught in her throat. *That's not fair…you're not being fair.*

Darry stood in her uniform amongst a wall of glowing orchids, lifting a flower within her hand into the moonlight. The light seemed to sink into the black silk she wore, and the white of her tunic matched the orchid she held, its petals heavy but delicate. On the edges of those petals, a ridge of bloodred lined their softness and bled back into the white, its color beneath the mixture of moonlight and distant lamps a deceptive blue. The stitching on Darry's jacket ignited strangely, and the panther seemed to move of its own accord and climb higher up her arm.

The rush of Jessa's emotions bled downward, the strength of her feelings lighting between her thighs and causing her lips to part at the sensation. Darry's skin caught the spill of the moon and its pale caress skated along her chin and ran like water down her neck, flowing upon her collarbone beside the chain of her necklace and the soft skin of her exposed chest, her tunic plunging open between her breasts.

I'll be sitting down now. Jessa tore her gaze away. *She wasn't so…so beautiful before, was she? Though maybe I wasn't…just breathe, Jessa.*

She walked into the clearing and turned around slowly before sitting on the grass with but a casual care for her dress. She closed her eyes and let her left hand fall to the earth, her heart easing somewhat as the slow pulse of the land beat heavy against her palm. *Such a thing is unfair and you know it. I prayed for a sign, not a bloody brick to the head. Essa, but she'll want me to speak.* Her tongue was thick within her mouth at the thought.

Darry unhooked her sword and walked to her. She knelt and set her blade and scabbard on the grass. Jessa heard the rustle of the sword but did not look up until she heard, "Your orchid, my Lady." Darry was offering her the flower. "Its beauty is matched only by the hand that was meant to hold it."

Jessa gazed at the flower, utterly overwhelmed.

"Take it," Darry said. "It was made by the gods just for you."

Jessa accepted the orchid, her fingers lingering against Darry's as she took possession. She placed the flower in her lap and put her hands beside the petals, almost afraid to touch it.

Darry frowned and shifted on her knee. She tossed her coattails out and sat cross-legged before her. "The story goes that my grandmother Marget decided she wanted orchids. Their beauty was a legend she had only heard of. And though they were not native to my land she was most determined they would be." Darry spoke as if for Jessa's ears only. "And it became a most terrible desire that would not go away. So one bright afternoon she announced to her husband, my grandfather Malcolm, that she would sail to the mysterious islands beyond Wei-Jinn where the Moonblood was said to grow."

Jessa heard the smile in Darry's voice.

"My grandfather, who was a very loud man, and quite large as well for he liked to eat very much, well, he forbid her such a perilous journey and told her that if orchids had been meant to grow in Arravan soil, they would be doing so already. This of course led to an argument so furious that my grandfather's voice rose to amazing proportions." Darry's arms went out as if to encompass the greatness of it. "Huge, booming shouts that caused my grandmother to cover her ears. So huge, in fact, that the ceiling stones and mortar in the throne room cracked."

Jessa smiled at that.

"He announced that no wife of his would *ever* sail so far upon the Sellen Sea. It simply wasn't done. It was a mistake, of course, for no one should ever forbid something *too* severely, at least not to the woman they love. It is asking for trouble.

"When he woke the next morning, all that lay beside him on the soft pillows was a single white tulip and a note written in my grandmother's hand."

"What did it say?"

"I have gone out for orchids and fresh fish for dinner. Love, Marget."

Jessa laughed. "It did not."

Darry smiled happily. "Perhaps you're right. But that's how the story goes, and you see? You have a Moonblood orchid at your fingertips, and the ceiling in the throne room still bears the cracks from his booming voice."

"Did she really go?" Jessa wondered at the courage such a journey would take merely for the beauty of a flower.

"She did. My grandmother was something of an adventurer. She sailed beyond Wei-Jinn to the Southern Isles and Artanis, an ocean voyage that took almost six months there and back, for ships then were not as they are now. My father has always said that she was forever on a quest for something new. She was very bold, but proper and always well-bred. They say I have her hair, though she was said to be very beautiful."

"It was a magnificent gift then, Darry," Jessa said. "But I don't think it was all that she gave you."

"Yes, I might have her feet as well. My toes are quite square, and it is said that my grandmother had to have special boots made."

Jessa laughed again.

"And I don't think I'm the sort of woman she would've liked," Darry said. "Whether I look as she did or not. I'm not very proper, as you already know."

"Do not say such a thing."

"It's true. I'm not as anyone expected when they looked at me in the crib. But a person can only be who they are, yes?"

Jessa had no answer to that.

"Though it's hard sometimes to be who I am. It troubles a great many people," Darry added. She looked down. "It troubles my father the most, but I cannot be who he wishes me to be."

"I don't think that's true, Darry. He looks at you with great pride."

"Yes. You're right, of course."

Jessa knew that Darry did not believe her and sensed that the subject was very private.

"People expect a great many things of you as well, yes?"

Jessa let out a breath of laughter. "Yes, well, they tell me what they want of me and I am made to do it. I would not call them expectations."

"Your Vhaelin teach that there is free will in all things, is this not so?"

The observation surprised Jessa. "Yes."

"Good. Then I will trust to your fine judgment and not worry so much upon the choices that will be laid before you. For one such as you, Jessa, whose beauty might pull the stars from the sky? A woman who is so clever that your thoughts spill from your eyes when something heavy is on your mind? I think then that whatever your future holds it shall be most interesting to see. And I will be very honored to be a part of it in any way you choose."

Jessa had never had such words spoken to her before. *How can you say such things so freely? Have you not a care for your heart, Darrius? And if not then your soul must bear many terrible scars. How is it that you've not learned to hide yourself better?*

Darry chuckled. "Why do you look at me so, Jessa? We are friends, are we not? There are no expectations within that. There is only what we would make of it, and the joy and comfort it might provide."

"You are…" Jessa pondered her words. "You are a most open woman, Darrius."

"Not so very, I think. But I am as you see me, for I can be no other way. Does this upset you? I can try to—"

"No!" Jessa said. "No," she repeated with a quick smile to lighten her words. "I like you as I see you. You must never think otherwise."

"Good," Darry said with a nod.

"*Jessa*?"

They turned at the voice in the distance.

"We're discovered!" Darry stood in a rush. "Emmalyn is like a bloody hound upon the scent. She'll find us for certain and within the Queen's own garden. Up now, quick!"

Jessa laughed. She took Darry's offered hands and was pulled to her feet with strength. She swallowed at the hand on her waist. A firm touch brushed at her skirt and her heart faltered. "Is it stained?" she asked, turning and trying to look.

Darry chuckled and moved with her. "Stop it, Jess."

Jessa put her hand on Darry's shoulder. "Radha will bloody well *kill* me."

"No, it's fine," Darry said. "And besides, I would protect you."

"Then Radha would kill *you*."

"I have no doubts as to that. She is a most imposing woman for one so tiny. Perhaps it would give you time to run, though."

Jessa laughed at the thought.

"Jessa?" Emmalyn's voice called out again.

Darry grabbed her hand and they ran to the ivy-covered door. Darry's boots slipped and Jessa seized her arm in order to steady her. "*Ah*!" Darry looked back. "My *sword*," she whispered, then seemed to swallow a laugh.

"Perhaps she's by the fountain," Royce said from beyond the hedgerow.

"No time," Jessa whispered, leaning close as Darry straightened beside her. Darry's left arm went around her waist from behind and she closed her eyes, letting her body fall slowly against Darry's lean strength. She slid her hand up the silk of Darry's vest and beneath the softness of her jacket.

Darry caught her breath as Jessa stepped close. Jessa's breasts pressed near her own, and there was a warm breath on her neck as Jessa's hair teased her flesh. She lowered her face, smelling the scent of Jessa's skin regardless of the garden they stood in and its riot of perfumes. Jessa's right hand moved up the small of her back and her body gave a tremble of response.

"No," Emmalyn grumbled, then laughed, a rustling of ivy and leaves following quickly. "*Royce*!"

"You taste very good."

Darry closed her eyes as her heart struck in a wild manner. *Please no, Gamar, not with her in my arms…bloody hell, she smells so good.*

"Dammit, Royce, you've already spoiled my hair *once*," Emmalyn said, which was followed by more laughter and a gentle struggle.

Darry gave a jerk at the sound of a slap striking true.

"Gods, woman!" Royce exclaimed.

Darry lowered her face as her laughter rose up. Jessa smiled as well and bit her lower lip. She pressed her fingers against Darry's mouth.

"I think you broke my hand," Royce said.

"Then it should not have been beneath my dress," Emmalyn replied evenly.

Jessa turned her face against Darry's neck. She could smell an elusive musk and, oddly enough, the scent of the ocean. It was not what she expected and sent a thrill along her veins. And then she recognized it, one more piece of her visions falling into place.

"It seemed a fine place for it to be, actually," Royce said.

"Shall we check the fountain?" Emmalyn said coyly.

"I'm not sure I want to go with you now."

There was a rustle of skirts and then, "What was that, my love?"

"Sweet *Gamar*, Em!"

Jessa lifted an eyebrow at the tone.

"Wherever you wish to go, my love." His voice was filled with strain.

"You're awfully brazen, Royce, with my father's guard so near at hand," Emmalyn said. "I have merely to cry out."

Darry reached slowly with her right hand.

"Yes, I know," Royce replied merrily. "It's why you love me."

Jessa looked up as Darry's touch floated softly against her face, pushing the curl back with a gentleness that caught at Jessa's breath.

"The fountain?" Emmalyn said playfully.

Jessa's hand trembled against Darry's mouth and then she caressed her mouth, moving slowly across her lips, tracing their softness from one side to the other as the blood raged within her ears. She could feel her heartbeat even to her toes, and she moved her touch down to discover the smooth dip beneath Darry's lower lip. *I know this*… She skated over Darry's chin and curled beneath as she brushed the backs of her fingers along Darry's throat.

"Then let us find Malcolm's Lyonese beauty and return her to the party." Royce sighed. "And where is Darry?" His voice was moving back along the path. "She enters like a summer storm and then takes her splendid clothes and disappears."

Darry swallowed and Jessa's lips parted with a breath at the sensation of Darry's throat moving beneath her touch.

"*Darry*?" Royce called out.

Both Darry and Jessa started and Jessa dropped her hand.

"If we don't find *either* of them, Mother will sound the watch bells." Emmalyn gave a snort of unladylike laughter. "We shall all be food for Amar."

Darry moved back with a slow step, trying to clear her thoughts, or at least push them into a more acceptable place. *She doesn't understand what she did. You've promised to be her friend, not a bloody fool...just be her friend.*

"This Amar fellow, he doesn't sound very forgiving," Jessa said.

Darry laughed at the statement, the words clearing the last of her thoughts. "Quick now, Princess." She took Jessa's hand and stepped to the door, pulling the gate inward and guiding Jessa forward. "Off you go and down the path."

"What of you?"

"I shall see you within."

"Do you promise?"

"I promise."

Jessa's skirt swept through the doorway. Darry watched her until she was gone, and then she moved back into the clearing to retrieve her sword. Her gaze caught on the ground and she stilled.

The Moonblood orchid sat in the grass at her feet.

She felt once again the sensual touch along her lips and throat, and a sweetness so absolute moved within her body that she had to close her eyes. Her arousal awakened further within her blood, her stomach tightening and her thighs tense. She had never meant for it to happen, but she knew as well that so much beauty held so close was cause enough for the heavy throbbing between her legs, whether she had wished for it or not. Her muscles clenched of their own accord and she caught her breath at the ache.

She's not like you, she's not.

Darry fastened her blade and picked up the fragile blossom, then placed it in the side pocket of her jacket as gently as she could. She crossed back through the night and closed the door, locking the memory of holding Jessa in her arms among the flowers and moonlight of her mother's garden.

❖

Jessa walked along the outer balustrade. Joaquin's hand was hard around her upper arm as they approached her chamber door. Her eyes were down as the stones passed beneath them, and for a moment she thought of refusing his authority and pulling free. She thought to defy him no matter the consequences. *And why shouldn't I? My rights are the same in this place, perhaps. We are no longer beneath the arch of the Jade Palace, you fikloche.*

"Next time," Joaquin jerked her about and Jessa was forced to look up as her shoulders hit the door, "you will not run away when your duty is clear, yes?"

Jessa said nothing, waiting, her own temper rising.

Joaquin yanked one of the clips from her hair. The veil fluttered across her face, revealing her features. "At the next fête you will sing until your throat bleeds, is that understood?" When Jessa remained silent Joaquin gave her a violent shake, her shoulders bouncing against the door. "Is that *clear*, you *sallah cunta*?"

Darry stood in the darkness of the curving corridor farther down the terrace.

"Will my voice so enrapture the court that the High King will weep and give you everything you want, Joaquin?" Jessa said at last. "Is that your best play? To sing him a lullaby?"

Joaquin opened his mouth to respond and then shifted to his left in obvious surprise. Darry stood but a few yards away.

"Lady Darrius." Joaquin let go of Jessa, straightening and taking a step back. "May I help you?"

A cold edge to her voice, Darry said, "Your manners are very poor, for a Prince. In the heart of an enemy land, hell and gone from the safety of your father's throne. Your men are camped almost ten leagues away, under close guard at Los Capos and outnumbered nearly ten to one. Not even your horse is at hand, should you feel the need for flight."

Joaquin lowered his hand to the pommel of his rapier. "And why would I wish to flee?"

Jessa watched her, standing so straight and certain, so very strong. Darry's stance was casual and yet Jessa knew that within the blink of an eye she might have her sword drawn. She looked at her brother. *Best watch your tongue, fikloche. You're not dealing with chattel anymore.*

"You have insulted me," Darry said.

"How so, Princess?" he said.

Darry smiled. "I watched as you danced with a dozen women, my Prince, and yet not one of them was me."

Joaquin laughed, pushed from his anger by the unexpected statement and the playful tone.

"Did you forget?" Darry asked sweetly, almost teasing him.

"No, Princess. I did not forget."

A slight pout crossed Darry's features. "And so you snubbed me."

"Only a little. You seemed so admired that I was jealous."

"You should not have been."

"Were you waiting for me?"

"I was."

For a moment, Joaquin was unsure if she told the truth or not, so delicate was her voice and so sensitive her eyes. He felt a surge of desire at her beauty. Despite her clothes the fact of her attractiveness could not be denied. *I would see you on your hands and knees before me, yellow hair*. He smiled at the picture within his head. *I would have you know my sword, yes?*

"Another time perhaps, good Prince."

"Yes, another time." *You do not lack for nerve, cunta, I will give you that much*. "Sleep well, Jessa," he said and turned to go.

Jessa waited until he disappeared down a staircase. She turned back and found Darry looking at her with curious, gentle eyes.

"I hope you'll not take offense," Darry said, "but I do not like your brother very much."

Jessa stared at her for a heartbeat, then laughed, covering her mouth.

"Are you all right?"

"Yes," Jessa said and lowered her hand. "Yes, Darry, thank you."

"I didn't cause you more trouble, did I?"

"No, Darry, you did not."

"Are you sure?"

"Yes. Joaquin is used to getting his own way. You interrupted his temper, and so now it will simmer in forgetfulness until he feels I've done something else wrong and he wishes to berate me."

"I could hit him on the head for you, if you'd like."

Jessa chuckled, wanting to reach out and straighten Darry's lapel, though it needed no straightening. "Yes, that might be nice."

"Off I go then."

Jessa grabbed Darry's arm. She tried not to laugh as she pulled her back. Darry stepped close and looked down at her, smiling in such a way that the dimple pressed into her left cheek, Jessa fought back a sigh at the sight of it. *Bloody hell, woman, it's only a dimple.* "Do not."

"No?"

"No, Darry."

"I only wanted to say good night to you."

"And saved me instead," Jessa said. *Again, I think, yes?*

"If you say." Darry was standing much too close and she stepped back abruptly, as if frightened. "I bid you only the sweetest of dreams, my Lady."

Jessa was caught again in the same swell of emotions she had experienced when her visions had blossomed in full, only this time she had no questions and very little confusion. Only a clear recognition and a dark heat of wanting at the surprising truth of it all. She remembered the softness of those lips beneath her fingers and the feel of Darry's throat moving, so much life reaching out to her within such a simple thing.

She responded without thinking and took hold of Darry's jacket.

Jessa placed her mouth on Darry's and kissed her gently, a slow, lingering taste of Darry's lips pliant against her own. Darry's hands brushed her waist and for a heartbeat Jessa wondered how it would feel to be held within those strong arms…but Jessa stepped back, their hands touching briefly before she turned and took refuge within her rooms.

Radha looked up from the comfort of the divan. Jessa covered her mouth with her hand as she collapsed against the door. "Jessa?"

The very center of her world was tilting, the wheel turning smoothly and slipping from its axis. She could even sense the threads upon the Great Loom pulling tight around her and was lost as the random runes of a hundred spells drifted through her head. The reality of what her life had always been began to rush away from her, as if caught by the current of a flooding spring river. *Vhaelin essa...she tastes as sweet as her words.*

Radha sat up. "I can feel your majik along my bones, child. Are you all right?"

"Yes." Jessa pushed away from the door and moved within the darkness, seeking escape among the blacker shadows of her dressing room.

CHAPTER TEN

Radha lifted her head and opened her eyes, her whispered prayer to the Vhaelin drifting into the distance upon the morning breeze. She pulled lightly at her shawl and the worn, fringed fabric slid from about her head, as she turned from the balustrade railing and returned to the rooms that were her and Jessa's. As she closed the door behind her she let her senses reach out, listening for Jessa.

The main chamber was silent and Jessa's bed was empty, the sheets and soft blankets in a tangled mess on the feather mattress. Jessa's tossing and turning had kept her awake until just a few hours past. It had been time for her prayers anyway, so she had risen in a gentle mood despite very little sleep.

She sensed Jessa's presence in the privy beyond the dressing room and approached the door, asking her question before advancing any farther. "Will you not tell me how the evening went?"

Jessa looked up from where she sat upon the edge of the tub. "Hmm?"

"You've said nothing since last night."

"What need do I have to tell you of a party you have no interest in? And besides, were you not drifting in the shadows?"

"Too many people," Radha lied. "Are you troubled? Did you not sleep?"

"I'm fine."

"But something bothers you?"

"Nothing bothers me."

"You did not have to sing?"

Jessa looked down at her hands. "No. I did not have to sing." *I was rescued by a beautiful woman instead.*

"I shall find the herbs today. We may work the spell tonight."

"Yes, that's fine, Radha."

"Do you not wish to see what the waters might hold?"

"Are they always true?"

"They offer but a path, you know this," Radha said, answering a question she had answered for years. "If you do not wish to follow the path offered, you do not have to. There is free will in all things and the Vhaelin never punish, should you not care for what is shown. You understand this as well as I, Jessa."

"I know."

"If you do not like what they—"

"I did not say that," Jessa said. "I never said that, Radha."

"They cannot tell you what is in your heart. If you are searching for the truth, this is yours to find. And you have the right to question whatever you would like."

"Yes, I know."

"What your heart needs," Radha said, "such a thing is your quest, and yours alone. It is not so easy, I admit this, but you will know when you find it."

"How will I know?"

"It will feel like nothing else ever has," Radha said, moving into the washroom. "It will throw you across a distance though you do not move. And you will wish to sit down, though you are sitting already. It will confound you and thrill you and make you dizzy with joy. And very angry at times as well, and you will forget your words. You will know it when you find it, I promise."

"It sounds annoying."

Radha laughed and kissed Jessa's cheek. "Yes, it is. Very much so," she said. "Take your bath now, child, and stop bothering me. You'll be late to break your fast and that is poor etiquette."

"Yes, Radha. And if I refuse to take a bath as you tell me, will you scold me and hit me on the head?"

Radha narrowed her eyes, pulling at a braid. "I might."

Jessa grabbed Radha's hand and held it between her own, studying the soft, almost fragile skin and the wrinkles of age. "I love you, Radha."

Radha put her other hand in Jessa's hair, petting her as she had when Jessa was a girl. "I know."

"Do you love me too?"

"Yes, child, you know I do. And that will never change."

Jessa's visions swarmed up and she allowed free rein as she held Radha's hand. She let them move through her and speak as memories do, feeling them stir her thoughts and her emotions. She wanted very much to know the truth of her heart. She could not hide from what had been shown to her, nor could she run away.

And more importantly, she had no desire to.

❖

They spent the day after the fête at their leisure. No official council meetings were held, and Cecelia declared that after such a gathering, no duties were so important that they could not be suspended until the morrow. That Malcolm and Joaquin had ridden to Los Capos for the day, and Owen and Armistad had disappeared behind closed doors in the early hours, had only made her decree easier.

Darry was surprised but she welcomed it. She wanted nothing more than to be in Jessa's presence. She had not slept well and her lack of rest was dragging at her. She felt in need of time, and a day of freedom seemed like the perfect remedy.

Jessa's kiss haunted her, and the taste of her lingered on Darry's lips long into the night. It had been a tender gesture of gratitude and nothing more, Darry understood that, but it followed her like a ghost nonetheless. And she felt her desire still, a low, heated pulse of want drumming through her veins. If she could just spend time with Jessa during a normal day, the passion of her feelings would fade, and her thoughts as well.

She had aching thoughts of how Jessa's body fit so perfectly in her arms, and quiet thoughts of a tender caress on her throat. How Jessa laughed and danced with Jacob at the fête, spinning so beautifully among the other dancers. Such a simple act, to dance with her. Darry's desire for such a privilege had been like a blow to the stomach. Jessa's movements had been so smooth and perfect, and the music had drawn around her as if it were a living creature, her black hair lustrous in the light.

Darry had wanted that for herself, to hold Jessa in her arms as the music played. But she had danced with Kingston Sol instead, and Sorren Fitzgerald, who was quite good. But wanting Jessa to press against her in the movements of a dance was far different than being led by Sorren Fitzgerald.

It was not the first time she had felt so utterly out of place at such a function. Bentley was always there, of course, and last night Arkady had been present as well. But she would never belong among the Bloods of court so long as she could not dance with the one she truly wanted. And even if she had, they would have been the object of speculation and rumors, and the whole thing would have become an epic disaster.

She had danced with Aidan once, at a small, informal gathering. But they had been young, and Darry had yet to declare herself backwards. Others had viewed it as a lark, and they had danced as girls often do, when no boys could work up the nerve to ask. Malcolm had ended it, however, and lectured her. If she could not stop pretending to be a man, she would no longer be allowed at family functions.

She had responded that she appeared to be a better man already than he might *ever* be. He had grabbed her jacket and shoved her, and it had been the beginning of the end for them.

Their mother had overheard their words and witnessed the confrontation, and Malcolm had been put in his place, though Darry remembered how frightened she and Aidan had been. They had hidden themselves completely after that, whether her family would have accepted their love or not.

Darry highly doubted that dancing with the woman who might well end up the future Queen of Arravan would have been accepted much better.

They broke their fast as a family, with Royce and Jacob present, and Alisha as well. And as Darry became lost in her thoughts yet again, she could smell jasmine and knew the weight of Jessa's nearness as never before.

They played Wei-Jinn afterward and she became caught up in the ease and comfort. She partnered with Emmalyn against their mother and Jessa, who soundly beat them in three straight matches. When Jacob announced that a match between the two unbeaten women be played, Darry stood and declared instead that Wei-Jinn was too tame for such a beautiful day and proposed a game of round ball.

Darry saw to it that the sticks for round ball were raised within the main practice yard beneath the noonday sun, and the teams made ready as the ladies took their seats upon a low rise of benches within the shade cast by the inner wall.

It was a game of speed as well as strength and Darry loved it, happy to be squaring off on a gorgeous day and hoping to find her balance within the purity of the sport.

Darry's team of Royce and Jacob stood in the center of the yard across from Bentley, Arkady, and Kingston Sol, who had taken up the challenge. Jemin McNeely placed the skin ball on the ground between them and announced that the match would be played to three sticks.

"I intend to whip your fine ass, kitten," Bentley said.

"You'll have to catch it first."

"What's the prize?" Kingston asked.

"What's the prize, Mother?" Darry asked.

"Another day without duty?" her mother said.

"Too tame, my Lady!" Bentley called. "We need more to inspire us. A clever man can always find a day off."

Jessa couldn't keep her eyes away from Darry. Her hair was tied behind her neck and her sleeves rolled up, and her body held a different sort of vitality than it normally did. She was not walking or dancing or being proper at the table; she was in her natural environment and Jessa's blood quickened to see it. Darry was a woman meant for action, not the quiet of courtly manners.

Emmalyn stood and slowly pulled the handkerchief from her bodice, then let the delicate lace and soft silk slide from between her breasts and catch the breeze. "Perhaps this will do?"

Alisha laughed at their startled faces and stood beside Emmalyn, unfastening her brooch, which glittered in the sun. "And this."

"Bloody hell," Cecelia groaned. "They'll kill each other."

"Jessa?" Emmalyn smiled at her.

Jessa stood and unbraided a plait of her black hair with practiced ease, then smiled at Darry's expression as she loosed a teardrop of jade and caught the delicate chain of its setting.

It was a polished gem of considerable size. Jade came from Lyoness alone, and within Arravan, its presence was as highly sought after as Blue Vale steel.

"Jessa, that's too much," Cecilia said. "It's worth a fortune."

"I may offer the prize I see fit, my Lady," Jessa said. "'Tis only a bauble of cut jade. I have more."

Cecelia lifted an eyebrow as she returned her attention to the yard. "Will that do?"

"Perfectly." Darry answered, glaring at her opponents.

Jemin stepped up. "No eye-gouging and no nut-busting." He looked at Darry. "And no tit-grabbing or hair-pulling."

"Thank you," Darry said, thinking only of Jessa's jade. To have such a token that had known the touch of Jessa's braids made her blood rise.

"Bloody hell," Bentley groaned. "Arkady, watch her clo—"

Darry burst forward and the game was on as she kicked the ball behind her with a heel and smashed her forearm into Bentley's chest, then spun back to her left and jabbed her elbow into Kingston's stomach.

The game was physical and often violent, depending upon the stakes, though for a courtly game Jessa hoped it would not be too dangerous. The dust from the practice yard stirred at once, and the players yelled and laughed as the general melee commenced.

Jessa tensed when Darry was involved in a play and admired her incredible speed and agility. She had seen nothing like it before and cheered when Darry outmaneuvered an opponent, just as she flinched when she was under attack.

Darry's team was two sticks up before long. Jacob was surprisingly accurate when kicking the ball, though he was the slowest runner Jessa have ever seen.

When in pursuit of Royce, Arkady swerved one way and then the other. But Darry caught him as he passed and took them both to the ground.

Arkady's legs tangled with Darry's, his weight on top of her in a rudely familiar manner. Jessa began to rise but caught herself, hesitating for a moment before she sat back down. *What sort of man would dare touch a woman of the Blood so easily? Bloody fikloche.*

A crowd was gathering on the other side of the yard, soldiers who were off duty and some that were not, and shouts of encouragement rained from the wall behind the benches as well.

Jessa followed the game as never before, feeling excitement and wonder and all the things she had experienced the previous night. That a woman participated so casually in a men's sport did not surprise her, for Darry seemed to allow very few restrictions in her behavior. Jessa was surprised that no one else seemed bothered by her involvement, however. Indeed, her comrades seemed to favor her, to judge by their shouts. They accepted her as one of their own, and Darry was easily the best player there.

And she was beautiful in her strength. Jessa smiled beneath her veil when Darry laughed, and the open affection with which she greeted her teammates charmed Jessa. Darry's femininity revealed itself in those moments and set her apart from the others in a most alluring fashion. Jessa had seen round ball many times in her life but never before had she been so invested in the outcome. She wanted very much to see Darry possess her jade and to reward her for her skill.

When the final stick was made, it was Royce who kicked the ball into a post and through the gate. Jessa forgot etiquette altogether and cheered with Emmalyn and Alisha as she experienced an unfamiliar swell of pride.

Then the winners sought out their spoils. Alisha gave her gold brooch to Jacob, along with a passionate kiss.

Emmalyn met Royce as he approached and held out her lace. Royce wiped his hands on his trousers before taking it and kissing the palm of her hand.

And Darry waited beyond them all.

"Do you not want your prize, my Lady?" Jessa asked. She had not missed the troubled expression or the timidity that had invaded Darry's posture as the others had stepped out and she had not. "It would appear that you will have to settle for my small token. I'm sorry."

Bentley stepped close with an easy smile, throwing his arm about Darry's neck and pulling her forward. "Might I see it?" he asked, and Jessa let him take it. "Well won, my Lady." Bentley set the jade in Darry's hand, smiling down at her. "I'm not sure what you'll do with it, though," he said, his eyes filled with mischief.

Darry raised the jewel in her dusty hand and looked up with a smile. "I do," she said, and Jessa laughed happily.

❖

The afternoon after lunch was warm, and Darry was still enjoying the freedom of a day without duties. Their group joked about Jacob's prowess on the field as they entered the massive courtyard beyond the kitchens. Darry kept very close to Jessa as they neared the kennels.

She had wanted the jade, but now she found herself pulled even further. She wanted a kiss as well, as she had received the night before. She wanted more of everything where Jessa was concerned, and though at first she enjoyed the rush of such emotions, as the afternoon progressed they troubled her because she was unable to push back her longing.

Gradually she put a distance between herself and Jessa, feeling hot in the sun as an ache began at the base of her skull. Jessa always found her, though, and occasionally brushed her arm or their hands would touch. And though Darry had no desire to escape such attention, her head spoke other words. Yet she became terribly vulnerable to the demands of her heart.

When they approached the kennels a wave of anxiety engulfed Darry when she realized where she was, and her thoughts sharpened into deadly focus. The long structure was open on both ends beneath a slanted pine roof, and as they left the sun for its shade, Darry's heart beat as if upon a bed of nails. She lagged behind the others, then stopped and backed away when she heard barking, her stomach churning at the heavy scent of the animals.

Jessa noticed Darry's hesitation and her pale color. When several of the dogs were released and moved about Alisha's legs with affection, Jessa followed in concern. "Darry?"

Emmalyn turned toward her holding a wolfhound pup, letting his small teeth nip at her hand. "Darry does not like the dogs," she said. "She never comes here."

Jessa understood such a fear all too well, though she was also aware that these animals were unlike Sylban's dogs. She slipped her hand in Darry's and held on. "I won't let them hurt you," she said, giving a tentative pull.

Darry resisted. "They don't like me."

"Why not?"

Darry evaded the question, her attention fierce upon the tall wolfhound that approached. The hound growled and the hackles on his back rose as he shook his wiry hair. He snapped his discontent and his bark filled the air around them, though he advanced no closer.

"Royce." Emmalyn pushed her leg at the dog as Jessa stepped forward, putting herself between Darry and the hound. Royce grabbed the dog's collar and pulled him back with a firm hand. The animal twisted and wagged his tail as Royce scratched his neck.

Jacob picked up a wayward pup. "They won't bite, Darry, I promise."

"When Darry was a girl, the dogs chased her," Emmalyn said.

"Tried to *eat* me is more like it," Darry said.

"Honestly, Darry." Jacob approached her. "I'd never let them hurt you again."

"They attacked you?" Jessa said. She knew the horrific damage that a dog was capable of inflicting, no matter their temperament.

"Yes," Emmalyn said. Darry stepped away as Jacob held the pup out to her. "The animal was innocent but it might have killed Darry if our father hadn't intervened. When he saw the blood on Darry's torn clothes and her injuries, he put down two of the dogs that day." She shuddered. "Jacob, stop it."

Jessa maneuvered between them and took the pup before Jacob could advance any farther. "I'm not a champion of dogs either," she said. "I've never known them to be kind."

The pup licked at Jessa's face beneath her veil and Darry's tension seemed to ease somewhat when Jessa laughed softly.

"Sylban's dogs," Jacob said, "I hear he keeps them…for hunting."

Jessa studied the pup's innocent face. "Yes. For hunting."

Darry stepped forward and tentatively reached out. If Jessa trusted the animal then surely she had nothing to fear, though her every instinct told her to back away. *It's only a pup…though the mother can't be far away.*

She knew they all watched but she made the effort. She had not touched one of the dogs since that afternoon years ago. Her hand hovered only a few inches away.

The puppy squirmed and Jessa smiled when the animal pushed her wet nose against Darry's hand and licked her fingers without restraint. Darry let out a breath of startled laughter. She pulled away, though, rubbing her hand.

"I like her," Jessa said kindly. "She has good taste."

"Then she's yours," Jacob said.

Jessa stared at him. "I beg your pardon?"

"She's just a pup, my Lady," he replied. "She'll be too small to hunt, and I'm not sure she'll have the heart. She's the runt of a large litter. One of the kennel lads has to feed her because the others won't let her eat. She's more suited to a lady's gentle hand."

Darry had to get away, so she had walked to the edge of the kennel. She felt almost savage as she glanced at Jessa and the puppy.

"Thank you, Jacob." Jessa's voice was a tad rough as she returned the pup. "I would like that, at least while I'm here."

The pup barked and struggled to return to Jessa, her legs kicking and her plump little body twisting about as Jacob laughed. "You see? She loves you already, Lady Jessa."

Darry saw the happiness on Jessa's face and the ache within her head returned. *And now you've made me ignore my instincts as well…*

"Look how tiny she is, Jessa." Alisha leaned over the pen as Jacob returned the pup to her family. "Perhaps she'll be a lapdog."

"My Radha would enjoy a companion, perhaps," Jessa said.

Darry watched as Jessa leaned over one of the cages and couldn't stop the erotic fantasy that blossomed in response. She saw herself claiming an open kiss as her spoils no matter the battle, her hands on Jessa's hips, pulling her close and feeling their bodies together. Letting her hands move lower yet. She wondered how perfectly Jessa's breasts might fit her hands, and if she would cry out when she—

Several dogs began to bark and one of the cages shook as the hound inside pounded at the gate in a sudden flurry of agitation. The barking spread, and the kennel erupted with a hard swell of noise as nearly every animal rose. Jacob shouted them down but they refused to obey. One of the kennel lads jumped over the nearest gate in order to calm the lead hound, whose fury was inciting the others.

And then they stopped.

As quickly as it had begun the barking died out. The dogs were restless and whimpering but no longer desperate in their passion to be freed.

Darry was nowhere to be seen.

CHAPTER ELEVEN

The next afternoon, Jessa walked along the edge of the great hall. They had eaten lunch a few hours before and now the room was filled with music. Alisha and her mother, Lady Bella, sat beside Emmalyn and Cecelia as a troupe of court musicians played. They sought to choose the songs and perhaps a singer for the wedding fête, and with music in the air for no special occasion it was a wonderful way to spend the afternoon.

Darry had been absent at dinner the night before, and it had been one of the longest meals of Jessa's life. She worried that Darry had been more upset by their visit to the kennels than she had let on. And today, Darry had barely eaten her lunch. Her movements had been almost fragile as she cut her food, very measured and precise. Darry usually had a wonderful appetite.

Jessa stepped inside the solar and searched the room. She found Darry near the wide doors that were thrown open to the gardens beyond.

Darry stared into the garden and her stomach was shaky. Her food was not sitting well and she was anxious beyond anything she had felt in some time. Not only was Jessa's presence upsetting, but her own frustration and temper troubled her as well. Frustration at the feelings she could only repress and anger that she had left herself so completely unguarded, that she was letting herself be so easily distracted.

She had spent the night reading from a book of poems that she loved well. The words of Eban Parrabas had blurred as her focus wandered, though she followed the letters regardless. She knew them by heart, she knew where they led and what they made her feel. Parrabas had written many works in his lifetime, but his poetry called to her like few scholarly things ever had.

Darry understood her limitations, but the words of his poems told her that such restrictions were a lie. They promised that the world and all its wonders were hers if she would just accept them. But she had to accept them without trying to change either what she encountered or herself.

Such a promise eased her heart and slowed her blood. She had sat on the floor, her back against the end of her bed, and read the words repeatedly, following the curve of the ink and seeing where the scribe had paused his quill.

She had spoken the words aloud until their cadence soothed her needs and her arousal faded. She had read until she no longer thought of Jessa's lips against her own, or of the fire in Jessa's eyes as she had offered her jade. She read until the peace of the poet's thoughts became her own, though in doing so she had barely slept yet again.

Darry had fallen onto her bed near dawn, and even then she had awoken in a violent manner, crying out from her dreams as she held herself, spending her spirit against her own rough hand. She had come with Jessa's voice in her head and the sheets tangled about her legs, confused and aching and not knowing what would happen next.

You need a good night's sleep, that's all. I'll read again and the words will—

"Darry?"

Darry flinched and turned at the soft voice.

"I'm sorry, forgive me, please," Jessa said.

"Yes. No, it's all right."

"Are you well?" Jessa asked as the music floated like a dream around them. "You didn't eat much."

Darry was staring at Jessa's hair and without thinking she had begun to count her braids. They were less in number than the day before. *Perhaps a bit thinner as well.*

"Darry?"

"Hmm?"

"You're not upset about yesterday, are you? I didn't mean to force—"

"Jessa," Darry said, and Jessa fell silent. "They're playing a Lyonese dance. Is it the Fortran or the Amendeese?"

"The Amendeese. The man twirls beneath the lady's arm, and the extra movement near the end, the quick-step turning?"

"They're hard to tell apart." Darry tried to see Jessa's lips beneath her veil. "I'm not so good with northern dances."

As if reading her mind Jessa released one of the clips in her hair, letting her veil flutter to the side. Darry's pulse intensified. *You shouldn't have done that, Jess.*

Jessa held out her hand. "Let me show you?"

Darry stared at the hand, taking a slow step away.

Jessa followed her, seeming determined to have her way. "You're not scared are you? Perhaps you're not as good a dancer as you think."

Darry smiled at the teasing. It was completely against etiquette to dance with her outside of a formal function, to be backwards and hold her as a man would.

"It's not proper," Darry whispered. *I don't want to touch you, Jess, don't make me do that.*

"Yes, and what of it?" Jessa said. "I think too much of etiquette. And my offer will not last long." She seemed unsure of herself yet bore an expression of triumph. "If you don't wish to learn properly, then you should say so."

Darry took Jessa's hand, ignoring her instincts. *Just one dance. Just this one thing.*

Jessa turned her head to the side as Darry stepped close. Her breath was quick as her left hand was raised in Darry's right, the heat of the touch at her waist burning through the silk of her sari. "Wait for the lute," she whispered.

As they stepped in the opening turn, Jessa looked up. Their thighs met for an instant and the muscles of Darry's left arm pressed against the side of her breast. Darry followed the steps as best she could, incapable of stopping her desire as everything shifted. The words she had spoken in the darkness of the night before were an insufficient defense as they filled her head.

Jessa smiled at the mistaken steps and they came to a stop. "The other way, Darry."

"I'm nervous." Darry adjusted her position. "I've never danced with a princess before."

They moved smoothly, turning across the solar to the bodhran's subtle pulse as the Lowland pipes rose in an ache of sound. "Neither have I," Jessa said softly.

Darry concentrated. *Just dance, Darry.*

Jessa let herself be led and wondered why she had never felt this before, the primal heart of the music. The pipes and the song were alive as she and Darry braided their movements within the beat, so effortless and easy with their bodies together. She was not thinking of the steps but, instead, of the softness of Darry's hair against the back of her fingers. When Darry stepped away she lifted her arm high and opened her hand. Darry's touch caressed gently in her palm as she turned beneath Jessa's outstretched arm. She stepped close after the second spin and they both smiled.

Jessa caught her breath as their bodies became flush with Darry's right leg between her own as they moved through the last movement of rapid steps and turns. "The quick-step turning?" Darry said.

"Yes." Jessa's face flooded with warmth. Darry's strength sang in Jessa's blood as it had done the day before.

The steps were swift and they eased to a stop as the music did. Darry was breathing fast. She smelled Jessa's hair with its earthy, clean smell. It was intoxicating and all of Darry's desire welled up, more powerful than the day before, perhaps even stronger than ever. She was going to kiss her and had no way of stopping herself. She knew it even as she struggled and knew that it would ruin everything. *I'm sorry, Jess.*

"Jessa?"

Darry recognized Emmalyn's voice, but it seemed very far away and Jessa's mouth was so close, her lips parted ever so slightly.

Jessa pulled back and Darry let her go, a lance of anger slicing through her chest at being denied. The urge to follow and take what she wanted was violent, and she battled to remain where she was.

"You're a very good dancer, Darry," Jessa said in an awkward breath of words. "You're very…graceful."

Emmalyn walked beneath the arch. "There you are," she said. "Alisha would like to…" Her gaze moved from Jessa's unveiled face to Darry, who turned away from them. "…have your opinion on the Lyonese dances. Do you mind?"

"Not at all." Jessa refastened her veil, her hands shaking.

"Darry?" Emmalyn called as Darry made for the garden doors.

"I have duties."

Jessa turned around at the words but found only Darry's back.

"She must be late," Emmalyn said as Darry disappeared.

"Yes," Jessa said. She needed to sit down. A sensual pulse beat low and heavy between her legs. She closed her eyes as she let out a long, slow breath.

"Are you all right?"

"Yes," Jessa answered. *Vhaelin essa.*

When Jessa made no effort, Emmalyn moved forward. "Come along then, my friend." She took Jessa's hand. "Let us have your expertise on the music from your homeland."

Jessa held on tightly, using the contact as her guide in a shining new world she was only now beginning to see.

❖

Darry prowled through her loft in the uppermost floor of the guard barracks, talking to herself as she paced the room for at least the hundredth time, her thoughts like a new sword that had yet to learn mercy.

It was dark and she had missed dinner again. The thought of food made her ill, and the notion of sitting proper and quiet at the table sent a dark flood of frustration through her. She had retched once already and washed her mouth out with a strong red wine. The bottle was half empty beside the hearth where she had sat and tried to slow her blood, hoping that the redolent taste of the grapes would hold her calm and ease the pain within her.

She should have said no to Jessa, no matter how badly she wanted their dance. She should have used more discipline. That she had been so careless yet again ignited an unstoppable rage in her.

When she neared her desk beside the window she let out a growl and clutched the edge of it. She lifted the heavy oak into the air, feeling the strain in the muscles in her back and shoulders. Only the presence of the divan stopped it from crashing to the floor.

"*Fool*!" she said. "You're a fucking fool."

She could smell the yards beyond, the scent of the earth strong and clean, though not enough to banish the dominant odor. The smell of flesh. The smell of a hundred men in the building below her—sleeping, breathing, their blood pumping, their scent pungent and crushing.

Darry stumbled to the side and fell to her knees. "I read here," she whispered desperately. "I read books and scrolls. Things a human being does. Only man does these things."

The dull taste of iron coated her tongue and she sat back on her heels. Her nose flooded with blood and she coughed, staining her hand red as her head exploded with pain.

Lips burned supple against her own and she gasped at the memory, her want clawing with renewed life. She stared at the carpet, seeing its pattern within the darkness. She should not have been able to see it without the lamps but she saw everything, every turn and crafted stitch. She tried to follow them, tried to get lost within the pathways and heavy thread.

She was wet with need and her stomach filled with fire. Darry closed her eyes in despair. It would only get worse now. Once the fire came she could never stop it.

She could feel Jessa within her arms and the scent of jasmine haunted her. She dragged a sleeve across her face and swiped at the blood, the memory of Jessa's breasts pressed against her too much to bear.

Blood was in her mouth again. It was the final blow.

"*Yes*," she said, her voice breaking as she scrambled to her feet.

Clothes. She was on her knees before the open doors of her bureau closet, staring up into the fabrics and colors. The textures were pronounced and rough within the dark and the colors askew, not quite what they should be. She flinched in pain and turned her face away. Tunics pulled from their hooks and spilled down as she clutched at them for balance.

Darry leaned against the bureau, trying to catch her breath, a cold sweat sliding down her back and soaking her tunic. Her legs trembled, everything trembled.

"Discipline," she whispered. *Don't move, just breathe.* "Just breathe."

The blade twisted in her stomach as Jessa's warm breath touched her throat.

Darry laughed, the sound barely contained, as she opened her eyes and followed the stairs that led to the high platform that held her bed. The bed where she had sat the night before, thinking herself clever and strong for having pushed back her blood. Thinking she had found her peace in the comfort of words.

"Poems to stop the blood." She laughed bitterly, wiping the blood from her lips. "And the dance you just had to have, that was so very clever."

She had to find Bentley. Bentley would help her. Bentley was *always* there when her majik came, and he could always figure out something.

❖

"Radha?" Jessa rose from her bed.

"I sense it, child," she answered. "Someone is working majik, yes?"

Jessa walked past the divan and stepped onto the small corner balcony. A secluded, oddly shaped courtyard below held the smell of summer and allowed her to look at the stars from the privacy of her own little space.

The distant power she could smell was very potent, holding the tang of something hidden. It should have been familiar. It *was* familiar.

"It's very old," Radha whispered, and Jessa turned from the railing as Radha stepped under the arch. "Old, child, like the bones of the earth."

"What is it?"

"I don't know." Radha held out her hand. "Come inside."

"It cannot harm me, can it?"

"Come inside *now*," Radha hissed.

"Radha, please, I'm fine.

"Take a breath, you foolish girl," Radha said harshly "*Havah seella do.*"

Jessa did as she was told and gasped, touching the arch to steady herself.

"How do you feel?"

"Afraid," she said. Whatever majik it was, it was deadly, and she knew it as surely as she had ever known anything.

"Aye," Radha said. "And you should be. The night is no longer safe."

"Radha?"

Radha turned back into the room. "Something goes hunting."

"Is it Serabee?"

"The stench of the Fakir is not so pleasant, girl, you know that. It is pleasing to you as well?"

Jessa's pulse was racing. Everything was too warm and something enticing hummed in her blood. She felt as she had when standing in Darry's arms, hidden behind the ivy of the Queen's Garden. A warm shiver moved down the back of her neck and her nipples hardened as she thought of Darry's hand spinning against her own when she had turned so gracefully during their dance. Her own majik stirred and the Vhaelin shuddered with life as she left Radha at the arch. "Yes."

"You have a secret," Radha said.

"Leave me be, old woman."

"You'll not tell me?"

Jessa sat on the edge of her bed. "What goes hunting then?"

"I don't know. That is why we return to bed."

After sitting for a time Jessa turned over and pulled up the sheet.

"What is your secret, child?" Radha said. "Tell me."

Jessa closed her eyes. "I have no secret."

"Your blood stirs."

"So does yours," Jessa said.

Radha's laugh scraped across the silence.

Jessa turned onto her back and stared at the ceiling. *Tell you what? That I've seen my visions clearly for the first time in my life? Would you laugh at that as well? And that the face I see...the eyes.*

Jessa had tried very hard just to be herself since the fête. To be with Darry and not pretend, to have no fear at what her visions had shown her. She had wanted to watch Darry and to study her as much as possible, to see if perhaps she was wrong.

But she was not wrong and the waters had not lied.

The way you looked at me, Darry...No one sees me like that, looking so deep, searching out something that is a mystery to me. Jessa closed her eyes, wanting to groan aloud at the strangeness of it, the unfamiliar sensation of physical yearning.

She reached beneath her pillow and closed her fingers around the delicate fabric of the handkerchief Darry had sewn. She moved it slowly between her fingers and caressed the softness of the thread, remembering Darry's smile as she had looked back from the door. She saw the shadowed hollow of Darry's dimple and her chest ached.

Everything ached and she turned onto her side again and brought her knees up. The damp flesh between her legs clenched slowly and sent a warm flood of pleasure through her loins and thighs. *Vhaelin essa…* she eased a hand between her thighs and cupped herself, biting her lower lip as her flesh reacted, begging for more as her left leg shifted smoothly against her right. *Bloody hell.*

What should I tell you, Radha? That the face I saw was a woman's? That the eyes that cause me to feel like I have never felt before are Darry's eyes?

"I can hear you thinking." Radha spoke softly.

"Then stop listening," Jessa said in a rough voice as she turned her face to the pillow.

CHAPTER TWELVE

Emmalyn turned at the sound of her name and draped the gold dress over her arm. She was not used to having Royce home, so close, so wonderfully solid beneath her hands that her world tipped. Her step was quick as she moved from the dressing room into her bedchamber. "Royce, if my mother walks—"

Emmalyn jerked to a halt beneath the desperate eyes of Bentley Greeves, then she stared at Darry. Darry's head lolled back and her right arm dangled limply as she lay in his arms.

Darry's tunic was stained with blood and Emmalyn's thoughts twisted as the memory of Wyatt and Malcolm carrying Evan's body into the great hall filled her head. His blond hair had been covered with blood and his neck bent oddly. She had known the instant she saw him that he was gone. Only his beautiful body was left, broken and cold beneath her hands.

"Please," Bentley said in a pained voice. "I can't hold her anymore."

Emmalyn's dress slid to the floor as she took a step backward.

"Emmalyn." Bentley's hold weakened and Emmalyn instinctively rushed close and put her arm beneath Darry's shoulders.

"The bed," she said, her thoughts gaining a bitter clarity as they moved. Darry rolled onto the top quilt and Emmalyn climbed on the bed beside her. "Darry?" She pulled Darry onto her back.

Bentley stumbled to the side and caught a hand on the carved post at the foot of the bed. "She's heavy. I carried her from the barracks by way of the far paddocks, hoping no one would see us. When I awoke before dawn she was passed out at the end of my bed, burning with fever and her tunic covered in blood."

"Bentley, she's on fire." Emmalyn pushed the limp curls from Darry's face, then pulled at the blood-stained tunic. *Baby, don't do this to me, don't you dare*. Her fingers refused to function properly and she let out a strange sound of panic as she yanked the shirt open and searched Darry's stomach for a wound.

"There's nothing there," Bentley said. "It's…it's not a wound."

Emmalyn set a hand on Darry's chest, the rhythm of the shallow breaths much too quick. She felt the pulse at Darry's throat. It was skittish and faint. "Healer," she said, and shoved from the bed.

Bentley grabbed her arm. "No!"

Emmalyn stared at him, trying to pull away.

"You must not."

"Let *go* of me, Bentley."

"You mustn't, Emmalyn, *please*."

Emmalyn struck him. Bentley staggered to the side but didn't let go.

"Don't do it," he pleaded.

"Let me go."

"No."

She struck him again and wrenched her arm free. "Are you *mad*?"

"Emmalyn," he said, "the healer will bring your mother. Darry will have to explain."

"Explain what?"

"What…what this *is*," he said. "It's not what…you can't, because that cannot happen, Emmalyn."

Emmalyn stepped close. "Explain *what*?" she said again, though she spoke less harshly. "Where have you been? Why is there blood on her clothes?"

He shook his head and looked down. Emmalyn was taken aback by his surprising refusal. He cringed at her approach but she merely put her hand on his chest, taking hold of his sweat-dampened tunic. "Bentley."

"She's not…" he began, then faltered. "There are times when—"

"Was she struck? Was there a fight?"

"No, there was no fight."

"Bentley, she has a fever." Emmalyn pulled at his shirt. "Either tell me what this is or I'm calling for help."

"It's but a fever," he said. "She's had others of this sort, but this one seems much worse, and I wasn't…I'm not sure that I can take care of her this time."

"Others?"

"You must ask her yourself, please. Don't force me to break her confidence, I beg you."

Emmalyn considered his words for a heartbeat, then stepped back to the bed, climbing onto the covers and pressing her lips to Darry's forehead.

"Lady Emmalyn, please. I'm sorry I grabbed you. I meant no offense."

Emmalyn touched Darry's face. "Get her boots off," she whispered, and wiped at her own tears, regaining her composure. "And close the bloody door," she added, her strength beginning to return.

Bentley refused to move.

"I shall clean her up, but we must bring her fever down. Bentley, I'll get help."

His face paled.

"Not as you think," she said quickly. "You must trust me. I think I know someone who'll not betray us."

❖

Jessa leaned against the balcony railing and gazed beyond the grounds, the late-morning breeze moving through her hair in a pleasing manner. She could smell in the air the many different trees of the land, each one holding a unique scent and power. In Lyoness the trees did not speak so loudly with the wind, nor did their essence travel so easily. The earth was too unforgiving for that and the sun much too harsh.

Amidst the allure of a rich new land, she understood at last what it was about Arravan that had obsessed Bharjah for so many years. Even a butcher could understand beauty.

Jessa recognized all too well what it was like to be deprived of what you needed most. Her royal blood meant nothing except what its presence within her veins might purchase for those who held power over her. She had grown up sequestered from her own lands, rarely leaving the Jade Palace except when she employed the Veil of Shadows. She had learned the twists and turns of its corridors and hidden pathways under the stern tutelage of Radha, and it had been as necessary to her survival as water on her tongue. To have freedom from her rooms, it had been a gift to her that she could never repay. As she had grown older she had been allowed more liberty, and Bharjah had of course seen the wisdom in teaching her what a woman needed to know.

She had learned to ride and dance, though she had done so under the eyes of Joaquin and his most trusted men. She had learned the art of etiquette, both Lyonese and what was acceptable within Arravan. She had learned the languages of her father's enemies and for several years had spoken only the strange words of the Arravan people and the patois of the Southern Islands until she was fluent with the cadence of each.

All things proper that a daughter of royal birth should know she had studied. And when her voice was discovered as she learned to play the instruments of her land and memorize its songs, her talent had been cultivated. Its sound was so beautiful that even Bharjah would stand within the shadows and listen.

She was taught all things Vhaelin as well, though her father had no idea to what extent Radha was guiding her knowledge. She had had maidservants over the years, though they had been old women, many of whom were without their tongues. Jessa had treated them all with kindness and respect, not only because this was what Radha taught her, but because they were her only daily contact. Those who could speak would tell her of the world beyond the Jade Palace, and some, after a time, would even tell her of the subjugation of their people. They were always careful in what they said, but Jessa had understood the words that were left unspoken. It was thus that she first began to understand that the people of Lyoness were unhappy.

Not until she was a young woman would Radha take her beyond the palace walls where she was able to see for herself what she had only heard in those stories. She learned, veiled within the shadows, that the poverty her people suffered was at times overwhelming and that her father was a sadistic man. She learned that his subjects lived in fear and that they would often disappear in the night never to return. She had seen women screaming in the streets for their lost sons, their high-pitched calls of grief piercing her ears. She had seen men tearing at their clothes as their daughters were forced into marriages because of their beauty or their station, or taken to serve in the *dreechakas* that serviced her father's soldiers. She had seen grief in abundance and it had made her weep silent tears.

For all of that, she had also seen laughter and stolen kisses, and lovers entangled in the sheets carried away in their passion, clinging together as they moved toward their release, their bodies slick with sweat and sex. She had seen men fight the Blooded Duel for honor's sake, and the victor pray above the loser and drop gold upon his chest for the family left behind. And she had seen what portions of life might never be hers.

She had begged Radha to take her and run, though only once, for Radha had made her confront the Waters of Truth as an answer to that plea. What she had seen haunted her still.

Jessa had seen her father's men moving through the streets in force and people slaughtered when they could not give the answers wanted. She had seen her maidservants hung from the gates of the Jade Palace and their children brought to the block, some with their own babes clutched in their arms, screaming as Sylban-Tenna's dogs were unleashed on them. Her brothers had sat upon their balcony and laughed as they tossed down their wine.

She had seen the price of her freedom, which was more than she had ever been willing to pay. She had seen, as well, the blade slowly pierce Radha's throat.

A fist of unease tightened in Jessa's stomach as she thought of Sylban-Tenna's black eyes, so much darker than her own. And Lybinus, their brother, who had clung to Sylban's shadow as if it were all he knew. They had been a dark pair, everything about them.

The night they had come into her rooms she had been but fourteen. Sylban and Lybinus had been adamant about what they wanted from her. She could still feel their hands on her flesh and smell the bitter wine on their breath. She had thought she knew fear before, but the instant they touched her, she understood better what it was to feel terror for one's life.

They had not violated her, but they had taunted her as she fought against them and tore her clothes. They had forced her close and pinched her tender breasts until the skin bruised, though they had not gone lower. She had scratched Lybinus's face, and his long black hair clung to the blood as he stared at her in shock. She could still feel the knife along the underside of her left breast as punishment for her attack.

It was Sylban who had taken the blade from their brother's hand and slit Lybinus from ear to ear in apparent retribution, leaving his body on the tiled floor to bleed out as Jessa huddled against the wall. Sylban had stood over his twitching body and cursed Lybinus for marking the flawless skin of their sister, and then he had knelt at her feet and smiled, holding out the knife.

He told her to take it, and she had seen something in his eyes that she would never forget. She had seen laughter and a terrible look of desire. It was then that he grabbed her between the legs and felt of her womanhood, pinning her against the wall. He had whispered in her ear that if she did not take the knife he would make her do things. He made her touch him, and she had wept in fear and revulsion even as he panted and groaned his pleasure against her face, his hand clutching her throat harshly. She had done as he told her, and as he spent his spirit within her hand she wanted to die.

When Radha had found her clutching the blade, her torn clothes hanging from her body and the gash beneath her breast still bleeding, she had not said a word. She had bathed her and stitched the wound, putting Jessa to bed. And then she had destroyed every piece of evidence that Jessa's brothers had been there, including the blood on the tiles. All evidence but for the dagger.

When the morning came, Radha had soaked its steel and bone handle in the Waters of Truth and the waters had let off steam and hissed in a boil, the stench of blood and something much darker leached from their elements. Jessa could smell beneath it all the sacred essence of the stag whose bone had been carved by such an expert hand to fit the deadly blade. She had closed her eyes and let its lost spirit wash through her as if her soul were the Ibarris Plains and the animal's hooves beat upon the soil that was her body. She plunged her hand into the steaming waters as Radha had cried out in warning.

The bone was cool to her touch, and when she lifted it free, not a single mark marred her skin. Radha had laughed then as Jessa held the weapon. Radha had bowed her head and seized the bowl from its twisted metal stand, shouting as if in victory as she threw the waters across the room. They had dissipated before hitting the tiles, hissing and misting about them both upon a wind that washed suddenly through the chamber.

That was what she knew of another's touch.

Sylban's hands harsh upon her skin and Lybinus his shadow, and the cold metal of a blade whose mark Radha had lessened with herbs and spells that were as familiar to her old lips as her raspy laugh. Jessa had never told Radha what Sylban had made her do, for not only was she deeply ashamed, she was terrified of what Radha might do in retribution.

That was what Jessa had experienced of passion, except for the Waters of Truth.

The waters had offered her many visions, and within their endless depths she had felt the loving touch of another. She had shuddered beneath its warmth for years, though never had she known the source. When she had begged for Radha's help, her pleas went unanswered. She was told that she was not concentrating enough or not meditating properly, and so the one thing she wanted most was always denied her.

When Radha asked, in return, why Jessa could not remember, Jessa had merely ducked her head and refused to answer. How could she tell her beloved Radha that she could not concentrate on such a thing? How could she explain that to do so was too painful? How could she tell her that she did not believe them, that she *would* not believe them, until her gods came out of hiding and showed her themselves.

And so she had lived with the shadow of warmth always beyond her grasp, sometimes waking in the night with a startled cry as pleasure blossomed wet between her legs and she spent, left to shiver within the darkness in its pleasing aftermath and hoping that her cries had not been heard. She would cling to her pillows and stare into the shadows, sometimes seeing a figure just beyond her sight, drifting like smoke. The tears she cried in silence would burn along her skin, though she had not cried in years now over a vision that had floated through the waters less and less.

Upon the sacred ground of the Lowlands, though, she had felt the old smoke of a familiar touch, and she had seen something she had never seen before: a face and a pair of eyes unlike any in all the world.

As Darry had entered the fête still her gods had hidden, but Jessa's heart had beat so fiercely she could barely breathe. As Darry had danced the Mohn-Drom and Jessa had watched her body move, so sleek and on display, her stomach had twisted with want and her hands had ached to touch her, to be the one who moved within the dance beside such loveliness. She had not thought it strange or wrong or even curious. It had merely been what she wanted, and it had been a very long time since she had wanted anything.

And then she had gazed across the room as Darry looked up.

Jessa smiled, almost laughing as she looked down at her hands on the stone rail of the balcony. *I hadn't even* thought *of that*. And then she did laugh, the sound quiet as she shrugged.

How many times she had been paraded before her father's guests she had no idea, wearing saris that were too revealing for etiquette and a burka that hid her face from their greedy eyes. She had stood before them and let her voice have its freedom as she searched their faces, wondering if among the dark-skinned men, and the pale as well, the face within her visions would finally reveal itself.

No passion had she ever felt when looking into their eyes, shielded from their fascination as she took in their clothes and their bodies, seeking something familiar that she never found. No tremble of desire had ever been inspired within her.

She realized now that she had found it, within the corridor beyond the door to her chambers when Darry had picked up her fallen shawl. Some deep part of her had recognized what she had always searched for. *A clever joke you've played on me all these years, my gods, to hide my visions in the body of a woman. Though perhaps the knowledge wasn't hidden at all. I merely didn't know that I was looking in the wrong place. And now to discover my passion within the sister to the man I am perhaps promised to? I should spurn you now and never bow my head to you again.*

She swallowed awkwardly at a surge of emotion, the memory of Darry's touch upon her face swarming through her insides with pleasure. *So soft and warm.* And then she remembered the brief taste of Darry's lips, just a whisper, and a wonderful ache laid claim to her heart. *Such simple things.*

The press of Darry's strong body as they had danced the Amendeese was still uppermost in her mind. *I don't understand as well as others, perhaps, but I could not have insulted you that badly. Or perhaps I did,* for Darry had been absent at dinner yet again. Jessa felt a tightness in her chest at the thought of having pushed her away. *I thought, Darry, that discarding my etiquette would—*

The knock on her chamber door made her jump and she spun about, staring into the shadows of the room. *Radha is prowling the streets of Lokey...you cursed old woman, did you know this? Is this why you wouldn't speak to me when I asked?*

Jessa was halfway through the main chamber of her rooms when the knock came again. She quickened her step to the door.

Jessa smiled at Emmalyn for but a brief second before her heart beat oddly and she met Emmalyn's hand halfway. "What? What's wrong?"

"Are you..." Emmalyn stopped. "We were told, I mean, Jacob's men said..." Jessa pulled her gently across the threshold. "I'm under the impression that you're a healer. Is this true, Jessa?"

"Yes. It is among the arts of the Vhaelin that I practice. It is a most sacred thing."

"All right then."

"Emmalyn, what's happened?"

"I need your help. And you cannot tell anyone."

"Is someone hurt? Is it Royce?" Jessa remembered Emmalyn's first husband and wondered if the fear that she saw was for yet another man she loved.

"Please, just come with me." Emmalyn's grip on Jessa's hand tightened. "Will you do that? Will you help me?"

"Of course," Jessa said. "I must get my things, yes?"

Emmalyn let her go. "Yes," she said, then pulled her back by the sleeve. "You mustn't tell anyone, Jessa, do you agree to that?"

Jessa nodded, though she did not understand. "I have many secrets, Emmalyn," she said softly, thinking that this was perhaps a part of friendship. She had never had any friends, however, save for Radha and the few maidservants who had taken pity on her. Sometimes she had laughed with them, but never had they given more. She was King Bharjah's daughter. "I think one more shall make no difference."

"Hurry then, Jessa, please."

Jessa gave a nod, then moved quickly for the baggage where her medicines were kept. A strange rush of foreboding moved within her.

CHAPTER THIRTEEN

The warm liquid filled Darry's mouth and she swallowed without thought. The hands. Flames moved along her throat and she coughed, trying to expel them.

"Hold her, please."

Strong arms went around her shoulders and pressed against her legs, and she fought them. She opened her eyes and a sea of faces filled her vision. And light, too much light that sent a stab of pain through her skull. "Darry, you must drink," came an unyielding voice, and she recognized the scent of her sister's flesh. *Emmalyn*.

She coughed but the fluid still filled her mouth. She had been thirsty for so long but not for this. Not for more fire.

"Wait."

Darry's head fell forward and she tried to hold her neck straight. Her back ached at the effort. She tried desperately to focus her eyes.

A gentle hand lifted her face. "Darry?"

The scent slammed through her and she spoke, though she did not understand what she said.

"Yes…please, Darry, you must drink."

The intense, appealing aroma flowed through Darry and the pain blossomed in the pit of her stomach once more, like an old enemy that never seemed to die. Her eyes burned with tears and she lashed out, trying to push it away, not wanting to fall beneath its strength. She had already done what it asked and yet still it clung to her bones.

There was heat against her face and then a breath beside her ear. Darry heard the words in her head like thorns. *You must drink, Akasha, and it will go away. I promise.*

The liquid filled her mouth once more and she obeyed, letting the flames coat her throat and burn deep into her stomach.

❖

Emmalyn stood at the end of the bed in the early evening light. Jessa sat in a chair with her legs drawn up beneath her chin and her arms wrapped around them. Jessa had pulled the chair as close to the bed as she could and barely moved for hours, keeping a constant vigil.

Darry wore one of Wyatt's old tunics, naked beneath its soft fabric and the sheets of her bed. Her beautiful hair had lost its shine as it lay scattered about her face. Her strong hands peeked out from the long cuffs as if she were a child again playing at being a king in one of their father's shirts. The memory pulled hard and lit upon the experience of earlier that morning when Darry had looked at her with unseeing eyes, her tears spilling as she begged it to stop.

Emmalyn had no idea what *it* was, but she had every intention of wringing the answer from Bentley's throat, if necessary. It would be easier than trying to get an answer from Darry, who could be as stubborn as a plough horse when her mind was set.

Darry stirred beneath the sheet and Jessa moved quietly, dropping her legs and leaning onto the bed. Her hand was tender as she pushed Darry's face free of her curls. And then Jessa sat back and brought her legs up once more, resuming her silent watch.

Emmalyn had not forgotten how she had reached out when Jessa first saw Darry in the bed. She steadied Jessa as she had swayed and her features paled. But it had been only for a moment that Jessa stared, and though she had tried, Emmalyn could not decipher the thoughts that had flooded her eyes.

Emmalyn had not missed the shock on Bentley's face either, when they had entered the room, nor the suspicion with which he regarded Jessa. It had not only been his worry for Darry, it had been something else, though he had done as Jessa asked.

"I must speak with my mother," Emmalyn said quietly. "I will make our excuses for dinner."

"Joaquin will try to find me if I'm not there."

"Then you must go."

"I will not," Jessa answered simply.

"It will be only an hour, Jessa. I'll be with her. I would not see you in trouble, nor have someone knocking at my door searching for you and finding my sister as well."

Jessa's eyes darkened and she looked to the bed without answering.

"She sleeps more peacefully," Emmalyn said gently.

"It is the sinjinn root. It relaxes the muscles," Jessa said. "The arbuckle is for the fever, though it has yet to take hold."

"And when it does?"

"She'll begin to sweat and the fever will free itself. It can be a dangerous time and we must give her much water, even if we must force her."

Emmalyn nodded. "I must go and speak to my mother now."

"I'll not leave until you return."

"I know."

Jessa watched as Emmalyn left the room. The heavy bolt slid with a turn of the key and fell into place, locking her in as she turned away.

Darry opened her eyes and Jessa's heart thudded violently. "Darry?"

Jessa saw a strange hunger in Darry's eye, and a flutter of excitement moved through her in reaction. She let her hand glide about Darry's jaw and trail along her neck. "All is well, *Akasha*," she said. "I'll not be gone for long, I promise."

Darry fought against the stones that dragged her down, but they were very heavy. She tried to speak, tried to tell Jessa something, but though it was very important Darry had no idea what it was.

Jessa smiled. "Thank you," she whispered. "Go back to sleep."

Darry closed her eyes to quieten the hum in her bones, smelling the fresh summer grass beneath her feet and the wind against her face. She could smell the stag and it crushed through her veins.

Jessa's shoulders jerked as the Vhaelin bit within her blood. Her head swam with a sudden rush of dizziness and the bed tipped beneath her.

"*Shivahsa*!" Jessa cried, and pushed back in a clumsy move. Her legs tried to find balance but could not. Jessa fell against the seat of a chair as it skidded away and she hit the floor. Her left hand caught in the blankets and kept her upright.

The scent washed over her and she gasped, her blood rising against the presence of another majik and her own power breaking loose. The rush of enchantment snaked heavily along her throat and blossomed within her chest as her ears popped.

Jessa felt the stag running, its powerful legs surging as she stared into a wild and vivid landscape. Her left leg kicked out in reflex and her stomach lurched as the stag leapt high and soared.

"*Antua zaneesh*!" she exclaimed, breathless as the power of the Vhaelin beat a fierce rhythm through her heart. "Darry."

❖

Darry dropped her legs over the side of the bed and looked about. She recognized the pitcher and basin on the table as her grandmother Lewellyn's, and the tapestry that hung beside the balcony doors. *Emmalyn.*

The sun was high at midday and the sky beyond the arch was a brilliant blue. She looked down at the tunic she wore and set a weak hand on its hem as it lay against her bare thighs.

Emmalyn was on the divan, the couch pulled away from the cold hearth and facing the bed. She was sleeping on its cushions with her face turned to a pillow. Darry pushed up from the mattress, found the floor with her bare feet, and took a step. Her head spun and she waited for it to stop.

She spied clothes on the bed stand and walked carefully, moving as slowly as she thought was necessary. She rested against the stones and stepped into her breeches first and then her trousers. She leaned her head back and stared at the ceiling after pulling them up. She could not remember ever being so exhausted.

"Let me do that."

Darry brought her head forward too quickly and closed her eyes. "Gods…don't do that, Em."

Emmalyn's emotions were thick within her chest and she tightened her brow as she walked across the room. Darry's hands fell away as Emmalyn fastened her breeches with a light touch.

"You seem very practiced at this," Darry said dryly.

Emmalyn smiled.

"How long have I—"

Emmalyn pulled Darry from the wall, wrapping her arms about her shoulders and holding tight as Darry returned the embrace. When Emmalyn loosened her hold Darry rested her forehead against her neck. "I'm all right," she whispered.

Emmalyn brought Darry's face up and searched her eyes, seeing only the clear light of Darry's unique gaze.

"How long, Em?"

"Three days," Emmalyn said. "No one knows, Darry. I took care of that."

Darry's head dropped onto Emmalyn's shoulder. "Thank you, Em."

"We need to talk," Emmalyn said.

"I'm sorry," Darry said. "Do you…did Bentley…"

Emmalyn waited but Darry did not finish. "I know where you were. All is well, Darry. Bentley brought you to me and asked that we care for you in secret. I don't know why…but it doesn't really matter for now, my sweet. Do you understand?"

Darry's shoulders pulled in and Emmalyn closed her eyes to blur the soft sound that followed, holding her once more as Darry tried to quell her emotions. It was a surprising and tender moment for Emmalyn. While Darry shared her joy quite easily, rarely if ever did she share her pain.

"Whatever happened, Darry," Emmalyn whispered, "you don't have to hide it from me. I will never judge you…or your love."

"My love?" Darry asked, and her voice was tired.

"Yes, well, I've been thinking," Emmalyn said quietly. "About a lot of things, actually. I wasn't sure if you would go up in flames upon my favorite set of sheets. The prospect made me thoughtful, all right?"

Darry smiled.

"About your passion, Darry, wherever you might find it, or with whom," Emmalyn whispered. "I realized that I've never said the words to you."

"What words, Em?"

"That I know you're not ashamed of who you are, or what you feel. And you shouldn't be, not *ever*. You don't have to hide that part of your life from me. It's only passion, and it's a wonderful thing, yes? And you're made for that." She smiled. "And I would see you have it."

"Should I be open?" Darry asked. "And push Malcolm's hatred into the light? Should I provoke our father and put him in a position that some might choose to ridicule and take advantage of?"

Emmalyn digested the words. They were not new thoughts, and over the past few days she had seen things from a very different perspective, one that she had either ignored before or not even considered.

She had seen the world through Darry's eyes, and it had caused her a great deal of pain. And shame. She had let the heart of her love for Darry become a stranger. She had been taking only the good and wonderful things, and leaving Darry to defend herself within the darker and more complicated aspects of her life. She had not been seeing her sister as the woman she truly was. *A woman with desires and passions and needs like my own. Dreams like my own. Wanting love, wanting to be touched, needing release.* "No, my darling. I don't know *what* we should do about those things. But you mustn't hide from *me*, do you understand?"

"I don't."

"No, I know. But Bentley is not your only friend, yes?"

"All right, Em."

"Good."

"Was Jessa here?"

Emmalyn heard the discomfort in her voice. "Yes. She said the fever was a passing thing but very dangerous." Emmalyn left out that she thought Jessa had lied for some reason she had yet to fathom. Nor had she forgotten Bentley's words, that Darry had been ill other times that no one knew about.

Emmalyn understood that Darry was frightened at having been exposed, though why, Emmalyn still did not understand. If she pushed Darry now for an answer, Darry would retreat within for Gamar only knew how long. Just as she had done since she was a child. It was never a smart move to corner Darry.

"I'm sorry I was sick," Darry said, looking down.

"Don't apologize, Darry." Emmalyn was content for the moment to ease Darry's worry with Jessa's lie. "But if it hadn't been for Jessa's help, we would've called the healer. She said it could've been something you ate."

Darry was still for a time and then her dimple appeared, her eyes filling with a dark humor.

"Don't say it!" Emmalyn laughed and pulled Darry into her arms once more, kissing her cheek. "Bloody hell, I know that look. Whatever it is, don't say it, you cad."

CHAPTER FOURTEEN

Darry sat on the balustrade rail and leaned against one of the blackwood posts, wearing a blue homespun shirt and soft gray trousers above her black boots. She had bathed and her clean hair was still a bit damp as it curled down her back.

She had seen Bentley. He had lifted her from the ground in a hug that probably bruised a rib, but it had felt good regardless. She remembered his smell and his touch while she had been ill, and she felt rich that he was her friend. She told him as much, and he had kissed her cheek and smiled down at her.

He said that Longshanks had given her several days of leave and she should take advantage of what was left. Longshanks had no desire to know what the problem had been; he had merely wanted to complain about his people being spoiled and fat, and not the least bit concerned that if the entire Lyonese army were to pour across the border they might actually have to put down their wine and do something about it.

Darry waited now for Jessa to return from dinner, unsure of what she would say. She had no idea what she might have said or done when the fever was full upon her. She remembered seeing Jessa's face and looking into her eyes as the scent of her flesh washed over her, and she remembered hearing Jessa's voice and trusting what it said. She remembered how beautiful Jessa was, then hoped she had said nothing to offend her. She couldn't remember anything else no matter how hard she tried.

Darry stared at her boots and sighed, troubled by a great many things, not the least of which was that her feelings for Jessa had changed.

"Darry."

She looked up in surprise but found nothing behind her.

Jessa jumped forward with a curse. Her right hand fisted in Darry's tunic and gripped her fearsomely, pulling Darry back. Darry grabbed the post and held on, righting herself.

"I want you in bed," Jessa said with authority. When Darry's brow went up in question, Jessa corrected herself. "I mean that you should be *in* bed, Darrius."

"I was in bed." Darry smiled. "Now I'm better."

"Yes, and almost fell thirty feet to your death."

"But you were here to save me…or perhaps cause me to fall. I'll have to think about that one," Darry said. "How can you sneak up on me when no one else can?"

Jessa became aware that she was standing close between Darry's thighs with her hand still wrapped in her tunic as Darry's left breast pressed against her arm. She let go and moved back, only to step forward once again and place a hand against Darry's face.

"Am I hot?"

"No." Jessa gave her a disapproving look.

"You seem disappointed," Darry teased. Jessa's eyes darkened and Darry made a face of contrition. "Sorry." She let her eyes wander over the golden sari that Jessa wore. Jessa's curves were extremely pleasing and the sari only enhanced them. Which gods had smiled and decided that one woman should be so perfectly proportioned? *Do you understand how beautiful you are, Jessa?*

Jessa dropped her hand, took Darry's, and pulled her from the railing. "Come inside," she said, and Darry followed without question.

"Thank you," Darry told her quietly. "For helping me."

Jessa smiled. "You're welcome."

Darry struggled furiously to remember what language she spoke. *You make it hard to find words sometimes, when you look at me so. Stop it, Jessa.*

"You have majik," Jessa said softly.

"What?"

"You have majik, Darry," Jessa repeated. Darry retreated and Jessa seized her hand before she could move farther. "Did you think I wouldn't feel it? I am a Vhaelin Witch, Darry. Like powers attract my gods."

Darry considered her words. "You lied to Emmalyn."

"Yes."

"Why?"

"Because she didn't know, so I thought you wouldn't want her to. I didn't like doing it, but to do otherwise might've betrayed you."

Darry had no idea what to say, seeing Jessa's sudden uncertainty.

Jessa had protected her when she had no real reason to. Jessa had kept her secret and done so willingly, as a true friend would, despite not knowing the consequences. Darry tightened her grip and Jessa's eyes lit up. "Thank you."

"You're most welcome, Darry."

"There's someone you should meet."

❖

They walked close, and Jessa saw how Darry moved slower than she had come to expect. When they descended the stairs Jessa held lightly to Darry's elbow, making sure that if Darry needed the support she would have it. It made Jessa nervous that Darry was out of bed so soon, but she supposed it could not be helped. As a soldier, Darry was not a woman to be held back, not even by illness.

They strolled along the path beyond the solar and entered the gardens. "My great-great, perhaps one more great grandfather Boris was supposedly a sorcerer of sorts," Darry said. "He built these gardens, and he was also very fond of puzzles."

"Puzzles?"

"A maze?"

"A *treesha*?"

Darry chuckled. "If that means a maze, then yes. A *treesha* is a sort of riddle that must be solved?"

"Yes. You have many words for the same thing."

"I used that argument once upon a time," Darry replied. "But my tutor would not relent and insisted I learn them all. It was very frustrating."

Jessa laughed and barely kept herself from brushing her hand against Darry's. The need to touch her in some way was almost irresistible, and Jessa was uncertain what she should do about it. The past three days she had touched Darry without thinking because Darry had needed her. But she knew that she had indulged herself as well, though only in the smallest of ways. *It hurt no one that I touched her hair.* But Jessa felt unaccountably guilty now that Darry was getting better. *Or that I caressed her skin, the hollow at the base of her throat where it is the softest.* Jessa swallowed and closed her eyes for a step. *Very soft, actually.*

"King Boris decided that he would make a riddle that no one could solve but everyone might enjoy," Darry continued. "He was of a dark humor at times, and he spent several years doing this, consulting architects and gardeners and any number of experts on such subjects."

"He made his riddle out of the garden?" The idea delighted Jessa.

"Yes. He even brought a man from Artanis here, who was said to be one of the most powerful wizards in the world. His name was Sebastian."

"I know this name," Jessa said. "Radha has spoken of him. She says he was a mystic of your god Gamar, and that his power was in the blood. Much majik is passed from generation to generation. If your ancestor had majik, Darry, perhaps this is where yours comes from. It is yet another gift."

"Perhaps. But I'm not sure I have majik as you think I do."

"How so?"

"I'll have to show you, and then perhaps you might decide for yourself."

"You're being very mysterious," Jessa said playfully.

Darry grinned. "Not really."

"Anyway," Jessa said, "your great-great, perhaps one more great grandfather Boris?"

"Yes. At the center of the main gardens, this is where Boris built his maze. It took him many years, as I said, and as it grew he wove within the hedgerows and plants, perhaps even the land itself, enchantments that pleased him."

Jessa brought them both to a stop. "He made a *living* maze? Why haven't I seen it before? I've walked these gardens many times, Darry."

"Yes. And you've not seen it because you don't know how."

Jessa searched the path ahead, its cut green trail winding into the distance. The hedgerows were lined with splashes of heather and periwinkle, even bluebells that hung heavy within the late-afternoon sun. "You have a living maze *here*?"

Darry took Jessa's hand. "What I have to show you is within the maze," she said. "It can be a dangerous place at times, for the hedgerows will change, as will other features, and strange things will happen there. It frightens many people. Malcolm doesn't like it, nor does Jacob."

"He would make a map of it, yes?" Jessa asked, knowing of Jacob's penchant for books and scrolls and all things written.

Darry laughed. "Yes, he tried for many years and then gave up. The pathways are never the same. Do you still wish to see it?"

"Very much, Darry, but will we find our way out again before it gets dark?"

"Perhaps," Darry said, a look of mischief in her eyes. "Will you trust me to bring you home again, Jess?"

Jess. The way you say my name, so unlike anyone else before. "Of course."

Darry turned, pointing with her right hand. "The maze is there."

Jessa followed Darry's hand and let out a hiccup of sound.

A thick arch stood some thirty feet away from them, the curving wood trellis dripping with vegetation, both ivy and twisted hamesroot sprinkled through with hundreds of white flowers. It stood where nothing had before, save the garden path.

Jessa started forward, pulling at Darry's hand. "*How*?"

"You need only find the center of the gardens and wish upon it, and so the trellis will appear. But you must know what the entrance looks like. You must have it in your head."

Jessa saw as they neared that the trellis was actually alive with thick, twisting arms of maple that rose from the ground and arched in a tangle of bark and ancient branches. "I can *feel* it, Darry."

"Does it ache along your bones?" That was what Darry felt upon entering the maze. It was a fine moment as she wondered what another person might feel who possessed a power not unlike her own. It was a question she had never been able to ask before.

Jessa's eyes were alight with anticipation. "Yes."

They passed beneath the arch and Jessa's hand brushed through the soft ivy as they stepped into a broad corridor bordered by heavy hedgerows. She stepped closer to Darry as the lane before them began to narrow and the hedges rose from the ground, heavy with life and weight, a weight that held more than just dense shrubbery.

There was majik there as well, and she could feel it just as Darry said, aching along her bones. The green brush was neatly trimmed despite its wild essence, its branches and leaves tangled and thick. There were flowers as well, though, their colors trapped deep within the walls and trumpeting their presence. "The rows are so thick."

"So you cannot see through them." Darry pulled them to a stop. "Most of the many paths lead nowhere, unless of course nowhere is the place you wish to go," Darry said. "There are only two paths to the heart and those you must work for. If you can see which path is wrong, it is not so much a *treesha* as a walk in the gardens."

"What is at the heart?"

"If I tell you, what fun would that be?"

"You're still too ill to be having so much fun," Jessa said, managing to scold while sounding terribly pleased.

"Yes. But I need to show you."

"Are you tired?" Jessa stepped closer. "You look tired."

Darry stared into Jessa's eyes for what seemed like a very long time, feeling happy that such a woman was worried for her. "I'm fine. I will sleep later, I promise."

Movement to the side drew Jessa's gaze and she let out a startled laugh. "*Shivahsa*, the hedge!"

"What?"

Jessa's eyes swarmed over the dense vegetation. "It *moved*."

Darry laughed. "It's an enchanted place, Jess. You may see strange things, as I said. This land is caught in a powerful casting."

Jessa spun and searched behind them for the archway. Bossa trees grew there, heavy with leaves and berries and a patch of heather that should not have been there. There was, however, no entrance trellis and Jessa laughed with pleasure.

Darry's heart swelled at the lovely sound. "There's nothing for it now."

"Show me," Jessa said with excitement. "Show me, Darry."

Darry nodded and regarded the path. "I must find my mark."

She pulled gently at Jessa's hand and Jessa kept pace close beside her. At times Jessa thought the light played tricks with her eyes. Where wild loosestrife had grown one moment, there would be foxglove or lady's slipper the next. At one point, when she thought they were moving straight ahead, Jessa realized they were being pushed to the left as the hedge beside them was actually shifting. She laughed, taking hold of Darry's arm. When the vegetation began to move faster than they did, they were forced to run ahead to avoid being trapped and having to go back. When Jessa spun to the side Darry caught her at the waist and smiled.

Jessa was breathing much too fast and she knew it, but Darry's scent of gentle musk was making her feel wonderfully alive. She placed her hands on Darry's arms, wanting to step closer and lean against her body. *It feels so very good right here. It feels…familiar, Akasha.* "You look flushed." She touched Darry's face. "Are you all right? Too much running?"

Darry nodded, out of breath. "Yes…and yes."

"We can rest if you need to."

"No, it's almost time."

"For your secret?"

"Yes."

Jessa saw something uncertain in her eyes. "What is it?"

"You mustn't be scared."

"Will I be scared?"

"You must trust me, yes? I would never let anything hurt you, Jess, I promise. So you mustn't be frightened."

"I won't," Jessa whispered. The primitive presence of majik in her blood was thicker and more compelling than she would have thought possible. It was the Vhaelin rising and yet it was something else as well. She recognized it from several nights past, when both she and Radha had reacted to its mysterious presence. Darry lowered her face and Jessa's heart nearly jumped from her chest, her lips parting slightly in anticipation.

Darry's cheek brushed against Jessa's. "Then look to the path, Jess, and don't move until I say."

Jessa felt a pang of regret as she pulled away, but she obeyed nonetheless. Her body jerked and she stepped back in fear as Darry eased in front of her.

A golden mountain panther stood in the path a mere twenty feet away, an enormous animal that looked to weigh two hundred stones or more.

Jessa raked her gaze over the cat's substantial paws and muscled front legs, her mind stuttering toward acceptance. The cat's fur was of the darkest tan, though where the setting sun speckled its light on her coat it was tawny gold. She was in the midst of taking a step, her long tail raised behind her and flicking lightly as if in annoyance. Jessa had never seen an animal of that size still alive and not mounted on her father's walls.

The cat's head was motionless as it watched them with ears back. Her mouth was open and she growled, her jaws stretching and her fangs bared as her long whiskers quivered. Her almond-shaped eyes narrowed as the sound rippled along Jessa's spine. Tears welled up and fell from Jessa's eyes; it was too much power not to react in some way to its aura.

Darry moved forward and Jessa's heart seized, her hands tightening on Darry's tunic. "*No*!"

"Jess, let go."

Darry turned her head and Jessa studied her profile, seeing how calm she was. "Darrius, you are *mad*."

"Let go, Jess. It's all right."

Jessa obeyed, the bones in her hands creaking in protest at her mind's seemingly ridiculous command. "Darry*, please*."

Darry walked slowly along the path. The panther's shoulders moved in a flowing manner as it approached Darry at an equal pace. Jessa put a hand to her mouth as Darry knelt and allowed the panther to advance. The cat's wide black nose twitched as she extended her face and Darry did likewise.

The panther leapt and Jessa cried out as the animal's front legs slammed against Darry's chest and knocked her backward. Darry tumbled to the grass with a shout.

Darry's laughter rang out as the panther lowered her face, laying a good portion of her considerable weight upon Darry's chest as she dragged her tongue across Darry's face. Darry's hands sank in the thick fur and pushed. The cat's hindquarters swayed and buckled lazily onto the grass. The panther let out a mewling noise and batted at Darry's head, taking her back to the grass in an instant. The rough-skinned paw sat heavily on the side of Darry's neck. A strange sound moved through the ground and Jessa realized it was a purr. The panther lay still and looked down at Darry with an imperious expression.

Darry pushed at the leg and tried to rise only to have the panther scoot forward on her belly and bite. Darry cursed as her hair was caught in the panther's teeth, forcing her to be still. The panther dragged her tongue once more along Darry's skin.

"Let me *up*, Hinsa," Darry mumbled, pushing at her face.

The cat tumbled onto her side and freed her, her long tail slapping the ground.

Darry sat up and scratched the panther's neck. She laughed and looked to Jessa.

Jessa's knees gave out and she reached back, catching herself as her backside hit the ground.

Darry's brow went up. "Jess? Come and meet my Hinsa."

Jessa shook her head.

"She won't hurt you, I promise." Darry smiled happily and then tumbled forward, laying her upper body across the panther and pushing her face into the golden fur.

The cat stretched beneath Darry, and Jessa stared into the animal's eyes as it returned her scrutiny, ignoring Darry's antics completely. *Very much as if I were your dinner.*

"Jess, you can move now."

Jessa was powerless to comply. Darry used the panther's body to push to her knees as she pulled at the fur beneath her hands. The cat shifted smoothly and vaulted to her feet. They walked forward and Jessa gasped as Darry moved as sleekly as the cat that prowled beside her. The animal stood mid-thigh to Darry, so much power in her long body that Jessa thought the ground was shaking as she moved. They stopped a few feet away and Darry knelt. The panther sat beside her in a rather polite manner as Darry's hand found the scruff of her neck.

"This is Hinsa, Jessa," Darry said. "Hinsa?" The cat's whiskers quivered as if she understood. "This is Jessa."

Jessa sat forward slowly, her fear evaporating as they both faced her. The knowledge of what they were quaked through her and stole her breath. Their eyes were the same, only opposite. Darry bore green upon the right and blue upon her left, while the panther's eyes were blue upon the right and green upon the left. "You are *Cha-Diah*!"

"Hinsa is my majik," Darry said, unable to keep the happiness from her voice. The panther began to purr once again, her eyes narrowing in pleasure as Darry scratched her ear. Darry leaned over and kissed Hinsa on the side of the face. "Go and say hello, biscuit."

Jessa gave a start as Hinsa pushed forward, extending her powerful neck. Jessa lifted her hand, her fingers trembling as she met the advance halfway and offered her palm. Hinsa let out a snuff of air, taking in Jessa's scent and sprinkling her skin with moisture.

The cat stepped closer and Jessa caught her breath, lifting her arms as the massive cat leaned against her, pushing her face within Jessa's braids. Jessa laughed, tears slipping free as she set her hands within Hinsa's fur.

"She likes you." Darry sat in the grass and crossed her legs. "But then how could she not?"

"Hello, Hinsa." Whiskers brushed across Jessa's lips. "*Salla shimbra ahbwalla... Vhaelin antua essa*."

Hinsa made a deep rumble of sound in her throat and stepped gracefully over Jessa's legs, rubbing against her. Thick golden fur passed beneath Jessa's hands as the panther's tail wrapped over her shoulders and slid along her neck. Hinsa turned about before sitting in the grass a few feet away, then flopped onto her side and stretched in contentment.

Jessa wiped at her flushed cheeks and smiled, looking up shyly. "How?" she asked. "How is she here?"

"There's a gateway in the hedge," Darry answered. "Or perhaps not so much of a gate." She frowned a little. "Maybe a window? I'm not sure what I should call it. She passes through it from where she lives in the Green Hills. She can feel me when I enter the maze and so she comes to me. Sometimes it takes awhile, and sometimes she's waiting for me. But she always appears. I can call her too, if I like, or she calls me."

"There is a portal here?" Jessa asked, shocked yet again.

"Yes, but only Hinsa knows where it is. It changes, you see? Like the rest of the maze. She always knows where it is, though."

"Have you ever gone through it?"

"Once."

"What happened?"

"I woke up in the Green Hills, in one of the deepest parts of the

Menath. I was twelve and I wanted…" Darry's voice trailed off, her eyes catching with emotion as she stared at the ground between them.

"What did you want, Darry?"

"I wanted to go with Hinsa and live with her. She took me but when I went through the gate, well, I'm not sure what happened." Darry shrugged. "I was there, though, and would've stayed with her forever if she hadn't made me come back."

"Made you?" Jessa eyed the panther.

"She can be very persuasive."

"I can imagine. Blood majik is an extremely ancient thing, Darry, or spirit majik as you say. How is it that you, I mean, how did this happen?"

"When I was five years old I came looking for the maze. My mother had brought me here several times and the place called to me. My brothers had been teasing me that I wasn't smart enough or old enough to find the heart of it on my own. I became angry, of course, and when my mother's attention was elsewhere I ran off. I found the maze easy enough for it was all that I was wishing for, but I became lost almost at once. As the day wore on and I could not find my way out, much less the heart of the maze, I began to cry. I wasn't very brave, I suppose."

"You were but a child."

"Yes, but I wanted to be like my brothers," Darry said. "Anyway, at some point I lay down and took a nap. Being lost can be very tiring, I assure you. When I woke the sun was going down and I started to cry again. It was then that Hinsa came to me. At first I didn't realize what I was looking at. She seemed like a very large version of the cats I knew from the kitchens, always stealing cream and underfoot. I was thinking that she must've eaten a lot of cream to have grown so big."

Jessa laughed softly, glancing again at Hinsa. The cat gazed back at her with Darry's eyes in a rather pleasant exchange.

"I ran over to her and smashed *right* into her." Darry laughed. "I think she was more startled than I was. She fell over and I climbed on top of her. She was very big even then and I was tired of being alone." Darry closed her eyes. "I remember…I remember pushing my face into her fur and telling her that I was lost, and could she please take me to my mother. She hissed and showed her fangs, all the while with me sitting on her ribs as if she were some sort of tiny pony. I punched her in the shoulder and told her to stop scaring me."

"And she did?"

Darry laughed. "Sort of. She grabbed me by the arm with her teeth and pulled me over as if I were a cloth doll." Darry loosened her left sleeve and pulled the material back, holding out her arm. The five distinctive scars on her skin were freckles of tissue thick and white with age.

Curious, Jessa touched them gently.

"I didn't cry, though it burned my skin and I was bleeding," Darry went on, her heart giving a pleasing flutter as Jessa's hand caressed her forearm. "She had trapped me beneath her leg and held me to the ground. I recall looking into her eyes, which were the most brilliant green. I wasn't scared, really, even though my arm hurt. She began to purr and it rattled my bones, but it felt good too. She ripped my shirt and began to clean the wounds.

"I felt very strange and dizzy as she did this and I tried to get closer. The earth beneath me was moving and Hinsa was very solid and safe. I fell asleep again. When I woke up next, my mother was holding me in the gardens by the fountain of the marble lady, and she was crushing me so tight I couldn't breathe. She was crying terribly, which of course made me cry too."

"What happened?"

"My mother says she found me all tangled and trapped beneath Hinsa's legs, bloody and not moving except to breathe. She was terrified but wouldn't leave me to go fetch my father or the guard, afraid that if she did the cat would either eat me or carry me away into the maze. After a few hours and a bath while I slept, Hinsa picked me up by the back of my shirt and dropped me a few feet from my mother.

"She grabbed me up and ran from the maze, which opened before her. I slept through the entire thing. Only when she reached the safety of the fountain did she stop and try to wake me."

"You are *Cha-Diah*, Darry. Do you know what that means?" Jessa asked. "It is a most rare thing. It's…Darry, it's *unheard* of. It is an old majik that has faded from the world."

"You don't need to explain what I am." Darry turned her eyes to the panther. "Since that day we've been connected, though I don't know how. I've not been just myself since I looked into her eyes."

"This was the fever then," Jessa said. "It was Hinsa."

Darry nodded. "If I fight it when her blood is high within mine, my body doesn't react well. It's not always easy to be both things. I'm not as strong as a panther. No one knows of this, though, no one but Bentley."

"The *dogs*!" Jessa exclaimed.

"Yes. I didn't realize the true depth of our connection until that day. When I was attacked I felt all of Hinsa's power in my blood, though it only made things worse. I was a wild animal to them, not a girl who only wanted to play. I was the quarry they'd been trained to hunt."

"But how can no one know?" Jessa asked. "Your eyes..."

"I became very ill shortly after that day. When I woke from my sickness my eyes were as you see them. The healer told my mother that it was rare but that it happened sometimes with such a high fever. They used to be blue, like my brother Wyatt's."

"Is what you see different than what I see?" Jessa asked.

Darry considered the question. "When my blood is high, definitely. And in the dark? The night is not so hidden for me."

"Why would you not share such a gift with those that love you? Why do you hide such an amazing thing from them?" *Though more importantly, why would you share it with me? Why do you gift me with such an honor, Akasha?*

"After what happened, after my illness, my brothers would tease me and call me the Golden Panther. It was a joke at first but it stuck. I would get angry that they mocked me. Even then I knew I was no longer just Darry, that in some way I was Hinsa as well. I thought no one would believe me, and even if they did, they would take her away from me. And the dogs taught me that Hinsa wasn't welcome in my world. I don't know, Jess, I was very young and I only knew that I must protect her. My mother was filled with fear by what had happened. After a while the name they called me was no longer in jest." Darry's expression was troubled as she tried to find the words. "I was afraid."

Jessa waited, seeing in the fading light how pale Darry still was.

"I was afraid that my father...he doesn't hear me sometimes. And she was something that was just my own," Darry whispered, and Hinsa moved suddenly beside them. The huge cat stepped close and rubbed against Darry's shoulder. Hinsa pushed her substantial weight into Darry, making her tumble over.

Jessa laughed as the cat lay on top of Darry, pressing her to the ground.

Darry let out a grunt and tried to free her arms. "*Hinsa*," she said in a strained voice. "Please, I don't feel well."

Jessa rose onto her knees and, without thinking, shoved hard at Hinsa's shoulder. "Get off, Hinsa!" she snapped. The panther hissed and Jessa flared in sudden challenge. "Let her up."

Hinsa's mouth curled and she hissed again, flashing her teeth as her ears lay back in warning. She shifted her weight to protect Darry more thoroughly.

"*Hinsa*," Darry said in a labored breath.

Jessa stared into the panther's eyes and did not back down, her temper high and fierce. She felt the Vhaelin move in her blood and called upon their strength. She slid her hand along Hinsa's neck as Hinsa's fangs seemed to grow in proportion to her annoyance. Jessa took hold of the fur and pushed, feeling the resistance and the coiled strength. "You should move now, my pretty."

Hinsa tried to twist her head away from the touch, and Jessa tightened her fingers in response. Hinsa slid her belly along Darry's ribs as she rose and stepped away. Then Jessa released her as Darry groaned and rolled onto her back.

"Are you all right?" Jessa asked.

"She's very heavy."

"It's getting dark," Jessa said. "And though I'm having the time of my life, Darry, I think you should be in bed now."

"When I wanted to tell someone, in the end, I decided on Wyatt and Emma," Darry whispered. "I wanted to share her like you said…but it was too late."

"Why too late?"

"I'd become a riddle that no one knew how to solve. Like the maze itself," she said. "Do you see?"

Yes, I see you, Darry. I see you so very clearly. "Let us go," Jessa said kindly. "Get me out of this *treesha* that your clever King Boris made just for you, I am thinking, and we shall ask Radha to make you a soup that will soothe your stomach."

"Will she tell me a story?" Darry asked, a touch of mischief in her grin.

"She'll probably hit you on the head if you ask her."

Darry rolled onto her side and pushed from the ground with less strength than Jessa liked to see. "Splendid."

❖

Radha stood beneath the arched entry to the balcony, her eyes on Jessa's profile in the moonlight. Jessa sat as she always did when thinking, her legs pulled up and her chin on her knees. She had done this since she was a girl and Radha understood that it was Jessa's form of meditation, though it was not as the Vhaelin would teach.

"Your Princess is quite charming," Radha said. She had not been treated with so much respect since last she had seen her home, which was too many years ago to remember properly. It had been springtime, and her mother had still been alive, though that was all she could recall that seemed important.

Jessa had an easy humor and to watch her laugh so freely had been truly wonderful. Radha had not missed the way Jessa had watched Darry's every move, her eyes hungry and longing.

Radha had smelled the blood as well, coursing thick through Darry's veins and betraying her. She had never thought she would meet a *Cha-Diah* in her lifetime. The Golden Panther was just that, and in a strange way it did not surprise Radha. That and Darry's beauty was a powerful mixture. Radha chided herself for not sensing it sooner. She had made broth and watched as they sat together on the balcony, Jessa making sure that Darry ate all that she was given.

"She is not mine," Jessa had whispered after Darry left, her eyes captured by the stars.

"If you say."

"I don't understand why I'm here."

"You still ponder Bharjah's deeper play?"

"I have my tea with Prince Malcolm tomorrow," Jessa said.

Radha grunted in assent. "Yes, it is time for you to be alone with him. They have followed etiquette quite well here, I will give them that. Their Queen is a formidable woman and knows the rules of the game. Are you frightened?"

"No."

"The Prince is why you're here, child, and Bharjah sees some—"

"I *know* what he sees," Jessa said. "He sees a child of his blood upon the throne of Arravan."

"Yes. And as you said, you have always been trapped and so it is no matter what you do." Radha pricked Jessa's temper with care. "So have your tea and smile at him, and look into his eyes. Perhaps you will like him. The rest of his family seems passable."

"*Passable*?" Jessa's tone was clipped in annoyance at the slight.

"All right, they seem quite lovely. Is that what you would like me to say?"

"Go to bed, Radha."

"Are you not tired as well?"

"No."

"Why not?"

"I looked into the eyes of a panther today," Jessa said, knowing that Radha would have spied out the truth of Darry's majik, for it still clung to Darry, and Radha was most wise in such things. It was Darry's majik they had sensed that night on the balcony, and the strength of her blood trying to free itself.

Radha laughed her raspy chuckle. "She was big? The girl's blood smells most powerful. The cat must be large."

"Go to bed."

"You as well, child."

"I will."

"You will wear the sable dress I made, yes? I think the Prince will like it."

"If it pleases you, Radha."

"It does not. Joaquin will come early to speak to you. Be prepared."

"Go to bed," Jessa said again. "You spend your days wandering the city and your nights prowling the corridors. You will fall asleep at the table in the middle of your dinner, and I shall have to wash your face and carry you to the divan."

Radha laughed. "I have a bird's bones. I am light."

"Do not make me afraid for you as well!" Jessa snapped. "And so when you're not looking and you're tired, I shall find Serabee bending over your throat like a wild dog."

"I am not so easy to kill, Jessa," Radha said gently.

"Yes, so you keep saying," Jessa countered quickly. "Though I've just seen the strongest person I may have ever met aside from you nearly laid low by her own blood. Do not let your arrogance be your undoing."

Radha was surprised by the words but her smile was quick. She *was* arrogant and she knew it. She had reason to be. "I shall go to bed then."

"Thank you."

"Should I—"

"Yes, put out the dress."

"It is only a tea, my child," Radha said, stepping into the darkness of their chambers. "Perhaps a lunch the day beyond and a walk through the gardens the next, and then they'll be gone for a week's worth or more, chasing the boar and the sacred stag and hunting in the Green Hills."

Jessa counted the stars of Attia's spear, following the constellation upward. *And they will discuss Bharjah's chattel come nightfall, no doubt, over spring wine and red meat. Discussing the price of my spirit and if it is pure enough and worth the price my father wishes. And what price could he possibly want?*

Why would the King of Arravan take me in exchange for the Lowlands of the Taljah, when I am the daughter of all that he hates? It is the only thing that Bharjah will want. It's all that he has ever *wanted, a foothold within Arravan. You're old now, Bharjah, yet you still claw at your power as if you're a man just come of age. Do you honestly think that the High King of Arravan will hand over his most precious lands for the hand of your afterthought? That he would think me worthy of his firstborn? You are a fool then.*

And should you be after a child of Lyonese blood upon the throne? Most likely you'll be dead and rotting before that day comes. A child will take too long, and your sons thirst for their day in the sun. Do you think they will see their feast given to a child in their stead? They have been begging scraps from your table for far too long, you butcher, to allow that to happen.

Jessa rubbed her forehead with the back of her hand, closing her eyes at the pieces that would not fit together. *Why am I here?*

As if in answer, the memory of Darry's subtle musk filled her senses.

CHAPTER FIFTEEN

Jessa stood beside the lilac trees in the courtyard and studied the arched trellis covered with ivy and hamesroot. It reminded her of the entrance to the maze and made her smile beneath her dark veil. The late-morning air was pleasant and heavy with the fading scent of the lilacs, the clusters of lavender blossoms still full as their perfume dissipated within the warmer summer temperatures.

She wore the sable dress that Radha had made, the silk an exact match to her eyes and bartered for at a great price. It was made in a similar fashion to her dress from the fête, the hem at her slipper boots shading to black as did the cuffs, though the skirt was not nearly as full.

She waited and felt as if the axe were about to fall, her mind racing with so many thoughts she could not follow them properly. Chief among them, however, was the image of her brother standing at the foot of her bed. Radha had warned her that he would come and she had prepared accordingly, though she had not been ready for that. He had been watching her as she slept, and the memory of such an insult would not let her anger fade.

"You should be up and preparing," Joaquin said.

Jessa held the sheet to her chest as she sat up, feeling instantly exposed in her homespun shift. "I'll be ready."

"Will you? Where is your ugly Vhaelin bitch? Should she not be attending you?"

"She seeks food to break my fast," Jessa lied.

"I should send Serabee to find her then, yes?"

"That is unnecessary."

"Do not tell me what is necessary, sister," Joaquin replied. "You have only to look beautiful and smile, not think. Never to think. You are but a sweet-smelling cunt to entice our Arravan Prince like a hungry

dog, do you understand? You have no power but what is between your legs."

"So I've been told," Jessa said. That she responded at all when he insulted her surprised them both. Her anger came alive at his words and part of her welcomed it. "Then I shall wash with even sweeter smelling soaps so that my scent is strong. Would that please you, Joaquin?"

Her response made him smile. "Now is the time for your charm then, sister, yes. Their women seem to dote on you, which is good. I had not expected that. But it is Malcolm you must worry about now, yes?"

"I know why I'm here," she answered.

His smile deepened at her words and she did not miss it. "You know nothing, as always. Do as you are told and I shall take Serabee with me to the Green Hills. Would you like that? To be completely free of his presence?" He taunted her, knowing how she loathed Serabee. "You'd not try to run?"

"Where would I go?"

Joaquin laughed. "Yes, where would you go?"

"Take him or do not take him, Joaquin. He is your dog, not mine."

He seemed to be genuinely insulted. "Dog? *He is a Lord of the Fakir."*

"If you insist."

Jessa reacted as he moved about the bed, and though her first instinct was to scramble for the other side and place the bed between them, she found her feet hitting the floor beside his own, stopping him short. His apparent shock filled her with satisfaction.

"You like to mock me, Joaquin," she said. "But you know I'm not a fool. I will do as our father bids me and snare him a prince. Then you may rise within the ranks of our blood, slitting their throats as you go. Sylban shall be happy for the company, I think, for he's not been the same since Lybinus disappeared. Perhaps you might become his new shadow. At least your scraps would be from a better cut of meat."

Joaquin grabbed the hair at the back of her neck, and Jessa's head snapped back as she was pulled against him. She did not make a sound. "Serabee has always said that you were hiding. You were wise to do so." His left hand reached up and slid with slow ease upon her right breast, cupping it before taking the nipple between his fingers and squeezing in a brutal manner. "But do not overtax yourself. You're only the rabbit, my sister, and you know this. You have no talent for playing the wolf."

Jessa stared into his eyes, the pain within her breast stabbing into her chest. "Then I will be a rabbit and bait your trap. How will that suit you, Joaquin?"

He laughed and shoved her away. Jessa fell to the bed and closed her eyes as he stalked to the door.

"Don't be late. Since your whore of a mother is dead you must meet them on your own."

Jessa lifted her face at his words and watched his back until the door slammed shut behind him.

She let out a groan of pain and pressed her breast close, and then she was up and moving, her blood surging. She took hold of the pitcher and basin from the table beside the bed and spun about, throwing one and then the other. The porcelain pitcher shattered against the wall with a splash of water; the basin followed but a heartbeat later. "Atta fikloche tu an atta zaneesha!" *She hissed her curse.* "Shivahsa fikloche!"

Radha laughed from the shadows beside the hearth as Jessa swung toward the sound. "Should I lay out your dress now?" Radha asked. "Or find you more things that will break?"

Jessa stood at the end of the bed and met Radha's eyes, though she was all but invisible within the cast of her spell.

"Find me food first." Jessa's voice shook with her fury. "Perhaps you will meet Serabee on your way to the kitchens, yes? If you intend to hide within your precious shadows when I need you most, then may you find the Blood Fires and be damned!"

Radha laughed. "Did you need me?"

Jessa stared at her.

Radha moved from the shadows and let her casting fall away as if it were one of her many shawls. "Did you need me?"

Jessa was stunned from her wrath by the answer.

"Princess Jessa-Sirrah."

Jessa turned smoothly at the voice in the courtyard, all thoughts but one disappearing at the sound of her name. *No, I did not need you*...and then, startled, she looked up into the warm gaze of the High King Owen Durand.

"I didn't mean to startle you, Princess," he said.

Jessa noticed his handsome silver coat and casual white tunic, his vest a deep black to match his trousers. She took a step back and bowed low.

"Princess, please don't do that." He extended his hand and gently pulled her to her feet. "My son is late, you see?" he said. "So I thought I might take a moment and give you my regards."

"Good morn, my Lord," Jessa said. She needed to clear her throat but knew it was bad form. He released her hand and she folded hers together at her waist.

By the Gods but you're a lovely girl, Owen thought. *How a vile creature such as Bharjah managed to get you I haven't a bloody clue.* It was the first time they had spoken in such a manner, and though he knew her already from Cecelia, he was glad of the chance to finally form his own opinion. "May I call you Jessa?"

"Yes, my Lord."

"Your dress is very beautiful, Jessa."

"Thank you, my Lord."

"How are you finding your stay with us? Arravan is very different from Lyoness, but perhaps you're discovering some of its many virtues."

Jessa was staring at his boots, which made him notice the sheen of dust upon them. He hoped she realized he was just a man with dust upon his boots.

"I like your land very much, my Lord. I am unaccustomed to so much color. The earth here is rich with rain."

Owen looked about the gardens as he clasped his hands behind his back, feeling relaxed. "Yes, it is very green. The land in Lyoness can be unforgiving."

"Yes," she said. "Much about my home is unforgiving."

Owen tried to decide if her comment held more than he heard. "My wife and my daughters, they've been kind?"

"Yes," she answered quickly, holding his gaze then looking down as if afraid she would offend him. "They have all been most generous, and the Lady Alisha as well."

Her words pleased him. "My wife was very nervous, you know," he said, bending toward her, "that you would not like her."

Jessa's surprise was obvious. "My Lord?"

"And Emmalyn as well. This is the first visit, you must understand, that your father has ever sanctioned. The royal blood of your line has never set foot so deeply within my country before."

"More is the pity for that," Jessa said. "For I find that your family is…" Her words failed her. *Your family is…*

"My family is what?" he prompted her gently.

"Your family is…a family."

Owen glanced at the trellis where his wife and Emmalyn spoke with Margery, no doubt discussing how the tea was to be served. "Perhaps not as proper as we should be at times," he said. "The Lewellyn blood that is my wife's family has always been, well, let us say *bold,* and we'll leave it at that."

"If love is bold, then yes, they are very bold."

"You will stop wearing your veil after today?" he asked. "It is my understanding that custom allows you to remove it, once you've spoken alone with my son?"

"Yes, my Lord. I may remove the veil."

"That would please me greatly," he replied, surprised by how much he wished to see her face. Her eyes were a wonder. "I imagine that eating must be somewhat interesting, wearing such a thing."

Jessa let out a breath of laughter. "Yes, my Lord."

"Soup. Soup must be difficult."

"Yes, soup."

"And creamed leeks," he said, wishing that she would look up once more. "I have a hard time keeping them from the front of my shirt, after which my wife scolds me like a child. It's very troubling for a king."

He hoped his feeble attempts to charm her were successful. He very much enjoyed trying to make her smile.

"Yes. Leeks are troubling all on their own, much less with sauce."

"I don't like them either." Owen laughed, and Cecelia and Emmalyn came into the courtyard, obviously drawn by the sound. "Ah, yes, now I've done it," Owen grumbled. Cecelia raised an eyebrow at him from across the courtyard. "She will see me talking with you, which I'm sure isn't proper in some way, and she will box my ears."

"Have a care for her ring then, my Lord," Jessa said.

Owen turned in surprise but she had lowered her eyes. He studied her closely, noticing her black curls and the braids that were scattered throughout. Her posture was perfect, yet she had a vulnerability about her as she stood before him, her hands together at her waist and looking as if she would flinch at the slightest provocation. She did not appear frail, but it seemed as if she waited for a blow of some kind, an anxiousness about her demeanor that made him want to take her hand. *Waiting for what, I wonder.*

They heard Malcolm's voice across the courtyard and Jessa's shoulders twitched just as he had predicted they might. *Waiting for that, I should imagine.*

Cecelia took Malcolm's arm after a few quiet words and they moved across the courtyard. Malcolm looked handsome in his black trousers and jacket with a green tunic, his thick hair brushed back and his mustache and goatee neatly trimmed. His blue eyes were on Jessa and he smiled as they approached. Jessa gave a low bow.

"Princess Jessa-Sirrah," Cecelia said, letting go of Malcolm's arm as he stepped close, too close in fact. She pulled at his jacket and Malcolm took a step back. "May I introduce, once again, our son, Prince Malcolm Edmund Durand, heir to the throne of Arravan and all the provinces held therein. Prince of Ishlere and Duke of Treemont. Liege Lord of Kenton and barrister to the High Court, and second to the High King in Council."

Bloody hell, woman. Owen scowled. *Why not just pound her on the head with a rock and be done with it?*

Jessa rose smoothly. Owen's eyes were drawn to her hands as she took hold of the jeweled clips within her hair and undid the veil, first one side and then the other.

The silk slid away and Owen saw her in full for the first time. *Sweet Gamar.*

"I am the Princess Jessa-Sirrah de Cassey LaMarc de Bharjah," she said, and met Cecelia's gaze. They held each other's eyes and Cecelia's expression filled with question at the lengthy exchange.

Jessa held out the veil to her.

Cecelia stared at the delicate silk for several heartbeats before taking it in a stilted manner. Etiquette demanded that the veil be handed only to Jessa's own mother or not at all. "Jessa," Cecelia said under her breath.

Jessa's attention returned to Malcolm. "And though I hold no lands or titles other than my name, I hold the hearts of my people with great care next to my own. Unlike my brothers, who are neglectful of such things. And unlike my father, who has forgotten them altogether."

Sweet seven hells. Owen could not remember when he had last been so intrigued by another person, unless it were Darry. But then his youngest child was her own sort of revelation and one that could not be compared to any other he had yet encountered. And though he felt he had ruined that well enough for himself, the surprising joy that was her wild blood, he could still admire it from a distance. Darry had taught him that much at least, though the lesson had come at a terrible price. Not everything was meant to be tamed, and one man's propriety could be another man's hell.

"I am most pleased to make your acquaintance once again, Princess," Malcolm said with an easy smile, though his eyes studied her with an awareness they had not held but a moment before. "Perhaps we might have tea?"

"I would like that very much," Jessa said, remembering how he had spoken to Darry upon the balustrade and his cruel tone as he goaded her.

How would you speak to me, *I wonder, if you knew that...if you knew that I would give all that I have at this moment to have your sister standing before me instead of you?* A terrible wave of panic moved through her and she felt like laughing as she realized the man before her might very well end up her husband. *And what would I do if he were? What would* you *do, Darry?*

Malcolm waited patiently for her to take his arm. She slipped her hand in the crook of his elbow and they moved away from his parents, walking to one of the far tables where the tea had been set for them.

Owen placed a hand at the small of Cecelia's back. "She cannot possibly be Bharjah's child."

Cecelia studied the veil, her heart pricked by the fact that Jessa had given it to her. It was the mother's honor to keep the veil, which symbolized that her daughter would no longer be hers and was a keepsake of immense significance. Cecelia swallowed over a tight throat and took a deep breath, honored and humbled. "Her mother was said to be the most beautiful woman in Lyoness."

"I remember," Owen said. "The girl from the Ibarris Plains."

"I imagine," Cecelia said as Malcolm held out a chair for Jessa, "that she's more her mother's than his, for all that she died years ago."

"You're to stay and chaperone?" he asked. "To make sure Malcolm does not insult her?"

"Yes. Emmalyn and I will sit within the solar."

"Perhaps just Emmalyn?" he asked in a tone of voice she recognized all too well. "My morning is surprisingly free."

Cecelia chuckled and slapped at his chest with the back of her hand as she moved away. "Go and do something stately, Owen, and let me attend to my duties."

"As you command, my love."

Owen watched Jessa once more and his humor faded as Malcolm poured the tea. Her shoulders were tight with the same anxiousness, only perhaps now it had spread. Jessa seemed to hold herself at a strange distance from what was happening around her.

Owen walked down the garden path, thinking upon his greatest enemy and the beautiful child he had sent in offer of a lasting truce, wondering what the price would be if his son chose to keep her. He understood the long-term payment, a child of Lyonese blood on his family's throne, but he knew as well that Bharjah wanted something more immediate. The Lowlands would never be Bharjah's unless he took them by force, so what would the Butcher of the Plains demand instead?

Jessa took up the teacup with a graceful hand as Malcolm began to talk. He was indeed quite handsome, as Jessa knew, but near at hand and with his attention on her, his eyes held a different sort of spark. He spoke of how glad he was that she was there, and that he was pleased at the opportunity to treat with her brother. She sipped her tea and smiled, as Radha had counseled, and searched his eyes. When she found them, he would look away. His reaction was discreet, but it was something she could not miss.

He spoke easily of Arravan and how when etiquette would allow, he would like very much to show her his city, for Lokey held many wonders that Karballa did not. He said this, and Jessa knew that he had never been to her city and could not possibly know what wonders it might hold. He did not ask her of Karballa or the Jade Palace, nor did he speak at all of Lyoness.

He smoothed his beard and Jessa noted that his nails were well-kept and his skin soft-looking. This was an affectation, she realized, that he would indulge when he was searching for something to say. He was polite, of course, but she saw almost at once that his mind was elsewhere. When her porcelain cup was empty of tea she waited as form dictated, but he did not fill it until his own cup was empty. She thanked him and he nodded absently, after which he engaged in more courtly talk.

He spoke of the Green Hills and how he hoped she would not mind that he would steal her brother away for the hunting. And then he spoke of his skill with the bow and how he hoped that they would bring down a stag, so that once more they might enjoy the rarity of its prized flesh. He asked how she had enjoyed such a delicacy, and when she expressed her appreciation in a lie, he leaned back in his chair, looking pleased.

After an hour or so he glanced at the trellis and Jessa saw that his councilor Marteen Salish was waiting. Malcolm nodded to him. He made his excuses politely and thanked her for the wonderful visit even as he rose from his chair. He stepped about the table and held his hand out, and she took it gently. She had to turn somewhat awkwardly from her chair, which he had not pulled out. When he asked if they might have lunch on the morrow and a walk within the gardens the next, she said yes.

Emmalyn was there then, taking her arm as Malcolm bowed and left them. He moved toward the trellis with more concern than Jessa had witnessed the entire time they had just spent together.

And within that moment Jessa knew the truth. She knew that Prince Malcolm Durand had no intention of marrying her and most likely never had. He had no interest in her at all, not as his future wife or even a friend. She knew it as surely as she stood there, and the knowledge struck her like a fist. If she was not here as a possible wife then why was she here at all? The question was the same as always, yet she had not expected it from the Prince himself. *What are we in the middle of, Radha?*

"That wasn't so bad now, was it?" Emmalyn asked.

"Might I go back to my rooms now, Emmalyn?"

Emmalyn squeezed Jessa's arm and stepped closer. "Of course," she said. "I'll come for you at lunch?"

"I don't think so," Jessa replied. "I did not sleep well last night, and I think perhaps…"

Emmalyn waited but Jessa said nothing more. "An afternoon nap," Emmalyn said with a friendly smile. "A splendid idea."

She led Jessa toward the trellis and the path that would take them to the residence, casting her mother a worried glance.

Cecelia felt a twitch at her temple in response. She had not missed Malcolm's breaches in etiquette or the fact that he had barely let Jessa speak. She could only imagine what he might have been saying the entire time, and she surmised that nothing was quite so boring to a prospective bride as talk of the millosha wheat harvest and the imported silks from Greymear.

"Dammit, Mal," she said softly, staring at the veil in her hands.

CHAPTER SIXTEEN

Darry pulled herself up with a grimace, gripping the turn in the stone firmly as she swung to the right. She threw her left arm up and grasped the top edge of the balcony rail, hauling her body after.

She rested her waist against the stone, her lower body dangling some thirty feet above the ground. She was just in time to see Jessa take down several dresses from the pole between the hearth and the balcony archway, freshly laundered and dry from the warmth of the hearth and the fresh summer breeze.

"Jess!" she hissed, as loud as she dared.

Jessa spun around, her body twisting to the side in mid-step. Her bare feet caught in the fabric of the dresses she carried, and she slipped with a strangled cry and fell to the floor in a heap.

Darry laughed. "Brilliant."

Jessa sat up and Darry swung a leg onto the stone of her balcony rail, then toppled over onto the smooth stones.

Jessa covered her mouth to stop her laughter and glanced toward the divan where Radha was snoring. She scrambled to her feet and hurried over the threshold as Darry got up. "What are you doing?" she said. "Have you lost your mind?"

"We have established that, yes?"

Jessa's blood was racing at the sight of her, her body suddenly alive and extremely focused. Darry had not been at dinner and Jessa had regretted her absence, especially because she was no longer wearing her veil and felt exposed.

"How was your day?"

"You climbed my balcony to ask me how my *day* was?" Jessa asked.

"Yes, and no."

"*Shivahsa essa*, Darry, you *are* mad. How'd you do that?"

Darry chuckled, glancing over the balcony as well. "It looks much higher from up here," she said. "So how was your day?"

"Fine," Jessa lied.

"I saw you in your sable dress. The color matches your eyes. Did you plan it that way?"

"Of course." Jessa was glad for the darkness, knowing it would hide the blush on her cheeks. "It's what women do. Why was your vest at the fête made of such a golden color if not for your hair?"

"It was the cheapest fabric," Darry said with a grin. "I was running out of coin very quickly."

Jessa laughed and glanced back into the room, searching for any sign of Radha. When she turned back Darry was reaching in her jacket. She pulled forth a flower with broad petals that Jessa recognized at once as the sunsdrop glory, a red desert flower that bloomed only in the sandy earth of Lyoness.

Darry held it out, fixing one of the bent petals. "I thought you might be missing your home."

Jessa took the flower by its thick stem. "Where did you get this?"

"The gardens at the Temple of Jezara. The Goddess is very fond of red."

Jessa's emotions rose at the sight of the broad petals she knew as well as her own flesh, lifting the flower to her nose. She closed her eyes as the scent of her homeland filled her senses, a swirl of unexpected joy born within the presence of a very old friend. Though she rejoiced each morning that the Jade Palace was a thousand leagues away, she had not realized until now that she did in fact miss Lyoness.

"And here is chicory for the Lady Radha's karrem," Darry said. Jessa was beautiful in the moonlight, her skin tanned and dark against the white of her shift, her hair a thousand strands of loveliness about her shoulders as a stray braid clung to the skin of her throat. Darry had to force herself not to push it aside.

Jessa took the small leather bag, her eyes finding Darry's. "Thank you."

"Are you...please don't cry, Jess," Darry said, panicked at the unexpected emotion. "Don't, don't do that."

"No. It's just that...I was missing my home."

"It's all right, you know." Darry held her eyes for a long time. "It's your home and you're far away."

"Yes," Jessa said.

"I should go."

"Where? Why?" she asked. "You've only just gotten here."

"I have six more saddles to clean tonight," Darry said. *And maybe this wasn't such a good idea. I hadn't counted on seeing you dressed as you are, or undressed, as the case may be. Amar's mustache.* She closed her eyes, but the sight of Jessa's body so scantily clad would not disappear. *What in the seven hells are you doing, Darry?* She had not considered the consequences of her actions, only that she wanted to make Jessa happy. "Longshanks is angry at me for being a princess."

Jessa grabbed Darry's arm as Darry lifted her left knee to the railing. "Take the bloody door, Darry," she said, loath to see her go no matter which way she went. *I hadn't thought to find what I was looking for. But by all the gods, for the first time in my life I understand.* "Take the door," she said again.

"And tip on my toes past the Lady Radha?" Darry asked with her rogue's grin, her dimple making an appearance. "Not on your precious life, Jessa, not on your life."

Jessa let go as Darry swung over the edge and lowered her body into the air. Jessa reacted quickly and covered Darry's hand, everything inside her pulling at her, begging her to lean down and kiss her. The thought startled her. Darry's lips looked so soft. *I would taste you on my tongue, Akasha.* And at that thought she caught her breath, feeling a deeper stirring that she recognized from her most sensual dreams. "If you fall, I will never forgive you."

"Not to worry, Princess. I do this all the time."

"Climb balconies when the moon is high and give flowers to women in their night clothes?"

Darry laughed. "Well, *no*," she said as she started downward. "Though it's not a bad idea."

"Come back," Jessa whispered, stretching over the rail and catching hold of Darry's eyes as she glanced up. "Come back again tomorrow, Darry."

"Yes…yes, all right."

"And the night after that as well."

"Perhaps I should find a ladder?"

Jessa tried to hold her quiet laughter in but it broke free. "Do you have other plans then?"

"Well, yes. I'm going to a party for Lucien."

"Lucien?"

"One of my men." Darry gripped more tightly with her right hand and shifted her weight. "It's his birthing day."

"I see."

"Would you like to come with me?"

Jessa couldn't speak.

"Sorry." Darry grinned. "Not proper, I suppose."

"No, it's not," Jessa said softly. "But I like being asked."

"Jessa?"

"Yes?"

"If I don't climb down now, I might be falling soon."

"*Shivahsa*, Darry!" Jessa bent farther over the rail. "Yes, *go*."

The material of Jessa's shift had slipped, revealing more than just a pleasing hint of her breasts. *Well worth a fall, I think.* Darry leapt from the wall and landed safely, then looked up to see Jessa still stretched over the stones. *You will pull the moon down, my sweet Jessa, looking so in its light.*

Jessa raised the flower to her nose. "Go," she whispered through the petals. "Go while I can still let you, *Akasha*."

Darry waved before she turned away and disappeared into the night.

❖

"The timing could not be better, Mal." Marteen Salish's brown eyes were bright with satisfaction. "Will she summon your father?"

Malcolm stared at the embers glowing in the fireplace across the room as if the small bit of light they provided could still hold back the night. "Yes."

"Then this is the perfect play. Stop brooding."

"It shall cause her a great deal of pain," Malcolm said, though the comment was meant more for himself than Marteen. "She doesn't deserve that."

"She's your mother and you love her, I understand that. But she is the past, do you agree?"

"Of course!" Malcolm snapped. "Is this not *my* plan? *My* play? This country has been sitting upon its laurels for nearly forty years. No one understands the need for young blood better than I. Try sitting in council with those old men day after day. They smell of boredom and bed death. My father must step away from his power now, before their inaction drags him down completely. At this rate the Durand name will fade into nothing but a footnote in history…all while Lyoness is ripe for the picking."

"Then you must *own* it, Mal. Very soon you will be the High King of Arravan. You may make amends to your mother when you sit on the Blackwood Throne."

"I need no lecture, thank you. Do not forget that my son shall sit upon *two* thrones when I am dead and gone."

"She's a beautiful whore, I will give her that."

"She is no *whore*, Marteen, of that I am certain. Though another woman must play her part first."

"So we make our move?"

"Have you spoken with her?"

"She will select her moment wisely. You needn't worry."

"She had better."

"This is her chosen field of battle, Mal. She is more deadly with her tongue than anyone I have ever known. It shall never be traced back to you."

"You seem overly fond of her," Malcolm said. He lifted an eyebrow, eyeing his First Councilor with suspicion. "You always have been, actually."

Marteen laughed. He dipped his right hand in his goblet, then reached out, staining the sheets red as he slid his hand along the soft skin of Malcolm's belly, pushing beneath the silken sheet. "Are you jealous?" he said, looking up at Malcolm from the middle of the bed.

"Should I be?"

Marteen wrapped his wet fingers about the shaft of Malcolm's cock. "Of course not."

Malcolm lifted their shared goblet and brought it to his mouth, then drank the last of it before setting it on the bedside table.

"It will all come together, Mal," Marteen said softly. "You'll see."

Malcolm relaxed back into the pillows, his eyes drawn to the movement beneath the sheet as Marteen stroked his shaft with a familiar touch. He could feel it within his thighs and his muscles tightened, his stomach filling with heat. The blood vessels beneath his flesh began to throb and his testes ached as Marteen stroked him faster, throwing the sheet back as he drew closer.

Malcolm's left hand slid up the back of Marteen's neck. "You will take it all this time…yes?"

"*Yes*," Marteen whispered, breathing quickly as Malcolm seized his neck in a grip of iron.

Malcolm smiled, his heart pounding as Marteen's mouth closed upon his cock, the heat and texture of his tongue fairly burning Malcolm's flesh. And then he began to thrust, his hips lifting then retreating with ever-increasing speed as Marteen held on, taking in the length of him until Malcolm spent his seed in one last, perfect thrust.

CHAPTER SEVENTEEN

Jessa leaned against the fence in the early-morning dawn. She was dressed in an Arravan skirt and simple tunic, one of Radha's black shawls about her shoulders. It was yet an hour or more before the first watch bell would ring, and she had risen early for want of a walk.

She had lain awake into the night before, waiting for something that never came—for Darry to scale the balcony so that she might be alone with her. She had waited for one more opportunity to touch her, though in what manner she had not wondered. Perhaps just to brush her arm or to feel the strength of Darry's hand as she slipped her own within it. *Or to see your dimple, Akasha.*

She had waited, but Darry never came. She knew Darry was at a celebration for one of her men, but still she had hoped. When she had finally fallen asleep it was late and she was alone, with not even Radha's steady breathing to ease her into the land of dreams.

Jessa had found no respite there either, her waking thoughts pushing into her mind and turning her dreams odd and frightening. She had felt a hand at her throat and she could not breathe. She had heard Darry's voice and felt fear at the words she did not understand. She was certain that Darry was in danger but was helpless to protect her.

She had awoken with her shift soaked through with sweat. Her hands had trembled and she wanted to cry out in rage, though she swallowed it down like bile and collapsed back onto the bed instead. She had spent the next hours fighting sleep, feeling the pull of the dream on the edges of her mind. She must have dozed at some point. When she rose with the sky still dark, Radha lay snoring gently on the divan.

Jessa had washed and dressed and left their rooms. At first she thought only to walk, but as her feet found the path to the stables and barracks she knew what she sought. She had watched the horses in the paddock moving along the fences and stretching their legs. She had smiled at their joy and trailed a hand against the white painted planks as she was drawn toward the barracks.

She had no intention of entering, but she wandered past the doors and farther south until she reached the fence about one of the practice yards. It was there that she found exactly what she was searching for.

Darry moved through the yard wearing brown trousers and a tight homespun shirt that hugged her upper body in a manner that broke all the rules. Sleeveless and cropped at her stomach, it was the garment that Jessa had first seen at the garden pond.

Her hair was held by a strip of rawhide at the back of her neck and it spilled down between her shoulder blades. Her sword flashed in a smooth arc as her body turned in a fluid manner. She moved through the discipline, her sword spinning in a deadly circle, whisking past her ear but an instant before it shaved the air beside her feet bare in the dirt of the yard. Her movement was constant yet measured, using only the energy that was needed.

Darry moved with confidence and left the ground, cartwheeling as her left hand found the earth. The tumble was graceful and she gained her feet without a stutter, her sword cutting through the air in a quick strike. She followed the weapon around and advanced into a second series of steps. Every move she made had a purpose and every step a destination.

The practice ground seemed to shrink in size. No distance was too great in order to attain the goal, no maneuver of the sword too complicated that the ground would not accommodate it. And all the while the sword moved, defending Darry against the air around her in arcs and smooth strokes, striking at an invisible enemy in deadly slashes. Moves that in battle would steal a man's life without causing a hitch in the blade's graceful movement.

Jessa watched the muscles of Darry's arms and the elegance of her hands as she switched the sword from right to left, then swung it smoothly behind her back. Darry spun to the left and turned with the same grace she had in the Mohn-Drom. Her skin was covered with a sheen of sweat though she did not appear to breathe at all, much less in exertion. Jessa recoiled as Darry's body twisted at the waist and her feet left the ground and flipped over her head once again. This time, however, both hands held the sword, the strike that resulted from the acrobatic move appearing deadly and without defense.

Her thoughts lost to the power of her desire, Jessa felt herself slipping. The sleekness of Darry's movements and the beauty of her body, the clean lines and power, Darry's breasts caught beneath the white fabric that had begun to darken with sweat. Jessa could see the raised flesh of

Darry's nipples and had to close her eyes. She was wet with her want and her desire moved through her body, spiraling through her stomach until it was enfolded into the heavy pulse between her legs. It was relentless, and Jessa was trapped beneath it.

She wanted Darry's flesh against her hands, she wanted the taste of her skin on her tongue. She wanted their bodies to move together and to feel Darry's hands on her. Jessa wanted to make her cry out like the lovers she had seen on the hot nights in the city of Karballa, as she had wandered cloaked in shadows and looked shyly through their windows at life. She wanted that life and she wanted Darry to show it to her. She wanted the terrible ache to go away, wondering if it would be replaced by something even sweeter.

When she opened her eyes Darry was moving toward the center of the yard. She turned in a tight circle, the sword gaining speed within its deadly windmill of movement. A grin flashed across Darry's lips and Jessa smiled, seeing her absolute joy in the gesture.

There was nothing but stillness.

Nothing moved. Not the sword, not the air around her, not a muscle or a twitch or a breath of wind. And then a large golden curl slipped forward along Darry's right temple and fell along her cheek as the tip of her sword was poised but an inch above the ground. Jessa had never seen a moment filled with more deadly promise, but for the sweetness of the curl. She had no choice but to smile.

"Is that you, Bentley?" Darry's said.

"No," Jessa replied, unable to find her full voice.

Darry opened her eyes and was nearly staggered by Jessa's gaze. She felt naked beneath its force. Her flesh reacted, her breasts chafing against the tightness of her shirt as the tip of her sword dropped slowly into the dirt.

Darry's blood rushed at the expression in Jessa's eyes. She could not mistake it in any way. The desire was blatant and completely unguarded. Darry's body answered its call and everything tightened with pleasure, arousal and need tipping the scales of her reason and good sense.

Jessa turned away and walked along the fence.

"*Wait*!" Darry stabbing her sword into the dirt and skidded around the west end of the barracks until she reached the edge of the dirt path. She stopped before the pebbled walk, eyeing the stones. She snarled and stepped on the stones, hurrying as much as she was able until she could jump to the scrub grass between the barracks and the main barn of the stables.

Darry searched the wide path that led to the residence but it wound empty to the trimmed hedges and beyond. Her disappointment was like a wave washing in from the sea and her thoughts shifted toward the common sense she had so easily discarded at a mere look. *Don't be a bloody fool.*

Someone shouted and she jumped. Darry smiled as a horse screamed in rage amidst more shouting. "That would be for me," she said, and retraced her steps, avoiding the pebbled walk and moving in the grass that grew close to the barn. She stepped into the massive opening of double doors that led from the barn to the paddocks.

Darry stepped back as a black filly skidded onto the planks of the main corridor and twisted to the left with a push of muscles and sleek flesh, her black mane swishing wildly. A groomsman stumbled from the stall and stretched for the halter rope, but the filly was too quick and he hit the boards with a thud.

Darry laughed as the animal raced past her. She gave chase, and one of the stable hands opened the wide gate to the lower paddock and waved an arm in an effort to herd the animal. Darry waved to the stable hand and the boy waved back, closing the gate as she sprinted past him.

The filly bucked and swung her head at the smooth rope that slapped against her flanks. "You cannot play all of the time, my pretty!" Darry called, slowing to a walk through the long grass.

The filly turned toward the center of the paddock and suddenly halted. Her head was held high, and her forelock of black hair fell across a brilliant, diamond-shaped spot of white between her eyes. She snorted and threw her head back as Darry approached, then took a step in the opposite direction.

"You mustn't be so cruel," Darry said, circling toward the far fence for a better angle. "They only wish to give you the grain I paid good coin for."

The filly walked toward the fence a few feet, stretching her neck out.

"And do I not bring you sugar every day?" Darry asked, reaching out her left arm as the filly tossed her head. "Small pieces that melt on your tongue and make you the envy of every woman around you."

Slowly approaching the fence, Jessa watched them both.

"Like kisses from Gamar that make you strong," Darry said to the filly. The horse moved forward a step or two, soothed by the sound of Darry's voice. "Look how beautiful she is, they say. How special she must be, to be given such treats. I wish I were as loved as that. Why am I not?"

Jessa had never seen a more gorgeous creature, despite the fame of the Lyonese steeds that were the pride of her people. The animal was utterly beautiful, every measure of her flesh filled with strength and muscle and her mane unusually long as it poured down her neck. She was blacker than black but for the splash of white between her eyes. Jessa stopped near the fence, holding her breath as the filly's nose hovered inches from Darry's hand.

"The girls will be so jealous," Darry said. The filly placed her nose in Darry's palm, her wet lips nibbling at the skin. "They will sigh with envy and turn away, for I will love only you, my pretty, and no other."

The horse stepped close and Darry smiled as she stroked the filly's neck.

"You have seduced her."

Darry spun beneath the filly's neck, eyeing Jessa as she stood on other side of the fence. The filly leaned farther over Darry's shoulder, still intent upon Darry's hand.

"No," Darry responded. "Merely intrigued her, I think."

"Are you certain?"

"No. But it seems more likely."

"Perhaps you don't know how persuasive you are," Jessa said. The bangles on her wrist clinked together as they came free of her sleeve. The filly reacted and threw her head out, but Darry caught the halter rope. "She has a name?"

"Not yet. She's one of yours. She's of the Ibarris Plains."

"Ah," Jessa replied. "Well met, then, Princess."

"Darry," she corrected her.

"No. I may call you what is fitting," Jessa said, smiling at Darry's bare feet. Her tunic was barely fastened and her shirt only half tucked in. Her hair swung forward over her right shoulder in a mess of curls that mingled with the filly's long mane, and her face was dirty from the dust of the practice yard she had dominated so easily. "At the moment, you are decidedly of the Blood."

"Why did you run away?"

"I ran nowhere," Jessa said, knowing without a doubt that she suddenly had a great deal of power. She enjoyed the exhilarating feeling very much. "I thought I would leave you to your friends. You enjoyed your celebration?"

Darry tried to find her tongue but Jessa's beauty shoved her thoughts out of order. The filly pushed forward and Darry was forced step closer to the fence. "Yes," was all she could manage.

"There was ale and wine?" Jessa drifted closer. "And dancing perhaps?"

Darry's heart gave a lurch. "Yes."

"And did you dance?"

"With Bentley," Darry answered.

"No women were there for you to dance with?"

Darry let out a breath as Jessa found her eyes and felt lost beneath them. *You look as Hinsa does, I think, when she sees a bird.* "Yes, but I didn't feel like dancing with them."

"No?"

Darry turned to the filly and scratched the hairs on her chin. "No," Darry answered, feeling strangely trapped, a part of her wanting to run as if the hounds were baying at her heels. She was the prey with nothing but open land stretching out before her. "And what did you do last night?"

"I had dinner and played Wei-Jinn with Jacob and Alisha, with Emmalyn as my partner," Jessa said.

"Did you win?"

"Of course."

"You didn't play with Malcolm?"

"Your brother had other things on his mind, I think. His advisor and my brother had his ear. I believe they were discussing trade routes."

Darry smiled ruefully.

"Why do you smile?"

"For one who will be a king, sometimes my brother is a fool."

Jessa laughed and her heart beat fast. Everything was new and it excited her beyond reason. Jessa had never seen Darry so openly shy and nervous, and her blood became incredibly hot. She fought against it, though, because she had no desire to hurt her in any way. She also had very little idea what she was doing and knew her recklessness might well come back to haunt her. But she could not help thinking what she did.

"I will see you today?" Jessa asked.

"You're seeing me now."

"With a fence and a wild horse between us."

"She's green broke."

"She is wild, Princess. That is why she likes you."

"I have duty later."

Jessa contemplated Darry's words, then spoke her mind. "Then I will see you when you're done, as before, if you please."

Darry's eyes were brilliant and filled with challenge, and she didn't look shy at all. Her expression was bold and wanting and extremely heady.

Jessa' s knees weakened beneath the strength of it. The new power stuttered through her veins, then ebbed away, leaving her feeling more than a little abandoned. The tables had turned and she stood helpless.

"Do not forget to give her the sugar you promised," Jessa said, and turned away. She could feel the strength of Darry's attention on her back and she straightened her shoulders, walking true. Vhaelin essa, *what did I just do?* She felt wonderful and was smiling like a fool.

Darry watched Jessa move, watched her curves and her supple body beneath her skirt and tunic, and the black shawl that might have been the Lady Radha's. She stepped away from the filly and took a few steps, but then stopped and tumbled into the long grass, which enveloped her.

The filly walked over and lowered her head, her lips flapping at Darry's shirttail. She grabbed it and lifted her head back, jerking Darry's body to the side. *I'm a dead woman.* She let out a tiny hiccup of sound. *Jezara's corset, my brother really is an ass. That doesn't bode well in the larger scheme of things.*

The filly pulled again and slowly towed Darry through the grass until her tunic ripped completely and the filly reared away from her, a chunk of green fabric between her teeth. The horse bolted, leaving Darry staring at the sky and grinning.

CHAPTER EIGHTEEN

Radha stood cast within her veiled charm even though the two women she watched were perhaps the only ones powerful enough to see through the spell. They sat against the far balcony wall, their shoulders touching. Darry's legs were stretched out with her ankles crossed, and Jessa's were folded before her, her left knee resting on Darry's thigh.

They had been that way for some time, talking as if they were lifelong friends. Darry spoke of a horse and how she had thrown the dice with a trader from Ibarris, waiting until he was drunk and then having the wicked Lord Greeves suggest a game of chance. The trader had bristled at the inference that a woman could best him and so, despite being in his cups, he had accepted the challenge. Darry had taken the filly as payment, much to the man's despair. Jessa laughed happily even as Darry did, trying to describe how he had wept and Bentley had been forced to console him or be found out.

Darry asked of Jessa's home and if she had seen the horse yards that were legendary even in Lokey. Jessa had shifted on some pillows and faced her, both knees resting along Darry's right leg as she described the vast prairie that was home to the breeders and their immense farms and ranches. She had not seen them, Jessa said, but she had walked the smaller yards on the northern edges of Karballa.

Darry asked her many things, about the flowers of her home and the music, and what of the sea? Had Jessa been to the sea, for Darry had heard that the beaches on the southern edges of Lyoness were of a black sand that would burn one's feet at midday. Jessa told her she had only been there a few times but never allowed to leave her covered coach. She had smelled the scent of the waves as they came in, though, and it had washed over her as if she were the sand itself. As she told Darry this, she let a curl of Darry's hair slide gently through her fingers.

Radha watched Darry closely and saw the heat in her gaze as she had looked at Jessa, though Jessa was lost in some stray thought. Darry had cast her eyes aside with some effort and an expression of shyness that Radha found terribly sultry.

She had looked just as beautiful the night before, as Radha had watched from a comfortable corner in Madam Salina's House, veiled within her spell as Darry had hosted a celebration for one of her men. She had treated each of her company with respect and affection, which they seemed worthy of. Radha had a skill for seeing to the heart of a man and knowing his worth, and Darry had chosen her friends very well indeed. Though they were considered outcasts for the most part, and bastard sons of powerful men, they seemed to mean the world to the Princess. They responded to her regard in kind, which had impressed Radha deeply. Darry had made them a family and a tribe unto themselves, a discarded generation of blood made kin by a woman's love and firsthand understanding of their rejection.

They spoke of the Queen and how Darry could fool almost anyone else, and then Darry asked, with great care, the name of Jessa's own mother.

Jessa had been surprised and her face showed it. Her smile had faded and a stillness settled within her body that Radha knew was Jessa's deepest sadness. Darry took Jessa's hand in her own.

"It is said," Jessa whispered, "that she rode a horse so black that the night sky would rise early every eve in search of its lost heart. Radha says the foal was named for the constellations and a prayer was said at her naming, for the Shaman swore the animal was blessed by the Vhaelin. When she was given to my mother a great celebration was held."

"Was there dancing?" Darry asked.

Jessa chuckled. "Yes, I'm sure there was."

"And your mother's name?"

Jessa glanced away and Radha wanted to call out across the room. *Speak it, child, and it will give you the freedom you so long for.*

Radha remembered well the day that Jessa had said her mother's name before Bharjah, and he had struck her with such force that her child's body had spun like a cloth doll across the tiles. He had followed her quickly and kicked her, then, as she lay gasping on the brightly colored floor, declared that the name was forbidden. Should Jessa ever speak it again, she would be given to her brothers and they would decide her punishment.

Jessa had been made to watch then, a girl of but ten years old, as one of the maidservants was brought forth to be murdered and torn apart by Sylban-Tenna's dogs. The woman's high-pitched screams had echoed off the jade-encrusted walls of Bharjah's throne room until at last her throat had been torn out. Jessa's brothers had laughed and goaded the animals to further violence until one of the dogs had to be slain when it would not leave its blood lust. Jessa had not spoken her mother's name since, not even within the secrets and privacy of their vast rooms and terraces.

"It is forbidden," Jessa whispered. "He said he would…that he would…"

Speak it, my child.

"I'll tell no one, Jess," Darry whispered in return.

Speak it, Jessa-Sirrah, take her back from him. Win your freedom with a single word.

"I swear upon my life," Darry said.

"It's not…I cannot," Jessa said, and Radha could hear the tears in her voice and the bone-deep fear that Jessa had never been able to banish. It was the last shackle she had left to throw off in order to walk free through the rest of her life.

Darry turned smoothly and faced her, still holding her hand. "You're in *my* land now, Jessa, not his. Within the walls of my home. If your father can reach across those leagues in the dead of night and a thousand stars away, then I'll protect you from his reach, no matter the cost."

Sweet child, how have they overlooked you so easily?

"She must've had eyes like yours," Darry declared softly. "I would know her name and hold it safe within my heart. I would know whom I should thank when you look at me so, with eyes the color of the southern seas at midnight."

Radha could see that Jessa reacted to the words, sweetly enticed by the honesty and strength of the woman she desired. *Sahla una patrice-ma, jhaloona fahdhee. You have a lover's tongue.*

"On my honor, Jess, I will hold it dear."

"Jhannina." Jessa spoke, then smiled. Sudden tears welled up and streaked her cheeks.

Jhannina de Cassey LaMarc of the Red-Tail Clan, Radha thought boldly. *Daughter to the slain warrior Tinsella de Sheen LaMarc and his widowed wife, priestess of the deepest bloodline reaching back to the blessed Neela herself. Neela, the greatest High Priestess the Vhaelin has ever known. Neela, who sacrificed what was left of her heart after the death of her beloved Tannen, only so that her power and blood would not be lost. Ancestor to my own Jhannina, a daughter to the Plains of Ibarris and a lost prophet of the Vhaelin. A prophet who sacrificed herself, in turn, so that our people would not perish beneath the sword of the Butcher. Lost blood and lost promise. Lost hope, until you, child. And oh, how she wept with joy when she looked into your eyes, holding you up to the stars as you wailed your fire like a battle cry into the night! She laughed as she blessed you and kissed your eyes, which were indeed her own.*

"My mother's name was Jhannina." Jessa spoke again, then laughed. And though the sound was quiet it was filled with joy. "And he can't hurt me any longer."

Darry caught a tear upon a careful thumb. "'Tis a beautiful name."

Jessa hid her face. "Yes," she said, wiping her cheeks.

"We don't seem to have such names here within Arravan," Darry said quietly, and Radha smiled at the clever turn. "Names filled with mystery and sounds that only a poet might understand. All I know of such things is the sea. I can only offer up the sea as having such rhyme. I would show you a beach that does not burn your feet, and you may walk within the surf for as long as you like. It will whisper as it washes against the skin of your legs, the names of the people you love. It will echo with the songs of fish so large that no ship may carry them should they be hooked upon a pole. So large that no net may hold them. It will tell you where the sun sleeps when it hisses into its bed at the edge of the world. Would you like me to take you there, Jessa?"

"Yes." Jessa accepted the invitation without hesitation. "I would like that very much."

"Then I promise that I will."

Darry talked of the sea and sat back as Jessa rested her head on Darry's shoulder. Still holding Jessa's hand, Darry told how once she had sailed on a great ship across the sea, seeing the Southern Islands and Wei-Jinn itself, and finding perhaps the place her grandmother had found. It was a place with a wall of orchids hidden in the mists beyond a fall of water so clear that Darry swore she could count the stars in it.

Radha left them and sat on her divan for a very long time, lost within her own vast memories. The touch of a hand smoothing down her back. The sound of a strong laugh and the sight of a child running in the sun, nearly lost within the wild grass. Each memory led to the next and she lay down eventually and rested her head on the pillow Jessa insisted she use, though Radha disliked such silly comforts.

I have seen your daughter become a woman, Jhannina. Radha spoke in prayer. *On this night, I have seen the deepest part of her childhood fear stripped away. I have seen her start upon the road to her freedom at last, and she will walk it beside the one who promised she would return. I have seen the birth of the Vhaelin's most sacred prophecy, and our power shall return now. Our blood shall usher in a new era.*

❖

Jessa lifted the shawl from the back of the divan and placed it over Radha's left shoulder as she curled on her side in a fair imitation of sleep.

"Have a care for her heart, Jessa," Radha said softly.

Jessa's hands stilled but she said nothing.

"She is a backwards woman and you're a most beautiful temptation. Your actions are inappropriate, child, do you understand? You're here for her brother, and Darrius has seen you with him, smiling and walking with him amidst the beauty of the gardens. It is very clear why you're here, at least to her."

Jessa's blood began to rise. "And?"

"And so you treat with her in the moonlight and touch her without reason to do so, but for your whim. It is innocent enough, though, perhaps, it is not so simple for her," Radha said. "If you have the intention of pursuing her then do so, but do not do it lightly, for you will pit her against her brother. There is bad blood between them and she is in danger from his hatred."

Jessa looked at the hearth. After a minute or two she shifted her legs to the side and sat against the divan, placing her right arm along Radha's.

"She is the one in your visions."

"Yes."

"A child of the Durand line."

"Not a son," Jessa whispered. "Not a son, but a daughter to the High King."

"Are you troubled that your desire lies in the body of a woman?" Radha asked.

"No. Not at all. Are you, Radha?" Jessa asked, her whisper filled with apprehension.

"I would bed her myself if I were not as old as the sea," Radha said.

Jessa let out a breath of startled laughter. "*Radha*."

Radha's raspy chuckle filled the air between them. "You had not thought, then, that you might be backwards?"

"It does not seem very backwards to me, Radha," Jessa said. "It feels like, like my want is…it feels very simple and honest."

"It is your heart."

"I hadn't thought of ever feeling anything like this," Jessa responded, amazed. "I had never thought that it would be so, so *much*."

"It's very lovely, isn't it."

"*Tua an ishla*, I cannot *breathe* when she is close," Jessa said, grateful to finally voice her feelings. "When she moves or when she laughs, I don't know, something breaks inside. And her hair smells like the sea and musk. Her skin is so soft that I wish to fill my hands with the touch of it. Such sweetness, Radha, she's the most magnificent thing I've ever known. Ever, Radha. I had no idea that one person could be so pleasing."

Radha's expression was filled with tender amusement.

"And her *mouth*," Jessa said, almost groaning on the words. "It's all I can do not to kiss her, and I am *dizzy* with want for the taste of her." She could not keep the despair from her voice, her words quickening with frustration. "Not that I have even the slightest *notion* as to what I'm doing. And the things I feel, they burn like nothing I've ever known before. Not even the touch of the Vhaelin compares. Not even that."

"And so this is desire, my child."

Jessa stared at her."Yes, thank you, Radha," she replied with quiet sarcasm. "I've managed to figure that much out for myself."

"What will you do?"

Jessa did not answer, laying her head on the cushion.

Radha touched Jessa's hair. "And if the Prince wishes you for his bride?"

"Malcolm does not wish anything from me, and I'm glad of it."

"He needs nothing but to find you beautiful to get an heir from you. He does not have to love you, Jessa. He does not even have to like you."

"I don't think that's why we're here. I am here as a ruse, at least for now. I am the excuse, Radha, though for what I cannot say. We're speaking of Bharjah's deeper play again, and I still haven't figured out what that is, though I'll swear by my braids that Joaquin spins at the center of it. He and Malcolm are devising something beyond the King's negotiations. I can see it when they speak. I *know* it. Joaquin with that clever look he gets when he's hiding something. And then I am brought forth like a bluff in a game of Suns, a shiny coin tossed before his secret wager in hopes of deceiving any eyes that may be watching."

"And if you're wrong, Jessa? If Joaquin finds his price and the boy's father agrees, if Bharjah agrees? What then?"

"I don't know." Jessa tried to see what the future held but was unable to do so. It seemed a very short road in her mind's eye and shrouded in darkness. "What if she doesn't want what I do?"

"If she does not love you as you love her?"

"Love?" Jessa asked in a breath.

"Do you deny it?"

Do I love her? It was not even a question, really, and Jessa knew it as soon as the words moved through her thoughts. It mattered very little that the feelings were new and strange and time had been short since that first moment she had gazed into Darry's eyes. *Love.* She knew very little of what it might be, but she knew enough to recognize it. The deep feelings she had when she merely looked at Darry were beyond desire. And though time had been short in the scope of her years, she had known Darry for a lifetime, if only from afar. Darry had easily fulfilled the promises given to her by the Waters of Truth, and then some. It was perhaps an unfair burden to place upon her, but it was the truth and Jessa knew it.

Love. Darrius.

"Do you love her?" Radha asked again.

"Yes." Jessa felt a profound thrill at the admission. "What am I to do?"

Radha was impressed that Jessa would accept this fact so freely despite all that she knew of life. Though Jessa had been sequestered, her seclusion had taught her a great many lessons that made her wise in the dark ways of the human heart. It had made her clever and trained her thoughts to follow hidden paths and long views that most did not even consider. By watching life as she had without truly being a part of it, she had become a dangerous woman in her knowledge of others.

For Jessa to be so near to her most precious desire, to finally be a part of that life she had only glimpsed from the outside looking in, her fear would be most formidable. "If you've not the courage to find out for yourself how she feels?" she said, "I'll not help you. Nor will the Vhaelin, I imagine."

"It is a reasonable question, Radha," Jessa said quietly.

"I know. But what if she does? You will have to choose."

"If she wants me that won't be difficult."

"There will be consequences," Radha said. "Hard prices to be paid, perhaps even violent ones."

"If she wants me, Radha, then let them come."

Radha smiled at the steel she heard and moved her hand gently in Jessa's hair. "You've grown into a very fine woman, Jessa-Sirrah," Radha whispered. "Your mother would've been most proud."

CHAPTER NINETEEN

The ladies of the Queen's Court moved through the crowded solar, their dresses between casual and formal. Though it was an official function it was decidedly private and unhampered by politics. The men were gone from the keep and it was a celebration of their liberty. The afternoon tea was somewhat of a tradition with the Queen when the Green Hills hunt was on, and the women present were her closest companions and Emmalyn's as well. A few names could not be avoided, but for the most part it was to be a friendly affair free of courtly pretense.

Tables were scattered about and the beautiful afternoon was filled with light breezes and summer warmth. There was wine, both warm spring red and cool Ravonese gold. The tea set on each table was merely for show, for if one were to pour and expect tea she would find a mild blend of Pentab Fire filling her delicate cup instead.

Musicians sat deeper within the gardens and out of sight, the lute and pipes seemingly drifting in with the breeze. And only the most delicious food was present: sweet breads and pastries and delicately spiced meats and cheese. The cooks had even prepared a plate of Lyonese rum sticks, the rolled bread heavy with the dark liquor.

Jessa watched the women around her with enjoyment, never having experienced such a gathering, as Bharjah's court was not known for frivolous functions. The Blooded women of her land were afforded little more station than the common people, for they were women, after all.

She smiled and was introduced to Emmalyn and Darry's cousin, Nina Lewellyn, arrived only that morning in Lokey. She was the daughter of Sulladon Lewellyn, Cecelia's brother, and Jessa liked her instantly. She had blondish red hair and freckles, and green eyes like Emmalyn, her sense of humor extremely bold and more than somewhat inappropriate. Jessa was still not comfortable with the laughter that always seemed to hover upon the edges of life in Blackstone Keep, but she considered it the most pleasant thing she might ever have to get used to.

She met the sisters to the infamous Bentley, and they were as beautiful as he was handsome. Alisha found her immediately, pulling her into their circle. She was a delicate woman and very pretty, and Jessa found her most appealing, liking her eyes and her sweet smile. And there was Melora Salish as well, who moved through the room as if she owned it, her brother's wife at her arm. As sister to Malcolm's most trusted advisor, Melora was a permanent fixture at any function no matter who the guest list might contain.

The older women of the court were present as well, friends who had been lifelong companions to Cecelia and a few distant relatives, recently arrived for the upcoming Solstice events. When Jessa was introduced they doted on her and she let them, treating them with the same ease and respect that she showed her Radha. Some had even known Owen's mother, Marget of the Moonblood orchids. One woman was Cecelia's own aunt, the only Lewellyn of her generation aside from Cecelia's father, who still lived.

When talk turned to Jessa's dresses and how they blended so beautifully the Lyonese and Arravan styles, she was most pleased to tell them that Radha had designed and made them.

As the afternoon wore on with no sign of Darry, Jessa could not help but feel her absence. As the talk about fashions continued, Jessa peered into her chalice and felt strangely abandoned, though she knew that was not the case. *How you must hate these parties, Akasha, and I don't blame you. The women all seem wonderful and kind and I'm having a surprisingly good time, but it's a lot of them in one place and all so unlike you.* Jessa turned as Alisha filled her goblet once more.

"Not to worry, Jessa." Alisha grinned. "'Tis a light vintage."

"Compared to what?"

Alisha's eyes lit up. "That's our girl."

But Jessa's humor did not last and she searched through the party once more.

Who is it that you're worried for, Jessa? Emmalyn liked Jessa's deep blue sari and noticed the curves of her beautiful body, somewhat on display though the dress fell within the rules of etiquette. It was the first court function that Jessa attended without her veil, and Emmalyn had heard more than one comment pertaining to Jessa's beauty. *You look decidedly forlorn, my friend.* Emmalyn glanced about the crowded room. *Perhaps a tad too much all at once?*

When Emmalyn suggested the party move into the gardens and

they enjoy the air now that the midday sun had passed over, the proposal was met with a cheer. The ladies mobilized as if they were a small army, Emmalyn taking Jessa's arm.

"You're not drinking enough, Jessa," she teased, wanting to make her smile.

"If I drink any more, Em, I'll be drunk. This would not please my Radha in the least."

"We're *all* getting drunk, my sweet," Emmalyn replied. "Welcome to one of my mother's afternoon tea parties. Now that the men are gone and the keep is ours, we have no intention of wasting such freedom."

Darry watched the party from the upper balcony of the great hall, finding Jessa the instant she stepped outside. The sari she wore was beautiful. Jessa was at the center of the inner circle and she supposed that was Emma's doing, which she was thankful for.

"Nina." Darry was surprised to see her cousin for the first time in just over a year. Darry had known that Nina was coming, but not when. She expected to see many of her relatives, as Jacob's wedding was barely two months away.

And then perhaps another wedding, most likely Winter's Eve if Malcolm isn't too much of a bloody fool. Or perhaps I'm the fool.

She had wanted to kiss Jessa so badly she was afraid something inside her would break, and she had thought at the time that Jessa had looked as if she wanted to be kissed.

And so what if she had? Are you to seduce your brother's possible bride? Sweet Gamar, I'm so completely damned.

She had returned to her loft in the barracks after leaving Jessa and sat on her small balcony for hours, watching as the stars wheeled their way through the sky. And she had prayed, which she had not done in earnest for many years. She had asked Gamar to give Jessa whatever she wanted. She deserved all that her heart desired and the world at her feet. She deserved love beyond all measure and good sense. Even if Darry could not be the one to give it to her, Darry wanted it just the same. She wanted Jessa to be happy and protected and to know every wonderful touch of a lover who adored her. *Even if it will not be me.*

The understanding of that fact cut deep yet again, and something inside her was bleeding at the knowledge.

"Hello, Darrius."

Darry's shoulders twitched but she turned smoothly.

Melora Salish smiled at Darry and rested against the balcony railing, the upper expanse of the hall spreading out behind her.

Melora's auburn hair fell in careful ringlets about her face and onto the shoulders of her deep russet gown. Her skin wonderfully pale and flawless, the delicate paint she wore at her eyes matched her dress and added to her attractiveness. Melora's smile deepened at Darry's appraisal.

"Hello, Melora." Darry answered, marshalling her thoughts. *Bloody hell, maybe I really* am *cursed. I hadn't thought of that.*

"I looked for you at the fête, but apparently I wasn't good enough for you to bother with."

Darry closed her eyes for longer than necessary, not wanting to open them.

"And we used to be such good friends," Melora said softly.

"That was a long time ago, Melora."

"Yes. But we were good friends, nonetheless."

"Yes."

"Before you felt the need to be a man."

Darry laughed.

"Have you found, I wonder, that this way is better?"

"No. It's just who I am."

"You're a woman."

"Yes," Darry responded. "I am decidedly so."

"And are you really satisfied by that sort of thing?"

At least you get right to the point. "Perhaps your many lovers, Melora, have not been doing it right."

Melora's smile was quick. "Yes, lovers. Shall we speak of lovers, Princess?"

"Do we want to play this game again?" Darry asked.

"And what game would that be?"

Darry let out a tired sigh. "The one where you try to make me feel ashamed, and I retaliate by slandering your husband's questionable skills in the bedroom. Which leads, then, to my reciting the list of your many affairs and your claws coming out. Are you not bored of that by now?"

"My husband is quite capable, thank you, Darrius."

"Is that why you refused to take his name?"

Melora gave a wave of her hand. "The Salish name is mine and I've earned it. I saw no need to give it up."

"And I respect you for that."

"Do you?"

"Yes."

"Why?"

"Why should you bend before a man's name when your own is more than ample? It's never made much sense to me. Least of all for you."

"Capitulation, yes. It can be troubling at times."

They stared at one another.

"You've never bent in your life, Melora."

Melora laughed. "Neither have you, Darrius."

"Not much, anyway." Darry smiled, the hairs upon the back of her neck prickling.

"Perhaps, though, you've found yourself upon your knees?"

"As have you, I'm sure."

Melora nodded with a sly smile and studied her chalice. "Had we known when we were girls that love would be so complicated, I wonder if we would've bothered thinking on it so much."

"Actually, I was rather occupied with learning the sword."

Melora let out a quiet laugh. "Yes, that's true."

Darry examined her closely, not liking what she felt, as always. She said the words yet again, as she had many times over the years, wondering if she would receive an answer this time. "I never meant to hurt you, Melora. I hope you know that."

"They were only rumors, Darrius. How could you know that by declaring yourself as you did that I would be tainted as well? At least for a time."

"I didn't."

"No. You didn't think, did you?"

"Still bitter, I see."

"Not in the least. I've found that it adds a bit of mystery to my reputation. Spice, if you will. I have a past now. Was she the lover of our backwards Princess? Did they kiss? It is only spice."

"A woman needs her mystery."

"Yes, it helps."

Darry thought of several responses but saw no use in voicing them. Melora wanted something or she would not be there. Prolonging their conversation was not high on her list of priorities for the day.

"You did bend once, though, didn't you," Melora said softly. "But I suppose that can be overlooked because of your station. It's hard, I should imagine, to defy a king."

Darry waited patiently.

"I was actually quite impressed at how you handled the Aidan McKenna affair. Much better than I thought you would've, considering your temper."

Darry let out a harsh breath. She could not have been more shocked if Gamar himself had walked up and kissed her.

"I would have thought you might've given up your charade after that and come to your senses. Perhaps married your Bentley Greeves for all that he's a complete cad. But you stayed loyal no matter what." She lifted her wine. "Cheers."

Aidan, Darry acknowledged, her thoughts stumbling. *You know of Aidan.*

Melora frowned though her eyes were bright. "You look pale, my dear. Are you quite all right?"

"What do you know of Aidan McKenna?"

"Are you trying to tell me that you don't know?" Melora asked, then laughed with obvious delight. "Your father and Malcolm, they paid her family a tidy sum of gold to leave Lokey. No doubt to avoid the disgrace and shame of your affair going public. I should imagine, actually, quite a *lot* of gold was paid."

Darry's pulse quickened with a violent surge of blood.

"She didn't want to leave at first, of course. After all, she *was* a backwards girl. Sharing her spirit with royalty was most likely something of a thrill. Someone of that ilk cannot find much better, I imagine. Marteen said that she wept terribly." Melora tipped her head to the side a touch. "They had to threaten her father's station in the end in order to make the poor girl see reason. It happened very quickly after that, as I'm sure you remember. As I said, I was surprised that you surrendered so easily to your father's justice. No matter what I think of you, you've always had a spine, which is more than I can say for most."

Darry swallowed and it seemed as if a dagger was lodged in her throat.

"I would've thought you'd chase after her, or some such romantic nonsense," Melora went on. "But for once you did the respectable thing."

"Who told you this?"

Melora recoiled at the tone. "What does it matter, Darrius?"

"Who told you this?" Darry demanded again.

"You cannot think that your father and Malcolm were just going to let you run *wild*, did you? Darrius, my sweet, you were sleeping with another *woman*. You were endangering your family's reputation and your brother's future. Best that you have a care for that sometime soon, for when Malcolm takes the throne no doubt things will change for you."

"You said…you said, Marteen? Malcolm's councilor?"

"You ran off to the sea." Melora sighed. "I suppose that was a bit romantic in and of itself. How did you find a ship full men? Did you try your luck, Princess?"

Darry reached back through the years for some sort of memory that would secure the crumbling ground beneath her.

"You did, didn't you," Melora said in subtle taunt. "Did the rocking of the ship ease the pain of that first time? Was his cock gentle? Were you quiet while the others slept and he pushed inside of you?"

"*Melora*." Darry was still trying to get her bearings. *That's not what happened. It isn't. Oh god, Aidan, tell me they didn't.*

Melora laughed quietly, a slight pout touching her features. "Poor Darry." Her voice was mocking. "I suppose you should've just found a man who was willing to be your wife. Your handsome Arkady Winnows seems an accommodating fellow, at least on the dance floor. Perhaps something there can be nurtured, if you're careful. Is a bastard more pliant? Perhaps he wouldn't mind if you wore a phallus, do you think?"

"I think you're lying."

"Really?" Melora countered. "How would I know, then, that your gentle little Aidan gave your father back the necklace? It was your grandmother Lewellyn's, wasn't it? A nice gold linked chain with a sapphire the size of a bloody walnut?"

A small sound escaped Darry's throat. "Your father told her it wasn't necessary, of course, but the silly girl insisted. She said something about honor and saving some small measure of it, or some such foolish nonsense."

"You *lie*." Darry's voice broke.

"No," Melora returned almost kindly, and then she laughed, the quiet sound very close to mocking. "You're making me feel almost guilty, Darrius. This is all too perfect."

"You're a liar."

"No," Melora repeated. "But if you think so then you should ask your mother, Princess. No doubt the Queen will have a prettier story for you, to soothe your heart and send you off to sleep. She's had plenty of time to think of one."

Darry stood unmoving as Melora pushed from the railing and walked toward her. She reached out and Darry flinched. Melora's perfume filled Darry's senses and she closed her eyes at the brush of Melora's soft skin against her cheek.

"You'll be lucky if your favorite courtesan doesn't meet the same fate," Melora whispered beside her ear. Darry jerked in reaction to her words. "Marin Corvinus, isn't that her name? Did you sneak back that night, Darry, and take what she offered at Madam Salina's? I believe that Malcolm is preparing a very swift horse for her even as we speak. Off into the night as little Aidan went."

Melora's lips brushed Darry's ear with the merest hint of a kiss. "It's too bad," she said, her breasts pressing close as her left hand slid beneath Darry's jacket. Her touch was suggestive at the small of Darry's back. "I imagine your whore was a much livelier fuck than your little Aidan. A woman like you? Timid was never your style, Darry."

Melora kissed Darry's cheek tenderly, her lips lingering before she stepped back. "Perhaps I'll have Garwyn bring the carriage around," she said softly. "Thank you for a full afternoon, Princess. Your mother's parties are always such fun."

She walked back along the balcony and Darry watched her go, holding on to her composure with every measure of strength she possessed. Only after Melora lifted her skirt above her shoes and swept down the wide staircase did she let go.

Darry let out a choked cry of anguish and grabbed for the wall beside her. She gripped the bound red curtain instead and bent at the waist in a rush of physical pain. The drape pulled against its golden rings and popped them one at a time in response to the sudden force. The curtain fell in a cascade of fabric from high overhead and poured downward.

She stood slowly, her head filling with the sound of the heavy material as it pooled on the floor beside her. She stared down the length of the empty balcony, lost within the brutal rush of her *Cha-diah* blood and more than happy to let it come. Her body trembled as her entire world turned on a heartbeat.

❖

Marteen Salish studied his sister upon one of the divans by the hearth, the lamp dusting her features in a pale glow. She still wore the dress she had that afternoon, though her shoes were off and he could see her bare feet, her right leg hooked casually over her left knee. Her eyes were closed and she rested the fingers of her right hand against her temple, looking for all the world as if she had dozed off.

"Is it done?"

Melora opened her eyes. "She hadn't a clue, Marteen, not a bloody clue. I have to admire the timid Aidan McKenna for a job well done. She must've been particularly brutal to have thrown Darry so far off the scent."

Marteen took off his jacket as he went to her. He tossed it on the couch opposite the one his sister occupied, then sat on the last cushion. "Don't tell me you didn't enjoy it, Mel."

"That's really beside the point." she answered. "I've just committed political suicide."

"Do you think she'll come after you?"

"Why should she? I'm not the one who betrayed her."

"Betrayed?"

"It will come out," she responded. "And I'll be banned from court. Most likely by Cecelia herself, for revealing her nasty little secret."

"Her circle is unimportant."

"Yes. It is Malcolm's that matters."

"Yes, it is. His is the court of the future. And I promise you shall have an elevated place in the accounting of it."

"He's not the King yet. Keep that in mind."

"Soon," Marteen replied. "Even sooner than some have predicted, I'll wager."

"Is he really planning to marry her?" Melora asked. "A woman of foreign blood? I can't see it. Owen will never allow it. He may be haggling now in order to buy time, trying to find out what Bharjah is thinking. But a child of Bharjah's blood upon the Blackwood Throne?"

"She's irrelevant, at least for now. It's Joaquin who is important."

"And in the meantime I'll sit in this house and wait, yes? Made a pariah by the truth." She laughed. "There's a first for me."

"No, Mel. Do you think I would let you be thrown to the wolves of the Queen without a care for your future?"

"I don't know, Marteen. I just stood before a woman I used to hold very dear and ripped her heart out. Though I hold no feelings for her now but contempt and pity, I'm not foolish enough to think I won't pay for that in some way. The deep repercussions for this may not be what Malcolm expects."

"How so?"

"I don't know," she replied. "This is what I'm trying to tell you. Darry has always been an unknown. It's why Malcolm hates her so, even more than her backwards bent. Malcolm has *never* known what she'll do, and he has always underestimated her power."

"Sweetling, she has no power."

"She has a great deal of power, and for all that you and Malcolm scheme and plot, it amazes me that you can't see it."

"What sort of power does she have?"

"The power of a favored child."

Marteen mulled over her words with a frown. "Perhaps, but that mea—"

"That means more than you think it does. And have you considered that she might go after Malcolm? Has *he* considered that?"

"Of course we have. We're counting on it."

Melora laughed, turning her attention to the empty hearth. "I've seen her fight and so have you. For all that it crushes etiquette and propriety under its boot heel, she's damned good at it, and most certainly better than *he* is."

"She would never challenge him in such a manner."

"Don't be so sure."

"Owen would never allow it."

"Owen has betrayed her!" Melora snapped. "Even though we hate each other now, I knew her well once upon a day. She has always been ruled by her heart. He can no more control her now than he could a dog that's turned. If her dagger winds up at Malcolm's feet, short of locking her in chains and stripping her of her rank and title, he can do nothing about it. And even then Malcolm must answer her challenge or be branded a coward, accused of using his station to avoid a reckoning for his actions."

Marteen smiled at her.

"What?" Melora demanded.

"And should Owen be forced to do such a thing, how do you think he will look then upon the throne? Such a great burden as that, being the architect of his own child's destruction. Forced to cast her out in order to protect the succession to his throne. Cast out like an orphan, poor little Darry. And Cecelia, our sad and noble Queen. Divided between her husband and her sweet little backwards girl? Their bed will be cold for months, maybe even years. It's happened before." He clicked his tongue. "So heavy is the burden of the crown."

Melora stared in disbelief. "You can't possibly be serious, though even if you *are*, Malcolm would still have to answer her challenge."

"He may choose a champion in his stead. And it is the King's right to step in if he feels so inclined, do not forget. What would you do, Mel, if your children went to war? Darrius would never raise her sword to her King, and Owen will know that, despite any bad blood. It is his right within the strictures of the Blooded Duel to usurp Malcolm's place on the field of honor. Standing in the yards, a sword in her hand as she faces her own father?" he said. "No matter what he's done to her she would forfeit and walk away. Even you cannot predict an outcome other than that. And then it's off into the night with you, little backwards cunt. One problem solved."

"So you hope."

"It's merely one scenario among many that play to our advantage."

"And so why is *she* here, Bharjah's little songbird?"

"She has a part to play, to be sure. But for now she buys us time."

"Time for what?"

"Time to sway Joaquin."

Darry sat in the far corner of her old chambers with her knees drawn up. Her hands would occasionally tremble and she would pull at the dark material of her trousers and hold tight.

The panther pulsed thick in her blood and every so often she would catch her breath and tip her head back at the brutal rush of its power. She would smile as well, now and then, as the hours passed, watching as if from a distance as her senses adapted and absorbed the primal force of it all. She could smell human flesh beyond the walls that she had once called her own, and the scent was pungent and dark.

She had not slept there since Aidan. They had made love in the bed more than a few times and discovered the pleasures that passion can bring. Discovered the secrets of love and the joys of yielding up one's body to the touch of another. After Aidan had spurned her she could find no peace in the familiar confines of her childhood rooms.

Darry could smell the smoke from the hearths in the kitchens, no matter that it was half a world away. She could smell the meat cooking. She could smell the blood and her stomach reacted. Her shoulders pulled inward against the onslaught of hunger.

She wanted to prowl. She wanted to move and strike and bend low upon the hunt, searching out her prey amidst the cold stones and dead timber.

But you will come to me, won't you?

She heard voices, distant and unconcerned in their conversation. She could smell the change in the world and knew the sun was rising.

I can wait.

CHAPTER TWENTY

Cecelia turned from the patio and walked slowly through the hall. She was considering the party from the day before and smiled occasionally, thinking it had gone rather well. *But for Darry's absence, though I'm not surprised. I know how you chafe at such functions, sweet Cat. Too many ladies and too much gossip. I would've thought you'd be there for Jessa, though.*

Cecelia pulled out a chair from one of the tables and sat down. *Gossip. That subtle blade has cut you too often.*

Jessa seemed to have enjoyed herself and been somewhat enchanted by Nina Lewellyn in the process. Cecelia grinned at the thought of her niece, so utterly without shame and as wild as Darry had ever been. *What a mouth you have on you, sweet girl. I've not heard such cursing since last I saw your father.*

She lifted her chalice and took a slow drink. *Where are you hiding, Cat?*

Movement caught her eyes and Bentley walked beneath the main entrance. His uniform was impeccable as always and he carried his shoulders back with an easy grace. *Bloody hell and hounds but is there a Greeves man who isn't beautiful?*

She could see his expression as he neared, and though she had expected his half-hidden smile at being summoned, she was greeted instead by a rather sedate look as he clicked his boot heels and bowed his head before her.

"Lieutenant."

"My Lady."

"Where is my daughter?"

"I don't know, my Lady."

Cecelia turned to face him more directly. "I beg your pardon?"

"It does in fact happen, my Lady."

"You had watch together last night. She didn't tell you her plans?"

Bentley's left hand tightened on his sword hilt. "No."

Cecelia regarded him closely, knowing him almost as well as one of her own children. "She was not at my party yesterday," she said, and his eyes darkened at her words, a tiny crease appearing above the bridge of his nose. "Nor dinner last night. Nor at lunch today, though she was expected. She was on duty with you, was she not?"

"She was on the roster, yes."

"Don't play games, Bentley. Was she on duty with you or not?"

"No, my Lady, she was not."

"But she was supposed to be."

"Yes, my Lady."

"She missed her turn at guard?"

"Yes, my Lady."

Cecelia sat forward in her chair. "What excuse did she give?"

Bentley said nothing.

"Answer me, Lieutenant."

"She gave none, my Lady," he replied. "No one has seen her since yesterday afternoon, when she left the barracks to attend your party."

"She came to the party?"

"She was not looking forward to it, if you must know. But she had every intention of attending."

Cecelia pushed against the table and rose, then walked several feet before turning back to him. "Well, where in the bloody hell is she then? Grissom must be livid."

"He's not pleased, my Lady."

"You've looked for her?"

"Yes, my Lady. Darry's Boys have been looking since last night."

"Don't tell me that she's drunk in a tavern somewhere, Bentley Greeves, or I shall strip the hide from both your bones."

"Bentley," she said with less heat, seeing his worry.

"No, my Lady, she's not drunk in a tavern somewhere."

When he said no more, Cecelia's concern escalated. "Bentley, please."

"I'm afraid something's wrong, mum, and I don't know where she'd go. Her loft is empty and the bed wasn't slept in. She would never disregard her duty, not *ever*. When she didn't show up I sent Arkady and Etienne to look for her, then later the others as well when they came back without her. The only place we haven't searched is the residence."

"Thank you, Bentley," she said quietly. "You may return to your duties. I will see to my daughter."

Bentley stood his ground, a look of stubbornness settling on his features.

"Then wait here. I'll send her along."

"You know where she is?" he asked quickly as she walked away, striding with purpose toward the main arch. "Mum?"

"Wait here."

❖

Cecelia stood outside the door to Darry's old chambers and stared at the handle, thinking of a day long ago when she had done the very same thing, the same fear moving even now within her breast.

Cecelia stepped across the threshold and into the shadows, closing the door.

The main chamber was murky and the furniture covered with tarps, the bed stripped clean and no doubt filled with dust. The chairs and the divan looked oddly sinister beneath their covers. The shutters were closed along the balustrade and Cecelia remembered when last they had been open.

Darry had stood before them so young and lean and looking as if she were about to break beneath all her strength. Cecelia had watched her lock the shutters and stood helpless as Darry had picked up her satchel of belongings. Darry had said she was going away for a few days and kissed her cheek and Cecelia had let her go, not knowing that a few days would turn into one of the longest years of her life.

The sea and all its terrible dangers had taken her daughter, and Cecilia could not do a thing once it was known. Darry had even left poor Bentley behind. The boy was absolutely lost without her and nearly found his own sort of destruction in her absence.

Cecelia moved into the main room. "Darry?"

Darry closed her eyes at the voice. Her mother's scent was heady and filled with fear. Darry tipped her head back against the wall and her stomach churned with violence. The stones were pleasing against her back, and she almost groaned at their coolness for her blood was very warm and not entirely her own.

Cecelia stood very still, allowing her eyes to adjust. "Darrius, answer me."

"I'm here."

Cecelia narrowed her eyes into the darker shadows beside the hearth and saw the white of Darry's tunic and then her hair. She walked to her, her fear rising like a knife when Darry's eyes met her own. She stopped several feet away. "What is happening here, Darrius?"

"What's happening here, Mother?"

The cruel mocking of Darry's tone startled Cecelia. "You've neglected your duty, Darrius, and you've worried a great many people. What are you doing in here?"

Darry laughed. "Duty, yes. I've neglected my duty, haven't I? And these are my rooms. Have I not the right to be here?"

"Yes, of course." Cecelia tried to find her footing without slipping. "They will always be yours. It's just…I thought you no longer wanted them."

"No," Darry said. "You're right. I would sooner see them burn than spend another night beneath your fucking roof."

"Stop this, Cat." She took a step closer. "What is this?" *What has happened?*

"I spoke with Melora Salish, yesterday," Darry answered. "Who used to be my friend. Who used to share secrets with me."

Cecelia let out a hard breath. *Melora.*

"She had one last secret to tell," Darry said. "I think she's been saving it, like a special present for Winter's Eve. Holding it tight to her breast for when it would please her most to give it to me."

"And this secret was what?"

"Her secret was Aidan."

The name stunned Cecelia to the core. *No, Cat. That's not what she told you.*

Darry's smile was savage. "*My* Aidan, Mother, and Melora clearly enjoyed the telling of it. The secret of my Aidan and what really happened to her."

Cecelia's heart twisted beneath the venom within Darry's voice, but she gathered her courage quickly. "What did she tell you?"

"What did she tell you?" Darry mimicked.

"*Darrius.*"

"*Mother.*"

"Answer me!"

"Answer me!" Darry repeated, and laughed, pushing from the wall then moving through the shadows. "Answer me, answer me…" she said, her voice fading in confusion as if the words themselves made no sense. She shook her head with a jerk, as if something pulled at her, and a strange, guttural noise moved past her lips. Cecelia flinched at the sound. "Answer me. Answer you what?" Darry faced her. "You should be answering *me*."

Cecelia understood then that she could do nothing but give in. Darry would never relent when so cornered. Never. The conversation they were about to have, that she was about to provoke by her next words, was to have never taken place, and that had been by her own desperate design. She savored the silence between them for as long as she dared. "Will you let me explain what happened?"

"I *know* what happened, my *Queen*."

Cecelia cringed at the tone and the disdainful use of her title. "Do not take that tack with me, Darrius Lauranna. I asked you a direct question."

"And I gave you a direct answer."

"Your anger will solve nothing, Darrius. Let us just talk."

"Talking and talking. I'm *done* with fucking *talk*ing!" Darry yelled. "I'm *done* with letting them pick at my flesh like carrion!" She pounded her fists against her temple as she began to pace back and forth over a few short feet of space. "Picking and picking…picking at me…"

Cecelia had never seen her like this. It was as if something in Darry's mind had broken loose. She had seen her temper before, yes, but not like this, and it caused her hands to tremble. Darry was speaking under her breath, lost within something powerful that Cecelia could sense but did not understand.

"Always trying to do what's best."

"Darry, please, just calm down." Cecelia stepped closer with great care.

"It's all meant nothing. *Nothing*."

"Darling, please."

Darry bent forward as she released her power and it filled the room with its brutality, her scream but raw noise. From deep within the far Green Hills Darry felt an answering howl of pain echo along her spine, and for an instant she smelled the depths of the wild land, thick and dark within her senses. Her world tilted as she stood in two places at once, a shaft of pain creasing behind her eyes.

"*Darry*!" Cecelia called.

The silence echoed with violence.

"Darrius?" Cecelia whispered.

Darry turned to her as if startled. "I am finished with hiding myself and turning away. And I'm done with my duty to your fucking liar of a husband, do you hear? I play no more at rebellion. It is in earnest until this is *over*."

The declaration sent a chill through Cecelia, and she tried to gather herself, frantically searching for the proper course. "What will you do?" she said, her own tone charged with emotion. "Challenge your—"

"I want blood!" Darry cried out. "Did Melora lie? Did you know? *Did* you?"

There it is, Cecelia thought with despair. *But I'll not play by your rules, Darry, not like this. You must breathe, you must just breathe, please.* "That she loved you?" Cecelia asked softly, barely finding her voice against the rage assaulting her senses. "That Aidan loved you?"

Darry said nothing, seemingly puzzled by the question. "Aidan."

"Yes, Aidan," Cecelia repeated in a soothing voice. "I knew that she loved you from the first moment she saw you. You and Wyatt walked in and Aidan looked up. It was as if she had seen the sun for the first time. I thought it was your brother, but you walked across the study wanting to see Emma's thread…and Aidan's eyes followed you as if they could look nowhere else." The shaking of Darry's body began to slow as she took a breath. "And the blush rose along her neck. I knew she was lost."

"What have you done?"

That's it. Just breathe, baby. "And Aidan laughed at something you said. Do you remember? And you smiled at her."

"Did you know, Mother?"

"After the spring moon I knew you were lovers," Cecelia said, ignoring the question yet again. "She was always so open and her eyes could hide nothing. Her smile—"

"Mother, *please*."

"Not at first," Cecelia said, her voice trembling. "Not at first, my darling."

Darry leaned forward at the pain in her stomach and clutched her tunic as the bile rose in her throat and she swallowed it. *I can smell your blood. I can smell it, Mother. Get away from me. Please, please get away.* She had wanted to let it come and so it had, but it was too much. *Hinsa!*

"I didn't know until you were gone on the *Zephyr*," Cecelia said. She knew she sounded desperate despite the fact that it was the truth. "Cat, please, I didn't know until it was too late."

Darry lashed out at the hands at her face. "Don't touch me!"

Cecelia felt pain in her right arm and a glancing blow against her temple, and she stumbled backward. She caught herself on the arm of a chair and spun back, staring as Darry advanced.

Darry stopped with a jerk. She stepped back in an awkward manner and grasped her head between her hands. *Hinsa, please…help me.*

"I thought…" Darry spoke in a strangled voice, trying to catch her breath. "I thought I wasn't enough." Darry tightened her hands on her skull, trying to keep it from splitting. "I thought she didn't love me anymore… she said…all those things she said, that I did something wrong."

"No," Cecelia said quickly. "No, my love, you did nothing wrong."

Darry felt Hinsa's presence in the maze and it invaded her very bones. Her flesh vibrated beneath the panther's elemental authority and her savage blood began to recede.

She closed her eyes and let out a long, slow breath at the blessed sound. Hinsa's divine purr of calm moved in her bones and she wiped at her mouth. "Yes, I did something wrong."

"You did *nothing* wrong," Cecelia repeated.

Darry took another long breath and everything flowed through her. She felt the wrenching need for blood lessen. "I believed."

Cecelia took a tentative step. "What did you believe, Darry?"

Darry wiped her face and stepped back in response to the approach, keeping the distance between them. "That I could have the love of my family and still have a love of my own."

"Darry, you can. I *swear* it is so," Cecelia said. "You must trust me, please."

"*Trust* you? You took the girl I loved and threatened her family with ruin should she see me again." Darry backed farther away. "You paid them in gold the price you thought my heart was worth. You let me think it was *me*! *Me*! And all these years I wasn't good enough. Not worthy of someone's love or their desire. I wasn't good enough."

"Darrius, no!"

"Your tongue is filled with lies, Mother."

"Yes," Cecelia answered. "But not this."

Darry's smile was bitter. "This was my fault."

"No, my love. No, Darry."

"So let's hear it, Mother. What's your excuse?"

Cecelia's heart tore open at the tears that rose in Darry's eyes and then fell. "Will you listen?"

"I asked. I'm not so weak as to turn away now."

The words were like bait before her, but Cecelia ignored them. "I did not know what Malcolm had done, or that your father sanctioned it. I didn't know until you were gone and it was too late to change it.

"And Malcolm was wrong in what he did, as was Owen, and I let them know my feelings emphatically," Cecelia continued. "But when you returned with the *Zephyr* the following year, you seemed happy, and I thought you'd made peace with Aidan's rejection. And you were home, Darry, and you…" Cecelia reached out to her, unable to stand it any longer.

Darry remained silent and utterly still.

Cecelia lowered her hand. "I thought it served no purpose to tell you what had been done, for it was over and there was no going back. There was no fixing it no matter how badly I wanted to. That was my decision, Cat, that we would keep the truth from you. I didn't want you broken from your father completely. He loves you dearly. Truly he does, Darry, truly he loves you. And I couldn't take it if you went to war with Malcolm. I would see neither of my children destroyed.

"But I had no idea that you thought such harsh and hurtful things. Such terribly untrue things, Darrius. And If I had known, no matter the consequences or the price, you and I would've had this discussion a very long time ago."

"She wanted to run," Darry said quietly. "Aidan begged me, while I held her in my arms. She bade me to disown my family and run with her and we would find a place to be safe. She was afraid of my position. We made love in this very room…and I told her no. I promised her we had nothing to fear from the people who loved me."

Cecelia closed her eyes. "No, Darry."

"I'll never make that mistake again, my Lady."

"Darry, *please*."

"I thought if I were strong and true and a good daughter that Malcolm could hate me all he wanted, but he would never be allowed to openly attack me. That even my father, in his confusion and uncertainty toward me, that even so he would never allow such a thing."

"I will see to your brother, Darrius," Cecelia said in a hard voice. *And Marteen Salish.* "And Melora will—"

"Don't bother," Darry growled. "Will you punish them for telling the truth?" Her smile was cold and her eyes were free of tears. "I should thank Melora, actually, though she would drop dead from the disappointment."

Bentley's voice sounded, close along the balustrade.

"Tell your son that if he approaches Marin Corvinus in any way he shall find my dagger in the ground at his feet," Darry said.

Cecelia's eyes darkened in question.

"He'll know. Make very sure you tell him that."

Marin Corvinus. Cecelia locked the name away. *A lover? Do you have a lover, my daughter? She is safe, I swear my oath upon it.* "Darry, you—"

"If he hurts anyone that I care for," she interrupted, "I swear by all that's holy, I shall meet him in the yards and gut him like a fucking Solstice pig. And then your poor King Owen Durand will have to decide, at last, what to do with his backwards *mistake* of a child."

Cecelia grabbed Darry's jacket, yanking her close as Darry stood unflinching.

"Not to worry, Mum," Darry whispered. "I'll be gone after the tournament."

"No."

"I would leave even now, but you see? I have a sudden desire to win the Laurel of Victory first. I will crown my father the truest heart, then forget that I ever knew him. No doubt it will be a huge relief to many, myself included."

Cecelia grabbed Darry's shoulders and pulled her firmly into her arms. "Don't do this!" she pleaded. "For the love of Gamar, Darry, don't do it."

Darry did not return the embrace. "I'm very angry, Mother."

"I know you are, baby. I know it."

"So just let me go."

"I cannot do that."

Darry pulled roughly at her mother's arms and wrenched free. She moved to the balustrade door without even a last look, then jerked the bolt and threw the door open.

Bentley pushed from the railing. He had never seen such an expression on Darry's face before. He waited as she walked to him. "What has happened?"

"It was not Aidan's choice to leave me."

Bentley looked up, watching Cecelia as she stood in the doorway. "Whose was it then?"

"My father's. And Malcolm's, of course. They threatened to destroy her family. They paid them gold when she spurned me as ordered. Blood money, for Aidan's love and mine."

"I'll go with you," he said.

"No, Bentley."

"Darrius."

"I'll find you, my friend. Don't be afraid."

"I'll come with you."

"See to my mother, please," she whispered. "Make sure that she gets to her rooms."

Bentley placed her hand against his chest, his fingers warm and gentle on her skin. "Don't leave me behind again…promise you won't do that."

"I won't."

She slid her hand free and walked away. Bentley saw within her movements every dangerous thing her strength had ever hinted at and the lethal grace of the mountain cat she was named for and whose blood ran within her veins. She disappeared beyond the curve of the stairs as she descended.

"What have you done?" he said as he spun about.

"Do not judge me, Bentley," Cecelia answered in a rough voice. "You don't know all that happened."

"What more must I know, Mum?" he said, refusing to back down. "She's been haunted by Aidan for years and punishing herself for something she refuses to share. I've always thought that Aidan wanted to run and Darry wouldn't. I know that Aidan was afraid of Malcolm."

Cecelia blinked at his words and closed the distance between them. "How do you know this? What did he want?"

"Aidan came to me. She was afraid of what Darry might do if she knew that Malcolm had approached her. She wouldn't say what happened or what he said, but for a long time she was very frightened and would avoid him. She wanted me to swear an oath to help keep it from Darry, but I wouldn't do it. She struck me, and we had a terrible fight. I agreed at the last for I saw there was no other way."

Cecelia could see his pain at the memory and she was astonished that Aidan would ever strike anyone. "It would appear, Bentley, that you're closer to my daughter than I have ever been. Though I thought differently but an hour ago."

Bentley could see the exhaustion and the blatant sorrow on her face.

"She has sworn to leave after the tournament," Cecelia said.

"Then we shall leave."

"We?"

"Darry's Boys," he answered plainly. "Where she goes we follow."

"But you have commissions, you all have rank. Some have families, yes?"

"No, Mum. We are the bastards or forgotten sons of those who don't want us. Those who may share our blood do so merely as a formality. We are the reminders of their mistakes or their desperation, or their drunkenness. Or we remind them of the woman they loved most but could not have. We are their anger and their disappointment."

His words hit Cecelia hard. "So what is my daughter?"

"She is the heart of us. She's given us a true family, and for some the only family they've ever known. She's given us love that we never thought to have and the respect of a world that would otherwise have shown us its back. And she's taught us that even though the daughter of a king may be tossed aside, there is still life for the taking if we would just be bold."

"She's not been tossed aside!" Cecelia exclaimed.

"You dare say that in light of the truth?" he said, ignoring her anger. "Aidan was her love." His voice rose as he took a step back. "Their love hurt nothing and no one. But they were deemed unworthy of the things that your other children partake of so freely and with royal fanfare. Aidan… To make her spurn the one she—"

"I know what was done," Cecelia said, stepping back from him. She began to walk away, reaching toward the wall in order to steady herself, but it was several feet away. Bentley watched as her steps faltered and he reacted without thought.

Bentley caught her, lifting her in his arms before she could fall. "My Lady?" he asked in fear. Her eyes were closed and she was beyond pale. When she did not answer he moved in a rush.

Jessa stood before him on the balustrade and he let out a grunt of surprise. He slid to a halt and took an awkward step to the side.

Jessa followed him and laid a gentle touch on Cecelia's brow. "What's happened here?"

"I think she's passed out, but I don't know."

Jessa took in Cecelia's pale face and stepped close as she pressed her hand more firmly on Cecelia's brow. She took a slow, full breath and let it out, then did so again, turning her mind toward the heat against her palm. She let her thoughts be drawn downward, let herself be pulled in, her eyelids fluttering as the air around them became thick with the scent of jasmine.

The spell was a difficult one but Jessa wove it quickly and with skill, falling within her own body as her mind followed the runes. She pushed them gently into a rope of connection that would bind them together. Her heartbeat slowed with a stutter and she took another breath, a shaft of pain lancing through her chest. She let the breath out slowly and another pulse vibrated into her palm, like the ripples from a stone dropped into a still pool of water. The pulse was Cecelia's, and after several seconds another throbbed along Jessa's veins, more focused this time and thrumming low within her chest. Her own heart absorbed the impact and began to pound in unison with Cecelia's.

Cecelia's heart beat hard and strong, though beneath it Jessa felt the presence of something black and cold that she recognized as fear. Her lungs tightened in want of more air so she took a breath and opened her mind further in search of the darkness.

Jessa took another cleansing breath through her nose, her head tipping back and her shoulders lifting as her lungs filled. Cecelia stirred in Bentley's arms.

Jessa could almost see the face, a flash of honey blond hair and a dress made of lace and silk the color of the bluest sky. She took another breath, as did Cecelia. Jessa thought she heard laughter and she smiled at the far-away sound, for it was a lovely echo in the back of her mind. She took another breath and opened her eyes slowly, her gaze steady as she watched Cecelia do likewise. The color returned slightly to her face.

"Princess?" Bentley asked in a whisper.

Jessa turned her hand over and slid it in a tender manner along Cecelia's cheek, allowing their connection to melt away. The runes dissolved within her thoughts as Cecelia took a clean, strong breath on her own. "She needs to rest, and consult a healer. A sleeping draught," Jessa said quietly. "She is filled with fear, and sorrow, I think. It presses against her and she's not breathing properly. Something is too heavy for her. She needs to sleep, this will help."

Bentley stared at Jessa, remembering her care of Darry as she had lain abed with fever, and the way Jessa had looked at Darry and smoothed the hair back from Darry's face when she thought no one was looking. And she had told no one, keeping them all safe when she had no reason to do so. "Is Darry your friend?"

"Yes."

"Is she?"

Jessa studied his expression and knew at once that something was terribly wrong. "Where is she, Bentley? Where is Darrius?"

"And are you her friend in return, Lady Jessa?"

Jessa's heart twisted and she pulled her hand from Cecelia's face, afraid that her emotions might affect her in such a vulnerable state. Something inside her began to tremble and it stirred the Vhaelin in her blood. She understood then the majik that hung so thick in the air. It *had* been familiar. It was Darry. "Yes."

"I don't know where she went, but she's been greatly wronged. I'm not sure what she'll do. I need you to find her, my Lady, please. She's very angry and I'm not…she is angry, do you understand?"

"The panther is awake, I can smell her," Jessa said. "I understand, Bentley."

Her comment startled him. *Sweet Gamar, she knows. She knows.*

"Go," she said. "Find the healer, do you hear? Tell him what I said. I left Emmalyn in the solar when we went riding earlier. My Queen will need her, I have no doubt. Leave *Akasha* to me."

Bentley frowned at the use of a name other than Darry's. It sounded terribly intimate, though he was ignorant of its meaning. *She loves her*. Jessa's heart was as open as the sky. *She's bloody well in love with Darry. Holy fucking he—*

"Go, you ass!" Jessa commanded, anger flashing in her gaze as she lost her patience. "May the Vhaelin help you for a fool, *move*!"

Bentley obeyed, hurrying through the door of Darry's old chambers, the quickest way to the inner keep. He managed the inner door and kicked it open, his voice booming as he shouted Emmalyn's name.

Jessa lifted her face and the heat of the Vhaelin moved within her blood. It was scorching and it was thrilling, her heartbeat hastening beneath its sway. Pulling her cloak tight about her tunic and riding skirt, she followed the scent of the panther.

CHAPTER TWENTY-ONE

The expansive stalls of the main barn were filled with anxious animals. Many of the horses shied away and tossed their heads as Jessa passed. A board was kicked and Jessa flinched but kept moving. Their instincts served them well. Something dangerous was in their midst and could not be ignored.

Darry threw open one of the farthest stall doors and disappeared within.

Jessa quickened her pace and as she approached, Darry reemerged, grabbing the blanket and saddle that sat waiting. Darry was pale and her eyes were distant, caught somewhere other than where she stood. Her body was torn between here and there. She disappeared into the stall once more.

Jessa was cautious as she grasped the gate. Darry threw the blanket onto the filly's back and tossed the saddle after it.

"I want to come with you," Jessa said.

"No."

"I want to come with you."

Darry pulled the cinch and the filly backed up. Darry followed and yanked again until the sash was fully tightened.

Jessa stepped to the opposite side of the gate and seized the bridle from its peg. When Darry turned she had no choice but to face her, though she eyed the bridle and refused to look up. Jessa held it out and Darry seized the leather. Jessa's grip tightened in response, and her refusal to let go finally prodded Darry to look up.

"I want to come with you," she said gently.

"Let go."

Darry could barely contain her wildness, Jessa could feel it. Darry's control seemed tenuous at best. "So take it."

Darry moved so fast that Jessa barely saw it. Darry's hands were rough on her upper arms and Jessa backed through the straw at her feet until the stable door was behind her. The filly screamed and threw her head up.

Jessa felt Darry's muscled thighs and breasts pressing close and moving as Darry breathed. She closed her eyes and lifted her face along Darry's skin, her blood pumping hard and pooling low within her body as her stomach filled with wings. "Take me with you," she whispered.

Darry's body was trembling and Jessa brought her hands forward as much as she was able. The bridle still dangled in her grip as her fingers brushed Darry's hips. Darry's lower body pressed closer in reaction and a wave of pleasure shuddered in Jessa's belly. Her lips brushed an earlobe and Darry faced her, then slipped her right leg between Jessa's thighs. Darry's hands opened and Jessa slid her own hands down Darry's slim hips, searching slowly for the leverage she intended to use to pull Darry nearer.

Their lips were so close Jessa could taste the warmth of Darry's breath, her entire world hanging on that single, aching moment.

Darry let out a strangled sound and backed away, ripping the bridle from Jessa's hand. Jessa leaned heavily against the door as Darry whispered to the horse. She slid the bit into the filly's mouth and the forestall over her ears, then did up the buckles with trembling hands. When Darry pulled her mount toward the gate Jessa stood in her way.

"Do you think you frighten me?" she asked.

"Jessa, please."

"I want to go with you."

"We cannot be friends anymore." Darry spoke harshly, her tone terribly cold, but Jessa saw something completely different in her eyes. "I cannot be your friend."

"That is fine," Jessa said. "You may do what you want, just take me with you."

Darry blinked. "Move."

"Take me with you."

"Jessa, *move*!"

"Take me with you."

They stared at each other. "If you have any feelings for me at all, please just move." Darry spoke in a trembling voice. "Please, Jess."

Jessa took a bold step forward, lifting an eyebrow in challenge.

"I meant *out* of the way," Darry said.

Jessa thought she saw a glint of something familiar move in those striking eyes. "You should be more specific. Take me with you."

"I don't know where I'm going."

"All the better."

Darry closed her eyes. "What must I say to make you go away?"

"There is nothing. Take me with you."

Darry stepped back and lurched to the side, grabbing the filly's mane for balance as the earth tilted beneath her. Jessa slid forward and reached out, but Darry rested her forehead against the horse's neck, using the filly to keep her feet. "Sweet Jessa, please…just let me go."

"Do you wish to go riding?" Jessa dropped her arm. "Or stand here for the next thirty years and argue with me?"

Darry tried to ignore the fear she could smell. The instincts of the animals around her were dense and violent. "Thirty years is a long time." The only scent that Jessa gave off was the hint of jasmine.

"I'm very stubborn."

"Seven hells!" Darry said, and threw the reins.

She stalked across the corridor and yanked open the opposite stall. The magnificent bay stallion within threw up his head as she slammed back the gate. He reared away as he caught Darry's scent. Jessa's heart leapt into her throat as the animal's legs lashed out, missing Darry's head by inches. Darry grabbed his mane and hit his neck with her fist. "*Talon*!"

Jessa was thinking fast as Darry calmed him and assembled his tack, moving with the same urgency she had the first time. She stepped into the filly's stall, holding out her hand, to which the filly lowered her nose. "Will you help me?" Jessa asked in whisper. "I need your help, my pretty."

Jessa took the reins, slipped her left boot into the stirrup, and mounted the horse. The filly snorted and stepped backward as Jessa ran a gentle hand along the horse's neck, feeling the power and enjoying the thrill it sent through her blood. She tapped a heel and the filly stepped forward obediently. Jessa lowered her head as they passed through the gate.

At the sound of hooves on wood Darry left Talon's bridle and stepped to the door. "What are you doing?"

Jessa looked down from her seat. "You would think to outrun me, saddling me with that *plough* horse?" she said, managing to sound insulted.

"Talon is no plough horse, I assure you."

"We will see."

Darry stared at her.

"Have you named her yet?" Jessa ran her hand along the muscles of the filly's shoulder. "It's bad luck to ride a horse without a name."

Darry did not answer, clearly uncomfortable at the question.

"You didn't name her something foolish, did you? Something like Sunflower perhaps?"

"Her name is Vhaelin Star," Darry answered with a rush of anger.

Jessa felt her face flush and her emotions rose as the filly stepped to the side. "*Hesta, Vhaelin Barrosha,*" she whispered. "Easy."

Talon burst from his stall with Darry sitting easy in the saddle. The filly reared, and Talon turned in a tight circle and threw his head back as Jessa leaned forward and pulled at the reins. Vhaelin Star's right foreleg pounded the boards.

Darry met Jessa's eyes. "Last chance."

"For what? To play the shy foreign Princess and retire to my rooms?"

"If it pleases you."

"Try to keep up."

Darry let out a shout as the filly bolted forward. She yanked at the reins in an attempt to wheel Talon to the side. Vhaelin Star slammed into Talon's shoulder and Darry slipped in her seat. Darry grabbed on as Talon backed up and shifted beneath her, saving her from falling completely like the well-trained war-horse he was. She kicked her boot back into the stirrup and dug her heels in.

Vhaelin Star thundered from the stables and onto the lane that led past the small paddock. Several groomsmen looked up and another jumped from the path with a shout of surprise. A moment later Talon shot through the doors in pursuit.

Vhaelin Star turned at the pull of the reins and the touch of a heel, wheeling to the right and heading for the gateway that led to the postern arch. A nearby stable hand yelled as he raced along the fence where the gate was still bolted shut. Vhaelin Star was too fast, though, and even as they neared, Jessa heeled her with purpose, feeling the filly gather her strength. She leapt, Jessa pushing back in her seat as they cleared the fence with several feet to spare. Jessa let out a hard breath as she was thrown forward in the saddle. She leaned into it smoothly and turned them yet again. Dust kicked up at their change in direction, but Vhaelin Star never lost her stride as Jessa glanced over her shoulder.

Talon cleared the fence easily. Darry took the jump with more ease and turned the stallion, letting him have his head.

Vhaelin Star flew beneath the postern arch with an echoing clatter of hooves and then she was gone, hitting her true stride as Jessa steered her from the road and into the grass. They were headed north where she knew there was nothing but miles of open land. Her hair whipped against her back as she kept low, her riding cape rippling out behind her. Darry kicked Talon hard in chase, her right hand on the reins and her left flat against his neck and urging him on.

The ground disappeared beneath them, Vhaelin Star moving with absolute power and grace as Talon slowly closed the gap, striding with equal beauty but not quite as much power as the Ibarris filly. Darry spoke to him as they ran. Something inside her burned with a new anger that they did not have open land before them but, instead, the backside of an apparently faster horse.

With a soft hand Jessa pulled back the reins, and the filly's gallop changed just enough to allow Talon to pull closer. Darry's smile was pure as she heeled her mount, letting him know what she wanted and that she needed more. His muscles responded, as did his heart, and they pulled alongside Vhaelin Star's thighs and then her rider. Darry looked straight ahead with a purpose that involved nothing but the hunger for freedom.

There were no limits then, nothing but tall grass and the setting sun as Talon took the lead with a final burst of speed and power. Darry let him run for all he was worth. Some dark part of her was content to let him race until they both folded into the ground; some part of her even wanted it.

Jessa stayed near but not too close, maneuvering the filly to the side and away from the stallion. She had not ridden this hard in years and had forgotten how exhilarating it was, not only for the danger it presented but for the abandon as well.

The ground passed away beneath them and after a time the landscape began to change. The hills in the distance that signaled the start of the Gonnard Forest became larger and more pronounced. When a stand of ancient maples gradually rose to the right, Jessa heeled the filly. "*Drassa matisse, Barrosha*!" she called. "*Drassa*!"

Vhaelin Star answered the call. Jessa smiled, knowing that she had never ridden a more splendid animal. They gained on Talon and Darry glanced over in surprise as Vhaelin Star passed them. She was forced to pull up as the filly cut across their path.

Vhaelin Star was on their left and they were being guided to the east. Darry saw the maple grove in the falling dusk and knew they had come nearly ten miles. Vhaelin Star was suddenly very near and Darry kicked Talon with a curse. The horse obeyed and Jessa adjusted swiftly. The filly swerved away. Darry heard the shout and looked back, sitting up straight and afraid she had cut too close. Talon's hooves dug roughly into the dirt as he slowed and Darry turned him roughly about.

Vhaelin Star bolted past them and Darry's heart jumped into her throat as the cloak was thrown and the heavy garment hit her in the chest and face. Talon skidded to the side and kicked out as Darry yanked at the garment. "*Jessa*!"

Vhaelin Star was racing toward the trees.

"Damn you to all seven hells!" Darry shouted, shoving the cloak against the saddle and kicking Talon into action. "*Hiyah*!"

Jessa did not look back as she guided the filly into the grove, letting the animal slow as she sat back in the saddle. She was breathing quick and resting the reins on the filly's neck. Talon thundered past them, terribly close, and Vhaelin Star reared and turned on her hind legs. Jessa was forced to grab the saddle.

Talon turned hard once again and Darry brought him around. "Are you *mad*?" Darry threw the cloak as they neared.

Jessa caught it and dropped it across the filly's shoulders. "You'll kill your plough horse, Darry. I would rather not watch that."

"Then go back."

"I didn't know you were cruel." Jessa's words cut through the haze of confusion in Darry's expression. Jessa saw a surge of pain in Darry's eyes and her heart ached for her. "I would not have thought you were cruel." She spoke with some effort, trying to gauge the effect of her words. *Give her back to me, Hinsa.*

Darry looked away as Talon stepped to the side and waited for a command. When Darry looked back, Jessa saw within her eyes the woman she loved.

"I'm not," Darry said, and pulled on the reins. Talon stepped to the left and moved away.

Jessa clicked her tongue and Vhaelin Star followed, weaving through the trees after them. Darry's shoulders fell a little and her head lowered as she gave Talon his head. The war-horse trotted for a time and the filly followed at a distance.

When the stallion stopped and lowered his face into the grass, Darry swung her right leg over his neck and jumped from the saddle. Jessa pulled the filly up as Darry approached. Jessa leaned down as strong hands took possession of her waist. She grabbed Darry's shoulders and slid from the saddle, her body descending along Darry's until her boots touched the ground.

Jessa's heart beat fast as their bodies pressed close and Darry held her firmly. Jessa found it hard to breathe and wanted very much to put her arms about Darry's neck.

"He's not a plough horse," Darry said in a quiet breath, and released her.

Jessa let her go and Darry moved beneath the massive maples, the savageness still within her body but not as it had been. Tamed somewhat by their wild ride, Darry's shoulders were not so tight nor her gait so fierce. Jessa followed at a distance, waiting until Darry stopped and touched the weathered bark of an ancient maple.

Jessa brushed past her and spun smoothly, then sat neatly in the grass. "You're right," she said. "He is made for more than farm work."

Darry lowered her face and Jessa thought she saw a smile.

"Come sit beside me, Darry."

"I cannot be your friend anymore," Darry said, stepping away from the maple and shoving her hands into her pockets. She pulled her shoulders in as if to protect herself. "I can't."

"As I said, that is your choice." A surge of frustration washed through Jessa that somehow their relationship was no longer within their control. Had it ever been? She wanted desperately to ask what had happened and to know the great wrong that Bentley had spoken of. "Come and sit."

"It's not my choice!" Darry raised her voice. "I can't be responsible." She swallowed awkwardly. "You cannot be near me anymore, do you hear?"

"I may do as I wish, Darry. I wish to remain your friend," she replied. *I wish to be so much more, do you not see?* "But if you cannot do that, for whatever reason, I trust your judgment." She ached for her, ached for Darry's touch again. She wanted that moment back when her entire world had hung in the balance.

"But someone I cared for was made to suffer. Someone I used to love…because she loved me in return. They hurt her. Because of me, Jess. It was my fault, my mistake."

"No, not because of you," Jessa said, certain of her words despite her lack of information. "It wasn't your fault."

"But if they…" Darry struggled with her words. From the moment she had seen Jessa in the stables, she had not thought only of Aidan. She had thought of Jessa, and all of the feelings Darry had for her swarmed up in her rage. "…if they…you and I."

"Darry," Jessa said, her tone unyielding.

Darry stepped close and dropped to her knees beside her. Jessa took hold of her uniform at the collar. "I don't know much, Darry. Not much of anything, actually, but I do know that at least. It was not because of you. Whatever you're thinking you're wrong."

Darry lowered her face and her shoulders jerked. Jessa pulled gently at the jacket and reached out with her other hand. Darry stumbled and Jessa caught her, pulling her near and wrapping her arms about her.

Jessa closed her eyes. "And if you don't believe me," she whispered, her heart breaking a little, "then I forgive you in her stead. Do you hear me, Darry? She forgives you. You are forgiven."

Darry shook within the embrace, a strangled sob slipping past her lips. Her arms slid around Jessa's lower back. "*Essa lana allah patrice ma*, *Akasha*." Jessa touched her lips to Darry's cheek in a supple kiss. *Do not hide so, Akasha, do not hide.*

The kiss broke her at last and Darry cried, giving in to her grief.

❖

Darry wiped again at her face and opened her eyes, feeling almost peaceful in the darkness. She had not expected to find such solace in being held.

Jessa's touch was like a whisper as she pushed a pale curl from Darry's face. She traced her fingertip along her temple and down her jaw, coming to rest on Darry's throat where she felt the slow and steady beat of her heart. "Did you damn me to your seven hells?" Jessa asked.

Darry took a deep breath and let it out slowly. "You threw your cloak in my face and then rode away on a faster horse."

The urge to claim Darry's mouth was close to overpowering, but Jessa knew it was not what was needed and had no idea if that was how to go about getting what she desired. It seemed to be, but she was not willing to ask just yet. "Ah, that."

"I wasn't intending to return."

"Then we shall keep riding," Jessa said.

"We'll go back," Darry whispered, a curious look in her eyes that Jessa did not understand. "It's all…everything is as it was meant to be."

Jessa moved her hand beneath Darry's chin. She turned her hand, tracing her fingertips along Darry's jaw once again. "Do you think so now?"

Darry swallowed and stared at Jessa's lips. *Do you know how beautiful you are? You should be told every day, until your eyes finally close a thousand years from now.*

"Do you think so?" Jessa asked again.

I would taste your lips just once before then. "Perhaps, but I'm very tired, Jess."

"Then sleep. I don't mind."

"Are you not tired as well?"

Jessa smiled. "No."

"Why do you always smell so sweetly of jasmine?" Darry asked, Jessa's fingers burning along her neck. "Do you wash your hair with it?"

Jessa's smile deepened. "Are you asking for my most well-guarded secret?"

"Is it a secret?"

"Why do you always smell of musk and of the sea?"

"I forget to bathe."

Jessa chuckled. "Yes, well, that probably isn't a secret you can keep then, is it?"

"Probably not." Darry sighed, shifting to rise.

Jessa lowered her leg and helped Darry sit up, her right hand lingering in Darry's hair before letting her go.

Darry wiped at her face again. "I'm sorry."

"For what? Things deserve their proper respect, yes? No matter the price. Tears are a better payment than most, Darry."

Darry accepted the words and then rose to her feet, offering both her hands. "Come now, my Lady. Let me take you home."

Home, yes. Jessa accepted the help and Darry pulled her up. Jessa stepped close as Darry grasped her waist. "We can still keep riding."

"I'm better now, Jess, truly."

"We can keep riding anyway."

Darry's smile was almost timid as she stepped back, but not before she wrapped her fingers about Jessa's hand again and held it tight.

Their return seemed to take no time at all despite the distance. They did not speak much as they rode. The silence between them was not strained or uncomfortable, but filled instead with a strange sort of promise, and when Darry would glance at her, Jessa's eyes would find her. It was Darry who would turn away and Jessa smiled when she did, happy for the darkness around them that hid her blush. When they rode at a gallop they did so with ease, both animals content to keep apace until one of them would settle and they would slow to a walk once more.

When they reached Blackstone Keep the postern gate had been left open for them. Darry thanked the guard as they passed beneath the arch, whereupon he saluted her. "Who won, my Lady?"

"She did," Darry answered with a grudging smile, and Jessa laughed with delight when the man chuckled and returned to the guardhouse. He announced the result to his comrades and their surprised laughter lifted into the night.

"I think you're not used to losing," Jessa said as Vhaelin Star walked with a high step as if she knew she were the victor.

Darry looked past the stables to the torches of the residence, a shrouded look on her face. "I don't mind this time."

Jessa glanced at the high walls of the keep. Did Hinsa wait in the maze, and would Darry go to her?

They dismounted at the stables and a groomsman came out and took their mounts, though Jessa was reluctant to relinquish the reins. Darry smiled a little when she saw this and retrieved Jessa's cloak from the saddle, then shook it open and held it out. Jessa stepped close, allowing Darry to lay the garment about her shoulders. She closed her eyes when Darry's fingers moved against her neck and her hair was lifted free of the hood. Darry carefully laid the curls and braids about Jessa's shoulders.

They walked down the wide boards of the stables and eventually along the path that took them to the residence. They moved along the stones in an easy walk, unhurried and quiet. When they reached her rooms Jessa opened the door and turned to speak, but Darry silenced her with a touch, taking Jessa's hand.

She brought her other hand forward as well and rubbed her thumbs on the soft skin of Jessa's fingers. Jessa's heart beat wildly at the caress and the hairs rose on the back of her neck.

Darry stepped forward and bowed her head, placing the back of Jessa's hand against her forehead. The quiet song of Jessa's bracelets filled the air between them as she let out a slow breath and closed her eyes.

Jessa reached out with her left hand but then hesitated, wanting to touch Darry's hair again but uncertain. *Oh, Darry, I love you, I do...but I don't know how to help. You must tell me if you can because, because I don't know how to do this.*

Darry lowered Jessa's hand and turned it over. Her fingertips skated lightly over the skin before she leaned close. Jessa's heart skipped as Darry kissed the center of her palm, her lips slow and lingering until etiquette no longer existed.

"Jessa," she whispered simply, then turned away and moved down the terrace.

Jessa closed her eyes, unmoving as she listened to the sound of Darry's boots fading into the distance. *Vhaelin essa.*

"Close the door, you foolish child," Radha said, though her voice held no reprimand. "You're late." Radha was in her favorite chair beside the small fire of the hearth.

"Mind your tongue, old woman."

Radha laughed. "Her attentions suit you."

"It wasn't like that," Jessa said, stepping away from the door and whipping off her cloak. She threw it onto the foot of the bed. "I must see to the Queen."

"She is well," Radha said. "She sleeps soundly with the Lady Emmalyn by her side to watch over her. She was given a draught of valerian root. Her heart beats strong and without pain, and her blood runs clean. She could not catch her breath. Part of her world came crashing down, yes?"

"I'm not sure." Jessa sat on the heavy lid of the trunk at the end of the bed. "But I felt a great fear within her, and sorrow."

"Not an easy spell to weave," Radha said. *Not even for me, my child. You weave spirit majik as if it were a trivial thing. Those runes can destroy as easily as they heal.*

Jessa gave an absent wave of her hand. "It was needed."

"Your Princess had a lover once, when she was younger."

"What do you know?"

"A girl named Aidan. The King and his Prince did not like it and so they threatened to ruin her family if she did not spurn the young Darrius. She did as was ordered out of fear for her family. The girl's father was given much gold and land titles, no doubt to soothe someone's conscience. They disappeared from the city one night never to be seen again." Radha watched Jessa's face as she spoke. "It was just today that your Princess finally found out the truth, that her father and his heir did such harm to—"

"Enough, Radha," Jessa snapped, rising from the trunk and stepping around the bed. She remembered Darry's pain all too well, and that it might now be the source of careless gossip did not please her.

"And that her mother knew, though too late to change things for them."

Jessa turned abruptly. "The Queen *knew*?"

"She did. She was not a part of it, from what I could learn, but she's known for some time. Your Darrius is now wise to her mother's lie."

Jessa tried to adjust her thinking. *My Lady, how could you?*

"It was her decision to hide the truth," Radha said. "No doubt to keep your panther from gutting her prick of a son. I would've done the same, may the Vhaelin bless her and keep her well."

"*Enough*," Jessa repeated, her temper quick. She unfastened her tunic as she walked to the dressing room. "Shall I ask how you found this out?"

"I was not exactly spying," Radha muttered beneath her breath.

Jessa stepped to the arch and glared across the room. "Answer me, Radha."

"For my own safety I shall blame one of the cooks," Radha replied as she turned to the warmth of the fire. "No one knows more than the cook, unless it's the laundress. Nothing tells a tale like a dirty sheet."

CHAPTER TWENTY-TWO

Darry sat back in the steaming water of the polished wooden tub and put her arms along its smooth edge. She gasped as she let her spine bow outward, the dark bruises along her lower back and ribs giving protest. They eased as her body relaxed, though, and Darry stared beyond the high window of the private bath, catching a glimpse of sky.

For the past three days she had done nothing but fight, every waking hour spent in the yards sparring with countless opponents. The sword, the mace, the spear and morning star, every weapon she had ever held before had come and gone, and every adversary had been punished and dispatched with little or no regard for their pride. No one wished to fight her anymore, and only Darry's Boys remained for her to choose from.

She still saw to her duties, though she had asked her peers of equal rank to take on most of them and they had agreed without question. When Longshanks asked for an explanation, she had fought with him as well. She had seen his concern but was incapable of stopping her temper. He had let her vent and then took her from the lists completely, telling her to spend her coin on some wine and a good fuck, for she seemed in need of both. It had been the only time she had laughed in days.

And in the night when she was too restless to sleep she would find the small yard beyond the armory and move through the Dance, the discipline of Honshi, even as she had done the morning that Jessa had watched her in the practice yard. Over and over she would glide through the steps and challenge their order. It was the first time in her life that she had strayed from the heart of the discipline. The patterns were new as she wove like a phantom among the crowded practice dummies. She had taken her obedience and set it free.

She did not attack the practice dummies outright but let her body move where it wanted instead, content to destroy them down to their posts when they entered her circle, and never once was there even the slightest hitch or hesitation in her actions. The Dance had adapted as if it were a living thing, and Darry used whatever maneuver befit the situation.

She felt fear at what had been done to her and fear at how she was to fight her way clear of it. Fear of what she would do when her father and Malcolm returned. Though as to her brother there would be no great change in their relationship, only that her restraint would now be gone. *I am the spear now, brother, not the thorn.*

She only ate because Bentley made her, or Arkady or Etienne. All of them had followed her about at any given time and she realized they were taking turns in watching over her. They were quiet about it, though, and unobtrusive, except for forcing her to eat at least a little. She could not argue against them, though the food sat like a stone in her belly. Only in the privacy of the baths could she find a true moment to herself.

Darry dipped a hand in the water and wiped her face, forcing herself to take a deep breath in spite of the cramp it caused against her sore ribs. *Whatever happens, it will be done...and I shall leave this place and not return.*

Darry frowned and for an instant she broke, the deep pain trying to claw its way free. She covered her eyes, taking a breath and then swallowing awkwardly on the hard fist in her throat. *I shall leave, when all that I still love is here.*

She dropped her arms in the water, letting the heat soak into her flesh. Her mother had requested her presence at dinner, a gentle missive of invitation written in her mother's flowing script. She had not begged exactly, but her words had been somehow pleading.

"*I thought it served no purpose to tell you what had been done, for it was over and there was no going back. There was no fixing it no matter how badly I wanted to.*"

She knew that her mother had spoken the truth, but it did little to ease the pain, learning that she had been a part of their betrayal, if only at a distance. Darry had tried to imagine what she might have done in her place, but it was too much and she could not see past the end results. It was too late to take back her words, and she was certain as well that she had every right and more. But it did not assuage her guilt at causing her mother pain, no matter her rights. Her mother had been ill because of her, because of her anger and...

Bloody hell, I hit my own mother. Darry tightened her arms about her legs. *Did I? She was so close and I swung out, and I...oh, Hinsa, your wants are too deep. I can't, I can't control them anymore, I just can't.* As if in answer her blood rose just a touch. Darry felt its wild, tempting power and fell into it. *And I don't think I want to.*

But with Hinsa's blood came the rush of her more furious emotions, and that was something she in no way wanted. With an effort she steeled her heart and her mind shrugged free, looking where it wanted. A soothing rhythm appeared in response, a cadence of thought that was natural to her now as she wondered how many braids would be held in Jessa's hair.

And so Jessa was there and flooding her thoughts like the sun.

So beautiful and clean of darkness, so untouched by anything but the sweet emotions behind her expressions, Jessa was all that Darry could truly see. It had been so from the first and she knew that now. Each moment she had spent in her company, each word shared and every innocent touch, they had only driven the shaft deeper into Darry's heart. She had looked forward to each hour she might steal with her and each meal they might share. Their nights on the balcony. She had even looked forward to the sewing, which should have been the first warning.

Her flesh sang with the need to feel Jessa's body against her own, and only her desire was strong enough to push away her rage. She had crossed that final line in Tristan's Grove as she had lain in Jessa's arms and wept. The satisfaction she found in Jessa's embrace, no matter the circumstances, had allowed her to grieve for Aidan as she had not yet done, regardless of the years that had passed.

The way you looked at me, sweet Jessa, there was no anger…and your hands on my skin. Did you know what you were doing? I've never been that way before, so at peace in another's presence that I felt nothing but stillness. Everything inside was so quiet. It's never been that quiet, not ever.

And she entertained the idea, at last, that Jessa might not be as she appeared. She remembered their moment in the stables and how her every instinct had shouted that there was want on both sides. But she had been wild and Hinsa's blood had been so thick she had no idea what the truth of it was anymore.

In addition, they were not just two women free to do as they pleased, even if Jessa did want more. There was royal blood to be considered. Jessa's etiquette and reputation were pristine and mired in the rules of her station. Even if her own honor was stolen now and her rebellion sincere, to tarnish Jessa would be a disgrace entirely her own.

She had felt it, though. She had felt the entire thing push her gently and she had fallen, knowing it as it happened. Knowing she could not turn back and praying to the gods that it would still be safe to be near her, to have Jessa within her life, even in some small way. Despite all that she wished to do, the things she longed so desperately to do. Despite the desire to know Jessa's flesh and to take her in her mouth, to taste of her spirit. To make her come and hear her cries, wondering how they might sound and if her sable eyes would darken to black in her passion. To know her as only a lover could. To show Jessa the true depth of her feelings.

To show you the strength of my... blessed Gamar, help me, Jess, but I've bloody well fallen in love with you.

Darry leaned back and the water splashed over the edge as her shoulders hit the wood.

"I'm in love," she said aloud, then laughed. "I've lost my mind."

But the words, the very fact of it all, filled her with a rush of warmth that stretched even to her toes. Love was here and had been for some time, and it was an amazing feeling despite everything.

I want to be inside you, Jess, one sweet measure at a time as your jasmine spins my head. I would have your mouth on mine as you cry out and spend yourself beneath me. I would have you claw at my back and feel your legs wrapped about my body.

"Sweet fucking Jezara."

Darry slid a slow hand between her legs and closed her eyes, letting out a moan of reprieve at the touch. Her hips rose beneath her own caress, her blood filled with need as her fingers traced the hardness of her desire and circled knowingly, everything swollen and aching as her thighs tensed and she pushed against the confines of the tub.

Her muscles ached as she strained, and her release appeared like a storm on the sea and just as violent. She could feel the silk of her spirit despite the water, and her body tightened as she braced herself, covering a breast with her left hand and teasing the nipple while imagining Jessa's long fingers in its place.

Her belly erupted in flames as she came. She bit down on her lower lip and strangled the shout in her throat as the water splashed around her. She jerked hard through the climax and trembled in its aftermath, desolate and incomplete regardless of the pleasure. She cupped her sex and closed her legs, trying to think beyond her senses and the overwhelming arousal she still felt.

She slid completely beneath the surface, wondering if everything that was still good in her life had just become a lie.

❖

Cecelia and Emmalyn spoke frequently throughout the meal and occasionally Jessa would join in, but Darry contributed very little and ate even less. Emmalyn noted this with troubled interest and observed their mother as well, noticing that when Darry did speak Cecelia would pay strict attention. She did not miss the tremor in her mother's hands or her nervousness. To others it might be overlooked, but it caused Emmalyn a great deal of worry. She had not forgotten that during their mother's illness, Darry had only shown herself at night when Cecelia had been sleeping, careful to keep her visits hidden.

When at last their meal was finished and a fine bottle of Ravonese gold was brought out, Darry pushed away from the table and walked toward the garden doors, both Cecelia and Jessa following her movements.

Bloody hell and drunken hounds. Emmalyn cursed in silence and pushed her chair back as well. She picked up her goblet and then Darry's and trailed after her. Darry moved beside the open doors, and Emmalyn handed her a fresh goblet of wine.

Jessa was greedy for the sight of Darry and indulged her need without reservation or caution. It had been three days and two nights since their ride, and she had been so severe in her want to see Darry that Radha had actually yelled at her. Radha scolded and hissed and barked and laughed, but she never yelled. Jessa longed for her though she had no say in it.

Cecelia touched Jessa's arm and Jessa flinched in surprise. "Not to worry, I'm only looking for company," Cecelia said.

"You are well, my Lady?" Jessa asked.

"I am." Cecelia smiled at Jessa. She was happy that Jessa no longer wore the veil. *Your face should never be hidden, Jessa.* "And I hear that I have you to thank for that, in part."

"No, my Lady, you do not."

"I do. Do not lie out of modesty."

"I'm not."

"If you insist then. And I hear that you went riding with my daughter several nights ago."

"I did."

Cecelia wanted to smile at the fire in Jessa's gaze. *Is it feelings for my Cat that gives you such passion, or was it always your own?* "Then I will thank you for that, instead. Darrius was—"

"Upset?"

"Yes." *You need not protect her from me.*

"This I know, my Lady, and she had every right to be."

Cecelia felt a jolt of surprise at the blatant challenge in Jessa's voice, though she knew it was deserved. "I'm not denying that fact, Princess." She found it interesting that Jessa seemed to know exactly what she was talking about, which meant that Darry had spoken of what happened. *What am I missing?*

"Then do not seek to dress your actions in courtly words."

Cecelia accepted the accusation. *No, you've had this fire burning in you for many years.*

"I'm glad that you're well, my Lady, truly I am. I would've taken your grief upon myself if I could have. But your guilt is your own and I'll have no part in it. As I shall have no part in manipulating your daughter into a peaceful resolution to your problem." Jessa rose from her chair. "I am a pawn already and on several fronts. I would not be used by you as well."

Cecelia took Jessa's hand before she could move away. "I didn't intend to ask such a thing, Jessa, I assure you."

"No? You weren't going to ask what Darry said? How she seemed, or what her intentions are? You should ask her yourself."

"Perhaps. But I have no avenue into her thoughts now, and it cuts at my heart as you can't possibly know. I wish to help her, if I can, to find some sort of peace with this."

Jessa sat back down, giving in against her better judgment.

"She told you what happened? Is she all right?" Cecelia asked. "That's all I ask. Is she well?"

Jessa tried to compose her thoughts into an answer that would not betray Darry.

"Is she all right?" Cecelia asked once more.

"She is trapped, I am thinking." Jessa chose her words with prudence. "Between then and now. If you denied her a love then, how might she have one now? How might she *ever* have one, yet still remain your daughter?"

Cecelia was struck not only by the words but also by Jessa's tone. *What are you afraid of, Jessa?* She searched across the room only to find Darry's savage eyes, an expression of such ferocity there that her heart tightened. "How indeed," Cecelia whispered, and rose as Darry moved across the hall. "Thank you, Jessa."

Darry stopped on the other side of the table, her eyes blazing as they challenged Cecelia. And then she turned and Cecelia saw them change instantly, filling with tender worry and question.

"Princess, are you well?" Darry asked softly.

Cecelia let out a startled breath.

Jessa smiled with absolute affection. "Of course."

Cecelia heard it in Jessa's voice instantly, like a clarion sounding into the silence of a winter's night. Jessa's expression revealed everything and Cecelia saw it all, even as she had those years ago when Aidan had looked up from her lace.

"I was considering a walk in the gardens perhaps, though I lack an escort," Jessa said.

Darry set her goblet on the table and moved back along its length, her eyes never leaving Jessa's as she did so. Jessa's smile deepened and she stood and followed on the opposite side.

Cecelia sat down rather heavily, staring after them. *Blessed Gamar!*

Emmalyn moved into the room as Darry escorted Jessa in the opposite direction. She saw how pale her mother was. "Mother?"

"I'm fine, my darling."

"You look tired. It's off to bed for you."

"I think not," Cecelia said. "Sit down, my love."

Emmalyn took the chair opposite.

"We need to talk."

Emmalyn raised an eyebrow and Cecelia pressed a hand to her right temple as it began to throb. *Bloody hell, why didn't I see it? Why didn't I see it? Sweet Gamar, what a fool I've been.*

"Perhaps this is a conversation best had in your chambers," Emmalyn said.

"For more reasons than one, apparently."

"Are you finally intending to tell me what in the bloody hell is going on?" Emmalyn asked. "It might be nice to know why my sister walks about like a caged animal. Or why she wears a weapon to her own table?"

Cecelia thought of the dagger on Darry's silver-studded belt, its leather hilt peeking out from beneath Darry's jacket. It had been a bold statement and she had not missed it. The knife spoke for Darry's true feelings.

"Or why for the last three days she has stalked the practice yards in a manner so violent that not even her own men wish to engage her blade?" Emmalyn continued. "Though they have, and I can only guess at the bruises she has as a result. I had to watch today as Jemin McNeely threw her across the yard as if she were a bloody child's toy, though only after she nearly killed him."

Cecelia's chest tightened with pain.

"Aye," Emmalyn said, trying to read what was in her mother's gaze other than fear. That in itself was enough to set Emmalyn on edge, but there was something more and she needed to know what it was. "It wasn't a very comforting thing to watch. Even Bentley was afraid. I don't think she knew what she was doing. I want answers, Mother, and I want them *now*. My sister is in pain and refuses to talk to me. I would like to know who caused it."

Cecelia set her hands on the table and pushed to her feet. "Upstairs, you're right."

"Was it…was it you, Mother?" Emmalyn asked, unsure if she wanted an answer.

"Yes," Cecelia said. "Among others."

"I'm not going to like this, am I?"

"No, you're not."

CHAPTER TWENTY-THREE

They walked along the garden path, Jessa glancing over at Darry every few feet. "I've missed you since our ride," Jessa said quietly.

"Yes." Darry tried to slow her pulse. "I've been thinking."

"About what?"

You. Darry's mind spoke with a silent groan of distress. *Of everything, of course, but mostly you, Jess. Gods, I just want to kiss you. Though it would never be enough.*

"Thinking about what?" Jessa asked again.

"I'm not all that sure."

"Though perhaps I don't truly wish to know. Perhaps I'm only with you now so that I may find a way to your horse."

Darry laughed as their eyes met. "Well, you may not have her. Besides, my price would be very high."

"I would pay it," Jessa replied.

Darry studied a line of heavy bluebells along the base of the hedge. *Just don't speak at all. Just hold your bloody tongue.*

As they moved farther along the turns of the garden path, the scent of foxglove filled the air and mingled with heather. "Perhaps we might go riding again?" Jessa said. "Would that be all right?"

"I would like that very much," Darry answered.

"You're not afraid to lose again?"

"Such a thing isn't possible, I think."

Jessa pulled the silken shawl from around her shoulders. "You're somewhat arrogant for one who has lost once already."

"That's not what I meant," Darry said quickly. "I didn't mean it that way."

"Then how did you mean it?" Jessa took hold of Darry's sleeve and gave her arm a gentle shake.

"I only meant…" Darry let out a breath of frustration. "I only meant that there can be no loss in time spent with you, Jessa. In your presence I find only happiness."

Everything inside of Darry cringed. *You're a complete ass, Darry.* She felt a blush creep along her neck, unable to stop it. *And I'm trapped; she has me trapped. Seven hells, I think I might die. Where's the turn to the patio? The fountain?* She glanced along the path and recognized virtually nothing. *I don't believe this. I'm fucking lost in my own gardens.*

Jessa still held to Darry's sleeve as they walked. "Thank you."

"You're welcome, sweet Jessa." Darry winced, realizing she had spoken the endearment aloud.

Jessa closed her eyes. *I can't take this anymore. I'm going to bloody well die.*

"Jessa?"

She fought hard to find her tongue. *One word, any word.* "Yes?"

Darry backed away, and Jessa was forced to let go of her sleeve. "I'm sorry but I can't do this, and I don't know how to make it stop anymore."

Jessa searched Darry's eyes, a touch of panic tickling at the back of her neck. "Do what? Make what stop, Darry?"

"*This*." Darry was cornered and she knew it, and for the first time in her life, she gave in without a fight. "I wanted only to be your friend. And though we've not spoken of it directly, I suppose, I understood from the first that you know me to be a backwards woman. That you've accepted me with such ease has been a great gift to me. I know the laws in Lyoness and I was afraid you'd be offended."

She swallowed roughly and continued before she lost her nerve. "And as I said, I wanted only to be your friend. To just *be* with you. You're so wonderful, Jess. I've never known anyone like you. Seven hells, I did needlepoint and *liked* it."

Jessa let out a breath of laughter.

"But there've been times when you've…" Darry struggled, letting out a heavy breath. "I'm thinking that you didn't know what you were doing perhaps and I was misunderstanding, though I was hoping as well, I admit that. I don't know, Jessa. I'm sorry."

Darry could see that she was making little sense. "And within the grove…" She charged ahead regardless. "I have no words to express how I feel about that, none that will do justice to your compassion. And though I'm still filled with rage…But even so I think, perhaps, that now I have a much greater problem."

"Might I help you?" Jessa asked, trying to decipher Darry's words.

Please don't tell me that you're leaving to find your lost love. The thought had occurred to her but a few hours after they had parted the night of their ride, and it had plagued her without mercy ever since. *Don't tell me that, Akasha.* "Or perhaps you meant it, when you said we could no longer be friends?"

"I'm trying to tell you, rather stupidly, I guess, that I don't know *how* to be your friend anymore. Because I cannot make this wanting stop."

Jessa's heart caught.

"I don't mean to offend you, *truly* I don't, but I can only tell you the truth. I may not understand etiquette as you do, but I know what's right and wrong. To do less than tell you the truth would be unworthy of you. And I'm fairly certain I'd never survive another pleasant conversation. It's very hard for me not to say what I want, it always has been. Maybe for others it's—"

"What truth?" Jessa had no restraint left in her. Whatever would finally happen between them would happen *now*, one way or another. "Darrius Lauranna, what bloody *truth*?"

"That I'm dying with want for you, Jess. That I long for your touch, even the slightest brush of your hand. And by that same token, it's all I can do to keep from just touching your skin." She closed her hands tight and lowered her eyes. "I'm sorry, Jessa, that I'm not stronger than this. Yet I must confess that these things are the *least* of my desires where you're concerned."

The balance of Jessa's world was sent reeling and she bit down on the torrent of words that tried to spill free. The silence between them was charged with tension. Jessa saw how absolutely exposed Darry was, standing in wait for her response. *Waiting to be rejected.*

And so it was that Jessa felt her future unfold before her, and it was more vast and unexpected than she had ever dreamt. Darry wanted her and she had confessed it, her gentle words opening a path through Jessa's heart that was wide and sprawling and filled with light.

Darry felt utterly lost, waiting for the axe to fall. *Bloody brilliant, Darry.*

Jessa's hands slid atop Darry's, her fingers spreading out and taking hold. "Open your hands, *Akasha*."

Jessa caught her breath at the intensity of the gaze. Darry's hands relaxed and opened at her command. Jessa guided them to her waist and stepped closer as Jessa slid her touch along Darry's face. "*Atta-loosha tu en fanta*," she whispered. "*Nessa anna*, Darry."

Darry's eyes fell to the fullness of Jessa's mouth. *Oh hell, that's done it, Jess.*

"These things you name? They are the least of my desires for you as well." Jessa felt dizzy to be speaking her desire aloud to the one who was its cause. "And so I would like it very much if you would just kiss me now."

Darry felt herself bending, unable to question the unexpected words. *Just kiss me now*. Her blood was rushing and a sweet want blossomed in her as their mouths hovered close. She felt Jessa's breath against her lips and the warmth of Jessa's hands on her face. She could smell jasmine and feel the silk of Jessa's sari like water beneath her touch. *Sweet Jessa, if I start I'll never stop.*

"Please," Jessa asked, "won't you kiss me?"

Darry brushed her mouth softly against Jessa's in answer.

The contact was spare as her lower lip teased with its presence, tasting slowly of Jessa's upper lip. The caress was hesitant at first, until Darry could not stop her tongue from gliding upon its delicate underside and Jessa opened to her, just slightly, just enough.

Her breath passed across Jessa's lips and Darry felt trembling hands in her hair. She could see the want in Jessa's eyes, and it was the key that released everything. "This is…a most pleasant development."

"Yes." Jessa spoke in a soft breath. "Thank you for finally saying something."

"Finally?"

"Well, yes, but I didn't mean you. It's just that I didn't know what to do, you see, and I—"

Darry covered Jessa's mouth, tasting in a slow, sensual manner until her tongue sought entrance. When it was granted and Jessa pulled against her neck, Darry complied.

Jessa felt Darry's arms slide about her back and the hard thighs against her own, their breasts pressing close. But it was the warm tongue in her mouth that made her weak, the tender strokes and soft lips. The taste of her burst in Jessa's mouth and she tightened her embrace, instantly wanting more.

A kiss. It was the thing that held Jessa's life in the balance and her heart beat fiercely at the reality of it. She gasped for breath as Darry pulled her lips away, though they returned for more within the next instant. Jessa followed her want and let her own tongue find pleasure in return. The texture and the heat, the flavor and gentle need, it was everything she thought it might be and more.

Jessa's knees were weak and her body was no longer truly in her control, her hand touching Darry's cheek as they gazed into each other's eyes. She saw the surprise and the need in Darry's gaze, and the hunger she felt mirrored within herself. She saw the vulnerability as well, hesitation warring with something primal and altogether lovely.

"It's all right," Jessa whispered, knowing suddenly that she had absolute power over the moment, over Darry's need. What happened next was up to her, but having power was not what she expected. It was not what she thought it would be at all, for the only thing she wanted to do with it was give it away. "Don't stop." *Blessed Vhaelin, please don't stop.*

Darry's thighs trembled and her blood was rushing. Jessa was so beautiful, her hair loose and dark about her face, her eyes filled with emotion. She could feel the press of Jessa's breasts against her and how Jessa's breath came fast. The moment was a singular one and she knew it. It was the second time in but a few days that her entire life had turned on a heartbeat, and the elation she felt now drowned out the heartbreak of the first with a power that might have stopped time.

"Darry." Jessa's voice was touched with a sweet misery that her words were not being heeded. "Will I always be having to beg? It doesn't seem quite fair. If you don't kiss me again I think I might die. I mean it."

Darry captured her mouth once more, and Jessa let out a startled sound at the hand at the back of her neck. Jessa surrendered completely, seduced by the lean power in Darry's body, suddenly at Darry's mercy and thrilled by it. The muscles of Darry's arms were hard and moving against her.

Jessa gasped at the pleasure that blossomed between her legs and into her thighs. Darry's mouth moved hot against her jaw and she tipped her head back. She blinked into the sky above and tried to breathe, the sensations raging through her body more pleasurable than she had imagined they might be. And then her eyelids fluttered as Darry's mouth opened beneath her left ear and tasted of the skin. Jessa pushed her hips forward. *Essa!*

Darry's strong hands eased low on Jessa's back.

"Drassa..."

Darry waited, her heart pounding as her lips brushed Jessa's ear. "Yes?"

Jessa's hand closed hard around Darry's wrist and moved the touch downward. "Yes," she whispered. "More, Darry...*drassa*."

Darry eased her hands onto Jessa's buttocks and took Jessa's mouth in another open kiss that was met with equal passion.

Jessa caught at a jagged breath as Darry's right thigh slipped between her own, and Darry's hands guided her against the muscled leg. Jessa gasped at the pressure against her sex, a stab of pleasure following close behind as Darry kissed her yet again. She found Darry's trousers and pulled, seeking leverage as Darry's thigh pressed harder and her tongue went deeper. Jessa arched forward with equal heat until they were both breathless.

"I want," Darry whispered into her mouth, "I want to do things to you, Jessa."

"What..." Jessa swallowed the taste of her, their lips clinging together. "What sort of things?"

"Wonderful things," Darry said, her hands cupping and squeezing and her lower body rocking forward.

"Things...things like that?"

Darry let her tongue taste of the shadows just beneath Jessa's left ear. "Even better."

Jessa pulled at Darry's hair and forced her face to rise. "Then do them, *Akasha*." Her body was on fire and she wanted more. "Do anything you want, just don't stop."

Darry's blood rose, a quiver of impending release a warning between her legs as Jessa pushed closer against her thigh. The expression on Jessa's face was beyond beautiful and Darry held her tight, forcing them into a tense stillness. "Sweet seven hells...Jess, *wait*."

"Never again. Please don't stop, Darry."

"Do you trust me?" Darry's voice was hoarse as she closed her eyes, pressing her lips to Jessa's cheek. "Do you trust me?" *Please say you do.*

Jessa did not understand why the question was asked, her lips claiming a kiss beside Darry's eye. "I love you, Darry, of course I trust you."

Darry's eyes opened and she pulled back.

Despite her uncertainty Jessa had to smile. She had not known that saying the words to Darry would cause such a pleasing swell of sensations. "Was I not supposed to say that yet?"

"You can say it again if you'd like."

Jessa's laughter was filled with delight.

"I love you too, Jess." Darry smiled. "I didn't know, but I thought maybe you...I mean, I was afraid you might walk straight, no matter how you looked at me. And I didn't want to ruin this, before, us being friends, I mean...so I've been trying to stop it. Oh, gods, Jess, I've been trying so hard."

"It would seem that you have nothing to fear." She felt as if she had been thrown across a great distance, just as Radha said she might. "So please stop trying, *Akasha*."

"I will, I promise."

"Did you just…did you just say that you love me too?"

"Yes." Darry smiled. "Yes, I did."

When they kissed, Darry's heart was pounding so wildly that Jessa could feel it in her own mouth. Everything ached and throbbed and Jessa wanted to laugh and cry, though mostly she just wanted more. She pulled away, though, her lips sore in their need for more of the same. "What…what were you about to say before?" Her hands trembled on Darry's face. She kissed her in a lush, yielding kiss. "Your mouth is so beautiful. And I've been wanting to kiss it for so very long. The night of the fête, Darry, it was so not enough."

"A bed." Darry's voice was uneven. "We need a *bed*."

"I have a bed," Jessa said quickly, her fingers upon Darry's lips, her eyes hazy as she watched the caress.

"You also have a Radha."

"She's very old, and a sound sleeper, I assure you."

Darry laughed. "And could no doubt turn me into a *goat* should she wake to find you screaming."

Jessa found it hard to breathe. "Actually, Radha is very fond of goats."

"Not really the point, love."

"Will there be screaming?" Jessa asked in a whisper, instantly weak at the thought.

Darry smiled tenderly, her expression so warm and filled with promise that Jessa's world tilted yet again. "Only of the sweetest sort, my love, I promise."

Jessa pulled back and Darry loosened her embrace. "Then find us a bed before something inside of me breaks. So we can…*Shivahsa*." She sighed and returned to where she had been, kissing her.

"No, don't do that," Darry pleaded, trying to free her mouth.

"But I like it."

"I can't think."

"You can't do both?"

Darry tried not to laugh. "My love, I can barely stand up."

Jessa smiled at the endearment and kissed her again, Darry holding tighter as she slid her hands along Darry's tunic.

"Jess…please, love…"

Jessa pulled back again. "I like the way you taste." She loosened Darry's collar. "I mean, I *really* like it, Darry." She slipped her right hand beneath the now-open collar of Darry's shirt and Darry stumbled backward, Jessa moving with her. They bumped into the hedgerow with a rustling of leaves and the snapping of twigs. "*Ahbwalla*, Darry!" Jessa laughed. "Where are you going?"

Darry groaned as Jessa pressed her leg between her thighs. "Bloody hell, Jess, stop this now."

"Or what?" Jessa asked, and tasted Darry's neck as Darry's head fell back. "*Essa antua*." Jessa moaned as she pressed her entire body as close as she could. "Does all of you taste like this?" She sucked on the skin beneath Darry's jaw. "Please tell me it does."

"Holy Gamar, Jess…*don't*."

"Have you thought of a bed yet?" Jessa ran her hand along Darry's jaw. "Everything is so soft. My blood is very hot, Darry. Is yours?"

"Yes." Darry took Jessa by the arms, needing her to step back but utterly helpless to force the issue. "Please, you must stop. I can't, you have to stop. Just for a minute."

Jessa pushed at Darry's hair, kissing her neck. "Why?"

Darry closed her eyes, letting out a harsh breath as Jessa's leg moved against her. "Because, please…Jess."

"You're so beautiful." Jessa's lips found Darry's ear.

"Jess, you'll make me spend," Darry managed, and Jessa stilled at once.

Darry tried to move beyond the thunder of her blood, opening her eyes as Jessa pulled back slightly. Jessa touched her face, her eyes filled with emotion. "I'm sorry."

"Don't be. It's just, if you could just move your leg away, that might be best."

Jessa tried to step to the side without actually letting her go. "I didn't…I didn't know I was doing that."

"I did." Darry felt like laughing as she pushed awkwardly from the hedge and Jessa pulled at her jacket. "It was bloody brilliant."

Jessa stared at her for a moment and then stepped close again, wrapping her arms about Darry's neck. "I feel it too. I feel like…I'm very…"

"What, what are you very?"

"I'm very wet, Darry, I can feel it," Jessa whispered, blushing as she said the words. "Are you thinking?"

"Thinking of what?" She was dizzy beneath her raging pulse as she pulled Jessa as close as she could.

"Of a bed."

"Yes, a bed. Say that again."

"A bed?"

"No, the other."

Jessa smiled, her heart flipping over. "That I'm very wet?"

"Yes, that's the one."

"I am."

"You have no idea what that does to me."

"Tell me." Jessa lost her breath. "Tell me, *Akasha*."

"I'd rather show you."

"Yes," Jessa whispered. "Yes, that would be nice too."

"You make me ache. Everywhere, Jess. You make me hurt in places I didn't know could hurt."

Jessa's fingers trembled against Darry's mouth. She wanted to feel her breath as she spoke such words. Words spoken just for her, because of her. "I make you feel like that?"

"Oh, yes, my love. Do you not know how sweet you are to me?"

"Like you are to me."

"Yes. And I hear your voice inside my thoughts, saying a thousand different things, asking me of Hinsa or laughing as you tell me of your Radha, and I feel you in my arms as we danced, or how I wanted to kiss you so badly within my mother's garden when you touched my throat that I thought, perhaps, falling on my sword might be less cruel."

"Less cruel than what?"

"Than knowing you would never be mine."

"I did not mean to tease you. I didn't mean to do that."

"I know." Darry smiled. "I know that, Jess."

"I'm feeling," Jessa's knees gave in slightly and Darry's arms tightened in response, "I'm feeling a bit faint, Darry."

"Yes?"

"Yes. Perhaps you should stop talking like this."

"Then I shouldn't tell you."

Jessa was breathing much too fast and she knew it. "No, you should tell me."

"Should I?"

"Yes, yes, I think that might be best."

"You make me want to come so badly." Darry's lips were but a kiss away. "I want to give you my spirit, Jess, over and over again. Only for you. In any way you wish, however you want me, I would have you take me."

"Bloody hell, Darry." Jessa moaned. "*Essa tua day-ha…*" She closed her eyes as Darry's mouth hovered against her own. "Are you, are you still thinking, *Akasha*?"

"Yes."

"About a bed?"

"That's part of it."

Jessa gathered all of her will into the center of her belly and made it obey. "Concentrate," she said in a rough voice, feeling weak and strong and wonderfully alive. "And think faster." She undid Darry's tunic and slid her open hand on the skin beneath. It was a slow touch and it stole her breath yet again, the utter heat and softness of Darry's flesh. Essa, *this is really happening to me. She loves me. Darrius loves me and,* Shivahsa, *but that taste! It tastes li—*

Darry made a sound in her throat and slipped her hand in Jessa's hair, tipping her head back and then kissing her. Her tongue opened Jessa's mouth and she took what she wanted.

CHAPTER TWENTY-FOUR

"Hold this," Darry said quietly, and Jessa took the taper.

They stood beneath the candle's dim glow deep within the darkness of a secret corridor behind the upper stacks and shelves of the Queen's Library. The stone walls were cold around them, but Jessa felt only heat. They had moved through back hallways and darkened corridors, and through them all they had been touching. Touching hands or thighs pressing close, Darry's mouth upon hers, tongues tangled and arms holding tight. When Darry had taken hold of her from behind after they entered the secret passageway and pulled her close, Jessa had wanted to weep with want. Darry's hand was upon her breast and caressed her through the material of her sari.

Her body had never felt as it did now. She stood within the candle's light and watched the woman she loved scowl in frustration as she searched the door for the catch of the lock. Everything was gloriously on fire and aching with deep echoes of desire, surges of physical pleasure that would blossom in her unexpectedly and delve between her legs or deep into her thighs.

Darry laughed anxiously. "If he locked this I'm going to kill him. I'll bloody well *kill* him."

Jessa yanked at Darry's jacket. "If you've brought me into this tomb and there is no *bed* at the end of it? I shall make you pay, I swear to the Vhaelin."

Darry grabbed her and Jessa dropped the candle. The taper hissed out, casting them in darkness. "*Zaneesha vash*!" Jessa cursed, then smiled as Darry laughed against her neck. "*Nahla tu en gitta pitton*." She found Darry's mouth in the blackness and kissed her boldly. Darry moaned and fell back against the door.

The latch clicked with a loud snap and Darry dragged her mouth away. They listened to the silence for any other signs of life.

"That sounded wonderfully depraved, Jessa," Darry whispered. "Tell me that you were cursing and I shall love you even more."

"Open the bloody door, Darrius." Jessa reached past her and pushed.

The hinges moved with a cracking at first and then swung smoothly. The door opened to reveal more shadows. Jessa could feel that it was a more open space, something decidedly different in its essence than the close corridor they stood within. Darry took her hand and led her within.

Jessa looked up and saw a second story. The circular room was lined with what appeared to be curved shelves, their contents inky and mysterious in the pale light from high overhead. "What is this place?" she asked softly.

"It's a private study." Darry stepped to the door and pushed it shut, locking the bolt. "Jacob and Wyatt found it when they were boys," she said, and struck a flint. The chamber came to light, the golden glow of a lamp flooding out and repelling the darkness.

Several tables were covered with scrolls and books, stacked neatly and well-organized. Next to the tables was a desk and just beyond a wrought-iron staircase that spiraled to the second tier. A circular balcony was built round and gave access to another level of shelves filled with more books and overflowing with parchments, rising to the ceiling where a small chandelier hung within the gloom.

"It was used by my great-grandfather, or so we think." Darry moved across the chamber as Jessa turned in a small circle, trying to find the ceiling. "The papers on the desk were his anyway. It's Jacob's room now."

"Radha says he is a true scholar." Jessa watched as Darry lit another lamp, this one on a small table beside an alcove carved into the stone. The gap was hollowed out in a high, deep oval of space that was opposite the entrance. "I think she likes him very much."

Darry smiled at that. "He sleeps here much of the time, for he reads late into the night and is often gone for days, lost in his scrolls. He turns up in the kitchens eventually, like a ghost in the middle of the night."

Jessa saw that the alcove was almost another room for its size and clean arch, and it contained a rather enormous bed, its mattress covered with a colorfully woven spread. There were pillows as well, and a tapestry was pinned to the wall above the spindle headboard, but it was the sight of Darry beside an empty bed that sent her heart into her throat.

"Alisha changes the sheets and blankets, and she cleans things for him because he forgets. I think they are lovers here, though I cannot say. Jacob is very proper and they're not yet wed."

Jessa pressed her hands against her thighs, hoping that would stop their trembling. *Lovers. We will be lovers, Akasha, you and I.*

Darry set the flint on the table and took a few steps, gazing at Jessa's long hair as it caught the light in a lustrous manner. "We may do as we please here, Jessa, without fear of being found out or spied upon. That is, if it still…if such a thing would still please you, of course."

Jessa let out a slow breath. "It pleases me very much, Darry. It's just…"

Darry tried to think of what she should say, wanting to use the right words. She had thought for so long now that she was not, in fact, worthy of a moment such as this one. Aidan had told her as much, and those words had clung like barbs to her heart, never truly letting go. All of the words spoken that terrible night had marked her, and she realized only now how deeply they had affected her behavior. *But they were lies, Aidan, all the cruel things you said.*

Jessa lowered her eyes to the floor.

"I love you, Jessa," Darry said. *At least I hope she was lying,* Darry thought with a flash of doubt. "Please don't be afraid…because I won't hurt you, Jess. I will never do that."

"I know, Darry. It's just that I've never…" It was all well and good to be bold in the setting sun and flowers, but Jessa was in foreign territory now. She was suddenly very afraid that Darry would be disappointed. "I think you must show me what to do."

Darry's smile was filled with tenderness. "But that is easily solved, my love," she replied in the softest of voices. "Because there is nothing we must do, only what we want."

Jessa remembered Radha's words. *If you don't have the courage to find out for yourself, not even the Vhaelin will help you.* So she moved forward, her heart skipping beneath the heat of Darry's eyes. Her touch hovered for an instant in the air between them, and then she took hold of Darry's jacket.

"What do you want, Jessa?"

"What I have seen in my dreams." Darry's eyes darkened with an infinite amount of color. "May we get undressed now?"

Darry smiled straight away. "Yes, my love."

Jessa slipped her hands beneath Darry's coat and slid her palms along the softness of her tunic, lifting the garment. Darry shrugged and Jessa pulled the coat free and tossed it aside, giving a nervous smile.

Darry's lips curled in her roguish grin, her dimple pressing deep. "Perhaps you might help me unfasten my garments? I don't have the patience for that, as you may recall, and you've made a good start of it already."

Jessa blushed as she remembered the gate of the hidden garden. She traced her fingers along the high collar of the white tunic and then slid downward, watching the play of fabric across Darry's chest and the raised nipples under the silken weave. She felt a tremor move through Darry's body and watched her eyes lift, green and blue so dark Jessa thought she might swoon. It was a terribly powerful expression, and the heat and the wetness pulsed hard between her legs.

Darry gathered her close, burying her face in her hair and breathing deeply. Jessa wove her arms around Darry's shoulders and slid up her back, grasping and pulling the shirt free of Darry's trousers. They were kissing, turning toward the bed in slow unison until Jessa felt the mattress bump against the back of her legs. Darry lifted the ties of Jessa's sari, the question within her eyes.

Jessa seized Darry's tunic and spun them about. Darry was forced to sit as Jessa balanced between her legs. Dark hair rained against Darry's skin and she accepted the deep kiss and reached around, caressing the backs of Jessa's thighs and moving upward.

"You really do taste wonderful." Jessa's breath seized as Darry's touch moved up her buttocks. "I know this taste of yours," she said, understanding yet another part of her visions. "I do."

"There's more," Darry said.

"Do you really love me?" Jessa asked, though she knew the answer. She could see it in Darry's eyes and she knew that her life would never be the same, never again.

"Yes."

"Say it, *Akasha*."

Darry had no idea what *Akasha* meant, but the name upon Jessa's tongue made her insides flip over in a delicious manner. "I love you, Jessa."

Jessa kissed her again and knelt between her legs. Jessa instantly missed the hands on her body but wanted something else even more. She sat back on her heels and took hold of Darry's left leg, her hands certain on the heel of her boot. It came free with a long pull and she tossed it to the floor behind her.

Darry grabbed the edge of the mattress, mauling the covers as Jessa moved to her right boot. She turned her ankle and tried not to smile.

Jessa frowned when the leather refused to move, and she tugged harder. "*Zaneesha seta-allah,*" she mumbled, and Darry's quiet laughter washed over her.

"Try again," Darry said happily.

Jessa's humor rose in her chest as the boot came free. She threw it behind her where it landed with a thud, then she loosed the sock as well. "I hope you're enjoying yourself." She was trying to scold and failed completely.

"Yes, very much, thank you." Darry grinned, her dimple sexy and deep.

Jessa rose upon her knees, her eyes on the fastener of Darry's tunic. She undid it slowly, took a breath, then moved downward, spreading the tunic open to reveal the skin down the center of Darry's body.

The rise of Darry's breasts drew her eyes and she touched the skin between them, trailing her fingers down its smoothness and wanting nothing more than to place her lips there. *There is only what we want.* She bent forward and kissed the skin, becoming lightheaded with the scent of flesh and the absolute softness beneath her mouth. She heard the moan from within Darry's body and felt trembling hands in her hair. *There is only what we want. Only what we want.*

As Jessa followed her desire she felt it, the quiver of pleasure in her sex as she traced the dark skin about the raised nipple of Darry's right breast. Darry's body flinched at the caress and her hands tightened within Jessa's hair.

"*Jess*."

The strain in Darry's voice caused another shudder of pleasure and Jessa pushed hard between Darry's legs, lifting the breast and savoring the tender weight within her hand. She took the nipple in her mouth and kissed it sweetly. Her tongue teased at the hardness of it, for it was what she wanted. "*Dennah nessa enna*, *Akasha*."

Darry let out a sharp sob, yanked the tunic free from her arms, and took hold of Jessa's shoulders. She was kissing her then, her hips pushing to the edge of the bed as Jessa's hands moved along her skin and cupped her breasts between their bodies, kneading them.

Darry dragged her lips away and held her face against Jessa's, closing her eyes tight as Jessa's hands continued to massage. "Jess." Her release was quivering hard, just an instant away. "Jess, I'm sorry." She pulled gently at Jessa's arms until Jessa was forced to stop. "But we must…I'll spend if you keep doing that."

"It feels good? Like before?"

"Take off your pretty dress, my love," Darry said gently, wanting this to be something that Jessa would remember. She wanted to give this to her as best she could; she wanted it for the both of them. "Let me show you."

Jessa closed her eyes, remembering the pleasure in her visions, remembering their potency and how the Waters of Truth had teased her with the promise of this very thing. She felt it again, the hard pulse between her legs and the heavy, throbbing ache that was everywhere. She wanted Darry's flesh against her own, wanted what she had waited so long to find. "I would like that very much, please."

She got to her feet and stepped back to kick off her soft boots and pull at the ties of her dress. The sari slid and slipped as it unwrapped, its silk material opening with a whisper. Her blouse and undergarments quickly followed. Everything pooled to the floor at her feet and Darry stood as Jessa's body was revealed.

Jessa's nipples were hard and waiting to be touched, her skin dark and smooth as her hair fell onto her shoulders in a silken mass of midnight and jasmine. The smooth curve of her hips and her flat stomach led Darry's eyes to the downy black curls nestled at the curve of her thighs.

Darry undid her trousers and pushed free of her clothes, revealing her body in kind. Her skin was clean and smooth, her firm breasts flushed in her want. Everything was sleek, lean muscle, announcing her strength and yet all so natural, so perfectly Darry. Even the bruises Jessa saw, though she felt a flash of worry at the sight of them, she could not consider them clearly. Her only want was to feel that magnificent body against her own.

"You're very beautiful, Darry."

"So are you."

They were together, embracing, skin against skin, everything pressing close and joining as Jessa knew it should. It was what her love was meant for and she trembled at the rightness of it. "*Arribas pahjlah-ne-ellow*." Jessa moaned and lifted her face along Darry's, the feel of flesh making her hold tighter. "Yes, *Akasha*, oh *yes*."

Jessa moved back on the mattress beneath her, watching as Darry set her knee on its edge and looked down at her. Darry's warrior body was even lovelier than Jessa had suspected and she tried to take in all that was happening, but she only wanted her close again. Darry caught up her curls and tied them loosely behind her neck, then moved toward her as if she had read her thoughts.

"Open your legs, my love," Darry breathed, both her mind and body clinging to the merest thread of composure. Her entire world tumbled into place. For the first time everything she knew and understood, everything she had ever dreamt of, every action she had ever taken made complete sense. *I've come home.*

Jessa obeyed and then gasped as Darry slid her body between her thighs, moving her skin on the heat between Jessa's legs. Jessa cried out softly and her thighs clenched in reaction. Darry's pelvis was against her own, moving gently, and her mouth was on Jessa's breast, hot and moist.

Darry thrust slowly and tenderly against her, lifting onto her arms. Jessa held desperately to Darry's neck, her breath coming in short bursts and fueling the heat that was rising between her legs.

"You're the most exquisite thing I've ever seen." Darry brought her mouth close. "It hurts me to breathe." And then she kissed her.

Jessa opened her mouth in total surrender, their bodies moving in rhythm as they kissed. But then Darry's hips pushed harder and she could no longer stand it. She turned her face at the shaft of pleasure that knifed through her. Darry kissed Jessa's neck, her lips taking her slowly downward. Jessa moaned and lifted her body, lost as Darry's breasts slid along her stomach. "*Tua drassa matisse*, *Akasha*."

Darry kissed her breasts, flicking her tongue on the hardened nipples before moving to her belly where her tongue teased the skin around Jessa's navel. Darry reached up and cupped her breasts, kneading them slowly and rolling the nipples between her fingers until Jessa's pleasure was close to pain.

Jessa felt it between her legs and deep within her thighs, and she smiled. The shadows played around the curved ceiling as she writhed on the covers, trying to breathe, though every breath lit a new and more furious fire. Everything trembled and jerked, and her hips pressed and retreated. She cried out when Darry's mouth closed upon her sex, and her shoulders lifted from the bed. She dug her heels into the mattress as she fell back and raised her hips into the kiss.

Darry's tongue moved to the fierce pulse in her mouth as she tasted Jessa's spirit. The flesh beneath her was swollen and glorious, and she explored it all, her tongue sure of what it wanted, her teeth grazing with delicate care. She needed to show her, she needed Jessa to understand that she was everything. To understand that she was the only thing that mattered.

The sounds of Jessa's pleasure filled her head and Jessa's thighs clenched harder around her body. Darry closed her eyes against her own violent need and wrapped her arms about Jessa's thighs as she sucked deeply.

"*Darry*…" Jessa gasped. "I don't…I need, I need to…"

Darry pulled away slowly, kissing her flesh before pushing up. She kissed Jessa's belly, opening her mouth and tugging on the soft skin. She tasted sex and sweat and a hint of something clean and dark beneath it all, knowing that it was the untainted flavor of Jessa's skin.

Jessa's hand was trembling as she touched Darry's cheek, then pushed gently.

"I want you to come in my mouth," Darry said.

"Yes."

Darry's hand was gentle but firm, and Jessa found it hard to breathe as her fingers circled and then teased through an ocean of spirit.

"Hurry, please…please, *Akasha*." Jessa implored within a harsh intake of breath, then cried out when Darry's mouth replaced her touch.

Unable to catch her breath, Jessa could only move and arch as the tears slipped from her eyes. She had never felt such things before. It was piercing and devastating and she wanted it to last forever, but there was a need she could not ignore and her flesh followed it, craved it, demanding to be released. The pressure built until her body could no longer contain it and she came, shouting and reaching a frantic hand into Darry's hair as everything seized and burst with pleasure.

She convulsed and her thighs clenched as she trembled on the bed. Darry's tongue flicked and coaxed from her body smaller shudders as her flesh dissolved and her hips wrenched. When Jessa finally began to still, Darry shifted and slipped her right hand between Jessa's thighs and massaged within the soaking heat. Jessa's thighs clamped tightly about the caress and Darry pulled her over. Her right leg went around Jessa's hips and she held her as close as she possibly could.

Darry kissed her, and Jessa filled with weakness and satisfaction and moaning at the taste of her. Her tears came unbidden, and Jessa turned her face and pressed it to Darry's neck. She gasped as the touch slid from between her legs and the strong hand slid up the small of her back.

"All is well, Jess," Darry whispered. "I won't let go."

Jessa lifted her face and put her hand on Darry's cheek as she fell from what seemed like the highest tower of the Jade Palace and left that dark place forever as Darry's eyes reached out and caught her. She caressed Darry's face and kissed her, sealing the features within her mind.

"Was that all right?" Darry asked.

Jessa kissed her again. "You are joking, yes?"

"You taste like paradise." Darry wanted to come so badly, but Jessa's satisfaction was perhaps sweeter than her own anticipation.

"I did not think…" Jessa's tongue stroked in Darry's mouth and then tasted of her lips in slow demand, "that you would do that."

"I've dreamt of having my mouth on you," Darry said. Jessa's left leg moved between her own and she caught her breath at the pressure against her sex, her body tightening as Jessa's thigh rubbed against her. "Jess, maybe you could…just…"

"*Akasha*." Jessa saw Darry's eyes and moved against her as she reached between them and slid her hand down the muscles of Darry's stomach. Everything was tense and hard beneath her touch. "I'm going to touch you."

"Yes," Darry said roughly. "Yes, whatever you want."

"Is that what you need?" Jessa asked. "Tell me."

"Whatever you want."

"I want to touch you."

"Then just…just touch me, please." Their bodies were together at last, the feel of Jessa's breasts against her and the heat and subtle dampness of her skin, they were sensations that pushed her into a new realm of need. "Please, hurry. Or I think I might spend without you."

"*No*." Jessa's hand slid through her curls. Darry's leg tightened about Jessa's hip as her body pushed forward. "No, don't do that, please."

Jessa caught her breath at the slick heat she found, and she stroked the hard length of Darry. She felt strong hands clutching and Darry's hips moving. Darry was beyond lovely in her passion and Jessa slid her hand farther.

Jessa felt the release and was stunned as velvet muscles seized about her fingers and her hand filled with Darry's spirit. She pressed the heel of her palm against the distended tissues and Darry cried out.

Vhaelin essa yellem ne-ellow! Jessa prayed, and Darry called out her name as if in response, clinging to her. *Vhaelin essa…by all the gods, Darry, you're so beautiful. Oh my love, you're perfect.*

Darry lay spent within her arms, exhaling the sweetest of sounds against Jessa's neck as her strength fled. Her body shuddered and Jessa moved her hand. Darry jerked and moaned in response. "Jessa."

Jessa rolled on top of her and plundered her mouth. Darry grasped weakly, trying to hold her properly. Jessa pulled away slowly, gazing into Darry's languid eyes and smiling as she tried to focus. Darry looked wonderfully dazed. "*Vhaelin essa yellem ne-ellow*," she whispered, pleased beyond anything she had yet felt. *I did that to you, Akasha.*

"Yes." Darry shivered beneath her. "Yes, me too."

Jessa kissed her again and this time Darry's arms were stronger.

Jessa draped along her body, their legs entangled. In time Jessa's heartbeat slowed and settled into a blissful rhythm, and she laid her head on Darry's shoulder. She could feel the smooth muscles of Darry's stomach under her hand. When Darry's right thigh rose along her own, Jessa's heart skipped.

"Well…" Darry said. "I suppose now I shall *have* to give you my horse."

Jessa laughed and met Darry's eyes, which were filled with love. "For certain." She laid her head back down, her body still shaking with humor as she took hold of Darry's waist and held tight.

"At least for an afternoon."

Jessa laughed harder and pinched her hip. Darry let out a hiss and grabbed Jessa's hand. They twisted together and rolled across the bed, where Jessa came out on top and sat astride Darry's hips.

Jessa pinned her arms to the mattress. "*Pootah en tua belowsh*!" She kissed her, releasing Darry's wrists and then took hold of her face. She felt Darry's hands on her hips as her tongue found happiness. Her feelings swelled beyond anything she had ever thought love might be. "More, please."

Darry lifted her shoulders from the bed and took hold of Jessa's waist as she was pulled up, moaning in the heat of their kiss.

❖

Jessa lay naked on the bed as Darry rummaged through the shelves by the desk. She had slipped on her trousers, but that was all. "This floor is bloody cold." Darry chuckled, moving some scrolls.

Jessa saw the deep bruises that darkened the skin of Darry's lower back. There was a strange mark on her left shoulder blade as well, a long welt, dark and angry and the blood stippled just beneath the surface of her skin.

Darry turned with several long candles in her hand. "We can save—"

Jessa stared at the bruise on her ribs and saw that it had darkened even further in the few hours they had been there.

"All is well," Darry assured her, moving to the bedside table. She lit the candles and placed them in an empty holder and blew out the lamp, then sat on the edge of the bed and Jessa pushed herself up and leaned onto her right arm. She slid her other hand gently along Darry's lower back, and the skin was abnormally hot beneath her touch.

Darry stared into the darkness across the chamber. "You must stop this," Jessa said, unable to keep the worry from her voice. "Do you hear me, *Akasha*?"

"I'm a soldier," Darry answered. "Soldiers have bruises."

"Not like these."

"Yes, like these."

Jessa moved her hand up Darry's spine and spread her fingers lightly over the welt. "And this?"

"That was an accident."

"What sort of accident?"

"Etienne's sword is very fast." She closed her eyes at the gentle touch.

"Why are you doing this?"

"The Solstice Tournament is soon. I wish to be ready for it."

Something in her voice sent a sliver of fear melting along Jessa's spine. "And then?"

"And then? And then I win."

"What will you win, *Akasha*?"

"My freedom."

Jessa said nothing. She stilled her hand at the small of Darry's back.

"After I win, I will renounce my title and resign my rank," Darry said, sounding very certain of her words. "And then I will leave this place and never return. I want you to come with me."

When Jessa said nothing, Darry turned and slid her hand along Jessa's neck. "They will never let us be, Jess, do you understand? You were brought here for Malcolm to judge. You're a daughter of royal blood, the blood that is a sworn enemy to my land. Your part in a marriage is meant to bring about a sort of peace that has never been. At least that's what Malcolm would like us to think, but I don't believe it, not for a moment. And even if we disregard such a thing, I've already learned that I'm not to be allowed what I want. They have let me play at my life, thinking perhaps that suddenly I will change my mind and wear skirts to the table and take up lacemaking."

Jessa smiled at the thought. "But don't they know you? There is love in your family, Darry, the likes of which I've never known for myself. I *see* it."

"I'm not saying they don't love me." A look of pain washed through Darry's eyes. "But my father and Malcolm, what they did. I'll not live under that yoke of dishonor, Jess. I love my family and the people of my country. Have I not chosen to serve Arravan with my very life if need be? But no more. All men are allowed the freedom to love as they wish and yet I am not? Who should care whom I steal my kisses from or find beneath me on the sheets of a warm bed?" Darry claimed a slow kiss. "None but the one who lets me steal them."

Jessa could hear the underlying rage in Darry's voice. She slid her hand along Darry's shoulder and down her arm, seeking to calm her.

"Were he anyone but who he is, Owen Durand would've been laid low for what he's done, and Malcolm as well. I'm shocked they've let me *near* you, so great their fear seems to be of who I am. I didn't understand that before, but I certainly know it now."

"What did you mean within the grove?"

"When?"

"When you said that everything was as it was meant to be."

Darry smiled. "That was about you."

"I don't understand."

"I love you, Jessa." Darry's thumb caressed lightly across the surface of Jessa's lips. "When I looked into your eyes in the grove that night, I understood why Aidan left. Beneath everything that was done, all the lies and the deceit, beneath the injustice, it was very clear to me."

Jessa waited, her heart hard within her throat as Darry took her hand.

"I loved Aidan very much, as she loved me. The way in which they broke us apart was filled with disgrace and cruelty, especially for Aidan. But in the grove, I understood something with a clarity I've never felt before. Aidan left because *you* were coming, Jess. She would've always left, no matter the circumstances that brought it about."

Jessa was surprised by her words.

"It could've been no other way."

"You speak of *Senesh Akoata*," Jessa said.

"I don't know what that is, my love, but I know what I felt. Whether you would have ever loved me or not, whether you walked a straight life or turned backwards, it didn't matter. It was as it was meant to be. My heart was meant for you. It was always so, I think, from the moment I was born, perhaps. I felt that in the grove, and it was not just my desire for you or some girlish romantic notion. It was something beyond that, something old and bottomless and so true I could feel it in my bones."

"This is a very deep teaching of the Vhaelin," Jessa said. "*Senesh Akoata* is the spirit woven on the Great Loom, and the soul travels along its threads even when the body is gone from this world."

"You mean fate?"

"This word of yours, it is not full enough for what I mean," she said, crossing her legs as she sat up fully. "When you…" Jessa stopped as she realized what Darry had said.

"And if I had walked a straight life?" Jessa asked, her thoughts disrupted by the full weight of Darry's words.

"It would not have mattered."

"If I had married your brother?"

"Does that mean you'll come with me?"

"Answer my question, *Akasha*. If I had married your brother?"

"I could not have stayed to watch that," Darry said. "But I would've always been close, somehow. And if you had need of me, I would've come."

"But you could've loved another." Jessa's blood turned fierce at the thought of another woman touching what was hers.

"No, Jess. I could not have done such a thing. I've been waiting for you, or at least that's how it feels. Waiting for you to find me. Now that you're here my heart is no longer mine to give. There would be dishonor in taking someone else's love and giving nothing in return."

"They will hunt us down and kill us. If not your family then Joaquin will find a way. Joaquin and his *Shivahsa* dog, Serabee."

"Does that mean you'll come with me?" Darry asked again.

Jessa smiled at the utter beauty of her expression, feeling a touch arrogant that she had managed to capture such a glorious woman. "Of course I'll come with you, *Akasha*. I've been yours since you danced the Mohn-Drom. But did you not hear what I said?"

"*Really*?"

"Really what?"

"Since I danced the Mohn-Drom?"

Jessa laughed. "Yes, since then."

"I didn't know that."

"Arkady Winnows almost lost his life that night."

Darry's brow went up.

"He kissed you and whispered in your ear," Jessa said.

"But you knew I was backwards."

"He kissed you and whispered in your ear."

"It was only a dance."

"He *kissed* you," Jessa repeated pointedly. "And he whispered in your ear. And the Mohn-Drom, *Akasha*, is not *only* a dance."

"Will you always be like this?"

"Like *what*?" Jessa said.

"This." Darry leaned back from her. "All possessive and scary Vhaelin

Priestess. Because if you become upset every time someone kisses me and whispers obscene suggestions in my ear, I'm not sure that we should share the fun of being hunted down and slaughtered together."

Jessa grabbed her by the shoulders and pulled her onto the bed. Darry laughed happily as Jessa climbed astride her body. "You are shameless, *Akasha*," Jessa said, unable to keep the love from her voice. She reached down and opened Darry's pants. "Were his words obscene?"

"No," Darry answered, hearing the threat within Jessa's voice. Her jealousy sent a pleasant thrill along Darry's spine. "They were merely off-color."

Jessa tugged on her trousers and Darry gasped as the seam pressed against her swollen flesh. "What did he say?"

Darry moved her hips slightly. "Oh, well…that's not really an incentive to making me talk, my sweet." She gave a hiss as Jessa pulled again. "A bit to the left, my lo-*oh*…yes, right there."

"What did he say?"

"Tell me what *Akasha* means and I will answer."

Jessa laughed. "Never!"

Darry cupped a breast in each hand and toyed with Jessa's already-rigid nipples as Jessa dissolved into the touch. "Tell me, *Akasha*," she said in a seductive breath.

"He said that my breasts were—"

Jessa pushed Darry's hands away and her right palm landed flat between Darry's breasts, stilling her words. Slowly, she trailed her touch downward. "What did he say to you?"

Darry thought her bones would melt. "He said that he had never danced the Mohn-Drom with a more beautiful partner."

"At least he's not a liar." Jessa gave a sensual smile. "I will let him live."

Jessa rose on her knees and yanked at the waistband of Darry's trousers. She lifted her hips and Jessa shifted to the side and pulled the pants free as Darry bent her knees. They were thrown to the floor as Jessa sat on Darry's right thigh.

Darry dropped her head to the mattress, smiling and catching her breath at the fingers that slid between her legs.

"You're very wet," Jessa purred with wonder and lust. "And I think it's time…" She moved her fingers in the heat and her own passion flared with a need that made her hips push against Darry's muscled thigh. "That I start learning what pleases you, yes?"

"If you say."

Jessa smiled at the sudden need in Darry's voice and tightened her fingers along the tissues beneath her touch. She felt the hardness and the pulse of Darry's want and saw her eyes go dark. Darry's breathing quickened and her breasts were flushed as she pushed against the caress, her nipples stiff and raised.

Jessa moved smoothly, lying along Darry's body and lifting her right thigh. Her breath caught at the spirit against her skin. Darry welcomed the touch and Jessa pressed high and hard against her sex as she took a ripe nipple in her mouth. Darry arched into her, her hands in Jessa's hair, and pulled her closer. Jessa obeyed the silent plea and sucked harder. She brushed her teeth against the taut flesh, quite certain that she had never tasted anything so splendid. She brought her right hand up and took the other breast with moist fingers, rolling the nipple between them as she feasted.

"Jess?"

"Yes, love?"

"That…pleases me."

The muscles of Darry's throat tightened when Jessa pinched the raised flesh between her thumb and forefinger. Darry's hips jerked against her thigh. "That pleases me as well."

Darry closed her eyes and let out a breathless laugh as Jessa's right hand slid down her stomach. "Blessed *Gamar*."

Jessa's fingers caressed and Darry's hips answered their call. "What do you want, *Akasha*? Tell me. Tell me now."

"Right there." Darry's voice broke as Jessa's touch worked the swollen tip of her arousal.

Everything became hard and Jessa explored, sliding along the stiff length of tender flesh and squeezing, dipping in the hot spirit and drenching Darry's flesh with it. She increased the pressure and returned to the place Darry had named, then smiled when Darry shuddered and jerked. Jessa found it hard to breathe as Darry rose toward release. She could feel it in Darry's flesh, in the way her legs tightened, and in the way Darry pushed into her hand. "More?"

"Put…put your fingers…inside."

"Please?"

"*Please*."

Jessa obeyed, letting Darry move against her hand. Her own spirit flowed in response and she felt her need in a wash of heat. She was aching fiercely and wanted to come. She had never seen anyone so completely beautiful before and it sent her reeling. She began to stroke with her fingers, wanting to make her come. She wanted to *make* Darry spend, not just allow it. She wanted Darry to feel her and to know that it was her.

That you are mine now, Akasha, and only mine. Jessa thrust her hand with more authority, unable to curb her need for complete possession.

The scent of Darry's spirit flooded Jessa's senses and she leaned closer. The sound of her fingers stroking sent her own need beyond her ability to call it back. "Are you…are you going to come?" She pressed her thumb hard and circled as she lifted her fingers, and Darry's entire body reacted. "Please, Darry, give me your spirit." Jessa moved and then moaned at the press of Darry's thigh between her own. "Only for me."

"Kiss me," Darry pleaded, and was given her wish.

Jessa had never thought it possible to feel so much for one person, to be so captured by another soul that all of her former life drifted as but a shadow and faded in the brightness of love. And as Darry moved beneath her, their bodies together, their flesh married in the intimate dance of need and desire, she understood at last what she had never been able to comprehend before. As she came against Darry's leg, unable to stop her own excitement as Darry stiffened and cried out beneath her, she understood what the Vhaelin had promised her.

Jessa understood freedom.

CHAPTER TWENTY-FIVE

Jessa stood in the sun of the solar dressed for riding and waiting on the Queen. The request had come just after dawn, and though Jessa felt a great affection for her, she understood the positions they were both trapped in. And beyond that, she knew what Cecelia had done to her daughter. Though perhaps more than Darry could ever comprehend, Jessa was now in a unique position to understand why Cecelia had done it. Jessa knew she would do anything in order to keep what she now had.

She closed her eyes and lifted her face to the light, remembering the night before and how she had parted from Darry. She remembered the tender words and the strong hands that had touched her face.

"I would awake with you in my arms," Darry whispered. "For the rest of my days I would know the sweetness of your body against mine as I open my eyes to the world. And with the strength that such a gift would bring me, I would ride out upon your magnificent horse and conquer that world."

Jessa's heart skipped. "And what would you and my horse do with that world?"

"We would lay it at your feet, where you could choose what things pleased you and which did not." Darry kissed her, tender and slow. "And then we would sit in the sun and watch you with your treasures, wondering what next great feat we might accomplish in order to prove our love to you."

"You needn't prove anything to me, Akasha."

"Perhaps not." Darry smiled in agreement. "You said you loved me."

"I do, I love you, Darry."

Darry kissed her lips. "And that makes me want to, I don't know. I want to sail into the deepest waters and find you pearls. I want to knock down mountains and bring you gold and jewels, then pick you flowers on my way home after such a long day."

Jessa laughed softly, looking into a gaze that held its colors despite the shadows they stood within. "No one has ever made me laugh so much before. I had no idea how such a thing would please me."

"The sound of your laugh makes my spine ache and I become desperate to kiss you. There's no great mystery why I seek to provoke it."

Jessa pressed her face to Darry's and put her arms around Darry's neck, holding tight. Darry pulled her close and her desire, still so near to the surface, heated Jessa's blood anew. "I'm not sure I can look at you without everyone knowing how I feel. Without them knowing what I want."

"But we're friends, are we not?" Darry asked beside her ear. Her lips pulled gently on Jessa's earlobe. "And so we shall continue to be. We must go with great care is all, until our plans are made and the tournament is over."

"When may I have my hands on you?" Jessa slid her cheek back along Darry's until their lips met. "I must know when I might touch you next."

Darry's mouth clung to hers and then she pulled back, a shrewd smile upon her face. "I've discovered your secret."

"What secret?"

Her hand moved in Jessa's hair and she pulled forth a thin braid. She drew her fingers along its length until she held its end, a small but plump round seed woven within the strands. Darry brought it to her nose. "Jasmine."

"You're too clever for your own good, Akasha."

"I've been told that before. Usually right before someone hits me on the head."

Laughter bubbled into Jessa's throat and she tried to push it back down.

Darry kissed her. "You see?"

"I'll not hit you on the head."

"How lovely." Darry grinned. "It shall be a pleasant change."

Jessa moved her hand down the front of Darry's tunic, pulled it open, and pushed her hand within. She glided her fingers on the skin of Darry's stomach. The muscles quivered beneath her touch.

"When, Akasha?" Jessa pushed her arm deeper beneath the shirt as they kissed. She moved her hand up the small of Darry's back and dipped low beneath the waist of her trousers. The feel of Darry's flesh incited

her lust and she pushed farther, grasping and pulling her closer. Darry pressed her to the wall, her hands strong as she held Jessa's hips and rocked against her. Jessa moaned and dragged her mouth away. She let her face brush against the soft skin of Darry's neck and took in her scent, feeling wonderfully lost. "When?"

"Tonight. When the moon reaches Attia's spear. I'll wait for you."

"Jessa? Are you well?" Cecelia asked, smiling at the expression upon Jessa's face. It was a mixture of many things, but mainly she recognized the heady look of desire. *I was right. Are you my daughter's lover, Jessa? Is that what I see in your eyes?*

Jessa's thoughts cleared as she pushed her hair back over her shoulder. "Yes, I'm fine, my Lady," she said. "Are you sure you're well enough to ride?"

"More than well enough, Jessa, and aching to see a bit of country. Let us go, shall we?"

"Yes," Jessa said, and followed.

"You enjoyed your walk in the gardens?"

"Very much, my Lady. Its beauty is a gift. In my country such excess is not permitted." They passed beneath the arch and into the great hall. "The ground in Lyoness can be bitter and many flowers do not like its taste."

"I hadn't thought of it that way before."

"I like your foxglove very much, and your *Fallon-oosh*? The purple flowers that flourish within the rest?"

"Periwinkle." Cecelia nodded.

"Yes, they do not grow in Lyoness."

"They're Darry's favorite. When she was a girl I would go into her room and find them everywhere. Petals and flowers strewn about the bed and chairs. I would ask her what she was doing, and she would always say that she was making a garden."

Jessa laughed. "She is fond of the gardens, yes."

"Has she shown you the maze yet?" Cecelia asked as they passed through the patio doors and onto the lower balustrade.

"Yes. And I've never seen before, what I saw within."

"Owen's great-great-grandfather Boris was a sorcerer of sorts, or so they say. I've seen enough within that bloody maze to believe without a doubt." Cecelia's tone was rueful. "It contains dangers as well as beauty. I almost lost one of my children there once, to one of his…well, I'm not sure *what* to call it, but I was not well pleased."

Jessa's heart beat fast in remembrance of Darry's *Cha-diah* mother, feeling again the weight and size of the panther and Hinsa's purr vibrating into her bones.

As they neared the stables Bentley came forth leading two steeds that were saddled and ready to be ridden. One was a magnificent white mare that was the Queen's own favorite named Dancer, and the other was Vhaelin Star.

"Bentley Greeves." Cecelia greeted him with a knowing smile. "Is this not a bit early for the likes of you?"

He bowed his head as she neared. "Times have changed as of late, my Lady," he said, without a hint of his usual charming smile.

Cecelia remembered his words and his expression of betrayal and outrage as he had confronted her. She took the reins with a pang of regret. "Thank you, Bentley." She rubbed Dancer's soft pink nose and the mare huffed at her and pushed forward.

The filly pulled suddenly at the reins and Bentley was forced to let go. Vhaelin Star stepped to the side with a wild toss of her head.

Jessa stepped forward without pause and held out her hand. "*Barrosha*!" she said, and the filly stretched out her neck, her nose blowing as she took in the scent. The animal stepped forward and lowered her head. Jessa smiled at the greeting.

"She cannot ride her, Bentley," Cecelia said. "She is but green broke and needs to be ridden more. She's too wild yet for—"

"She may ride whom she pleases," Darry said, walking from the stables. "She'll always be wild, my Lady, but she gentles to a hand she trusts. She would run into the ground for that hand unless she be mistreated."

Jessa's heart doubled its beat as Darry approached. She could see the struggle at once. Darry's eyes were hard upon her mother with a look that Jessa had never seen from her before, a violent anguish that Darry seemed to be trying very hard to hide.

Cecelia rubbed at Dancer's nose, Darry's words striking true. "Then we shall have a spirited ride."

Bentley moved about the beautiful mare and held his hand out. "Let me help, Mum?"

Jessa gathered the reins and moved to the saddle as Darry neared.

"You don't have to go with her." Darry spoke for her ears only.

"I would not have said yes, Darry, if I did not wish to go. A hand, if you please?"

"Of course, Princess, my apologies."

Jessa accepted the lift and dropped into the saddle, then reached back down to adjust a stirrup that needed no adjusting.

"Anything else, Princess?" Darry said.

"I'm sure I will think of something."

Cecelia looked down from her saddle. "We will see you at lunch, Darrius?"

Darry spared her but a cold glance. "I practice with the spear. Some other time."

"I will expect you for dinner then, Darry," she responded, a flare of frustration tainting her words. She regretted it instantly. *No, Cat, don't.*

Darry turned on her and Bentley stepped smoothly in between. "I will see that she's not detained, my Lady."

Cecelia held Darry's furious gaze and some part of her reacted instinctively as the mother she was.

Darry pushed Bentley aside. "Is there something you wish to say, my *Queen*?"

Cecelia was suddenly trapped and she knew it. "Please don't take that tone with me, Darrius."

"Or what?" Darry said. "You'll take my sword away next?"

Vhaelin Star screamed at the scent that filled her nose, and Jessa maneuvered her to the side with an expert hand. Dancer shied as well and Cecelia pulled the reins as they backed away.

"Will you tell your husband I've been a disobedient child?" Darry said, Hinsa's blood rushing within a heartbeat. It was heady and dark, and it felt clean and right. It was as if she could wrap her arms around the world and crush it if she wanted. "Perhaps he can think of a more fitting punishment this time for his deviant offspring, yes? Lock me in the dungeons until I go blind and swear to change my ways? A marriage to some weakling Lord? Perhaps all I need is the prick of a man's cock, yes? Perhaps he can *fuck* me into being who you want!"

Bentley pulled Darry away from the mare. "*Ride*," he ordered Cecelia in a hard voice.

Cecelia jerked the reins and Dancer obeyed, spinning to the left and then bolting at the touch of a heel. Bentley turned but Darry was walking along the barn, yanking her jacket off as she went. He looked up. Jessa was tense in the saddle as she watched Darry round the corner of the stables and disappear.

"You must go with the Queen, my Lady."

Jessa studied his face, his hand on the stirrup. "Where is Darry going?"

"The yards. She'll try to stop it, but most likely it's too far gone. I've never seen her so easily pushed before, my Lady. She'll have to fight it out."

They stared hard at one another and Jessa saw his absolute devotion to Darry. He, in turn, clearly saw all of her passion. Neither could hide even the smallest part of their affection nor deny their love in the presence of the other. Without a word their bargain was struck.

"If I find but one fresh mark on her body, Bentley Greeves, you will answer to me," she said with confident menace. "Do you understand?"

Bentley smiled at the threat. "I shall do my best, Princess. I swear upon my love for her. Or should I swear upon yours?"

Jessa saw the true depth of his famous charm. "Either will do," she answered, and turned Vhaelin Star. The filly jumped forward in compliance.

❖

Cecelia walked among the grove of poplars as a pleasant breeze washed over her. Jessa strolled behind her at a short distance, seemingly content at the silence between them and occupied elsewhere. She would kneel in the tall grass and study the wildflowers that bloomed. Or she would walk off to the side, intent upon some goal that Cecelia could not fathom. When after a time Cecelia sought her out, she found her sitting with her back to one of the poplars, gazing up into its foliage.

Cecelia sat in the grass close by and Jessa said, "This is a very peaceful place. It seems to know you."

"It should. I've been coming here for many years."

"What is it called?"

"The Queen's Grove."

Jessa glanced up into the leaves. "Yes, of course."

"When I'm feeling lost, it always seems to find me."

Jessa said nothing, thinking that perhaps Cecelia wanted to talk and wondering if she had been summoned for that very purpose.

"I used to come here every day, after my daughter died."

Jessa hid her surprise at the unexpected revelation and pulled slowly at a long blade of grass.

"Her name was Jacey Rose." Cecelia paused. "She was four years old when she was taken by the marsh fever. She had dark eyes like yours and hair as black as pitch. Very much like yours as well, actually."

"I had a sister once, or so I'm told," Jessa replied, thinking that she could share in kind if only a little. This was Darry's mother, after all, whether they saw eye to eye at the moment or not. "But she was killed when I was very young. Radha says I was but one or two when she was born."

"She became ill?"

"No."

"I'm sorry."

Jessa considered the blade of grass she held. "Sometimes I wonder what she might've been like. If we might have been friends."

"I'm most certain you would have. You would have made a fine older sister."

"Like Emmalyn."

"For certain. But you have other siblings as well. Twelve brothers, Jessa. It is a large family."

"They are many, this is true. My father had four, no, five wives before my mother. They are but half blood to me."

"But not a one to be your friend?"

Jessa did not answer.

"And Joaquin?"

"Joaquin is closest to me in age." Jessa tossed the blade of grass aside and chose another. "He is my keeper."

Cecelia frowned at the word. *There's no love between you, that I can see.*

"When my father saw I had a sort of value, for men found me to be beautiful, he appointed Joaquin to be my guardian until he could find a suitable use for me. This has never pleased Joaquin. He sees no opportunity to advance in our father's eyes with such a weight about his neck."

Jessa's graceful fingers folded the delicate stem of grass. She was indeed stunning, and the thought that Bharjah considered her as nothing more than chattel pricked hard at Cecelia's temper.

"How old was Darry, when your Jacey died?"

"I became pregnant within the same year, actually, and it was too soon, perhaps. I'm afraid that a burden was placed upon my Cat that no one should have to endure." Cecelia found it sinfully easy to talk to Jessa. *And you should know these things, if you will love my daughter.* "Owen took his grief strangely. When Darry was born it was very difficult for him to leave her. He was extremely protective, which I understood, but he found it difficult to show his affection as well. Even though he loved her desperately from the start."

"He was afraid?"

"Perhaps. He was nearly broken when we lost Jacey Rose. He had doted on her so. Jacey looked so much like him and he would take her everywhere, even to his council meetings. She would sit quietly in his lap while he discussed land contracts and Gamar knows what else. When she eventually started talking, discussing nonsense most times, he would listen very intently. He would let a room full of Blooded men wait until she and he finished their conversation of dresses and dolls and pretty flowers."

Jessa smiled at the picture she described.

"She was such a gentle child, always very ladylike. She didn't like her hands to be dirty and would hold them up if they were, until someone would help her. She liked Emmalyn to do it, actually. She worshipped Emma."

Jessa could hear the stark sadness and her throat tightened. It was perplexing yet lovely to see a mother's love so on display.

"Darry was very different from the first. She was a complete mystery to Owen. Her will has always been so bloody strong, and she chafed at being held back in any way. He would try to protect her, and she would look at him as if she were seeing something that no one else could. She would say then, 'I will love you, Pappa, even if you say no.' And he would relent and say, 'Fine, then, do as you wish.' She was always so fearless."

"It is her nature," Jessa replied. "She cannot be otherwise."

"I know. And I would have her no other way."

"Her fire, I think, is much like yours."

Cecelia took the compliment with a smile. "Perhaps. The Lewellyn blood can be somewhat wild at times."

"Like your Nina," Jessa said. *She is much like my love, I think.*

Cecelia chuckled. "Yes, like Nina."

"And when Darry began to fight?"

"Yes." Cecelia sighed. "When she first took up the blade Owen was furious. And he was quite angry with me as well for I'd given her my permission. He allowed her to do it, though, for he thought it a passing fancy. Her brother Wyatt and Darry are thick in their blood, and he became her champion. When Jacob found his passion in learning and Wyatt in the ways of the sword, they stopped being boys together. Darry had followed them about like a ghost for many years, and though they adored her completely, she was but a girl to them."

"And when did they see her differently?"

"When she bested Wyatt during practice. It was a heated battle of wooden swords, and Owen and I watched from the fence. Cat moved so beautifully, and after a time she began to fight within the steps of Honshi. Do you know this?"

"The Dance, yes," Jessa replied. "My brothers have all trained in its ways, though only Kaliq and Sylban follow the discipline. It is very difficult to master, Radha says. You must let go of yourself and take on the will of your weapon."

"Yes, well, it was then that things changed."

"She had proved her skill." Jessa remembered Darry's deadly beauty in the practice yard.

"Owen realized it was not just a passing thing," Cecelia replied. "We argued terribly and I lost. He could not be swayed or convinced to allow her such a dangerous thing. Later that day he called them both into the throne room and forbade her the sword. It was a horrible fight between him and our son, and he charged Wyatt with seeing that his wishes were obeyed.

"They were both yelling so fiercely, but Darry merely stood there and watched her father. When Owen demanded in his rage if she understood that she was to fight no more, she simply said no. Twelve years old and she stood before the King in all his fury and calmly defied him. 'I'm sorry that I'm not Jacey Rose,' she said, 'but I will never be her. You must let me go my own way now.'"

"What did he say?"

"Her words threw him because of their hard truth. He lost his temper and reacted badly. He asked her to repeat herself and Darry said quite clearly, 'Jacey Rose is dead.'" Cecelia closed her eyes. "He advanced on her and I yelled, stopping him, but Darry held up her hands and said, 'Do you see, Pappa? My hands are dirty and I'm happy that they are. I'm not her and you can't make me so.'" Cecelia opened her eyes, an expression of regret on her features. "He struck her and she fell to the stones."

Jessa looked down at her hands, hoping to hide her emotions.

"He had never hit one of his children before. I was rooted to the floor with shock, though when I spoke his name he turned…and he was so pale, so horrified by what he'd done. He went to help her up, but Darry hurried away before he could. Her nose and mouth were bleeding badly. He had struck a true blow, as a man sometimes strikes another man.

"She didn't cry, though. She just let the blood run down her face. Wyatt was there and put his arm around her, and I will never forget how he looked at Owen, *never*…

"I ran to her and she let me lead her away. She was shaking and I wanted desperately to hold her, but she wouldn't let me. Wyatt was there and she took his hand. I cleaned her up and Wyatt took her to her rooms.

"After about an hour I went to her, whether she wanted me there or not. She was sitting near the hearth amidst complete destruction. She had destroyed everything that could be destroyed and her hands were bleeding from the shards of one of the broken lamps. Then she began to cry and reached out to me. I held her until she stilled and I saw that she had passed out. Her face was terribly bruised and her lips cut and swollen.

"I rushed her to my own chambers and the healer came. Owen sat beyond the door as she was washed and given a draught to calm her emotions. Her wounds were tended and she seemed to sleep.

"I went to Owen and we stood in the corridor as he struggled against his regret. 'We should not have had another child,' he said. 'If this is how I am, if I can cause such pain it was a mistake to have her. Another child was a mistake.' He walked away before I could respond. When I turned back to our chamber, Darry was standing near the door."

Jessa closed her eyes. *Akasha.*

"I tried to explain to her what he meant, that he was frightened and didn't mean it as it sounded. But Darry just stared at me." Cecelia looked puzzled, even after all this time. "And to this day, I still cannot decipher her expression."

Jessa's thoughts filled quietly with Darry's voice. *I was twelve, and I wanted to go with Hinsa and live with her.*

"The damage caused that afternoon still lingers between them. Owen has never forgiven himself, and Darry cannot forget the words he spoke. It had nothing to do with her and everything to do with his fear and shame at what he'd done, not knowing how he might undo it."

They sat in silence as the leaves spoke above them, a dance of movement within the breeze.

Jessa formed the words within her head, debating her tone for an instant and preparing her tongue for the innocence she wanted to convey. Joaquin would pursue them, she had no doubt, but she wanted desperately to have some idea of Cecelia and Owen's reaction when she and Darry broke from Arravan and Lyoness. Darry was set in her mind and was protecting her honor, but perhaps she was not thinking clearly enough about the consequences of their actions. This would fall to Jessa, and she was more than willing to shoulder that responsibility. She never lost at Kings and Jackals either, which resembled the long game she and Darry were soon to engage in. She asked her question. "Why did he break her from Aidan?"

For many reasons, none of which were good enough, and he knows it. "In the end?" Cecelia was impressed that Jessa would ask the question. *Well played, my girl.* "I believe it was for the same reason he tried to deny her the sword."

Jessa was shocked. "He thought her being backwards was a passing thing?"

"I'm not certain, Jessa, but this is what I believe. It's not something we talk of, though that will change now."

"But it's *love*, my Lady, and love is…" Jessa stopped before she spoke her mind on the subject. "Perhaps he has yet to learn his lesson then."

"Perhaps. And what do think he should learn, Jessa?"

"That is not my place to say, my Lady."

"Owen is not a hard man, Jessa. If I've given you that impression, it was unintended."

"Not a hard man? Yet his actions thus far concerning his daughter might say otherwise."

"He's but a man, Jessa, and men make mistakes. That he is the King does not change that fact."

"And yet Darry is the only child that he has struck, according to your own words. And it was Darry's lover that he threatened and their affair that he destroyed, denying her love that is the birthright of all men. It is Darry's heart that he has wounded, perhaps beyond repair now that she knows the truth. I wonder what else he might do to her that you would consider but a simple mistake."

Cecelia wanted desperately to smile, for either she would tell Jessa the truth as she saw it or defend Owen and reveal the truth just the same. In either case, Jessa could then predict what to expect from them. *So you will leave with her then, yes, Jessa? But if I tell you that Owen will most likely do anything within his power to make amends, how easy will it be for you to take my daughter and disappear into the night? Darry will never forgive him for Aidan and I've always known it.* "You have no intention of marrying my son, do you?"

"Your son has no intention of marrying *me*, my Lady. None whatsoever."

"And how do you know this?"

"Because he refuses to look me in the eyes. And when he does I see evasion, and indifference as well. He is more enamored of my brother than of the thought that I might share his bed."

Cecelia recognized the truth within Jessa's words. *Malcolm, what are you playing at then?* "Yes, I suppose that would trouble a prospective bride. Though you don't seem very troubled."

Jessa said nothing.

"And if he did look you in the eyes?" Cecelia challenged her openly, and either Jessa would lie or she would reveal everything. "If Malcolm wanted you in his bed? What would you do then?"

Jessa didn't answer, for it was a trap and she knew it. But she had learned patience at Radha's knee and was certain that Cecelia wanted something from her, though what it was she would need time to decipher.

"You would be a queen, Jessa, as your mother was."

Jessa's expression became fierce at the comment, the color dark within her face.

A tremor of unease moved through Cecelia but she forged ahead. "And a queen wou—"

"I was tempered within the cold fires of the Jade Palace, my Lady," Jessa said. "When Bharjah learned that my mother had not given him a son, he took her from me and kept her prisoner until she was with child again. I was suckled upon Radha's breast and so never knew my mother's touch. When she bore him a second daughter, he crushed my sister's skull on the stones and slit my mother's throat when she tried to stop him."

Cecelia stared in open shock.

"The prospect of being a queen holds very little appeal to me," Jessa replied, with steel in her voice. "And at the moment, it does not appear to have done you much good either." Jessa shifted smoothly and rose to her feet. "I would like to walk among the trees now, my Lady. When you wish to leave, if you would let me know?"

"Of course," Cecelia answered, still stunned by the intimate revelation and the cutting observation as to her own plight.

Jessa bowed her head in respect before walking away.

CHAPTER TWENTY-SIX

Jessa stepped into the corridor behind the upper shelves of the Queen's Library and closed the secret panel behind her, shutting herself within the gloom. She lowered the cowl of her cloak, whispering a spell as she did so.

The air before her reacted to the quiet words and began to move, churning slowly. The utter black of the corridor seemed to melt away as a swirling point of air began to glow, rotating smoothly at first and then picking up speed and forming a small orb of substance. The atmosphere thickened around her as the radiance of the witchlight became more dense. A white core of energy pulsed slowly from its center as Jessa dipped her fingers in it. The sphere reacted as water might and bent inward. Small veins of blue light bled away from her touch, adding depth to its light and illuminating the corridor.

Jessa spied the door, then caught her breath in surprise. The sphere pulsed and exploded outward, doubling in size in a heartbeat and then tripling within the next. The blue veins split and burst free, splintering like lightning toward the secret chamber in the distance. The air cracked like the breaking of branches as they traveled, and Jessa stumbled against the wall. The majik slammed against her as the witchlight crawled on the surface of the door. She struggled to regain her balance and slid forward, speaking the counterspell in a rush of words.

The ball of light bent strangely in response and collapsed inward with a noise not unlike the blowing of the bagpipes. The sound was low and discordant as Jessa winced and turned her face away, and her hair blew back as she lifted a hand to protect herself.

"*Shivahsa*!"

The witchlight moved upon the door as if it were a wild animal. Its blue claws scraped the wood and found the weakest point, flooding within an old crevice and pouring downward as she stared. The light broke apart near the floor and spilt to the stones in a shower of sparks and hissing streamers, filling the air with the pungent tang of a summer storm. The iron handle of the door was glowing, white light snaking about the metal with a high-pitched sound that sang along the wrought iron.

Jessa stepped forward and spoke the counterspell again, the strength of her voice filling the corridor and echoing along the stones as the witchlight gathered in a molten pool at the threshold and then disappeared, bleeding in a rush beneath the door.

"*Darry*."

She ran, closing the distance, then seized the door's handle. The metal froze against her skin as she threw the door open, and the light dripped free from her fingers as she stepped within the chamber.

Darry was crouched against the far curve of the wall beside the bed, her right arm extended before her as the witchlight swarmed about her hand. The blue light threw her features into extreme contrast against the golden glow of the lamp.

Jessa stumbled against the door as the Vhaelin within her blood surged up at the heavy scent in the room. It was torrid and filled with a potent, seductive musk of power that caused her heartbeat to stutter and then lurch within her chest.

Darry stood up slowly as the witchlight slithered up her arm. She shook her arm and the light splattered against the floor at her feet. An abrupt sound, the warning bark of a panther, echoed high into the upper expanse of the chamber.

Darry flung her arm violently and the light left her with a splash, thrown free. It clung to the wrought iron of the spiral staircase where it hissed and fell away in defeat, dropping to the stones and dissolving into nothing.

Darry turned and met her eyes.

She wore but brown trousers and a white tunic that was only half tucked in, her hair tied behind her neck in freshly washed curls. Her feet were bare and she had never looked more wild, her eyes alive with an abundance of color as they moved down Jessa's body and claimed what was hers.

Jessa could smell it, the *Cha-diah* blood. It assaulted her senses in a way she had no chance of stopping, a buzz of dizziness pushing up from the base of her neck and making her sway. She leaned more heavily against the door, grasping for the handle.

"Shut it," Darry ordered.

Jessa stood completely still, uncertain if she should move, uncertain if she even could. The majik in the chamber was unbearably thick, Darry's scent a living thing as it reached out to her. The musk moved against her skin, and when she took a breath, it poured down her throat like the brazen touch of Pentab Fire.

Jessa tipped her head back and parted her lips as she exhaled in a push of breath. A quiver of arousal slid along her sex and everything tightened, aching with need.

"Shut the door, Jess."

Jessa's spirit flowed at the command and she was instantly wet. Her grip twisted on the handle of the door and she took a tentative step, then another, pulling the door around and then pushing against it until it swung shut. The click of the latch was like a mountain falling within her head.

And then she waited, resting her forehead against the wood and closing her eyes, faint beneath her own heartbeat. She heard nothing, but when Darry's scent intensified she knew she was close, and her blood knew it as well.

The breath was hot beside her ear. Just that. Just a breath.

Jessa's majik rose up in self-defense. It faltered at first but then pumped with confidence through her veins. *Essa tua Vhaelin*, she prayed, and felt a profound swell of fear at the absolute force of it, at the raging in her ears. The *Cha-diah* scent wove itself within her own blood, lush and wild. Jessa let out a low moan of appreciation. *Is this how you feel, Akasha? Bloody hell…*

Another breath. Just that. Just a breath.

Jessa wanted to be touched, and she pushed back, her hips finding what she needed.

Darry slid an arm about Jessa's waist and stepped against her, thrusting her pelvis against Jessa's backside and pinning her against the door. She pushed the dark hair aside and rubbed her face against Jessa's neck. And then she tasted her with her tongue, and Jessa's entire body jerked and her hips pushed back yet again.

Strong hands were at her throat and the brooch that held Jessa's cloak came free, both the garment and the pin tossed aside. Just the slightest brush of Darry's fingers against her throat and Jessa thought she might spend.

Darry took her by the shoulders and turned her about, their eyes meeting as her hand found Jessa's stomach.

"You won't hurt me." Jessa took a quick breath, seeing something other than desire in Darry's gaze. Her breasts were aching and her legs heavy with need. Jessa was unable to feel anything but her want. She was more than willing to risk whatever she had to for satisfaction. Though looking into Darry's eyes, she wondered if surrender might have consequences that her majik would not submit to. "You may do as you like."

Jessa let out a cry as Darry yanked her tunic open. Her body jerked forward. Darry's open mouth was on hers and Jessa was trapped against the door beneath Darry's strength, beneath a kiss meant to consume her.

She pulled blindly at the tie in Darry's hair and freed the curls and shoved her hands within them. She moaned at the stroking heat in her mouth and the fierceness of the full lips against her own. Darry reached between their bodies and ripped the stitching on Jessa's skirt. Her right hand slid beneath the waist and undergarment, then her fingers moved through the soft hair between Jessa's legs.

Jessa pushed against the caress, tightening her hands in Darry's hair and yanking her head back. She had never been so seduced by the aura of another power, not ever. No majik had ever enticed her so completely that she had no control over her own reaction to it.

"I thought you were a panther," she taunted her, then hissed at the fingers that squeezed her flesh, slick within her spirit. "Where are your claws, *Akasha*?" she asked, then smiled, her Vhaelin blood exploding with life. *We shall see, my beautiful panther, yes? What we're both made of.*

Jessa had never experienced its like before, though she had always felt it waiting within the distance of her soul. It was the majik she had never been able to summon no matter how hard she had been pushed, no matter how fervently she had prayed for its release. It screamed now through her body in answer to Darry's need, rising to meet the *Cha-diah* majik that assailed the very heart of her being.

Darry was silent as she pushed against the restrictions of Jessa's clothes, her fingers insistent as Jessa's passion fell beneath the raw darkness. She was slow as she entered her body, but Jessa moved hard against the touch, thrusting back as Darry's fingers pushed deep and began to stroke.

"More," Jessa implored, and pulled Darry close. Her vision had turned deep and piercing, and Darry's eyes were fairly glowing. *Bloody hell, Akasha, what have you done?* "I thought…the panther was fast, yes?" she said, and kissed Darry fiercely, biting Darry's lips and her tongue as her world caught fire.

Darry jerked at the sting and shoved against her, driving into her more quickly and taking what she needed, discarding all tenderness. The flesh about her hand was so swollen and wet that Darry's own release rippled hard between her legs.

Jessa's mouth opened against Darry's as she cried out. The door rattled in its frame as she was taken. She clawed at Darry's neck and shoulders, shouting as her head fell back against the door. Her climax rose around the strokes of Darry's fingers and burst like a storm beneath the fast press of Darry's palm. Darry bit Jessa's neck and sucked the skin.

"*Akasha*!"

Darry beat the heel of her palm against Jessa's flesh and Jessa came with a broken cry. Darry held her up as she spent. Jessa's hips strained as everything opened wide inside of her, freeing more than her spirit.

"*Yes*!" Jessa cried out, and laughed, breathless. "Did you," she swallowed and pushed the hair back from Darry's face, "did you feel that?"

Darry let out a growl of need and yanked free of the touch, lifting Jessa up and forcing her legs open. Jessa's thighs tightened and she leaned away from the door, grabbing Darry's face and coercing her mouth wide as Darry carried her across the room beneath the scorching kiss.

Jessa bounced on the mattress and Darry slid on top of her. Jessa pulled at Darry's tunic and the fabric ripped as the garment came open and Darry's breasts moved against her own. They moaned in satisfaction as their bare flesh met. Darry moved against Jessa's thigh and Jessa pulled at her, clawing at Darry's trousers and then grabbing her hips.

Jessa's blood sang with her majik and she closed her eyes, letting it come, letting it flow into every part of her body. "Yes." A burst of light flared within her head and seared through her skull. Jessa was transfixed. "*Akasha, yes*!"

Darry's thrusts were furious and Jessa urged her on, meeting her with equal strength as Darry's strangled sob broke free and she spent her spirit, lifting onto her arms and then slamming into her release. Jessa watched in awe as Darry arched back with muscles straining, her violent shout of liberation filled with a passion that clawed at the darkest depths of Jessa's power and pulled it free.

Jessa caught her as she fell. Darry moaned as her hips jerked and she moved through the waning of her climax and fell to the side. Jessa closed her eyes and tried to breathe, unsure if she could control what raged inside her. Unsure if she even wanted to.

"Did I…did I hurt you?"

"*No*." Jessa pushed her hair back with a trembling hand, witchlight bleeding from her fingertips and moving within her hair, weaving through her braids. "No." The tightness of desire was still rising, wrenching at her as she smiled. "*Akasha*?"

Darry's hand slid along Jessa's belly and Jessa arched upward as the hand closed upon her breast. "I want more." Darry spoke in a ragged breath. "I need more, Jess."

"*Nessa abwello,* so do I." Jessa groaned in deliverance, rolling over and claiming Darry's mouth. Her hand was rough as she yanked open Darry's trousers and shoved within them. Darry thrust into the contact.

"Can you?" Jessa gasped, her hand drenched in Darry's spirit. "*Shivahsa*, Darry!"

Darry pulled at Jessa's skirt. "Get this…*off*…"

"Wait." Jessa laughed, breathless as she freed herself from her skirt and breeches and climbed on top of Darry. She wore but her boots and torn shirt, which fell from her shoulders.

Darry let out a shout at the demanding touch between her legs and Jessa reveled at what she saw, Darry's body coiled tightly, so much strength at her mercy. "In my hand, *Akasha*." Jessa rose onto her knees and Darry's hips thrust tightly between Jessa's legs, clenching and straining upward as Jessa pushed her to the verge. "Let me feel you spend."

"*Jess*."

Jessa's left hand landed firmly between Darry's breasts. "You're so hard." She smiled, feeling altogether dark and lush. Darry's scent was inside her, a living thing. The panther was inside of her and her majik had awoken at last to meet the challenge and throw back the invasion. "Can you feel me?" Jessa's heart had never beat so fast. Darry's head pushed back into the bed. Her throat was exposed completely and the sight of the offering filled Jessa with a rush of dominance as well as love. "Come for me."

"Jess!"

"Come in my hand, do it *now,*" Jessa demanded, Darry's flesh opening beneath her quick, forceful fingers. "Darry."

Darry grabbed Jessa's thighs as her entire body seized and gave in.

"*Akasha*." The *Cha-diah* majik swarmed over Jessa in a sensual haze and she soaked it in, feeding on it.

Darry's body trembled and Jessa felt her power like never before as she settled on Darry's thighs. She felt the power of the Vhaelin and the strength of her blood reaching back through the generations, of her majik released and claiming her at last. She felt the sway of her love and lust for the woman beneath her. The woman who had stirred into life so many things inside her, the least of which might have been her majik. Jessa brought her hand up and slowly tasted her fingers, smiling in absolute victory.

Darry grabbed Jessa's waist and Jessa looked down at her, dipping her hand between them once more and playing for a moment. She painted the hard muscles of Darry's stomach with the evidence of their passion. Her heart gave a push as the flesh quivered beneath her touch, and she rubbed herself against Darry's abdomen. "If you touch me but a little, my love, I will spend," she said. "I want to come on you."

Darry licked her lips. "You…you do it."

Jessa obeyed, her right hand slipping between her legs.

Darry watched as she stroked herself, her hand becoming a blur of motion. She had never known a woman so beautiful or so dangerous. Jessa threw her head back as she spent, half laughing and moaning her bliss.

Something ancient trembled along Darry's bones and she knew it was majik, though whether it was hers or Jessa's she had no idea. All Darry knew was that they were both in trouble. She smiled at the joy of it and held Jessa close as her mouth tasted of the sweet flesh on the inside of Jessa's left breast.

Strong hands fisted in Darry's hair and Jessa's trembling voice filled her head. "Did you feel that?"

"Yes." Darry groaned. "Yes."

"I want your mouth next, *Akasha*."

Darry laughed helplessly.

"Will you taste what I have for you?"

"You'll kill us."

Jessa laughed, the sound low and wanton. She took Darry's earlobe in her teeth, rough for a heartbeat as her tongue savored and then her lips soothed at the mark. "Maybe," Jessa whispered. "Maybe just you."

Darry's body shook with startled laughter.

"Did I not say I wanted your mouth?"

Darry was at Jessa's mercy and liked it. "You want me to fuck you with my tongue?"

Jessa smiled at the deliberate words. Darry slipped her fingers inside her, slow but certain. "Is this how you talk, Princess?" Jessa took a heated kiss from her. "Is it?"

"Sometimes." Darry searched for more when Jessa pulled away.

"I like it," Jessa said. "Yes. I want you to fuck me with your tongue."

"If I start, I'll not stop until you beg me."

"Fair enough."

"Until you can't even scream. Until all you know is my tongue."

Jessa thought she might spend then and there, all her senses locked tight upon the slow touch within her body. "You really need to stop talking now."

Darry freed her hand and took Jessa with strength, throwing her onto the mattress as Jessa laughed in surprise. She propped herself onto her elbows and watched as Darry stood, stripped from her clothes, and dropped to her knees beside the bed. She grabbed Jessa's booted ankles and pulled her toward the edge. Jessa smiled as her head bounced against the blankets and her braids scattered.

Darry's hands smoothed up her thighs and Jessa swallowed roughly, catching hard at her breath. Darry placed Jessa's legs over her shoulders and began to taste her way along Jessa's inner right thigh.

"You're right," Jessa said within a gasp. Darry gave her exactly what she had asked for. Jessa grasped one of the spindles of the headboard and the wood creaked at her violent pull. "This might not..." She let out a glorious cry of pleasure that turned into a wild laugh. "Might not, *Shivahsa*!" Darry's mouth was like a red hot flame. "Not...not *end* well."

Jessa let the panther have her way. She let Darry have her way until she had no idea how many times she cried out; she only remembered that she had not begged. She could not remember how many times they both came or even when Darry's blood finally relented. The Vhaelin within her was sated and she hummed with approval that she had tamed the panther into submission. And with the taste of Darry's spirit on her tongue Jessa let her sleep. Darry lay thoroughly defenseless and yet never more protected along Jessa's body.

Jessa held her with reverence, caressing the strong arm that was thrown lax across her stomach, unable to refrain from still touching her in some way. She sensed the slumbering force of Darry's body and knew the softness and heat of her breath. Darry's breasts pressed against her and the lean muscles of the leg draped between her own.

Darry was more pure in her essence than Jessa could ever imagine being herself. Darry let her see everything, not only giving over her body, but her heart and soul as well. Jessa had seen it as they had made love, so furious and with such utter abandon. Jessa had seen it in Darry's eyes.

Jessa understood that she was inexperienced at such things, at love, but she was not innocent. From the first throat Jessa had seen torn out by Sylban's dogs, she had not been innocent. She recognized the fragility and the wasteful, cruel nature of life. She had known no mystery since witnessing that first violent act, and she had no illusions as to what life could be. Without reserve and caution one's chances of becoming a casualty were extremely high. Or so she had thought. Now she was not so certain.

Radha had been wrong. *What need do people have for dreams that don't come true? Every need, old woman. Vhaelin essa, there is every need.*

And even the Waters of Truth had not shown her this, and there Radha had been right. The truth of her heart had been hers to discover.

Darry stirred against her, and Jessa closed her eyes in quiet joy as Darry's body shifted smoothly, skin against Jessa's skin. Darry's arm tightened about her waist and she opened her eyes and lifted her face. She was still caught within her sleep. Darry's eyes were nearly black within the now-fading light from the lamp, her face serene yet filled with a fierce beauty.

"Majik?"

"Yes, my love. My majik is more than yours," Jessa said softly, shifting and kissing her.

She studied Darry's face and pushed a strand of her hair to the side. She placed the softest of kisses on Darry's left cheek, knowing very well where the dimple hid in wait for Darry's roguish grin.

"*Nessa-ahna allah sheetun, tua de Akasha*…my love." She held her face against the heat of Darry's, breathing in her beguiling scent. *You are the wish, Akasha. The wish that I never knew enough to make.*

CHAPTER TWENTY-SEVEN

The tantalizing smell of strong *karrem* filled Jessa's nose and she woke slowly. She lay sprawled upon the sheets of her bed in only her torn shirt, her disheveled hair scattered across her face. She moved her head along the pillow and spied the cup of steaming *karrem* on the bedside table.

"You look satisfied." Radha's voice was rough and she laughed, sitting in the chair beside the bed and studying Jessa with amused eyes.

Jessa turned her face into the pillow, her laughter rising.

"I suppose I should scold you for arriving so late last night, or should I say early this morn?"

"Leave me be, old woman," Jessa said as she shifted about and pulled up the sheet.

"Perhaps I should ask what bit you?" Radha pointed out the bruise of a kiss on Jessa's right breast and another near the base of her neck.

Jessa pushed onto her right elbow and rested her head against her hand, her hair falling in a black tumble down her arm. "And if I were to say a cat did?"

"I would ask what sort of cat?"

"A golden mountain panther."

Radha laughed, the sound like someone scraping on stones. "You have no modesty," she chided her. "Lying about half-naked in the middle of the morning."

Jessa considered her open shirt. "I feel very tired still." She fell forward into the pillow, her voice muffled. "*Vhaelin slova tu an hezza*, Radha."

"Yes, and while you were off being eaten by your panther," she smiled as Jessa laughed, "I was sitting here waiting, wondering where you were. I even went looking for you."

"I'm sorry, Radha."

"It's all right. I found other things during my search to make it worth my while, a few things for my scrolls. This place, this land even, is rich in secrets and new knowledge."

"More philosophy, my Radha?" The traveling trunk that carried Radha's things was more precious than all of their baggage combined, even Jessa knew that. All of her life she had lusted after the spells and scrolls that marked Radha's immense wisdom, but though Jessa desired to know what secrets they might contain, she respected Radha's rank. Radha was a High Priestess of the Vhaelin, and she was still but a student. "You will let me read them now, yes?"

"You may read them when you are ready."

"I am ready *now,*" Jessa said. *I am more powerful now than even* you *had imagined, my sweet. Can you not feel it?*

"Do you think so?" Radha's voice took on a hard edge. "Now that you have a lover, is that it? Now that you know love, you are wise in all things? But even so, little girl, what other than that has changed?"

Jessa narrowed her eyes. "I have come into my power, old woman."

"Have you?"

Jessa hesitated at the rigid words. *Have I?*

"Do not live so fiercely in the moment, Jessa, though it is sweet. And yes, I smell your power. It is like the pepper spice seeds beneath my nose and it makes me want to sneeze. But power without control is disorder and ignores the structure of things. We have yet to test your new strength, and we have no safe place within these walls to do that. So I ask you, when does the song of the lark become silence?"

"When the hawk is near."

"Yes, and we are in more danger now than ever. If I can smell your power so easily, then Serabee will find your scent with very little trouble. But that does not mean that you cannot savor this moment." She smiled, her words losing their edge. "You can still feel her kiss?"

"Yes," Jessa whispered.

"And her touch?"

"Yes."

"And so life is good, *ashanna essa*?"

Jessa smiled almost shyly. "She loves me."

Radha chuckled. "Yes, I know. And where were you? Were you safe?"

"I'm not sure that I was safe, exactly…but the place was secure from prying eyes so you needn't worry."

"She did not hurt you in any way, did she?"

"*No*." Jessa spoke firmly and gazed down the length of the bed. She felt the blush rise along her neck. "She would never do that, Radha."

"I only mean that *Cha-diah* can be very dangerous, child. Remember your place in the order of things. Blood majik can turn quickly, and no doubt she's been pushed by what was done to her. You must mind the strength and the nature of the animal that is within her and have a care when her power is high. The panther is a wild creature, always remember that. Do not *ever* forget that, Jessa, or you might both regret it."

Jessa took note of the counsel and rolled onto her back, stretching her entire body and groaning as her muscles shuddered. She smiled yet again at the sensations humming through her body. Her shirt fell open and slid down her arm as she pushed onto her right hip.

"*Chindonna!*"

Jessa followed Radha's gaze and laughed, for yet another bruise from Darry's mouth was on the inside of her left breast. She closed her eyes for a moment and remembered the getting of it, and her stomach flipped over in a very pleasing manner.

"I hope you gave as well as you received."

Jessa remembered the scratches on Darry's back and how she had laughed in astonishment, only to find another along Darry's neck. Jessa could still hear the sounds of their lovemaking and her heart beat fast. "Yes, I believe I did."

"Do you have any idea what time it is?"

"No. And I don't care."

"Today you meet with the Lady Emmalyn and her dressmakers, and have a late lunch with the Lady Alisha and her mother to discuss her wedding."

Jessa cursed and threw back the sheet, sliding to the edge of the bed. When her legs flopped over the side she sat still, considering how sore her body was in any number of areas.

"You need a bath," Radha said.

Jessa narrowed her eyes.

"You smell like your lover."

Jessa laughed and stepped to the chair, kissing Radha soundly on the cheek. She received a hard slap on her bare thigh for her troubles and stepped away quickly. "Do not be jealous, old woman. It doesn't suit you."

Radha marveled at how Jessa moved, seeing the difference in the way she held herself—with a blatant confidence Radha had long prayed for. She could, in fact, smell the Vhaelin swarming like a maelstrom in Jessa's blood, unleashed at last and singing like nothing she had ever encountered before. The power was unlike any she had even imagined and beyond her most fervent hopes.

It was Jessa's passion that had set it free, and Radha chided herself for not seeing it sooner. Often the greatest power was buried the farthest out of reach, demanding something primal for its release.

Radha gave a curious grunt and then laughed. "*Cha-diah*."

Jessa stuck her head through the door of the washroom. "What?"

The volume of Radha's amusement intensified as she glimpsed Jessa's disheveled beauty. "*Cha-diah*!" she barked.

"What of it?" Jessa demanded, her eyes smiling. "You have no idea, love, none at all."

Radha tried to catch her breath. "I might."

Jessa shook her head and disappeared within. "*Essa tua nessa*…I can barely walk, Darry." She stepped naked to the tub and climbed in, cringing as she sat in the steaming water. "*Shivahsa*!"

Radha appeared in the doorway. "Too hot?"

Jessa moaned her pleasure as she stretched back. "*No*." She sighed. "No, it's perfect, my sweet…absolutely perfect."

Radha's curiosity won out. "Does *Cha-diah* taste as pleasing as its scent?"

Jessa took a breath, sinking beneath the surface and refusing to answer.

"Ungrateful child."

❖

Joaquin sipped his *karrem* and watched the soldiers in the courtyard as they prepared for the day's hunt. One of the private balconies of the expansive Blackwood Lodge gave him a wonderful vantage point, and he considered the amount of timber that went into its construction. Such a building in Lyoness would be for the richest of the court alone, though even then, few could afford it. *I shall have to build one myself.* He gave a slow smile. *And let them fight to be invited to my door.*

The day was becoming hot and it was not yet noon, and he pulled at his silken dressing robe. He was naked beneath it and wondered if he should bother with a bath. He could still smell the spirit of the kitchen girl he had fucked before dawn, and though it was an amusing scent, he doubted if his new peers would approve.

He hated the Green Hills. He hated everything about them, especially the dampness. And the insects were everywhere, inescapable. They were large and they bit, and the back of his neck was covered with small welts he had scratched in his sleep. The girl had placed a cool, soothing lotion on them, and he had repaid her well. Not every lowly serving wench could lay claim to having a Prince's spirit within her womb. Joaquin chuckled and tossed his braid back with a turn of his head. *Perhaps my seed will find root in these rotting hills and grow.*

"My Lord, you called for me?"

Joaquin turned in the sunlight at Serabee's voice and gazed back into the shadows of his room. "Yes," he said, and his thoughts cleared. "And you took your time about it."

Serabee bowed his head. "My apologies, my Prince."

Joaquin tossed the karrem from his cup and left the balcony. "What say you then, Serabee? Can you carry out my orders?" He walked to the chair beside the hearth and turned about with a swish of his robe before he sat down. "It is time I made my play."

"Yes, my Lord, your plan should work."

"Should?"

"Nothing is ever certain, young Lord, unless the gods allow it."

"And so does the Fakir bless my glorious ascension to the Jade Throne?" Joaquin knew that his tone was far from respectful. Serabee stared at him with cold, calm eyes and fear fluttered deep in the pit of his stomach. He looked away and spied his clothes for the day on the end of his bed. "I meant no offense."

"Of course not." Serabee spoke quietly. "My man will arrive at Blackstone Keep sometime near dawn on the morrow. He will wait for his moment, then carry out your orders."

"Do you wish the old crone dead as well?" Joaquin thought that he might gift Serabee with something he would appreciate. "No one will miss her."

"That is not necessary," Serabee said with a careful smile. He was dressed in his usual black with his brace of throwing knives about his waist. He had a vest on as well. The man wore at least three layers of clothes. "Thank you for the thought, my Prince."

"I would think you would want her dead," Joaquin said, then waved his hand at him. "*Fickloche aladda*, man, aren't you sweating in all of that?"

"The Lady Radha is not so easy to kill," Serabee said. "And no, I am not sweating, my Prince. You are perhaps used to a dryer heat."

Joaquin frowned. "This fucking forest, I don't know why anyone bothers to take a bath when all you have to do is walk outside." He looked into his empty karrem cup and considered Serabee's words. They were not what he expected. "What do you mean she is not so easy to kill?"

"You must trust me on that point," Serabee said. "As I am a Lord of the Fakir, so is she a High Priestess of the Vhaelin. It is good to respect your enemies at times, my Lord. This my people have learned at a great cost, where the Vhaelin are concerned. Though if she gets in the way, I suppose my man can deal with her."

"You suppose?"

"Yes, he should be fine."

"I don't want him to be *fine*, Serabee," Joaquin said with heat, and pushed up from his chair. "I want him to murder my cunt of a sister." He stepped close to the Fakir Lord and hit his fist against Serabee's lean, hard chest. It was a firm blow for emphasis and he held his hand there. "And I do not want some slack-mouthed fool of yours making an attempt and failing."

"No, my Lord." Serabee took Joaquin's hand with a gentle touch.

Joaquin blinked and felt the sun from the balcony on the side of his face, then a cool, dry breeze that drifted up from the floor. It washed beneath the hem of his robe and felt wonderful, easing the tackiness of his flesh in the humidity. He heard the horses in the courtyard below and someone laughing, and he remembered the tightness of the kitchen girl's body and how she had called out his name as he had rammed his cock inside her. She had been a pleasant distraction and so he had not punished her for her lapse in manners when she forgot his title. She had been tight and wet, and she had smelled like kitchen flour. "And grapes," he whispered.

He felt dizzy for a moment and then looked to his left to find Serabee as they stood beneath the arch to the balcony. Serabee had put his arm about Joaquin's shoulders in a friendly gesture and Joaquin felt a surge of pride. Serabee had never touched his father so. "But if you think that I should go with him, to ensure that the Lady Radha does not interfere, it might be wise."

Joaquin followed the logic as he turned away from the balcony and walked slowly to the end of the bed. "Then do it," he said, picking up his shirt and giving it a shake. "And then Lyoness shall ride to war over the murder of their beloved Nightshade Lark, and my brothers will tear each other to pieces in the process." Joaquin turned as he draped his clothes over his arm. "And here I shall be, protected in the arms of Arravan."

"Yes, my Lord," Serabee said. "It is the most important play of all, and well thought out. They shall not expect it."

"They all have their own plans." Joaquin felt tired. He had not felt tired with his karrem, and he wondered if the kitchen girl had worn him out more than he thought. It was the bloody humidity. "All of them, even Jessa, I should imagine."

"Yes."

"Malcolm would see his whelp of a son sit on my father's throne, while offering me the privilege of being the little pig's counselor. He would put me there to do all the work, and then he would ride in and take what is mine after I have cleaned out the rats for him. Does he think that I cannot see what he's doing?"

"This way is much better, yes." Serabee's voice was oddly soothing. "And after this, your position will be secure, for Malcolm will have no other of Bharjah's blood to help him complete his plan for Lyoness. He will think to use you as his puppet king, but he does not know you, my Prince. He does not understand how cunning you are."

"Yes." Joaquin said and sighed as his anger ebbed away. "Yes…yes, see to things, will you, Serabee?"

"Yes, my Prince, I will see to things."

CHAPTER TWENTY-EIGHT

Jessa sang softly in the early afternoon sun as Darry lay on the ground with her head in Jessa's lap. She braided together several strands of Darry's hair, happy at last to have the opportunity. Draped along Darry's thigh and purring a strange sort of accompaniment to the ballad, Hinsa lay at her leisure, her eyes lazy and staring down one of the twisting paths of the garden maze. Darry absently scratched the giant cat's head, and its long tail flicked against Jessa's legs.

Darry opened her eyes, listening to the Lyonese words she could not understand. Jessa stopped as her lips hovered above Darry's, then continued her song. Darry grinned at the tease as Jessa let her fingers float through Darry's hair. Jessa's humor moved within her voice as she sat back and wove the seed of periwinkle within the tightly wound braid.

Darry took hold of a thick curl and pulled gently, and Jessa let her words trail off as their lips met in a pliant kiss. When released from the gentle demand Jessa sang the remaining chorus, which spoke of two lovers on their wedding day. The panther tipped her head back and let out a low rumble, drawing Jessa's attention.

Hinsa huffed through her nose and yawned, baring her deadly teeth as her long whiskers shivered. Jessa laughed and stretched her arm out, feeling the wet nose against her palm and then Hinsa's rough tongue as the cat sprawled back onto Darry's stomach. Darry grunted at the sudden shift in weight.

"She is too heavy?"

"If I had my choice?" Darry responded, "I would rather it be you lying atop me."

Jessa dropped her hand onto Darry's stomach. "You'll hurt her feelings."

Hinsa flopped her head back, seeking her touch once again. Jessa obliged and ran a careful hand down the animal's face, feeling the black skin of her jowls quiver.

"They did not lie," Darry said.

"Who did not lie?"

"The one who claimed your voice might drive men mad and so named you the Nightshade Lark."

"Have I driven you mad?"

"Sort of." Darry grinned.

Jessa kissed her once more. "That is the first time I can remember that I have ever sung for the simple joy of it." And then she kissed her yet again and stroked her tongue against Darry's before she tasted her lower lip. "Thank you, *Akasha*."

"Tell me what it means."

"Smile as you just did."

Darry's dimple appeared once more. "Please?"

Jessa sighed happily and ran her fingers along the cheek. "I am thinking that I like this smile of yours very much. It is different from your others, and though all are very beautiful, this one most makes me want to kiss you."

"I am at your leisure then, Princess."

Jessa sat back and began to sing once more as she searched through Darry's curls for more suitable hair.

"No?"

Jessa ignored her plea.

"You would leave me unsatisfied?"

Jessa stopped singing. "Are you not satisfied?"

"I have duty this eve. I'll not be able to meet you."

"You cannot…what do you mean you cannot meet me?"

"The senior officers walk the wall with Longshanks," Darry said. "And though I've been taken from the lists, I must attend. I'm sorry, my love. I cannot get free of it without causing suspicion."

Jessa did not like what she heard, not at all. "I'll not be able to touch you until when?"

Darry ran the backs of her fingers down the skin of Jessa's neck. "Until I say," she answered, then laughed at the dissatisfaction that greeted her. Hinsa gave a growl low within her throat and shifted her weight. She pushed to her feet and padded through the grass. "Are you angry with me?"

"Perhaps."

"I should make it up to you then."

"And ruin my dress? I think not."

"It would not be the first lady's dress I've ruined."

Jessa laughed, remembering her words at the pond. She slid her right hand down the front of Darry's shirt until her hand stopped upon Darry's belt, which she fingered in contemplation. "Perhaps it is time for your uniform to be ruined, yes? I rather like this dress."

Darry crossed her legs together at the ankles and sighed, trying to look casual as Jessa's fingers pulled at the leather and loosed the flap. "Leave off, woman. I'm not interested now."

Hinsa sat in the grass several feet away and extended her neck, letting loose a rather plaintive yowl.

Jessa laughed, glancing at the panther and then back to Darry in understanding. "I think you are lying, yes?"

"Don't listen to her. She's just a cat."

Jessa pulled the belt open and settled her touch at the top of Darry's trousers. She yanked them open and slid her hand beneath the material. "Is she?"

"Yes."

"You're being led astray, Lady Jessa."

Jessa enjoyed the flush of color that darkened the skin of Darry's neck as she slipped her hand farther. Hinsa's purr rattled in the air around them and Jessa laughed again at the sound. "I'm finding this revealing in more ways than one."

Darry lifted her head from Jessa's lap and gazed down the length of her body. "Bloody hell, biscuit, *stop* it."

Jessa took the opportunity to kiss her, stealing just a taste. "Will she stay while I touch you?" She was terribly aroused at just the thought and slid her hand even lower, slipping between the tightness of Darry's legs as Darry squeezed her thighs together. "Do not be stubborn, Darrius."

For a moment Darry's eyes were clouded and Jessa sensed her majik.

Hinsa pushed to her feet and walked close. She crowded against them both and rubbed her face along Darry's. The sound of her purr was jarring, and the back of Jessa's skull vibrated as Hinsa opened her mouth in Darry's hair.

"*Ouch*!" Darry exclaimed. Several strands caught in Hinsa's teeth as the cat bit and pulled away, causing Darry's head to jerk to the side.

Jessa grabbed Darry's waist as Hinsa ran off down the path. "Did she hurt you?" she teased, but let out a startled cry as she was seized about the waist and pulled into an awkward tumble of tangled limbs before Darry settled along her body in the grass.

Jessa turned her face as Darry's hair glided across her skin and teased her lips. She ran her fingers through it. Darry kissed Jessa's throat, her breath warm and her mouth tender, her lips pulling sweetly on the skin. Her tongue tasted briefly and her teeth grazed.

Jessa let out a breath of surprise, smelling the heady scent of the Lowlands for an instant. She had not heard the words in her vision and her heart was fierce with anticipation as Darry's lips brushed against her ear.

"Everything I am is yours. I love you, Jess."

"I love you," Jessa said, finding and claiming her waiting lips.

"Why didn't you send for me sooner?" Owen asked quietly, staring into the cold hearth from his favorite chair. He sat with his legs extended and his shoulders slouched in the familiar leather cushions.

"I thought I might change her mind," Cecelia answered from the balcony arch. "And I was afraid."

A wave of guilt followed her words, but Owen accepted it with little argument. *Taking the brunt of the rage that was meant for me. That I deserve and no one else.*

"Do you understand yet, my love, what you did?"

"I knew what I'd done when Aidan wept. I just didn't know how to take it back."

"And do you still believe our son?" she asked. "That to allow Darry the rights and privileges that our other children enjoy with fanfare and freedom will somehow damage five hundred years of your family's rule? To openly accept another kind of love will weaken his position for the future?"

"I still see her in my dreams sometimes, handing me back your mother's necklace."

Cecelia moved across the room then knelt beside him and placed a hand on his leg. "You must accept her, Owen, for who she is. Not who you wanted her to be."

"You mean Jacey?"

"Yes, my love."

"She's nothing like Jacey was."

"She never was, Owen."

"I know that. I've always known it."

"Then why have you always fought her so?"

"Because she loved me the same." He said the words he had never spoken before. "She looked at me the same way, right through me.

I couldn't help but think of them in the same breath, though I knew it was unfair. I kept thinking she would change, even though you told me she wouldn't. Even though I knew it as well. I never wanted her to be Jacey."

"The sword is her destiny. And as to how she loves, it is only that, Owen. It's love, and the heart does as it pleases. No man has a say in this decision, and no woman either. She could no more change the path her heart follows than you could, my darling."

"I know it. I just thought, well, here is yet another thing I cannot protect her from," he admitted at last. "Here is yet one more danger she'll walk into alone, and I must watch as the world tries to destroy her, if only a little at a time."

Cecelia lifted his hand and placed it against her cheek. "Owen."

"I thought at the last that at least I could teach her fear."

Cecelia was startled by the words.

"The fearless die young, my love," he said. "She had no fear. It was my brother's fate as well, to walk through the world without fear. Though he finally found it at the end of a sword upon the field. If he had held but a measure of caution, Malcolm would be King now and you and I would've lived a different life entirely.

"He was as she is, a natural with the blade. I knew it that day, the day I struck her. I knew her completely when she held her wooden blade to Wyatt's throat and smiled down at him, waiting for him to yield. And I've never been so frightened in all my life. I saw her laid low, but a girl still, for she would rush in as Malcolm had. Not arrogant, but unafraid of losing. She doesn't understand it. She had no concern for such a thing as failing.

"And when she declared herself backwards? I saw it yet again, though it was *my* fear for her that led to all of this."

Cecelia saw his mind at work. She saw the shame he felt at his actions.

"That she kept their love hidden for so long, she had learned to fear and I didn't see it. It was my fear that listened to our son. I wanted him to be right. I wanted to believe that the council would turn against me. I wanted the Bloods up in arms. I wanted Aidan's father to break from the Guilds and campaign against me on the strength of his disapproval. If they did these things, I would not be wrong in my own displeasure at their love, for how could that be love? How could I protect her from something I didn't understand?"

"Owen."

"No, Cece," he said. "But I knew when Aidan wept. When she looked at me and spoke of saving Darry's honor, no matter what it cost her. Bloody hell, she was just a girl."

"Owen, you must finally answer for what you did. And we must deal with Malcolm for what he's done. That he shared such things with Marteen and Melora. It was a cruelty that Darry will seek satisfaction for. It was in the worst form possible and unworthy of him. We've made a terrible mistake in allowing him his feud. It is founded only in prejudice. It serves no purpose but to torture them both." She felt fear at her own words. "And I think it's made him careless, Owen, and cruel."

"I see it," he said. "It's in his voice when he loses patience. A distaste and contempt for the opinions of others. An arrogance in his manner that's dangerous."

"I think we should look more closely at what he's doing," she said, remembering Jessa's words from the grove. "I've reason to believe that Mal plays a deeper game here, one that neither you nor I has any knowledge of."

"The girl."

"Yes."

"I know it. He is too focused on Joaquin. There's a play that runs deeper, and our Lyonese peacock is up to his neck within it. As is Mal, I fear. He has that look he gets when he's living in the distance. When we thought he would court Celine, he had the same look…dreaming of the future and making grand plans. It's time that Mal and I had a talk."

"But Darry first," Cecelia said. "You must answer to her first or she'll be lost to us, do you understand?" Her tears slipped free. "Don't let her run, Owen, *please*. I can't lose another child. I can't do it."

"I never meant to hit her."

"Owen?"

"Yes, love?"

"There's something else you need to know."

He took a deep breath at her words and let it out slowly. "Of course there is."

Chapter Twenty-nine

"Your rooms are good then?" Emmalyn looped her hand in Nina's arm as they walked.

"Bloody hell, Emma." The freckles across Nina's nose glowed as her cheeks lifted in a smile. "If my sister brings any more luggage I'm going to shove her lovely ass into the biggest trunk I can find and send her back home in it."

Emmalyn laughed. "And the house was fine?"

"Of course. They sent me ahead to do a serf's work, as always." Nina spied Jessa moving down the stairs. "Where in the seven hells is Darry, anyway? Jessa!"

Emmalyn lifted her arm free and pushed her to the side as they walked. "*Princess* Jessa to you, water rat!"

Nina's eyes flared. "Don't start *that* again." She growled, sounding both annoyed and amused. "I like the water, what of it?"

Jessa came down the last steps into the foyer. "Am I late for our lunch?" she asked, knowing already that she was.

"You cannot be late, Jessa," Emmalyn said. "It's only lunch."

"You look damn fine, Jessa." Nina took her elbow. "Let us find a few bottles of good spring wine, shall we?"

"Yes, let us have it, Lady Lewellyn," Jessa said.

"Fucking hell and hounds." Nina laughed. "Call me that again, Jess, and I shall never speak to you again. Even if you do marry my *fool* stick of a cousin. He may be the King of Arravan one day, but he'll always be a stick."

Emmalyn laughed and stepped close, putting a hand over her cousin's mouth. "Ignore her, please, Jessa. She's a smelly street urchin we picked from the gutters and has yet to learn her manners."

Nina's eyes narrowed in a threatening manner.

"Will you behave?"

Nina mumbled against her hand and Emmalyn released her, whereupon she turned to Jessa. "Have you seen Darry? I'm here for days and days and not even a kiss hello? She can't escape me now. I've taken over the north wing and intend to root myself here until after Solstice. Father can look after his own bloody house when he gets here. Do you know where she is?"

"I imagine not far behind," Jessa answered, "knowing that you've arrived. She's had duties that must be seen to, though most likely she was thinking of you while she did them."

Emmalyn stared. Jessa's voice as she had spoken of Darry filled with something familiar and altogether intimate. She had spoken as if answering for Darry were as natural to her as taking a breath. *She answers for her lover. Mother was right. Bloody hell, Mother was right.*

"Darry is a rogue and a cad for ignoring me," Nina said.

"Yes, she's a cad for certain," Jessa said in a faraway voice.

Emmalyn saw it in Jessa's eyes. She recognized the emotions and the tell-tale signs of desire. She knew what it was like to be unable to control her body's response to Royce's touch, or even the thought of it in an unguarded moment. *This will spill like blood to the foot of your throne, Father. My sister's blood, and now mine as well. All of us.*

"Emma?" Jessa asked.

"I'm starving." Emmalyn turned her thoughts as smoothly as she could. "Off we go."

The three of them moved toward the great hall and Nina started the tale of opening her father's house in the city and preparing it for her family's arrival. Her language was peppered with curses and phrases both hilarious and decidedly ill-advised, considering her rank. Neither Emmalyn nor Jessa could resist their laughter, however, for Nina's charm was too great and her enthusiasm for the tale far too amusing. When Emmalyn mentioned the impropriety of her language, Nina shrugged.

"I can't help it, Emma," she said. "Everything is so big inside it just comes out that way."

"I rather like it, water rat, if you must know."

"Water rat?" Jessa asked.

"Don't you start too, Jess," Nina said.

"Nina!"

Nina turned quickly at the voice and looked back the way they had come, then gave a whoop to rival a war call, lifting her skirt as she ran.

Darry watched Nina, impressed by her speed as she closed the distance between them, and laughed as she braced herself for the impact. A few seconds later Nina was in her arms and clinging to her neck.

"*Darry*!" she cried happily and Darry whirled in a circle. Darry felt kisses on her face and laughed harder, setting her down. "Darry." Nina smiled, breathless. "I've missed you."

Darry pushed the hair away from Nina's beautifully freckled face. "And I you."

Nina stepped back and let her hands slide along the lapels of Darry's royal blue jacket and trousers. "Cocks and balls, Darry, but you look bloody fucking handsome."

"And you're even fouler than last time we met, my sweet."

"I've been practicing in the pubs," Nina proclaimed. "Where my tongue is given the respect it deserves."

"I stand in awe," Darry replied. "You cut your hair."

Nina shrugged. "It was very heavy. Too hard to swim."

"My champion paddler. I would see you race a tiger fish in the Sellen Sea," she said. "Auntie Phillipa must've had a bloody seizure."

Nina leaned against her. "You have no idea."

"Seven hells, the wedding. On Winter's Eve?"

Nina made a sour face. "Yes, and it won't grow back in time. I've heard it all, you must trust me."

"How is Hammond?"

"He's fine. He's always fine. Gods, Darry, but our foreign Princess is bloody-well beautiful. I like her."

Darry followed her gaze to see Jessa smiling as Emmalyn spoke to her. "Yes," she said simply. *She's everything.* "So do I."

"Does she really intend to marry Malcolm?"

"She will marry someone, I think." Darry pulled at her hand. "Come on. I'm dying for my lunch."

"I hear you danced the Mohn-Drom, cousin."

Darry let out a startled laugh as they followed Jessa and Emmalyn. "Yes, and it was perhaps ill-advised."

"Practically fucking on the dance floor, Darry. You're even more shameless than I am, and with a *man,* no less!"

"But you were not here yet, my sweet, or I would've danced it with you."

"And I probably would've let you take me afterward as well," Nina said with a touch of wickedness. "The Mohn-Drom is a very serious dance."

"You're my first *cousin*, my love."

"Cousins have fucked before," Nina said, coyly lifting an eyebrow. "How else can you explain my sister's husband?"

Darry laughed and seized her waist as they passed beneath the arch.

Nina let out a startled cry as Darry swept her up. "Poor Bernard, you're worse than I am, Nina."

"I know, isn't it grand?"

They danced a step gracefully to the music of Nina's laughter.

Emmalyn stood beside Jessa on the far side of the dance floor as Darry led Nina through their steps, both women extremely graceful as Nina pressed against Darry rather shamelessly.

"I like your cousin very much," Jessa said. *Though she presses too closely.*

"They've always adored each other," Emmalyn replied. "Stuck together through thick and thin, and alike in so many ways."

"Yes, they're both wild at heart and honest."

Emmalyn felt instantly threatened at Jessa's words and the adoration she heard within them, and a swell of dread rose in her throat. She wanted to cry out as Darry and Nina danced, afraid it would all come crashing down. Everything, and her sister's life would hang in the balance.

Darry and Jessa were alone, and Emmalyn would not allow it despite her mother's order for silence. Their father would be home by now and it would all end, one way or another. She made the decision with very little difficulty. If Darry and Jessa were truly in love, it would not be only Darry who disappeared into the night.

Jessa looked down as Emmalyn took her hand fiercely.

"Don't take her," Emmalyn said. Jessa paled and Emmalyn saw that she was right. "Please, Jessa, don't run."

Jessa tried to pull her hand away but Emmalyn held tighter.

"Whatever must be done, Jessa, I'll help you. I *swear* it. I'm on your side, do you hear?"

Jessa stepped back but Emmalyn followed as Jessa looked at the dance floor.

"Jessa?"

You'll not take her from me. Jessa was panicked. *I will see you all burn before that happens.* She returned to Emmalyn, trying to arrange her thoughts about her sudden reaction. "What do you mean?"

"That you're backwards as well? That you love my sister? Don't be afraid, Jess. I couldn't be happier. She's as dear to me as the sun, and I hold you very dear as well."

"Who else knows?" Jessa demanded.

"Mother. Our mother knows."

"*Darry*!" Jessa called, yanking her hand away.

Darry faltered within their dance at the sound of her name spoken in such a manner.

"Jessa, I'm not your enemy."

Darry moved instantly, crossing the floor between them with a startled Nina close at her heels. Jessa took several steps to meet her and Darry took her hand. "She knows," Jessa said.

Emmalyn recognized the dark expression upon Darry's face and stepped forward. "I know you want to run, Darry. I know it and I don't blame you. I know about Aidan."

Darry's left temple twitched. Jessa tightened her hold on her hand and Darry returned the pressure.

"I won't let that happen again, Darry, do you hear me? I won't." Emmalyn held out her hand, seeking to calm the storm that rose within Darry's eyes. "You promised. You promised you wouldn't hide from me."

Darry was torn. More than anyone it was Emmalyn she had always wanted to be like. It was Emma she had always revered as the woman she wished to emulate, if only in some small way.

"Yes, it's only me, Darry," Emmalyn whispered. "You've nothing to fear."

"Mother knows?"

Seven hells. "Yes."

Jessa's eyes were fearful as Darry touched her cheek, but above all Darry saw love, and she let it wash through her with so much strength that she felt her majik rise. "Go and find Bentley, Jess. He'll be in the yards. Find him and tell him what's happened."

"I'm not leaving you."

"You must go, Jess, please."

"*No*."

"If you find Bentley I'll know you're safe. I can't do anything that must be done if you're not safe, my love."

"*Akasha*, no."

"The game is over," Darry said. "We must go now, we can't stay. Our plans have changed, do you understand? We're in danger and I'll not have it."

"I'll take her," Nina said. "I'll go with you, Jess."

"Go with Nina," Darry said, never looking from Jessa. "Do you understand, Nina? Bentley Greeves and no one else."

"Aye, Darry, I'm with you. Just like always, cousin."

"Find Bentley, Jess, and tell him. You must tell him."

Jessa looked long into her eyes, seeing purpose and a steady confidence, a calm strength that eased her own fear. She had been waiting her whole life and now her freedom was near, whether she was ready for it or not. She took hold of Darry's neck, pulled her close, and kissed her with passion, deeply and without reservation.

"Amar's breeches," Nina said. "Bloody Darry."

Jessa released her and walked away.

"Nina," Darry said firmly.

Nina started and rushed forward, chasing her.

Darry turned back to Emmalyn. "Whatever you're thinking, Em, it's not enough."

"You can't know that, Darry, you can't."

"She *lied* to me," Darry said. "Father and Malcolm, what they did, they've stolen my honor. As if it meant *nothing*, they took it. I would no more stay here than I would cut my own throat."

"But *I* am here," Emmalyn said. "And Jacob, and Alisha…and Mother."

"Weren't you listening?"

"Yes," Emmalyn answered with force, stepping closer. "And I was also there when she told the tale and wept as she did, cursing herself to Gamar for her part in it. She is guilty of trying to spare you pain, that's all, Darry.

"How she went about it I can't condone, but I'm not sure I would've done it differently. She had nothing to do with breaking you from Aidan. She tried to pick up the pieces, that's all. And I was there when she told me about you and Jessa, for neither of you can hide what you feel from a mother's eyes, nor mine now that I look for it. I was there when she spoke of trying to help you both and swore an oath upon her own blood that she would see it through. Don't run, Darry. Stay and fight."

"Emma, you've lost your mind. Fight? Fight for *what*?"

"For your birthright. You're of royal blood and you have a place here. If you don't want that, fine. I will give you Evan's lands and gladly, and you and Jessa may live there in peace. But don't break from this house or the ones that love you. Don't do it, Darry, please."

Darry's expression softened at the unexpected words. "She is a daughter of Lyoness, Emma. She's Bharjah's only daughter, don't you see? *Bharjah's* daughter. She is his most valuable piece of jade to barter with. There'll be no peace for us if we stay in the open. We will be the stag in the hunt."

"Well, yes, that's a bit of a problem. I see your point."

"You'd give me Evan's lands?"

"I would give you anything you ask for," Emmalyn said simply. "I love you. I even love her, I think, for she's bloody well wonderful."

"This I know."

"Let me help you."

Darry was torn as she felt the pull of it, the desire to have such strength on their side. "No. You would be pitted against Malcolm and that cannot be. Your children will be in line for the throne should he have no heir."

"I've lost one sister already," Emmalyn returned fiercely. "I did not like it."

Darry's heart gave a painful twinge. "Jacey."

"Yes, Jacey Rose. I watched her die and could do nothing to help her. And so you would leave me as well without a backward glance? And what of Wyatt? He's a thousand leagues away and yet when he returns home to learn that you're gone from him forever? It will kill him, Darry, and you know it."

"Emma, don't put it in such a way, please." Darry couldn't conceal her pain. "She is my *love.* Jessa is my love, even as Royce is yours. Even as Evan was."

"But that's what you must do if you run. You must give up one for the other."

"Then I choose Jessa. I will always choose her. I'm sorry, Emma, if that hurts you. If it hurts Wyatt."

"Stay and fight for what is yours!" Emmalyn said. "You'll not fight alone, I assure you of that."

"There is nothing here that is mine, as it was meant to be," Darry said with quiet truth. "That was made very clear to me. I have only what they allow me to have, out of conscience, perhaps, or guilt. Or perhaps no choice at all, for my blood is as you say and cannot be denied. What scraps they would throw me I no longer want."

"Do you mean that?"

"Malcolm will just calmly allow the woman brought here for him to judge to share my bed? To publicly scorn him in preference for his backwards sister, whom he hates and thinks of as diseased?" Emmalyn's shoulders fell slightly as she absorbed Darry's words. "No matter that he doesn't want her, he'll not allow it. And he's proven his ability to sway whomever he must to his cause. Aidan is proof of that. What they did is proof of many things."

Emmalyn's frustration showed in her eyes. "No."

"The end result of that, Emma, would be our brother dead and my neck upon the block. I'll kill him if he tries to take her from me. Jessa is mine, even as I am hers. No one will break that. I won't allow it."

Emmalyn had no rebuttal.

"And I've known our father's feelings toward me since I was twelve years old. I'm not Jacey Rose and he's never forgiven me for that. As a girl I used to put flowers on her tomb, and I'd whisper to her of our father and how he missed her. I would apologize for not being good enough and swear to try harder."

"Periwinkle." Emmalyn said. *The periwinkle was you.*

"I don't do that anymore, Emma, because I *am* good enough and I needn't try harder to prove it. It's he who is unworthy. For though I'm not the daughter he wanted, neither is he the father I needed."

"No one has ever wanted you to be Jacey," Emmalyn said carefully. "Did he tell you that?"

"Quite clearly, actually, upon the end of his fist."

Emmalyn was shocked by the statement. "When?"

Darry could see her thinking, searching back through the years. "It doesn't matter, Em, it doesn't. We would be free and that can't happen here."

Emmalyn remembered. She remembered quite clearly Darry's battered face and her cut hands, and their mother's words that she had gotten into a fight and fallen. That she had struck her face against the stones and cut her hands as well. She remembered how Darry had refused to talk about it no matter how hard she had pressed. "You didn't fall," Emmalyn whispered, extending her hand. *And he wouldn't touch you. Even at Solstice he pulled away.* "You didn't fall."

"I fell a great distance, actually."

"You should've told me."

"I loved him." Darry took Emmalyn's hand. "I forgave him."

"Darry."

"He wouldn't allow me the one that I loved, though she had no true standing in the world but for her family's good name. Do you think he'll let me love a daughter to the King of Lyoness? That he will allow?"

"But how can—"

"What if it were *you*, Emma?" Darry said. "And they took Royce from you, because they decided in some back room that your love wasn't pure enough? That you were sick because you loved him and it was easier for everyone if the problem just went away altogether?"

Emmalyn felt everything beneath her begin to crumble. *Father, what have you done?* "I'll give you Evan's lands. Don't leave until I've given you the deeds. Do you understand?"

"You don't have to do that, Em."

"Take the land!" Emmalyn snapped, trying to wrap her thoughts around defeat. "Bloody hell, I'm sorry, love. Just take the land, Darry, please. Whether you go there or not, at least it will be yours. You'll always have your own place. And in the meantime you may leave missives for me there, and the seneschal will see that I get them. That is something, at least, and I would know that you and Jessa are well."

"I'll find you, Emma," Darry promised her. "And I'll find Wyatt and Jacob as well. After we're safe and free from harm."

"And where might that be?"

Darry spun about at the deep, familiar voice, reaching for her sword.

CHAPTER THIRTY

Jessa moved along the fence, searching through the crowded yard as the sound of weapons and laughter filled the air. She saw Bentley standing by a sword post. His shirt was off and his muscled torso shone with sweat as he handed a sword to a younger man.

"Bentley!"

"Princess." Bentley smiled beneath his mustache as he neared. His pleasure at seeing her faded quickly. "What's happened?"

"They know," Jessa said, and his expression hardened in response. "She sent me to find you, but I'm afraid for her. Please, Bentley, we *must* go back. I cannot leave her to face this alone."

"Yes," Bentley said. His eyes narrowed in scrutiny, seeing Nina. "And you are?" he asked as she stood on the fence.

"Nina Lewellyn," she answered. "And whatever trouble my cousin is in, I'm in it with her. So would you fucking step it up, please?"

Bentley's eyes flashed. "As you wish, my Lady." He stepped back into the yard, lifting a hand to his mouth. The whistle that rang out was piercing. Across the yard Darry's Boys came to attention, their weapons falling still. "To Darry!" he yelled, his voice booming and filled with command.

Nina jumped to the ground as Bentley ran to the fence, grabbed the top rail, and vaulted over. He took Jessa's hand. "Off we go then, my Lady. Off to keep our girl out of trouble."

❖

Owen Durand watched Darry's hand fall empty to her side. *Lucky for me, I think.* He walked across the dance floor, holding her eyes even from a distance. *But unfair yet again.* He unhooked the clasps that held his sword. When he came to within a few yards he tossed the weapon.

Darry caught the scabbard with her left hand as her right curled about the hilt.

Standing in judgment at last, Owen put his right hand into his pocket and then pulled free, opening before Darry as Cecelia stepped close behind him.

Darry bared her teeth at the sight of her grandmother's sapphire, and she pulled on the blade. The steel pinged from the scabbard as she met her father's eyes. Her blood rose and she clutched the sword so tight she feared she would bend it. "Why?"

"Because I was a fool."

"Yes. So was I."

"No, Darry, never that."

It really was for nothing, all of it. The sudden clarity stunned Darry. *Wanting your love, wanting you to be proud of me. Always waiting for your slightest nod of approval or your touch on my shoulder as when you would praise Wyatt. For even just a smile to show that you understood me, if only a little. Always begging for the scraps of your love, my whole life, desperate for even a kind word and my pride undone when you never gave it. And where has it left me?*

My name was once Durand, and I know the blood of Kings.

Darry threw the scabbard behind her and set the blade against her left hand, just beneath the guard. The deadly edge bit into her flesh in a smooth line as she pulled. Her blood slid down its polished steel. She threw the blade on the floor at her father's feet.

She delved in her own pocket with her wounded hand, wrapped her fingers around the gold of her family medallion, and brought it forth. She studied it, the writing and her family's crest stained with the blood it represented. It felt good, the wound, for she could hold it out for the world to see and no one could mistake that she had taken a blow.

Owen watched the blood slide through her fingers, all of his hope sinking in the reality of what was happening. He had expected her rage, but not this. Not the decision already made. He had never meant to corner her, but that was exactly what had happened, and even as before he could not undo it. *What a cock-up you are, old man.*

Darry tossed the medallion.

The gold crest spun oddly with its heavy linked chain and hit the floor between his boots with a solid clank.

"I relinquish my title as a child of the Durand line," Darry announced in a calm voice, squeezing her fingers tight as she held out her hand. The blood began to drip on the stones before her boots. "And I resign my commission in the service of my King, who is no longer my Lord. And if

I could drain the blood that is yours from my veins and still walk away, I would do it, just to be free of you at last."

"Darrius, *please*." Cecelia's voice broke as she stepped forward.

"I love you, Mother." Darry's words stopped her. "For whatever part you played, I forgive you. And I ask for your forgiveness in return. Please excuse me for my disrespectful words and my lack of kindness toward you. I was wrong to have blamed you. You did nothing except seek to protect me, even if you lied to me in the process." *I can give you that at least, but no more.* Darry remembered Jessa's words in Tristan's Grove and how they had soothed her, how they had made the difference when she had not wanted to believe. "And I forgive you in Aidan's stead as well. She forgives you."

"*Darry*," Cecelia pleaded.

"Thank you for loving me so," Darry said, her voice thick with feeling. "Thank you, Mother, for giving me my sword."

Cecelia's tears slipped free. "You're most welcome. Please don't do this."

"Your mistake is corrected at last, Owen Durand. And the child you once said you should not have had? You have no more."

He seized her by the wrist before she could step away, his hand marked with her blood. His anger flared, seeing the truth of it and that Cecelia must have known. A profound panic stirred in his chest that Darry had heard his long-ago words. The words he bemoaned thinking, even more than he regretted what had come before. "Forgive me, Darry. Forgive me."

"Let go of me."

He released her instantly.

"If you truly seek forgiveness, seek it from Aidan McKenna. That you would injure me so I should've expected. But what you did to her fills me with shame. Not because you're my father, but because you were my King and I thought you to be a good one. A man that I was willing to give my life for, no matter the troubles between us. That you could abuse your power and position so easily and bring it to bear against a girl who had no defense against you? That was a truly dark thing."

"I know it."

They stood in silence. Owen knew that she would not change her mind. Darry turned and walked away, never looking back.

"Owen," Cecelia said.

"I cannot *force* her. She was there. She heard what I said."

"Yes."

Emmalyn took a hard breath, Darry's words singing within her head.

The child you said you should not have had. She swallowed her emotions and shock, wanting to deny it. But their father's words echoed close behind. *She was there. She heard what I said.*

Emmalyn approached the sword and knelt down. She studied Darry's medallion stained with royal blood, sealing the image hard within her memory where it burned clean and unforgiving.

"Emma, please."

The child you said you should not have had. Oh, Darry, I'm so sorry.

Emmalyn picked up the necklace with a trembling hand. "Here, my Lord," she said, and Owen held out his hand. She placed the bloodied crest in his palm and lowered the chain after, letting it swirl with a gentle clinking of the links.

Owen saw the shame in her eyes and the anger as well, twisted and confused among her pain. There were tears but they did not fall. "Emma."

"You should put this next to Jacey's," Emmalyn said, her voice cold.

He closed his hand as Emmalyn walked away, following her sister.

Chapter Thirty-one

Darry!" Jessa called, and everyone slowed at the sight of Darry walking beneath the timbers of the high terrace above.

Darry smiled at the sight of Jessa and the company of her friends and wanted to laugh despite the ruin her heart was in, despite that she had just forsaken her entire life. *For a better one.* With a quick, certain breath, she opened her arms as Jessa neared. *For you, Jess, and me as well.*

Jessa let out a soft sound of joy as Darry put her arms around her waist and lifted her up. "I'm all right, love."

Jessa touched Darry's face, not understanding the roguish expression, though her heart skipped as always at the sight of Darry's dimple. "What is it?"

"Perhaps I should introduce you."

Jessa frowned and Darry turned her around. Jessa let out a deep breath and stepped back into Darry's body at the sight of their audience. Darry's Boys and Nina Lewellyn smiled at her. Several of the men looked down at the blush that crept up Jessa's cheeks.

"Darry's Boys? This is the Princess Jessa-Sirrah de Cassey LaMarc de Bharjah, and she is my love. Jessa? These are my Boys," Darry said. They all bowed their heads to Jessa, smiling like playful youngsters and looking a bit too happy about things.

"You are my love," Darry whispered beside Jessa's ear.

"What does this mean, Darry?" Arkady asked.

Darry took a deep breath and straightened. She met Arkady's eyes and then looked to each of her friends in turn, landing upon Bentley at the last. No one was smiling anymore. "I have just relinquished my title and given up my rank," she said. Jessa turned into Darry's side and stood closer, sliding her arms about Darry's waist. "I've had words with the King, for he returned early from the Green Hills—" Darry looked down as Jessa grabbed her collar, her eyes filled with concern. "All is well."

She returned her attention to her friends. "There are many reasons for what I've done, but you should know that I'm not to be allowed a love of my own. For political reasons and perhaps hatred as well. I am backwards and will not deny it, and maybe this doesn't sit well with some. Their reasons are their own and I cannot change them."

It was not exactly the way of things as they stood, but the words were true enough and Darry felt comfortable with them. "And I'm very tired of trying. I'm tired of it. That my love is not good enough for them? I find this unacceptable, and so I've broken with my blood and my King."

Bentley saw how Darry held her hand back and saw the blood on her sleeve and staining the leg of her trousers. He was not the only one. He narrowed his eyes as he searched past her, seeing Emmalyn standing beneath the entrance that led to the foyer and the staircase beyond.

"I won't ask you to give up what you've earned, for I am so very proud of you. I can't tell you how proud." Darry's voice became rough as she stared at the floor, unable to face them now that she was finally saying the words. She shook her head and a long minute of silence stretched out. "I love you," she whispered, though they all could hear her. "I love you all so very much. I am humbled when I look at you, for the happiness of such a gift, your friendship." Jessa's arms tightened around her and gave her strength. "I was born a Durand without any say and so made royal blood by the will of Gamar, but it was *you* that taught me what that could mean. And taught me the honor of such a thing. And I shall miss you all, more than you'll ever know."

Arkady spoke gently into the silence that followed her words. "Why will you miss us?"

Darry swallowed over the fist within her throat, still refusing to face them.

"We would go with you, Captain," Theroux spoke up.

"Aye," Jemin said. "I've had enough of this bloody uniform anyway. It has never fit me right. It'll be good to move free once more."

"There are horses to be caught upon the plains," Matthias said. "And gold to be made when we catch them."

"And pubs I've yet to see," Lucas added, smiling. "And women that have yet to mock me."

"I shall hit you in the head, Darry," Tobe Giovanni said, "if you leave me at the will of bloody Longshanks."

"Who will fight me in the Dance?" Etienne asked. "Not these clods."

"Who'll braid my *hair*?" Orlando sounded genuinely disturbed. "Bentley?"

"Gamar save us all," Lucien muttered, and there was quiet laughter as Bentley actually blushed at the comment.

"You would abandon me as well?" Sybok stepped forward, his voice thick with disbelief. "You would leave me, Darry?"

Darry closed her eyes and Jessa touched her cheek. "*Akasha.*"

"We're not Darry's Boys," Lucien said plainly, "without you, Darry."

"Perhaps you're thinking that because you're no longer a princess or a captain, that we cannot follow you?" Arkady asked.

"Bloody hell," Darry said beneath her breath.

"But *you* are a princess, Lady Jessa-Sirrah," Arkday said, and Jessa looked at him in surprise. "Are you still of Lyoness?"

"Darrius is my country," Jessa said. "I am LaMarc, no longer de Bharjah."

"Then we could swear our oath to *you*, Princess," Arkady proclaimed.

Jessa could not have been more shocked had he struck her.

"No doubt your consort could find a use for us, my Lady."

Darry's eyes filled with tears though they never fell.

Jessa's heart ached at the struggle of it, at seeing her so helpless and vulnerable. *You shall not give up everything for me, Akasha, not this as well. I'll not allow it.* "On one condition."

"Anything."

"That you never, *ever* dance the Mohn-Drom with my beloved again."

Darry gave a breathless laugh, pulling Jessa into her arms and burying her face in dark curls and the scent of jasmine.

Every one of the men stepped forward and bent to a knee. Darry stepped back and left Jessa to stand before them. Jessa appeared decidedly uncertain and out of her depth.

"You must accept their oath." Darry smiled from behind her, her right hand at the small of Jessa's back to keep her from stepping away.

"And then what?"

"We pack our things, my love."

"Do you accept us into your service, Princess?" Bentley said with a bold grin. "We are a drunken lot and our manners are poor, but we're loyal unto the grave and would serve you until you'd have us no more."

"Or we die clogging a gutter somewhere," Tobe mumbled happily, and there was laughter, including Darry's.

"Take us, Lady Jessa." Arkady smiled up at her. "And I promise never to dance the Mohn-Drom with your beloved again. Though I would ask for another dance now and then, for she's cracking good."

"Not even that."

Arkady frowned. "You're too harsh, my Lady."

Jessa gave in. "Perhaps just one."

"Say you accept us," Bentley said kindly. "My knee is beginning to hurt."

"I accept you." Jessa stepped back as they surged to their feet at her words. Darry's right arm slipped about her and held her safe as they all stood close.

Names were given then, one at a time as they approached. Jessa smiled and accepted their hands in introduction. They bowed their heads to her, and when she told them in an irritated voice to stop, there was happy laughter.

"Go and see to things then," Darry said when they stood waiting for their orders. "We'll leave the day after tomorrow. I would see us gone before the others return from the Green Hills. If you'd like to bring anyone with you, it would appear that one or two more will make no difference."

"My sister?" Jemin asked, his voice hopeful.

"Always, Jemin. Marlee is most welcome."

"Let's go." Bentley ordered and started pushing them back. "Let us go and give our lovely Grissom a seizure when we all resign at once, eh?"

"Should I see to your hand, Darry?" Tobe approached, reaching out.

Jessa saw the blood for the first time and grabbed Darry's left wrist. "*Tua Nahla en gitta!*" she cursed, and her eyes blazed as Darry stepped back from her. "*Zaneesha hoonta*, Darrius Lauranna."

Darry gritted her teeth. "It's nothing. Just a cut."

Jessa inspected the wound and saw that it would need stitches as fresh blood seeped forth. She understood at once that it had been self-inflicted, a symbolic breaking of her blood. The Durand line had been sliced apart.

"*Nothing*?" Jessa snapped, trying to ignore her sadness. If there was a line of the Blood that did not deserve such a thing, it was the line of Durand. She had learned that much at least. Despite their mistakes and their rivalries, they had shown her what a family could be. "*Patra sillas*, I am loving a *fool*." She growled and then scolded her again as laughter rang out among the soldiers around them watching Darry humbled and berated beneath her lover's worry.

Darry grabbed her and kissed her, and though Jessa tried to argue against it, Darry's tongue slid past her lips and Jessa moaned, giving in. Their love had been declared and they were free.

Bentley chuckled, reaching out as his boot crowded another foot. Nina Lewellyn stepped back from him and looked up as he brushed her elbow. "Would you care to give your oath to the country of Darrius?" he asked her with a grin.

Nina stared at him.

His smile faded as he regarded the pain in her eyes, a flush of heat moving through his chest at the sight of it.

"I've just lost a kinsman, Lord Greeves, and one of my favorite people in all the world." The insult was clear within her voice. "And though my heart is full that she's found love at last, no doubt I'm about to watch as my family is torn apart. Your careless charm is not welcome, thank you."

"I'm sorry, Lady Lewellyn," Bentley replied in all sincerity, stepping closer as Etienne bumped into him from behind. "Honestly, I meant no offense. I love this family well. I know the pain here, most certainly better than you do. I wasn't making light of it."

"Weren't you?"

"No. But I'm happy at the hope of a new life for us all, and my dearest friend has her love well in hand. I'll not apologize for feeling joy at that."

Darry's Boys retreated the way they had come, their talk bursting forth as to their unexpected future. There was laughter and most definitely joy. "I would not have you apologize," Nina replied in a quiet, sullen voice. "I'm sorry at my tone."

"What would you have me do then, to make your eyes smile?"

"Try putting on a shirt," Nina answered dryly, and walked away.

"You stink as well," Etienne said, stepping up behind him.

"Shut your mouth, Blue."

Etienne laughed and set a hand on his shoulder. "The pretty girl doesn't like you, I think. Perhaps she might find blue eyes more to her pleasure."

"No doubt," Bentley replied. "How do you feel about buying some wagons?" He turned away from Nina's retreating figure.

"We should get Theroux."

"All right, do it. I'll meet you in the yards."

"What about you?"

"Why, I'm going to find a shirt, of course," he replied, spinning Etienne about and following him close. He glanced over his shoulder, but the Lady Lewellyn appeared to have forgotten all about him.

❖

Jessa lay on her left side, her arm propped on the pillows of her bed. Darry lay beside her, tucked close along her body. Jessa held her left hand, the heavy gauze brown with the stain of the herbs she had applied over Darry's wound. "Not exactly how I wanted you in bed."

Darry smiled. "The night is still new."

Jessa enjoyed the suggestion, though she could hear Darry's pain beneath it. "Yes, well, I think you've had enough excitement for one day."

Darry turned her head toward her. "Thank you, Jess."

"I did nothing."

"They're my friends."

"They love you even as I do. And besides, the trouble that my Radha will cause will be twice as bad. They shall all rue the day."

Darry laughed quietly, turned her face back to the pillow, and shifted closer. Jessa obliged her and lifted her right knee, accepting Darry's leg between her own. "She's not even said that I'm suitable for you. We might have a problem if she finds me lacking."

"I promise, my love, that will never be an issue."

"Are you sure?"

"Yes, I am, and aside from that, my Radha loves me. She'll not say no."

Darry lifted her head from the pillow and glanced toward the end of the bed. "She's not in here *now*, is she? Using some Vhaelin trickery?"

Jessa laughed. "No."

Darry flopped her head back down. They lay in silence for some time and Jessa saw how tired Darry was. She wished that she would sleep. Wished that she could take away the pain. "Will Hinsa come with us?" she asked. Darry's eyes darkened and filled with tears. Jessa's heart twisted and she bent over as a tear slid across the bridge of Darry's nose. She kissed it away. "You must ask her."

"A better life, Jess." Darry spoke softly. "We shall find a better life."

Jessa smiled and pulled closer. "You have already given me that,

Akasha," she said, and was happy despite the uncertainty of their position. "Let us find a life of freedom as well, yes? It is a full moon this night, a night of prophecy. 'Tis a good promise to make, yes?"

Darry nodded and kissed her again. "Yes…yes, that sounds right."

About the Author

Shea Godfrey is an artist and writer working and living in the Midwest. While her formal education is in journalism and photography, she has spent most of her career thus far in 3D Animation and Design.

Books Available From Bold Strokes Books

Wind and Bones by Kristin Marra. Jill O'Hara, award-winning journalist, just wants to settle her deceased father's affairs and leave Prairie View, Montana, far, far behind—but an old girlfriend, a sexy sheriff, and a dangerous secret keep her down on the ranch. (978-1-60282-150-7)

Nightshade by Shea Godfrey. The story of a princess, betrothed as a political pawn, who falls for her intended husband's soldier sister, is a modern-day fairy tale to capture the heart. (978-1-60282-151-4)

Vieux Carré Voodoo by Greg Herren. Popular New Orleans detective Scotty Bradley just can't stay out of trouble—especially when an old flame turns up asking for help. (978-1-60282-152-1)

The Pleasure Set by Lisa Girolami. Laney DeGraff, a successful president of a family-owned bank on Rodeo Drive, finds her comfortable life taking a turn toward danger when Theresa Aguilar, a sleek, sexy lawyer, invites her to join an exclusive, secret group of powerful, alluring women. (978-1-60282-144-6)

A Perfect Match by Erin Dutton. The exciting world of pro golf forms the backdrop for a fast-paced, sexy romance. (978-1-60282-145-3)

Truths by Rebecca S. Buck. Two women separated by two hundred years are connected by fate and love. (978-1-60282-146-0)

Father Knows Best by Lynda Sandoval. High school juniors and best friends Lila Moreno, Meryl Morganstern, and Caressa Thibodoux plan to make the most of the summer before senior year. What they discover that amazing summer about girl power, growing up, and trusting friends and family more than prepares them to tackle that all-important senior year! (978-1-60282-147-7)

In Pursuit of Justice by Radclyffe. In the dynamic double sequel to *Shield of Justice* and *A Matter of Trust*, Det. Sgt. Rebecca Frye joins forces with enigmatic computer consultant J.T. Sloan to crack an Internet child pornography ring. (978-1-60282-147-4)

The Midnight Hunt by L.L. Raand. Medic Drake McKennan takes a chance and loses, and her life will never be the same—because when she wakes up after surviving a life-threatening illness, she is no longer human. (978-1-60282-140-8)

Long Shot by D. Jackson Leigh. Love isn't safe, which is exactly why equine veterinarian Tory Greyson wants no part of it—until Leah Montgomery and a horse that won't give up convince her otherwise. (978-1-60282-141-5)

In Medias Res by Yolanda Wallace. Sydney has forgotten her entire life, and the one woman who holds the key to her memory, and her heart, doesn't want to be found. (978-1-60282-142-2)

Awakening to Sunlight by Lindsey Stone. Neither Judith or Lizzy is looking for companionship, and certainly not love—but when their lives become entangled, they discover both. (978-1-60282-143-9)

Fever by VK Powell. Hired gun Zakaria Chambers is hired to provide a simple escort service to philanthropist Sara Ambrosini, but nothing is as simple as it seems, especially love. (978-1-60282-135-4)

High Risk by JLee Meyer. Can actress Kate Hoffman really risk all she's worked for to take a chance on love? Or is it already too late? (978-1-60282-136-1)

Missing Lynx by Kim Baldwin and Xenia Alexiou. On the trail of a notorious serial killer, Elite Operative Lynx's growing attraction to a mysterious mercenary could be her path to love—or to death. (978-1-60282-137-8)

Spanking New by Clifford Henderson. A poignant, hilarious, unforgettable look at life, love, gender, and the essence of what makes us who we are. (978-1-60282-138-5)

Bold Strokes
BOOKS
WEBSTORE
PRINT AND EBOOKS
Romance
Mystery
Intrigue
MATINEE BOOKS
LIBERTY
EDITION
BOLD
STROKES
BOOKS
Adventure
victory
EDITIONS
AEROS
e
Erotica
Fantasy
Sci-Fi
http://www.boldstrokesbooks.com